About the Author

Anna Charlotta Efverman was born and raised in Stockholm, Sweden. She lived and worked in many different countries for a number of years before she finally settled in Australia year 1996.

During her time of travel, she saw and experienced many things; in one horrific moment she had a gun pointed at her head – and so she writes from her experience of being a victim of crime, as well as drawing from her extensive imagination; plus many many hours' research of criminal psychology, real-life murderers and police procedures.

Her crime fiction novels contain the same main characters, and the stories take place in her home town Sydney.

A.C. Efverman is also an artist – she paints with oils and acrylics – and she utilizes her artistic view of the world in her writing.

GAME

A.C. Efverman

GAME

First published in Australia 2015 by
A.C. Efverman

Copyright © 2015 A.C. Efverman

The moral rights of the author have been asserted.

All rights reserved. No part of this publication may
be reproduced or transmitted by any person or entity
(including Google, Amazon or similar organisations),
in any form or by any means, electronic or mechanical,
including photocopying, recording, scanning or by any
information storage and retrieval system, without the
express prior written permission of the copyright holder.

In loving memory of Siw Efverman.

A.C. Efverman

Prologue

Brian and Sally are walking through a landscape of shadows: lit up only by distantly spaced street lights. Beyond the sidewalk the night is densely dark like an empty blackboard. An illuminated window up high on a facade is a white square that hangs suspended amidst the black surrounding. The deserted street is a contrast to the brightly coloured lights of the casino that is now out of sight behind them.

Brian had looked at the time display on his mobile before he turned the phone off in the bar's men's' room and the time was ten to two am then: that would have been about an hour ago, he thinks now.

Sally talks and Brian pretends to listen: he even manages to fit in a laugh where it's needed.

Sally finally falls silent as they walk into a black shadow from a wharf building and Brian takes the opportunity to slide his hand over Sally's back: he lets his fingers travel up to her shoulder and down to her breast. Lights from a car move towards them and for a second they are spotlighted before the dark body of the car sweeps past them. As the red tail lights are swallowed by the night, Brian's hand squeezes Sally's breast and she turns to face him. A warm wave of euphoria races through Brian's stomach and down to his genitals as his tongue slips inside Sally's wet mouth: the pressure is building and he desperately needs to release it. He takes Sally's hand. "This way, I know a place where no one can see us."

GAME

Her hand suddenly yanks his as they step out on the boardwalk and for a moment he thinks he has misread her signals: that she is not coming with him.

"Wait my shoe..." Her hand leaves his. "The heel is stuck between the planks. I need to take my shoes off." For some reason she is whispering.

Brian exhales. The glow from a street light reaches them where they stand and he watches as Sally crouches down to unclasp the small buckles on her high heeled shoes. There is a clucking sound as waves make contact with the wooden poles under his feet. The wind has picked up and clouds cover the stars on the black sky. Further out on the wharf is a lit up entrance: why is the light on? Brian looks up at the wharf building but he can't see any other lights. Sally has taken her shoes off: she takes his hand and they walk towards the light. Inside an illuminated glass door they see a stair well where wooden steps lead up into darkness. When they have passed the entrance everything turns black.

Sally clings to Brian's arm and giggles. "I can't see a thing. Where are you taking me?" She is surprised to feel his body stiffen.

"What the *hell*?" Brian tries to adjust his eyes in the dark: he has stepped on something that is soft but firm – not like rubber, but he feels his weight mangle what-ever-it-is to the ground. He quickly takes another step and almost trips over as his foot touches a larger soft mound: another step and both his feet are back on wooden planks. A stench is in his nose now: he has registered the smell seconds earlier, but then it was a part of the many odours that are rising from the water below. It smells like *dead rat*. But Brian knows that he hasn't stepped on a dead rat.

Sally stares into the compact darkness without seeing.

A.C. Efverman

She stopped when Brian's hand suddenly let go of hers. She can't move forward because she can't see: it's so bloody dark. And her feet are cold. What the hell is she doing here and why has Brian moved away from her? She's an idiot for coming here with him: he has hardly said a word to her all night and then he takes her here; where it is so dark she can't see – he has obviously planned to have sex with her... and now he has abandoned her. "Hey, what are you doing? What's going on?"

Brian ignores Sally's angry questions and crouches down. His fingers are stiff and uncooperative as he tries to light his cigarette lighter – the small flame finally ignites and reveals much more than he wants to see. He gets to his feet and takes a few unsteady steps in the dark. As the half digested meal of fish and chips splashes the water surface below, Sally gets down on her knees and in the light from the flame on her own cigarette lighter she sees what has upset Brian's stomach: Sally has never sobered up so quickly.

GAME

1

Morgan is in a bush fire: he is surrounded by tree trunks that seem to dissolve and change shape as he looks at them through a veil of grey smoke. There is no wind. Charred pieces of bark and black leaves rain over him and he is scared that some of them might still be on fire – *set him on fire*. It's painful to breathe: the fire is eating the oxygen in the air. Why is there no wind? The heat stings his eyes and nose. He coughs and looks up: hoping against all odds to see rain clouds but all he sees are burned trees tops against the smoke filled sky. It's eerily quiet: the forest is dead and all animals must be gone. Suddenly he hears fire truck sirens in the distance: rescue – finally. The noise gets louder and louder and then it abruptly stops: then it starts again. This time Morgan slowly emerges from his deep sleep and recognises the sound for what it is. He squints with his eyes in the dark: the red digitals on the alarm clock read ten past four. If this is about a fire I won't go, he thinks as he stretches his hand towards the phone on the bedside table.

"DS Callaghan?" a male voice asks in his ear.

"Yes." Morgan's voice cracks. He has a remnant feeling of inhaling smoke and vivid scenes from the dream are still with him as he clears his throat. "Yes, speaking," he repeats and then the dream slips away like a silvery fish under water: he is wide awake now and has a suspicion about what will come next.

"This is Detective Osbourne. A naked female body

A.C. Efverman

has been found on a wharf in Pyrmont; the exact address is thirty-two Pirrama Road on Pyrmont Point. They're taking the photos now but I thought you wanted to see the scene 'as is'."

Morgan's suspicion has been confirmed. "Okay. Thirty-two Pirrama Road, Pyrmont Point, got it. I'll be there in twenty minutes. And Osbourne…"

"Yes?"

"Make sure no one touches anything until I get there, alright?" Morgan hangs up and goes to the bathroom. Eight minutes later he is showered and dressed. Fragments from his dream flash past under the surface of his conscious thoughts as he grabs his keys and wallet from the hallway table on the way out. How many times has he been woken by a phone call in the middle of the night, he ponders as he walks down the stairs. He suddenly wishes he is one of the neighbours that sleep without interruptions behind the doors he passes: he would like to see how the bush fire dream ends.

There is hardly any traffic and the streets of Sydney look wider than usual. The morning is still a few hours away and the dark city outside the car window looks like a painting in black and grey tones with yellow spots of light dotted randomly on the skyscrapers. Morgan drives slowly past Hyde Park where fairy lights decorate large fig trees: adding more yellow dots to the dark background. Flying foxes look like vampire silhouettes in the sky above.

Morgan decides to take the scenic route as there is no traffic and he needs more time to organize his thoughts – the phone call that woke him has sparked a monologue in his mind and memories of texts and pictures fly chaotically in and out of his thoughts. One important fact suddenly stands

GAME

out: the body has been found a short distance from where the detective headquarters are located. Sometimes in a crime investigation there are no coincidences and sometimes there are only coincidences: Morgan smiles at the irony of this thought as he drives down George Street and enters a part of the city that has been built by settlers and convicts. The water in the harbour looks like a black mass through the car window and the top of the harbour bridge disappears into the cloudy night sky above. When Morgan has passed The Rocks he speeds up, drives around Darling Harbour and turns onto the main road that will take him to Pyrmont Point Park. He hopes that someone at the crime scene has brought coffee: if not, there is a convenience store in the wharf building he knows, but maybe it's not open this time of night?

Police cars on the side of the road reveal the location of the crime scene. A cold wind touches Morgan's face as he steps out of the car and he is grateful it's not raining. His desire for warm coffee is strong now, but a quick glance at the corner of the wharf building confirms his suspicion that the convenience store is closed. He passes the shop and walks out onto the wharf.

"Morgan!" Amanda materializes out of the darkness like a tall red-haired wish-granting angel, handing Morgan a Styrofoam cup half filled with black coffee. "You're on the wrong side, we're over here." She starts walking and suddenly disappears out of sight. Morgan sips the warm liquid as he follows her, when he walks around the corner of the dark mass that is the wharf building he sees a bright light further out on the wharf. As he gets closer he sees a semi circle of human silhouettes under the lights. A man and a woman – they look to be his own age: in their late thirties

– sit on the boardwalk outside an illuminated entrance about ten meters away from the crime scene. They have blankets over their shoulders and sip coffee from Styrofoam cups. Morgan walks past them and taps with his fingers on a back that he recognizes. The man turns around. "Hey Morgan, take a look."

The naked woman lies on her back. Morgan notes that her head is tilted to the side, her arms are positioned along each side of her body, her palms are faced down and her legs are bent slightly sideways. Purple stains on the face, groin and stomach area contrast sharply against the otherwise pale skin. There is a large open wound on the throat, and the neck and hair are covered in black, dried blood. There is no blood on the wooden planks under or around the body as far as he can see. For a second he gets the impression that the naked woman has fallen out of the dark sky and landed on the boardwalk.

Morgan walks around the body, grateful for the coffee cup in his hand and the warming lights set up by the forensic team. Clucking sounds from the water below is all that is heard as the group on the wharf stands silent.

Morgan is blinded by the lights when he looks up. "Where's Osbourne?" he asks, shading his eyes with one hand and trying not to breathe through the nose as he speaks: there's a pungent odour of rotten flesh despite the wind.

"I'm here," a voice says behind him. "We haven't touched anything. The couple who found her told us that they didn't touch her either. Well… apart from when the guy accidentally stepped on her hand… and then on her stomach."

"Okay, noted." Morgan drinks some coffee and stares down at the body again. "Alright, I'm done here." He turns

GAME

to face two detectives. "What's the story with these two?" he points with his thumb in the direction of the man and woman sitting on the ground.

"They found the body," Ricketts, one of the detectives, replies.

"I gathered that much. You and Stone need to take them home. If you haven't taken their statements yet, you can do so in the car. Don't forget to record their ID's. And ask if they need counselling: they must be pretty shook up by what they've seen."

Detective Stone leans in closer to Morgan and whispers: "The man refuses a lift home by us: he wants to be driven to a taxi rank and take a cab home."

Morgan frowns.

"He's married, but not to..." Stone gestures with his hand towards the woman. "And he's terrified that his wife will find out what he was doing here tonight."

"Okay, drive him to a taxi rank but take his statement and his details first." Morgan realises that the man and woman probably can hear what he is saying, but doesn't care. "Tell both of them that they cannot disclose anything they've seen or heard here tonight and that we'll be in contact with them if we need further information. Lay down the law if you need to, but make it very clear to them that we do not want to read about this on the Internet tomorrow morning, not on bloody Twitter or Facebook, not in any paper, not on the news: not anywhere, okay?"

Stone nods. "Okay, we'll let them know. What do you think happened here?"

"We'll talk about that in the office later. Get those two out of here: now." Morgan dismisses Stone and turns his attention to two men dressed in dark blue jumpsuits. "I want you to wrap the whole body before you put her in the pouch," he tells them and then he addresses the medical examiner: "Do you have an estimated time yet?"

George Demitriades zips up his windbreaker so the collar covers the lower half of his face. "Looks like she's been dead for about one to two weeks, but for all I know she might have been stored in a fridge. Don't know how long she's been out here for." His words are coloured by a slight Greek accent and the collar muffles his voice. "You'll get all details after the full examination: I'll courier the report to you."

Morgan nods. "Thanks. I'll leave you to it then." He suddenly notices some tables and chairs that are folded up and chained to the wall of the wharf building. He turns to face Osbourne. "This restaurant here, or café or whatever it is... Find out what times they're open, and let the owners know they won't be open today or tonight. I think there are some more restaurants on the other side of the wharf: check them out too, and while you're at it check if there are other businesses in this building. We need to establish the time the last person was in this area today, or that would be yesterday now wouldn't it... Last night I mean. And gather all information such as possible prints, drag marks, blood, et cetera. You know the drill. I want it on my desk in two hours. And send the photos to my computer. Okay?"

The young detective nods.

Morgan walks back over the wharf. As he approaches the asphalted sidewalk he sees that two uniformed police officers are rolling out plastic blue and white tape to seal the area off.

Morgan turns his computer on, puts a grease-stained

GAME

paper bag on his desk and heads off to the kitchen to make a cup of instant coffee. As he comes back to his room he registers that the in-tray on his desk is full, but other things will have to wait: he needs to get on to the Missing Persons' page as soon as possible to try to establish the identity of the body. His thoughts are still with the dead naked woman on the wharf and he wants to load his eyes with new and different images: even if they are just old and not very good photographs of faces that no one has seen for a long time.

He recalls the boardwalk where the dead woman was lying: there were no items of clothing and no blood – the naked body was there alone. The strange image of the dead woman falling out of the dark sky comes back to Morgan. He recalls two crime scene reports he has read recently about other dead women, but he knows it's too early to voice his thoughts: more information needs to come to light first. The pressure is on Morgan to identity the dead woman on the wharf as soon as possible. But first thing first, he thinks as he puts the coffee cup on his desk and bites into a warm croissant.

The sun is on its way up when Detective Andrew Osbourne enters the office. Morgan has decided that he needs a private library of all missing women in Australia and has sent the whole file to the printer: as a result, 689 pictures of faces form a stack of papers that is quite high and resembles the leaning tower of Pisa on the corner of his desk. Gruesome images of the naked woman on the wharf are spread out on his desk and copies of the photos are blue-tacked to a whiteboard behind him. The lower half of the whiteboard is covered in scribbled notes. Morgan is looking at a page of convicted females that have prostitution listed as their occupation and is drinking his third cup of coffee.

"So Andy, what have we got?" Morgan offers a croissant with a gesture towards the paper bag and gets up from his chair to stretch his back: the air-conditioned room is cold and he feels stiff.

"The autopsy report will be here in the afternoon, as well as the finger prints and dental images. A preliminary examination show bruises on the woman's legs, arms and torso. And it looks like she's been tied up, according to marks on her wrists and ankles. There is a strong possibility of sexual assault." Osbourne takes a croissant from the bag and tears it to small pieces that he eats quickly as he continues: "You got the photos I see," he gestures with a piece of croissant towards the pictures on the whiteboard. "Demitriades thinks that she was between twenty three and twenty six years old, but he wouldn't say for sure. You know what he's like."

Morgan nods as images of naked dead women flash through his mind, but he isn't prepared to share his thoughts with Osbourne – not yet. "Okay... While we wait for the autopsy report, you should write a report from the statements made by the couple that found the body. What were they doing down there anyway in the middle of the night? Kissing and cuddling?"

Osbourne swallows the last bit of croissant and rubs his palms against his thighs to get the grease off his hands. "They were going down there to make out, they said. I think they had more than kissing and cuddling on their mind before they discovered the body. But whatever they were up to, it seemed soon forgotten when they stumbled upon the body... The guy called triple 0 from his mobile and the call was directed to our unit from Ultimo police station. The

GAME

guy's not likely to blab as he's married and was out fooling around. But Stone told me that the woman needed some legal threats to convince her to keep her mouth shut about what she's seen."

Morgan touches the stubble on his chin with the back of his hand as he sits back down in his chair. "We'll get the legal team to draft a document for the witnesses to sign. We need a leak to the media like we need a hole in the head right now."

Osbourne isn't sure what to say to this so he settles for the safe option of a smile and waits. But Morgan swivels his chair around, stares out of the window and seems lost in thoughts.

Osbourne finally clears his throat. "I'll contact the businesses in the wharf building so we can establish what times they're open and if anyone has seen anything out of sorts then."

Morgan turns his chair to face the desk and lifts some papers from a pile. Osbourne senses that his attention has gone somewhere else. "You'll get all details in the report," he says as he leaves the room.

The office begins to fill with people around eight o'clock, when the first morning shift starts.

Morgan calls for a meeting in the boardroom: this is usually a sacred place used by Superintendent Travis when he wants to butter up officials, but Travis is officially on holidays and Morgan's currently in charge. The power must be going to my head, Morgan thinks, the decision to use the boardroom is not a great one: when all detectives are gathered along the walls around the oval table there is not much room left to move – or breathe for that matter. Morgan

A.C. Efverman

decides to keep the meeting short: without details he briefs everyone on what has happened, informs the detectives of his theory of a serial killer and finishes the meeting by announcing that he will delegate work by email.

Morgan has sent a request to the Police Intranet hours earlier: when his senses were still filled with the dead woman on the wharf. In this email he asked for an update on missing persons who still haven't been added to the missing persons' file – but as yet there is no reply. The search engine on the missing persons' webpage is unpredictable he knows by experience, and he doesn't bother to do a computerized search there. Instead he spends an hour going through his printouts and tries to match them to the photographs he has of the body on the wharf: it feels like he is playing Memory, but at least the pile that once resembled the leaning tower of Pisa has shrunk a little since he now has an official estimated age of the dead woman.

Amanda knocks on Morgan's door at two pm: she takes a step into his personal space and a layer of perfume follows her arm as she hands Morgan a thick yellow envelope over the desk, he thanks her and opens the envelope by breaking the Medical Examiner's logo that is stamped on the back as a seal. The room still smells vaguely of jasmine flowers as Amanda closes the door behind her. Morgan skims through the autopsy report quickly until he finds the most relevant part.

'Female', the report reads. *'Dental images indicate age to be 27 years old. Hair colour: fair brown. Eye colour: blue. Weight: 54 kilograms. Height: 174 centimetres. Shoe size: 6. Dress size: 8. Blood type: O negative.'*

Morgan writes the information on his keyboard and continues to read.

GAME

'One existing scar below bellybutton, one existing smaller scar located in pubis area; concurs with internal scar tissue build up on left ovary – my conclusion is a keyhole operation: surgical removal of cystitis or similar.

One existing scar from vaccine injection on left shoulder: similar to that of an injection of Tetanus and Diphtheria vaccine. No other visible scars or tattoos. No sign of broken bones in the past.' This concludes the identification part of the report. Morgan stops reading and concentrates on copying the information he has entered in the computer. He then pastes the text into a new email message that he addresses to a message board on the Police Intranet and he also scans a dental print, a picture of fingerprints and a photo of the dead woman and encloses them as attachments in the email. When the email is sent he realises that he should forward the information to Interpol as well: a lot of Australians have had Tetanus and Diphtheria injections he knows, but he guesses that people in other parts of the world must also have had the vaccine. He locates the Interpol email address on Intranet and then copies the text and pictures from the drives on the computer and pastes them into a new email message.

Morgan knows that it will be hard to match the dead woman's fingerprints as they are far from complete and he is impressed Demitriades has still managed to get a picture of five-point prints considering the decomposed state of the body: even though the woman's skin looked intact under the strong lights on the wharf, the purple stains coupled with her time of death indicate that the skin is in the dissolving stage. Their best bet for identification will probably be dental images, he thinks as he picks up the autopsy report and continues to read:

'Cause of death: Carotid throat artery severed causing

blood loss. Two incisions made with sharp, straight blade (large blade, exact size undetectable), no rust detected in wounds. Irregular bruises on upper thighs, upper arms and torso are pre mortem. Marks on both wrists and both ankles indicate victim has been tied up before time of death. Small amount of seminal fluid present and some vaginal bruising: sexual activity took place before time of death. Fragments of dark blue cotton-fibres (100% cotton, common dye) found in victim's mouth, indicates she was gagged. No stomach content found that could be analysed, due to prolonged time of death. No fingerprints found on body. Time of death: seven, possibly eight days ago. Place of death: unknown.'

Under this remark, at the bottom of the page, are some handwritten notes in what Morgan recognizes as Demitriades' handwriting:

'Possible time for the body to have been lying in the position we found it: at the most: four hours, at the least: two hours.'

Morgan leans back in his chair and stares into the infinite blue sky outside the window. The information he has just read is almost identical to two other autopsy reports he has read recently. The next step is obvious: he needs to ask Demitriades to match the seminal fluid found on the dead women. Morgan puts his hand over the phone on his desk when it startles him by ringing: he involuntary makes a small jerking motion before he puts his hand back on the receiver and for some reason he doesn't say his name when he picks it up but remains silent until the caller speaks.

"DS Callaghan?"

GAME

"Yes, Callaghan speaking."

"Hi, it's Travis. I need to speak to you. Can you meet with me this afternoon? I'm at home and can have my driver pick you up at… shall we say three thirty?"

Morgan stares out through the window again. He is mentally detaching himself from the conversation and it feels like he is floating – he is probably just tired. "Yes of course, I'll wait outside."

"Good. See you later then."

Morgan tries to imagine why the Superintendent would want to see him, but then he realises that he needs to talk to Demitriades and picks up the receiver again. "George," his voice is recorded by the medical examiner's voice mail, "this is Detective Sergeant Morgan Callaghan at the detective headquarters in Pyrmont. I'm calling about the autopsy report you sent to our office earlier today: the twenty-seven year old female. I want you to try to match the seminal fluid found on her body to the seminal fluid found on Rochelle Stevens three months ago, I don't have the case number here but should you have any queries you know where to find me. I'm in a meeting from three thirty, so if you can't reach me leave a message on my voicemail. Thanks." He ends the call and reaches for his diary, scribbles a few notes in it and looks at his watch: three fifteen. He gives the autopsy report to Amanda and tells her to copy it and hand it out to the detectives. He also tells her that he is still logged in to his computer and that she should keep an eye out for replies from Interpol and the Intranet site. On the way back to his room he walks past Osbourne's desk and tells him to go home and get some rest as he looks like he's falling asleep. Morgan then records a new message on his voicemail: saying that he will be contactable after five pm on his mobile, and leaves

A.C. Efverman

the building via the stairs.

Outside, he lights a cigarette and inhales the smoke deeply into his lungs. The nicotine rush instantly relaxes him but he also feels a pang of guilt and shame: he knows full well it's politically incorrect to smoke these days. Graphic pictures of the harm smoking causes, shown on TV frequently, are constantly in the back of his mind: so much so he fears the images have such a powerful impact on him that his body might create the very diseases he is so terrified of.

A dark blue Mercedes drives up next to Morgan and stops. The driver puts his head out the window. "DS Callaghan?" he asks. When Morgan nods, he adds: "Get in."

Morgan steps on his cigarette and kills it together with all cancer thoughts. He gets into the backseat. The car has tinted windows that give relief from the glaring sun on his tired eyes: still he leans back and closes his eyes. The lack of sleep is a buzzing vibration in his body. He feels like he is gliding through the air: the body of the car doesn't exist and he's floating a metre above the road, past the glittering water down below in Darling Harbour. He has never been to the Superintendent's home before and doesn't even know where Travis lives: where he's going. He opens his eyes and sees that the car is moving into the shadows from skyscrapers in the city centre. The driver changes lane and drives up onto the Sydney Harbour Bridge. Preparations on the bridge for the upcoming World Cup are well underway: a giant circular shape on the top span makes Morgan suspect it will show a picture of a soccer ball: the image will probably be lit up at night during the cup.

The harbour view outside the window disappears and shortly thereafter the driver turns right at the Kirribilli exit

GAME

and drives down towards Neutral Bay.

Tall trees flank the yellow house and provide effective screens toward the neighbouring gardens and the outside world. Not only is it an exclusive address: it also has exclusive privacy, and privacy doesn't come cheap in this city, or in any city for that matter, Morgan thinks as the car drives into the garden on a tiled driveway. Inside, Morgan is introduced to two small girls that turn out to be Travis' granddaughters: very serious, still in their school uniforms and plaid hair, they both shake his hand before Travis shows Morgan to a balcony on the second floor that has views of the harbour, gestures to a canvas chair and asks if Morgan wants coffee or something stronger to drink. Morgan accepts the offer of coffee and leans back in the chair while Travis goes inside. He closes his eyes for a few seconds and when he opens them again he notices that the railing around the balcony is very low. For a dizzy second when he leans forward he thinks he is falling down into the garden below. Is it wise to have a low railing around a balcony when there are small children in the house, he wonders. He stands up and moves his chair closer to the house wall when Travis comes out on the balcony holding a tray. Travis places the tray on the floor and pours coffee from a thermos into two cups and hands one of them to Morgan.

"Three murdered women are left in central places around the city," Travis moves a canvas chair closer to Morgan's chair and sits down in it, "and at the same time more than half of Sydney's police force is on security training in Canberra for the upcoming World Cup. I don't know about you, but my first thought was terrorists: could this be some kind of terrorist attack?"

A.C. Efverman

It is a rhetorical question and Morgan remains silent.

Travis pours sugar into his coffee and stirs it slowly with a spoon. "We're expecting thousands of overseas visitors, and the press will be watching us from all over the world in less than three weeks' time: it's a hell of a situation. Did you know that an estimated 715 million people watched the televised final of the last soccer World Cup?"

Morgan shakes his head and takes a sip of coffee: it's too hot to drink so he puts the cup on the floor next to his chair.

"It's the world's most watched sporting event." Travis takes a sip of coffee and makes a face before he too puts his cup on the floor. "But I don't want to jump to conclusions about terrorist attacks: even though it's a high risk with the World Cup. What can you tell me about the investigation so far?"

Morgan desperately wants to light up, but there's no ashtray and he doesn't want to ask for one. He pushes his nicotine addiction to the side: he knows that he should concentrate on what's happening now. He needs to show that he is in control of this investigation. Although Travis is officially off work for holidays, Morgan knows he is unofficially on stress leave due to a mental breakdown. He also knows Travis well enough to know that he will never leave his position: as things are, it's a delicate situation. "Well first of all, we suspect that all three women were killed by the same perpetrator. From what we've learned so far it looks like they were killed by a serial killer who kills for sexual pleasure. If it's part of some kind of terrorist attack, I can't tell you. I guess it's possible that the women were raped, murdered and left in public places as some kind of message: maybe as an attack on how Australian

GAME

women live free lives, I don't know... it seems unlikely, but then again: when it comes to terrorists, who knows?" Morgan makes a gesture with his hands to emphasise his words. "I've contacted the medical examiner and asked him to match the seminal fluid that was found on two of the women. We'll search the register for a DNA match. There should have been a search made when seminal fluid was found on the second victim three months ago, but the first two murders were investigated by different police units and the connection between the two cases was not detected at once." Morgan shrugs his shoulders. "I guess everyone's been busy preparing for the World Cup." He looks at the sailing boats that float past below on the harbour. Who are all these people that can afford to spend a week day sailing, he wonders. Then his perspective turns and he sees himself sitting on the balcony looking out over the water: if someone sees him there they will think something similar, he thinks. He suddenly becomes aware that Travis is quiet and turns to look at him. Travis is squinting with his eyes: Morgan doesn't know if the afternoon sun is bothering him or if it's a sign of annoyance.

"Well we can't rule out the possibility of a terrorist attack, so just keep it in the back of your mind. I want you to continue to lead this investigation with the resources that we have at present. But we can't afford any more mistakes or delays." Travis stands up and pulls his chair out of the sun, into the shadow of the house. When he sits down again Morgan sees that his pupils are unnaturally large and he wonders if Travis is taking anti-depressants.

"You will report directly to me every night from now on. As you know I am officially on holidays, but you can reach me here at home. And I want the names of everyone who's involved in this investigation."

Morgan nods in a way he hopes looks obedient. "Understood. So the decision still stands to not go public with the murders? What about the public's safety?"

Travis bends down to pick up his cup. "It's not up to me. With the World Cup coming up it was a political decision. And until we receive a thorough profile of the offender I don't see the point of scaring the hell out of the public: right now we don't have any information of what people should look out for anyway." Travis takes a sip of coffee and resumes:"And as I said before: we don't know if this is part of something bigger, like a terrorist attack. We also need to take great precaution when gathering evidence to make sure that when we do catch the killer we have an air tight case against him: we don't want the media mudding the water for us, or the public getting involved in any way. Plus, if we are in fact dealing with an insane serial killer, I think that media coverage might trigger him to commit more murders. You can have a word with the psych department and see if you can get them to commit to making a profile report urgently. But for now we need to keep a lid on this and make sure that all police units report suspicious deaths on a secret radio channel, so the media won't get a whiff of what's going on."

Morgan freezes as he thinks back to the emails he has sent earlier that day. "What about using the Intranet? And Interpol, are they safe to contact?"

Travis nods. "Everyone within our Intranet is safe. We have just installed new firewalls to all our computer and phone systems. We've also updated everyone on the security issue."

You didn't update me, you bloody idiot, Morgan thinks, but he stops the words from coming out loud and asks

GAME

instead: "What about external personnel, like the medical examiner?"

"The medical examiners' office is an exception and it's safe to forward information there over the net." Travis frowns. "But you need to take care not to forward sensitive information over the phone or net to anyone else outside. Is that understood?"

Morgan nods again as he wonders why everyone except for him has been informed about the new security systems. "So the call from Ultimo police station came over a secure line to our unit, is that right?"

"That's correct. The Commissioner has outlined severe punishments to anyone who steps outside our new safety regulations. It's a serious security issue." Travis pauses for a second before he adds: "And this includes everyone in your unit. It will be up to you to update everyone there." It is an order.

Morgan nods. "I will make sure of it." The local police stations have been updated about the new security systems before him. The situation is sliding into full view: he is playing a role in a charade. He wonders if Travis has made a mistake, but his instincts tell him that Travis is having a power trip: out of spite because he no longer has full control. Maybe he should check with higher command if Travis still has authority to give orders. Or this could on the other hand be some kind of test to see how Morgan will handle the situation: only time would tell. The only thing that matters now is that he's still in charge of the investigation, and that it might lead to the promotion he deserves. Morgan knows the game rules after almost fifteen years in the force: it's all a game. He takes a swig of coffee and gets up from his chair. "Thanks for the coffee. I should get back to the office. You can trust me to look after this."

They walk together through the house. As they reach the hallway Travis pulls out a drawer in a side table and hands a printed card to Morgan. "Here are my contact numbers and email address. I can be contacted any time for any reason you feel necessary. My email is secure and I want you to report in writing every night from the office, I don't trust other peoples' home computers or iPhones." Travis puts a hand on Morgan's shoulder as he opens the front door. "Remember: no contact with the press. Should there be a leak I'll handle the media. Just make sure we keep a lid on this."

"Understood."

They shake hands in the doorway and Travis gives a wry smile. "Good. Paul will drive you back to the office."

The charade is over.

Morgan allows his body to relax as the Mercedes drives over the bridge. Tiredness falls over him like a wet blanket and he is suddenly ravenously hungry. He looks at the harbour view and concentrates on clearing his minds of all thoughts. He is so tired he can hardly keep his eyes open.

When the driver has dropped Morgan off outside the detective headquarters, Morgan smokes a cigarette: the nicotine has a stimulating effect on him and gives him the energy to take the stairs up to the office to tell Wendy – an older lady who does admin work in the evenings – that he is going home and he asks for any messages. Amanda has left a printout of the reply from Interpol on Morgan's desk: he grabs the report and leaves the office for the day.

Traffic is bad in the CBD and Morgan curses the driver

GAME

of a delivery truck that is parked in his lane. Finally at home, he puts a frozen pizza in the microwave and makes a drink of bourbon and coke. With the glass in one hand and the Interpol report in the other, he walks into the living room and sinks down in the sofa. The red light on the answering machine blinks madly to catch his attention but he can't be bothered to listen to messages: instead he sips his drink, puts the glass down and starts to read the report. Beeps from the microwave wake him up minutes later: to his own surprise he has fallen asleep.

He eats the pizza quickly with his hands and afterwards he decides to have a hot shower and then read the report in bed. In the bathroom he studies his face in the mirror: the eyes seem sunken into their sockets and stubble creates the illusion of more dark shadows over the jaw and cheeks. My face is a landscape of shadows, he thinks as he looks into the reflection of his eyes. "Who are you?" he asks out loud. As soon as he has said the words he feels silly.

Morgan scrubs his body vigorously in the shower to get the blood circulation going. Feeling warm and clean, he then wraps himself in a morning gown and steps out of the bathroom just as the phone starts ringing.

He spends the next ten minutes on the phone: talking to his girlfriend Lisa. He briefly entertains the idea that Lisa can come over and spend the night before he realises that he still has to read the Interpol report.

A.C. Efverman

2

Morgan wakes to glaring sunlight and the familiar sound of screaming seagulls. The hot sun through the window forces him out of bed: nature is a good alarm clock when the bedroom window faces east. The bright daylight continues its fall through the door frame and illuminates dust particles on the hallway carpet: Morgan watches the dust bounce around his feet as he walks to the bathroom and realises that it's been a while since he vacuumed. As he waits for the warm water to come through in the shower he recalls what he has read in the Interpol report the night before. The dead woman on the wharf has been identified through dental records: her name is Else Henriksen and she's a Danish citizen. Else held a three year working permit in Australia and she spent two of those years working as a graphic artist in Sydney.

The Danish police had apparently submitted a missing persons' notice to the Australian police through Interpol last week when Else didn't respond to her family's attempts to contact her. Well, their notice hasn't turned up on the missing persons' page yet, Morgan thinks. If it had, he would have seen it yesterday when he searched the file.

Else Henriksen was born in Copenhagen and she was the youngest of three daughters. She graduated from Copenhagen School of Art in 2001 and she worked for various companies in Copenhagen as a graphic artist before she started to travel in 2005: she worked in England, Sweden

GAME

and Belgium before she came to Australia.

There was a photograph of Else Henriksen included in the report, submitted by the Danish police. The picture showed an attractive young woman with sparkling blue eyes and a vibrant smile that reminds Morgan of the American actress Kirsten Dunst. Else's parents would have been notified by now that their daughter has been murdered, and Morgan is relieved that he isn't the one who has to deliver this message: in this case Interpol would contact the local Danish police, who in turn would inform the victim's family.

Morgan drives into the detective headquarters' garage and parks his dark blue Magna in the usual spot. He then takes the elevator to the street level to get his morning coffee from a café down the road. While he waits for his coffee he skims through a newspaper and to his relief he sees nothing in the paper about the murders. He thinks back to his conversation with Travis: why wasn't he told earlier about the media silence and the new security systems? Morgan had assumed that Travis was in his holiday home in Queensland, resting after his nervous breakdown: not acting behind the scenes of the investigation. And now he has to report to Travis – it's a frustrating thought but at least he is in charge at the office: for now.

Morgan takes the lid off the paper cup and sips hot coffee while he listens to telephone messages and writes names and phone numbers on a large post-it note. He turns the computer on and as he waits for the start-up process he makes some notes in his diary. He then dials Amanda's extension and asks her to gather everyone for a meeting at nine am. This time he chooses the meeting room – as the

A.C. Efverman

name suggests it is just that: an appropriate venue for a meeting.

Nine o'clock comes around quicker than Morgan has anticipated and he is still on the phone when Amanda comes into his office and points at her wristwatch to indicate the time. A few minutes later Morgan enters the meeting room where all the detectives have gathered. He goes straight to the whiteboard where he writes "NO PRESS CONTACT" in large letters with a black marker pen. He turns around to face the detectives who have grown silent: their attention directed at him.

"I will expect all of you to follow this order, the last thing we need now is mass hysteria with the World Cup coming up. No one will mention this investigation outside work, and you will take great care when you talk to members of the public about the murders. Anyone who doesn't comply with this order will be punished severely. Our computer and phone systems have been upgraded with new security systems, but you still need to act with caution at all times when you disclose information that concerns this investigation. The only people who know that we have a serial killer in Sydney right now are the people in this room… And I want it to stay that way." Morgan pauses as he realises that his words aren't entirely true, but rather than to complicate things he decides to leave it. He also decides there and then that he will not mention the possibility that the murders can be part of a terrorist attack: he has never entertained the idea seriously. "Okay and now to the investigation. We have identified the third victim: the woman found on Pyrmont wharf. Her name is Else Henriksen and you will all get copies of her details later, but I can tell you now that she was a Danish citizen and that she was on a working holiday here in Sydney. We

GAME

know where she worked, and I will personally interview her colleagues this afternoon. We also know where she lived here in Sydney. Now, I want everyone who's signed up for other investigations to speak up so I know what we're left with. Needless to say: this case takes priority and I appreciate any time you can put into it."

Six detectives put their hands in the air: Morgan asks them to write reports of the cases they are signed up for and how much time they have allocated for it.

He then asks two of the detectives, Stone and Ricketts, to go to Else Henriksen's home address and interview her neighbours discreetly, without letting on that Else is dead: "Ask them if they saw a boyfriend or a male that hung around her place, make out that you are looking for him, but also ask questions about her. If anyone asks, tell them that she's gone back to Denmark."

Stone and Ricketts nod and take notes.

Morgan turns to the whiteboard. He writes the times the murder victims were found, where they were found, their names, ages and some other details. "As you can see," Morgan turns to face the detectives, "were all three women in the same age-group. They were all single, and they were killed in exactly the same way. The killer probably used the same weapon on all three occasions. The only exception to these three is Anne Miller, the first victim, as there was no seminal fluid on her body. Anne was found six months ago, Rochelle Stevens three months ago, and now Else Henriksen. You can see the pattern." Morgan clears his throat. "The bad news is that the seminal fluid is not on any of our records for convicted felons. The records are, as you probably know, far from complete as it's still a touchy issue to get DNA from prisoners. And unfortunately there were no prints at any of the murder scenes so we don't have a lot to go by at this stage... And when I say murder scenes I mean the places where the victims were found, as we know that they were transported there when they were dead. I have searched the register of convicted felons country wide and have requested further information of known rapists and murderers and I'm still waiting for a reply to see if anyone who fits the profile for these murders are out of jail at the moment." Morgan looks up from his notes. "Detective Osbourne, you were contacting the restaurants and businesses located in the wharf building on Pyrmont Point where Else Henriksen's body was found. What did you find out?"

Osbourne stands up and reads from his notebook: "On current leases in the wharf building are two licensed restaurants, one café, one convenience store, one architect firm and one boat building firm. Plus there is a fruit and vegetable market held on the wharf boardwalk every third Saturday. The office rooms of the architect firm are located on the second floor of the building and yesterday their office closed at 5.30pm. The entrance to the architect's office is located close to where the dead woman was found. The boat building firm have their office rooms on the ground floor in the middle of the wharf building, and the entrance to this office is at the street front of the building. The last employee to leave the boat building firm yesterday was the MD, and he left at 6.45pm last night. The convenience store closed at 9pm last night, there was only one employee working there yesterday. Then there are the restaurants... 'Khali' restaurant is located on the other side of the wharf building from where the body was found, the restaurant is fully licensed and is open for lunch and dinner Monday til Saturday, closed on Sundays. The last employees to leave the restaurant last

GAME

night were one chef and the bar maid and they left together at 10.40pm. The second restaurant is called 'Blue Juice' and is located a few metres from where the body was found. Blue Juice is open for lunch and breakfast six days a week, closed on Tuesdays. The last employee to leave the restaurant yesterday was the owner and she left at 3.15pm. There's also a café called 'Frothy Coffee': it's located next to Khali restaurant on the other side of the wharf building from where the body was found. Frothy Coffee is open for breakfast and lunch seven days a week and close at 2pm every day. None of the employees of any of these businesses had seen anything out of the ordinary yesterday."

Morgan nods. "Okay, and who is the landlord of the wharf building, did you find that out?"

"The wharf building is heritage listed and is owned by the city of Sydney. The leases are handled by the council."

"And what did you quote was the reason for your questions to the business employees?"

"I quoted 'suspicious activity' in the area as a reason. A few of them got worried and asked about terrorist attacks: I guess they were thinking along those lines as we've got the World Cup coming up."

"And what did you tell them then?"

"That they had no reason to worry about terrorist attacks on their businesses and that they need to speak to the council about any rent reduction for the time that the businesses need to keep closed."

"Well done. The forensic team have finished their investigation of the wharf so the businesses will be able to open again tomorrow. Hopefully this will be a forgotten event soon."

"Okay, I'll let them know."

"Thanks Osbourne, that will do for now. Are there any questions?"

Osbourne raises his hand as he sits back down in his chair. "Just one question: do we get details of the other two victims as well? Can we see investigation reports from when they were found?"

Morgan nods. "I've received the files from the local police units and I'll include those in the material I'm putting together for you. We are now officially in charge of the investigation of these three murders. Are there any questions about this?" He pauses. When there is no reply, he adds: "I will update each of you on email with what I expect you to contribute to this investigation on a daily basis. That's all for now."

When the detectives get up from their chairs and leave the room, Morgan collects his notes and goes over to Amanda's desk: he asks her to type the notes into a report that can be forwarded to the detectives and to collate the reports of Rochelle Stevens and Anne Miller and give them to him as soon as possible. Back at his own desk he picks up the phone and dials the number to the forensic psychological department. He comes through to a receptionist, asks for Camilla Rogers and is transferred to a voicemail where he leaves a message.

Camilla calls back within minutes. "Hello gorgeous", are her first words and Morgan closes his eyes when he hears her voice.

"Camilla," Morgan tries to switch off his feelings. "Good of you to call back so quickly, I know you're busy."

"For you, any time," Camilla purrs.

"That's good. Look, I know I'm a bit late with it, but can you do lunch today? I've got something I want to discuss

GAME

with you. Is it possible for us to meet around twelve down in Darling Harbour?"

"Hang on darls, I'll check my diary." He hears that she puts the receiver down and rustles some papers around and then her voice is back in his ear: "I'm free at eleven thirty, but only if you take me to Jordan's, okay?"

Morgan sighs. "I haven't made reservations or anything: it's a business meeting for Christ's sake!"

"Okay, see you eleven thirty at Jordan's."

The phone goes dead in Morgan's hand. He instantly makes a new call to reserve a table at Jordan's seafood restaurant.

Camilla still has an effect on him even though it's been more than a year since their relationship ended. He thinks back to the few, intense months when they were seeing each other: he'd felt like he was in his twenties again – the passion and drama they'd shared was the closest he'd come to a Hollywood version of love. He knows now that he mistook his physical pleasure for deeper feelings and that the movie recipe for love is purely fiction. He doesn't regret their relationship when he thinks back at it, but he realises now that he was very naive to believe they could stay together. These sober thoughts don't cloud the fact that he's looking forward to seeing her.

Morgan focuses on his notes for a while and prints the end result. He then dials Detective Osbourne's extension and tells him to keep his afternoon free so he can accompany Morgan to Else Henriksen's former workplace.

A soft rain is falling outside but Morgan decides to take a brisk walk down to Darling Harbour: it isn't far and he feels like he needs a cigarette. He holds his briefcase under his arm and keeps close to the house walls where he can feel the warmth from the sun that has built up during the day. When he reaches the harbour the rain is pouring down. He tries to quicken his steps but the wet boardwalk is slippery and he feels soaked when he turns up at the restaurant. Camilla isn't there yet so he goes to the men's' room and dries himself with paper towels. After taking his jacket off, he doesn't look too bad so he goes back into the restaurant and orders a gin and tonic at the table: his feet are wet and cold and he tells himself that he needs something to warm his stomach.

Camilla turns up a few minutes later. She hands her wet umbrella to the waiter and sits down opposite Morgan. "A glass of chardonnay," she orders and turns to Morgan. "What happened to you? Doesn't the force supply umbrellas for their employees?" Her smile reaches her eyes as she takes her trench coat off. Her long, blond hair is curly from the moisture in the air and the soft blouse under her suit jacket clings to her breasts. She looks great, but up close Morgan can see that she has dark circles under her eyes.

They study the menus and order food, and then Morgan takes his notes from the briefcase and hands them to Camilla. She sits quiet for a while, reading. When she finally looks up she turns around to see if anyone is close enough to overhear their conversation. They are seated in a corner and the closest table is at a safe distance a few meters away: it is occupied by an older couple. After calculating the risks, Camilla leans over the table as she speaks. "Interesting", she says. "This is your first serial killer, isn't it?"

Morgan nods. "Yes, it is. I've never seen anything like it."

She studies his face and their eyes meet for a few

GAME

seconds before he looks in another direction; which happens to be out through the window. There is no one on the other side of the window glass: the rain has cleared the decks. A few sea gulls stand in a puddle, huddling together in the pouring rain. Camilla has always been able to see straight through him, he thinks. Her eyes make him feel naked, no: her eyes make him want to be naked. He sips his drink to hide his feelings.

"What about you?" he asks. "A change from the serial rapists for you as well?"

"I've encountered serial killers before: in my early days up in Queensland, and also in Melbourne a few years ago. In both cases the perpetrators evolved from serial rapists to serial killers." Two deep lines appear between Camilla's eyebrows as she frowns. "I need to have a look at the case files but from reading your notes I would think that you're dealing with an organized killer. In other words: the murders were planned and the victim's weren't chosen at random. Is that your impression too?"

Morgan shrugs his shoulders. "I haven't reached a conclusion in regards to that as yet. The killer seems to inflict the women's' injuries in a ritualistic way, and with that in mind I would tend to believe that the killer didn't know his victims. But on the other hand, there's nothing to suggest that the killer was in a rush. It seems he had full control over his victims. He also spent a long time with them after they died. The MO is very similar on all three murders."

"Yes, statistics show that when serial killers kill people they know, there is seldom a sexual motive or any rituals involved. What we have here is a killer who repeatedly rapes and murders women: and that leads me to believe that the he is living out a sexual fantasy. And when it comes to serial killers' fantasies, they tend to see their victims as objects rather than people: which is easier done when they're dealing with a stranger as there is no emotional attachment or memories that can confuse the fantasy. Or it could be that they are fantasising about another person and are figuratively speaking killing them over and over again: in that case the victims all play the role of this person. Either way: serial killers can spend some time looking for a suitable victim and that's called the trawling phase, it's very much part of their fantasies. Once a victim has been selected, the stalking phase begins. But I'll go more into detail about that in my report, and I'll also include a theory of who you should be looking for, the killer's motive and his background." Camilla's face suddenly breaks into a smile. "You do understand that I will have to take your notes with me and do some more research before I can forward an official report to your office?"

Morgan is thankful that the waiter arrives with their food and interrupts their conversation. He isn't sure why he has asked Camilla to meet with him in a restaurant: he could have forwarded the papers to her office as standard routine is. Perhaps his own Modus Operandi reveals that he is after some flirting after all.

Morgan picks at his parrot fish with ginger and shallots. His appetite has departed in company with his sensible mind, he thinks: good thing he didn't order oysters. Camilla quickly empties her plate with Moreton Bay bug cakes and crab and avocado salad. The rain is still pouring down outside and the restaurant is warm and steamy from the food and condensation from many bodies cramped together in the small dining room. Morgan's second gin and tonic is starting to go to his head and he feels sleepy and comfortably warm. Camilla looks at him over the rim of her wine glass: he holds

GAME

her gaze for a few seconds and then looks down. To his horror he can feel an erection grow between his legs. As she bends forward and touches his knee with hers, Morgan can clearly see the cleavage between her breasts. Let the games begin, he thinks and he knows he is getting drunk.

"Do you want to leave?" she whispers. Her eyes look straight into his and he feels her energy like a hot wind that blows straight through him: there is no escaping it.

Morgan nods. He feels faint. "I'll get the bill."

"I think I'll better pay. You don't want everyone to see that you've got a hard-on," she whispers. She takes her trench coat from the back of her chair as she stands up and walks over to the bar.

Morgan quickly drains what's left of his drink. He takes his jacket and folds it over his arm as he stands: covering his crouch. He decides to wait for Camilla by the door.

Morgan's hand pokes out from underneath a white sheet and pats Camilla's bedside table in search of his cigarette packet when a mobile ring tone interrupts him. "Damn," he mutters as he gets out of bed. He picks up his phone and watches Camilla's naked backside as she walks out of the room. He hears running water as he presses the green button on the mobile. "Sergeant Callaghan speaking," he says briskly.

"Um yes, this is Detective Osbourne. I was just wondering what time you want to meet this afternoon."

Morgan sits down on the bed and reaches again for the cigarette packet. "Good of you to call, Osbourne. How about meeting me there at, let's see…" he looks at his watch as he lights the cigarette, "three o' clock? Have you got the address?"

A.C. Efverman

"Yes, it's in the report that we received this morning. I'll meet you in the reception area then?"

"Okay, I'll see you there." Morgan turns the phone off and lies back on the bed and drags on his cigarette. His thoughts turn to what he and Camilla were doing minutes earlier and he gets excited thinking about it so he decides to join her in the shower. She has her back to the door and doesn't see him as he enters the shower cabin. He grabs her from behind and pushes himself inside of her with a grunt as the warm water hits him. Her inner muscles squeeze his penis and pull it deeper inside of her. He presses her up against the wall and holds both her hands tightly behind her back as he pushes himself deeper and deeper into her wet slippery body. The steam in the shower cabin is so dense he can hardly see her, and he doesn't want to: he just wants this warm good feeling to last forever.

"No, stop." Her voice sounds vague: like it comes from a distance. "Morgan stop, you're hurting me."

He lets go of her and takes half a step backwards, ending up outside the flow of warm water. He shivers as the cool air hits his wet skin and he feels his erection die. "Sorry. I didn't realise…"

She turns around and looks at him as she rubs her fingers over a red mark on her breast. Her hair is slicked to her scalp and thick smudges of black mascara line the bottom of her eyes. "What got into you?"

No honey *I* got into *you*, Morgan thinks. He shakes his head to clear his thoughts: what *is* he doing? What is he thinking? "I'm sorry. I didn't realise I was hurting you." He is overcome by a strong instinct to flee. He steps out of the shower cabin and grabs a towel from a rail on the wall. Camilla stays in the bathroom as he quickly dries himself

GAME

and gets his clothes back on in the bedroom. He knows he has to concentrate on work: he's meeting Osbourne at three o'clock in Strawberry Hills. He needs a coffee to clear his head before he can function normally again, he thinks.

Camilla comes into the room: she has a small towel wrapped around her body, her hair is towel dried and the mascara under her eyes is gone. "Listen honey, I'm not angry with you. Are you alright?"

Morgan can't help staring at her long tanned legs under the towel. "Look, I'm sorry. I'm tired and stressed, I haven't slept much lately." He turns away from her and grabs his things. "I'll leave the notes with you then, so you can make an official report. I've got to go, but I'll give you a call later." As he turns he sees that she's sitting on the bed: the expression on her face is sad. He walks over to her and kisses her forehead.

"I'll talk to you soon, okay?"

She nods. "You can call me if you need to talk about… you know, about anything."

He bends down and kisses her lips quickly. It doesn't feel right: it's another charade.

"Right, I've got to go. I'm meeting a detective in Strawberry Hills at three o'clock."

Camilla looks up at her wall clock as Morgan walks out the door: it's ten to two.

Morgan takes the elevator to the ground floor. He walks into a café next door and orders a long black. He grabs an ashtray from the counter and a magazine from the wall-stand and sits down outside by a table on the pavement, next to the wall: from there he has a view over a small park across the road. He lights a cigarette and thinks that he

A.C. Efverman

is polluting the air that trees and people breathe. The TV announcements come back to him again: pictures of blood clots in brains, emphysema sufferers who can't breathe and people in wheel chairs... Somehow these images makes Morgan think of another TV campaign that was shown in the 80's: about AIDS. He recalls a scene where the Grim Reaper strikes people down with a bowling ball. What is he doing screwing around behind Lisa's back? He doesn't know who else Camilla has slept with. He knows that these thoughts are pure paranoia: a way for his sub-conscience to keep his guilt at bay and push the blame over to Camilla. Who started the flirting anyway? He isn't sure now and he doesn't want to think about it.

The coffee arrives at his table. He takes a writing pad and pen from his briefcase and starts to make notes for the questions he is going to ask Else Henriksen's colleagues.

Detective Osbourne is talking to an attractive blond girl that sits behind a reception desk. Morgan watches their body language from a distance: he isn't surprised that the girl shows interest in Osbourne as he's a good looking guy. The girl says something and Osbourne laughs. Morgan decides to interrupt their love bird activity.

"Osbourne," he says loudly as he approaches the reception desk. "Time for work mate, you can flirt on your spare time." He blinks at the girl.

Osbourne spins around and Morgan sees that his face flashes red for a second. "I was just asking Tina here which floor Else Henriksen worked on."

"Right mate, good work. Let's go up then, shall we?" Morgan doesn't bother to hide the irony in his voice.

The girl stands up behind the counter. "As I was saying

GAME

to Andy: it's on the seventh floor and the lifts are around the corner to your right," she points with her hand.

Morgan nods. "Thanks Tina, I think we'll find it." He puts his hand on Osbourne's back as they walk across the marble floor. "So, *Andy*," Morgan clears his throat loudly, "what plans did you make with that young lady for tonight? A late dinner at your place, followed by some moonlight strolling… holding hands?"

Osbourne swings around and shakes Morgan's hand off his back. "None of your business, so what if she was attracted to me, is that my fault?"

"Makes sense," Morgan nods as they get into the elevator. He pushes the button for the seventh floor. "With your charm the girls have no chance."

The lift reaches the first floor and two men wearing business suits get in. The rest of the way up they remain silent. Morgan's thoughts turn to the task ahead as they enter the office of Thomas & Sons graphic design studio. With Osbourne by his side he walks up to a desk where a large built woman sits. She is dressed in a shirt that is made out of a shiny blue material and Morgan notices to his surprise that her lips are painted purple.

"Hi, I'm Detective Sergeant Callaghan and this is Detective Osbourne," Morgan makes a gesture with his hand towards Osbourne. "We're here about Else Henriksen."

The woman looks up at them over the rim of her glasses. "Oh yes, I've been expecting you. I'm Sarah: we spoke on the phone earlier. I'll show you Else's desk and then I'll give you a room where you can talk to the staff." She gets up and moves around the desk with some difficulty. Morgan and Osbourne follow her through a door. The first thing Morgan sees is a row of desks with large Mac computers in different colours. There are about twenty people in the room: most of them sit in front of the computers and a few are scattered around a sofa group in the corner where a chocolate cake seems to be the main attraction.

"This was Else's desk," Sarah says. "I don't think it's been touched since she was here."

Morgan walks up to the desk: it's a neat area with papers in piles and a box filled with graphite pens and erasers. A large computer screen with an orange frame dominates the desk top. There are no personal items or photos. The two desks on either side of Else's are vacant.

"What was she working on before she left?" Morgan asks Sarah.

"She was working on a campaign for a telecommunications company for the last few weeks before she…" Sarah's voice trails off. "I don't know what to say. I mean, Else was a part of our team. We didn't socialise outside work, apart from the odd drink down at the pub on a Friday, but we all liked her very much. She was so young and full of life… " Sarah bites her lip and lowers her voice to a whisper. "How did she die?"

Morgan raises his eyebrows as he theatrically whispers back: "I can't give you any details." He raises his voice to a normal tone again. "Who was her manager?"

"Oh," Sarah blinks behind her glasses and seems taken aback for a few seconds. She blows her nose into a green handkerchief that has magically appeared in her hand. "Marc is out of the office for the day. Marc Pearson, that is. He's in Melbourne meeting with a client. He should be back tomorrow. I can get him to give you a call when he gets back if you want."

"That would be good," Morgan says. "Now, if we can

GAME

have a quiet room to ourselves where we can conduct the interviews, that would be great."

"Sure," Sarah leads the way from the art studio and into a small room through a frosted glass door. "I've made a list of the employees," she nods towards a sheet of paper that lies on the table. "Would you like some tea or coffee, or is there anything else I can do for you?"

Morgan looks at Osbourne.

"A cup of tea would be great," Osbourne says. "White with two sugars please."

"Same for me please." Morgan takes a seat by the table and looks at the list with names. "And if you could start sending people in one by one, in order by this list, that would be great."

Sarah closes the glass door on her way out and Morgan takes two note pads from his briefcase. He tells Osbourne to take a seat by the table, in the corner of the room, and leaves an empty chair facing them both. "Here's what we'll do," he says. "You'll observe while I ask questions. And if you think of anything that I might have missed, an expression, anything, point it out to me when the person has left the room, okay? Meanwhile, I want you to take notes of what is being said. Not the questions, but the answers of course." He pushes a note pad and a pen over the desk.

Osbourne nods. "Sure."

The door opens and Sarah enters the room. "This is Sean Walker, a colleague of Else's." She bends down to put two cups on the table and a young man wearing brown leather pants and a tight blue T-shirt becomes visible behind her. "Sean, this is Detectives Callaghan and Osbourne. It's alright, go on in." Sarah almost pushes Sean into the room with her large bosom as she squeezes past him through the door frame.

"Hi Sean, take a seat." Morgan nods towards the empty chair. "We need to ask a few questions about Else Henriksen. Firstly: how well did you know her and what was your relationship with her?"

Sean puts his elbows on the table and pulls his fingers through his white-bleached hair. "I… I work with her." He looks up. "What's this all about? Isn't she on sick leave?"

Morgan meets his gaze. "What I am about to tell you is strictly confidential, do you understand?"

Sean nods.

Morgan holds the eye contact. "Else Henriksen is dead, she has been killed. I can't give you any details at this stage. You'll have to bear with us and just answer our questions, as we're in an early stage of the investigation."

Sean leans back in the chair and raises his eyebrows. "No way! I mean… I was told the other week that she was on sick leave. I haven't been in the office that much this week and I just came back from a meeting with the printers, but surely someone would have told me if she was dead! Did you say that she was killed? What happened?"

Morgan nods. "As I said… We're in an early stage of our investigation. She was found just a short while ago. Look, I would appreciate if I could be the one asking the questions from now on, as I can't answer any of yours." He pauses but Sean doesn't say anything. "So, as I was saying before: how well did you know Else Henriksen and what was your relationship with her?"

"We work… worked together. I mean, she had her own assignments and I have mine but sometimes we helped each other with various things. Else… she was good with forms and shapes and I'm good with colours, so sometimes

GAME

we helped each other in the final stages of putting things together. I really didn't know her as a person very well, I mean outside the office. She was very professional and didn't talk much about her personal life... She had a great sense of humour though, she used to cheer me up sometimes when I was feeling low or stressed." Sean falls silent and draws a deep breath. "I liked working with her." His exhale is a sigh.

"Okay," Morgan says. "Did you ever socialise with her outside work?"

"No. I mean, sure, she would come to the pub sometimes after work when a few of us from the office went, but that was rare. Actually, she only came a few times and she didn't stay long."

"Do you know if she had a boyfriend, or who her friends were outside work? Did she mention any names?"

Sean seems to think about this as he sits quiet. "No," he says finally. "She never mentioned any friends or a boyfriend. She was quite a shy person. I don't know what sort of life she had outside work. I know that she painted though: she mentioned that she was going to have an exhibition somewhere. When I asked her where, she told me that she hadn't finalised the details with the gallery yet. She didn't seem to want to talk about it, so I dropped it."

Morgan looks attentively at him for a few seconds. "You mentioned earlier that Else had a great sense of humour, and Sarah said that Else was a lively person. But you're also saying that she was shy... It doesn't make sense to me."

"What I mean is that she was shy in the sense that she never spoke about herself. She could be lively and crack jokes sometimes, yes, but that was all superficial, on the surface, if you know what I mean. You could tell that she kept her true personality to herself."

"Right," Morgan says. "Okay, is there anything else you want to add?"

"Yes, I don't know if it means anything," Sean scratches the side of his neck, "but Else was quite moody the last few times I saw her. That would have been... Yes, it was about two weeks ago. Someone said that she was on sick leave, had the flu or something like that, so I didn't think about where she was."

"Okay," Morgan interrupts. "Go back to the moody bit. How could you tell that she was moody? Did she say something, did she tell you why?"

Sean shakes his head. "No, she just didn't talk much. She muttered answers when I asked her something. And when I asked her what was wrong she snapped at me... She's never done that before and you know... it shook me up a bit. So I stayed away from her."

Morgan sighs impatiently. "What did she *say*?"

"She told me to stay out of her business. I was just asking when she was having her art exhibition. She was a really friendly person and that was not like her *at all*. So I left her alone..." He adds quietly: "That was probably the last time I spoke to her... Yes it was."

"Alright Sean." Morgan looks up from his notes. "That's probably all for now, unless you can think of anything else that would be important?"

Sean shakes his head slowly.

"If you think of anything, anything at all," Morgan hands him a business card, "you can contact me any time, okay? Thanks for your time, and please tell Sarah to send in the next person."

Sean leaves the room and is without earshot when

GAME

Morgan asks Osbourne: "Anything you want to add?"

Osbourne looks embarrassed. "I got the feeling that he's homosexual. I don't know if you noticed the falsely imitated female voice and the body language?"

"I'm not blind. But I'm glad you noticed it too, my dear." Morgan smiles. "Anything else?"

"No." Osbourne stares down at his notes.

There is a knock on the door and a woman who looks to be around thirty years old enters the room. "Hi, I'm Helen Robertson. I was told that you wanted to see me?"

"Hi Helen, have a seat. This is Detective Osbourne," Morgan nods towards Osbourne, "and I'm Detective Sergeant Callaghan. We're here to ask a few questions about Else Henriksen. This is a strictly confidential matter, do you understand?"

Helen nods as she takes a seat.

"Good, then we can start. How well did you know Else Henriksen?"

Helen clears her throat. "Well we never really spoke. She wasn't the talkative kind, if you know what I mean. So I guess I can tell you that I didn't really know her at all."

Morgan fidgets with his pen. "I find it hard to believe that you never spoke to her when you worked together in the same office."

"Well, alright. We exchanged a few phrases like 'Can you delete your redundant work so it doesn't take up all space on the hard-drive' or something along those lines, if you know what I mean."

Morgan sees the anger in her eyes. She is transparent like a jelly fish, he thinks. "So you didn't like Else. Is that a fair statement?"

"Yes, I guess you can say that. She had a snobby attitude

and was a bit up herself, if you know what I mean, like she was better than everyone else."

"Alright, is there anything else you can tell us about her, did you notice that she seemed a bit moody a few weeks ago?"

Both Morgan and Osbourne are startled as Helen suddenly gets up from her chair. "As I said, I didn't speak to her and I didn't know her. Now if you'll excuse me, I've got a deadline. I've just been given Else's project and I already had too much work."

Morgan looks at Osbourne when she has left the room. "What do you think?"

"Well," Osbourne avoids eye contact and looks down at his notes. "I reckon she was jealous of Else. I've come across that behaviour before. You know, when women compete at work. Who's the youngest, most beautiful, et cetera... If you know what I mean," he adds, imitating Helen's voice.

Morgan nods. "Alright," he says. "So what have we got so far? Young and full of life, professional, shy, great sense of humour and stuck up snob – I think I know which description I would take out of the equation. Else Henriksen sounds like a nice girl. What do you think?"

Osbourne's face is dead pan as he looks at Morgan. "I don't know. I've only met her as a non-verbal, bruised and not-so-attractive corpse."

"I meant of course from what we've heard so far today, dummy!"

"Oh yes, that does make a difference."

Morgan shoots him a glance like he wants to say something more, but is interrupted by the sound of high heels that are moving over the floor towards the room. He looks down at Sarah's list. "You must be Elisabeth Reese,"

GAME

he says as a young woman dressed in a black dress comes through the door. "Come in and have a seat."

She gives off a vague scent of perfume as she sits down and crosses one slim leg over the other. The quick movement as her fingers flick her long fringe to the side of her face makes Morgan think she has made the gesture many times.

"I don't know what to say, I'm still in shock." Her voice is strangely deep: it's almost masculine and doesn't match her feminine exterior. "I can't believe that Else is dead."

Morgan introduces himself and Osbourne and explains why they're there. "I'm sure you understand that this is a confidential conversation and I expect that everything we say will stay in this room. We would appreciate anything you can tell us about Else Henriksen."

Elisabeth crosses her arms and looks up into the ceiling: the movement of her breasts reveals that she isn't wearing a bra. "Else has worked here for about two years, I think." She glances over at Osbourne who is taking notes. "She was good at her work and she usually met her deadline with no dramas. Not like some of the other people here... But I didn't really know her. She was very professional and never talked about her private life. I mean, she would have a conversation with you, but that would always be about work. It was like she was scared to let anyone in under her skin. Some of the girls here go for coffee and lunch together down at the café, but Else always bought her coffee takeaway and drank it at her desk while she was working. And she always brought lunch from home as far as I know."

"Someone mentioned that she had a good sense of humour, that she would crack jokes and cheer other people up. Would you say that would be true?" Morgan asks.

Elisabeth taps her front teeth with a long red-painted

nail. "I don't know... I guess she had a sense of humour, she used to laugh at other people's jokes but I've never heard her tell a joke."

"Where is your desk compared to where Else's desk stands?"

"Oh, it's probably about five metres between them I guess..." she pauses. "I see what you're getting at, but we're not bound to our desks here. We circulate quite frequently around the room and use different equipment and interact with other members of the team."

"But Else didn't interact with other members of the team?"

"No, not really, sometimes she would ask for advice or help someone else, but she had her own assignments."

"Okay. Did you notice that Else was a bit moody a few weeks ago?"

"No. As I said, I didn't know her that well. The person who probably knew her best here is Sean. His desk is next to Else's and he is quite new here. Else used to help him a bit sometimes I think."

Morgan hands her a business card. "We would appreciate if you would contact us if you think of anything else. I need to stress that you cannot discuss this matter outside work."

The afternoon is long. Person after person comes through the frosted glass door and tells the same story: Morgan hears repeatedly that they didn't know Else Henriksen very well, that Else did her job well, and that Else didn't socialise or interact much with her colleagues. Morgan gets the feeling that Else Henriksen was very different to them all: like she closed herself in and hid her personality from the people that she worked with – and he can't work out why. A piece

GAME

is missing in the puzzle that was Else.

It is twenty minutes past five when Sarah comes into the room and tells them that most people are going home for the day. Morgan tells her that they will leave too: he will call her in the morning and set up a new time for interviews.

As they walk over to Osbourne's car Morgan lights a cigarette and drags on it greedily: the rush of nicotine instantly calms him. Osbourne drives Morgan back to Pyrmont and Morgan tells Osbourne to go home for the day. Morgan still has to write a report for Travis so he takes the elevator up to the office and sits down in front of his computer with a cup of instant coffee.

It takes most parts of an hour to gather all notes and reports, scan them, copy the relevant texts and then paste the information into a Word document. Morgan finally adds some personal comments. When the computer blinks and declares *'Email sent'*, Morgan stretches his arms up in the air and yawns. His work is done for the day. He follows an impulse and picks up the phone and dials Lisa's home number: she answers on the third signal.

"Hi there, I haven't seen you for a while. Are you hiding from me?"

Morgan realises that she is reading his number on her number display. "Not at all, I thought we could have dinner tonight. Alright if I pick you up in about an hour?"

"I just got home from work. But I guess I can make the effort to slip into something seductive."

"Sounds good, see you in an hour then?"

"Okay, but I'm not getting dressed up to go to that Scottish restaurant with the yellow M on the roof."

A.C. Efverman

"Don't worry I can do better than that, see you soon." He hangs up and saves the Word document in his personal file on the computer before he logs off. He decides to ignore the messages on his desk, switches the phone to voice mail and leaves the office.

Lisa lives in a small unit block near the beach in Coogee: it's a fifteen-minute drive from the city when there is no traffic. Morgan is always impressed by the view when he drives over the top of the hill and sees Coogee bay below. Tonight, as the sun in sinking towards the buildings, the light blue sky looks stretched out and thin around the edges. The water in the bay lays turquoise and calm. A small group of people are playing volleyball on the beach. Morgan wonders if he would walk around barefoot and take up surfing if he lived here: maybe life would feel like an eternal holiday if he could spend every night on the beach. On the flip side it would probably be harder to go to work every day and leave all the wonderful possibilities behind, he thinks as he drives up in front of an apartment building and beeps his horn three times.

Lisa sticks her head through an open window on the second floor. "Come up for a while, I'm not ready yet!" she shouts.

Morgan parks his car on the side of the road and goes inside. He has had a quick shower and changed his clothes as he felt paranoid about if Camilla's perfume had stuck on his clothes or he had lipstick marks on his body. His hair is still wet and he smells of Issey Miyake aftershave as he climbs the stairs in the old Art Deco building: up to the second floor where Lisa's door stands open.

"Come in and shut the door, I won't be long," he hears

GAME

her say from inside.

He goes into the living room. The apartment is small and doesn't have a lot of natural light, but the wooden floors are shiny and the walls have recently been painted white. An entire wall in the living room is taken up by a large bookshelf that he's helped Lisa assemble from an IKEA flat pack.

Morgan is studying book titles in the book shelf when he feels Lisa's body press up against his back. He turns around: she is wearing a simple black dress and her blond hair is pulled from her face into a ponytail. She puts her arms around his waist. "I've missed you," she mutters into the side of his neck. "You smell nice, is that the Issey Miyake I gave you?"

"I only wear it for you," he teases.

She breaks the body contact. "Sure you do. Do you want some wine before we go?"

He looks at his watch. "Okay. I've made a reservation at Barzura, but we still have time." He sits down on the sofa as Lisa walks out of the room. He feels comfortable around Lisa: she makes him feel good. His thoughts suddenly slip back to the afternoon in Camilla's apartment and he notices that his palms are sweaty when he takes the wine glass that Lisa hands him.

"How's work?" he asks as she sits down next to him in the sofa.

"It's alright; we're not that busy… What about you?"

Morgan sips his wine. "I can't talk about it, but let's not talk about work anyway. I need to relax."

"Want to come outside for a smoke?" Lisa gets up.

They sit on the concrete floor on the tiny balcony and drink wine, smoke cigarettes and admire the view over the beach. Seagulls scream above their heads and winds from the ocean are cool but not too cold.

"Don't you get sick of living in the city with all the pollution and noise?" Lisa tugs at her dress hem to cover her knees.

"The good thing about my work is that I'm never home long enough to suffer the place. No, but really, it's okay. I get a sea breeze through my window too: it's just mixed up with some pollution. I need to be close to work anyway." Morgan realises that Lisa might have been hinting at the fact that they don't live together, but he can't think of anything else to say.

Lisa keeps her eyes on the ocean that is a few shades darker now that the sun has disappeared behind the roof tops. "It must be hard for you to never be able to talk about your work when you see so many terrible things every day," she says finally.

"Yes it is. But we're trained to cope with it. I talk to the other detectives and that helps. It's important to separate work from your home life though, if you can't do that you won't last long."

"So you mean that you have to be two different people: one at home and a different one at work?"

Morgan thinks about this as he drinks some wine. "Yes, pretty much. I guess I am a different person when I'm at work: I think differently when I'm there."

"I'd like to meet that different person one day." Lisa leans her head against his shoulder. "I want you to know that I'm here if you need to talk though… About anything, you know."

The same words said by Camilla's voice echo in Morgan's head as he looks down at Lisa's face. "Thanks, I know you are. Shall we get going, or we'll miss our table."

GAME

***

The sound of traffic and screams from flying foxes outside the window are night time noises he is used to: he feels safe inside the walls of this house. He looks at his reflection in the mirrored built-in wardrobe doors and sees the shell that is his body. The mirrored image looks wrong: it's distorted and doesn't reflect who he is. No wonder no one understands him when not even he himself can see his true reflection. The polished surface has served him well though: he admits this in his thoughts. He sighs and lies down on the bed. It's good that the acute pressure has been released. But he knows that he is sinking back into depression. He has that floating feeling again and it's happening faster this time. He can't hold on to the feelings of ecstasy: the memories are fading and he can't recover the moment of release in his mind. The pressure will start to build up soon and then the cycle will start all over again.

He needs to sleep: he can sleep for a hundred years, he is so tired. He turns the bedside lamp off and the room turns black for a second but a street light throws a white glow through the window and his eyes soon adjusts to see through the dark shadows. He stares at the reflection of his eyes in the mirror until he falls asleep.

Ninety minutes later his mind slips into REM sleep and his first dream begins. He sees a red bird that sits on a rock in the distance. He hears chirping. But then he realises that the bird isn't singing: it's talking. He has to get closer to hear what it says. Like a camera that zooms in he gets closer and closer to the bird frame by frame, and now he hears that the bird *is* singing. When he hears the words he wants to scream: to tell the bird to shut the fuck up, because it's singing out to the whole world what he has done. He has to kill it. He moves in closer and is about to grab the bird when he sees that it isn't red: it's covered in blood. The head has been cut off and sits loosely on top of the body. And it isn't singing at all: it's crying for help.

GAME

3

Morgan has a hangover. It's six o'clock in the morning when he leaves Lisa sleeping in her bed – he quietly gets up and puts his clothes on: watching her as she lies on her side. The sheets have twisted around her stomach as she moved in her sleep. He hasn't felt her move around: he hasn't realised that he was not covered by the sheets either. He drank too much wine and must have slept like a dead. Lisa's breasts and most of her legs are bare and Morgan feels vaguely ashamed looking at her when she is unaware and vulnerable in her sleep, but at the same time it excites him as he recalls how they made love the night before.

Alone in his car he is tired and weary. The effect of last nights' wine pounds in his head as he drives along Anzac Parade towards the city centre. There are only a few cars on the road. A crow screams from somewhere within the park to his right. In only an hour or so the morning traffic will cover the roads and city noises and pollution will fill the air again.

Morgan drives past Woolloomooloo where grey battle ships lay sleeping in the green water, swings up towards Potts Point and parks his car outside the apartment building he lives in.

Inside, he throws his clothes on the floor and stands under the shower for a long time, letting the warm water massage his body. He then walks naked into the kitchen and

A.C. Efverman

pours water into the coffee brewer. As the aroma of coffee fills the apartment, Morgan irons a shirt and gets dressed. He drinks his coffee standing in front of an open window that overlooks parts of the harbour. Seagulls sail on winds over the water and make occasional dives for fish. The sun is warm but there is a chill in the wind that blows in from the ocean that makes him shiver.

It's a quarter to eight when Morgan drives into the garage under the office building. He takes the lift to the street level. Some rosella parrots have gathered on a branch of a tree that grows out of a hole in the asphalted side walk: they scream in his ear as he walks past. At the café he orders a take away coffee and a blueberry muffin at the counter, turns around and sees that Detective Osbourne is sitting by a table in the corner. Morgan walks up to him. "Good morning."

Osbourne looks up from his half eaten fried breakfast, chews and swallows. "Hi. Good morning, I didn't see you. Do you want a seat?"

Morgan shakes his head. "No I've ordered take away. I've got to go upstairs and go through a few things before the meeting. I need you to get a report from Stone and Ricketts, from yesterday's interviews in Newtown. You know the one?"

Osbourne nods as he bites into a buttered piece of toast.

"Good. I'd like you to go through the report and put the important facts in point form. You've got until nine o'clock when the meeting starts."

A waitress appears with a brown paper bag and a paper cup in her hands: Morgan pays her and looks at Osbourne. "Can you do that?"

GAME

Osbourne wipes his mouth with a paper napkin. "Okay, I'll be right up."

The surface of Morgan's desk is covered with yellow post-it notes. He reads the messages as he waits for his computer to start up. The first message is from his mother, asking him to call her back: he puts the note to the side. The next message is from the medical examiner, telling him that he will store Else Henriksen's body in his cool room until claims for the body are received. Morgan makes a note in his diary: 'Follow up on when/ if parents are claiming body.' He reads a few more messages and then notices a print-out of an email. The email is from the Danish police and it reads:

'Please be advised that Mr and Mrs Bo and Kristine Henriksen, parents of Miss Else Henriksen, will arrive in Sydney on Friday the 29th of May. They have asked the Copenhagen Police Department to provide them with a contact of the Australian police, whom they can contact upon arrival in Australia.

Mr & Mrs Henriksen will be staying at the Palisade Hotel on George Street, Sydney. Please get back to me with a name of a contact person before the above-mentioned date. Kind regards, Sergeant Kim Stroetter, Copenhagen Police.'

There is an email address at the bottom of the page, but Morgan decides to reply later. He has to get ready for the morning meeting, which, he notices after a quick glance at his watch, is approaching fast. He dials Osbourne's extension. "Andy, are you finished with that report? I'll need it soon."

"Not yet, give me a few more minutes and you'll have it on your desk." Andrew Osbourne sounds stressed.

Morgan frowns. "Okay. But I'll have it in the meeting

room instead." He hangs up, makes a few more phone calls and then quickly sorts through his notes.

At nine am the meeting room is filling up with detectives. At three minutes past nine Morgan closes the door. "Alright," he looks at the twenty or so men that have gathered in the room. "Firstly, I'd like to mention that these meetings will take place daily from now on, so you may as well pencil it into your diaries for at least a few weeks ahead. This is where we will go through what we have found so far on the serial killings, and we will also discuss tactics for coming parts of the investigation." Morgan pauses and looks around the room. "I will expect all of you to take notes during these meetings, to make sure that you are updated. You will get a printed report every day with all new facts, but these reports will not cover our discussions in the meetings."

There is a rustle of paper as several diaries and note pads are opened.

Morgan clears his throat. "Okay, let's start with the interviews that Detective Osbourne and I held with Else Henriksen's former colleagues yesterday afternoon. All in all, we didn't get a lot of new information about Else, apart from a few glimpses of her personality at work. But I still find this important as we're trying to establish how she was as a person and with who or whom she spent her time, so I will include this information in today's report." Morgan turns to Detective Ricketts, gives him a nod and sits down. Ricketts gets up from his chair and walks to the front of the room. He reads from a notebook that he holds with both hands.

"Me and Detective Stone went, around two pm yesterday, to the address in Newtown where Else Henriksen had resided.

GAME

We found it was an older style, two-storey building with a façade of red bricks that consisted of eight apartments. We spoke to residents in five of the apartments. We were unable to contact residents in the other two apartments, so we left notes under their doors asking them to contact us. We went to apartment number one first: it is located on the ground floor. The tenants' names are Trudy Tagiello and Angela Cook, and they are twenty-one and twenty-four years old. They are both students and have lived in the apartment for eight months. Their apartment has a window facing the street front of the building. They recognized Else Henriksen's face when we showed them a photo, but they didn't know her name. They both said that they had seen her and had exchanged greetings and small talk, but they didn't know her. When asked if they had seen other people with Else, or other people going in or out of her apartment, they were sure that they had never seen her with anyone. Else was always alone according to them. They weren't sure if there had been other people in her apartment at any time, as Else's apartment is located on the second floor, and apparently a lot of people walk in and out of the building. Trudy Tagiello said however that, quote: she 'had seen a good looking guy around the place the last few months' and she remembered wondering who the guy was visiting, as she had only seen him there at night and never during the day. When asked if she could describe this male, she told us he was in his mid-twenties with dark hair, and she thinks he had blue eyes. He was further quite tall, 'Anglo-looking' and well built but not overly muscular. She also mentioned that he was always pretty well dressed... something I gather would stand out a bit in that neighbourhood. When asked if she ever saw a car that the male drove, she could only describe the vehicle as dark coloured, quite large and plain looking. She never noticed the license plates and didn't know what brand of car it was. The last time Trudy Tagiello or Angela Cook saw Else Henriksen or this male, was at least a couple of weeks ago." Ricketts looks up at Morgan, turns page and continues to read:

"At apartment number two there was no one home so we proceeded to apartment number three, which is located on the ground floor directly underneath Else Henriksen's apartment. The tenant there is a single male named Eric Haggins, aged fifty-two. He's an unemployed bricklayer and has lived in the building for two and a half years. Haggins recognized Else Henriksen's face on the photo that we showed him, as, quote: 'the pretty girl upstairs', but he didn't know her name. He said that he had talked to Miss Henriksen only a few times when they had met in the entry of the building or outside by the letterboxes. He had seen her together with a young man aged in his late twenties one night when they had entered the building at the same time. Haggins described the young male as very tall, with dark hair and a handsome face. Haggins told us that he heard shouting from Miss Henriksen's apartment a few weeks ago. And her front door had been slammed shut a few times. Haggins said that the other tenants frequently slammed their doors, but, quote: 'never the girl upstairs and when she did, my walls shook.' When asked about the shouting incident, Haggins told us that it went on for days. He had assumed that the girl and her boyfriend were having an argument. As he put it, quote: 'there is nothing abnormal about that, sometimes people have to let some steam out.' But when Haggins didn't see the girl, or the guy she was with that night, again, he assumed they had broken up and moved on. Haggins never

GAME

saw a car that the young male drove." Ricketts looks up from his notes. "As a reflection from myself and Detective Stone, I'd like to mention here that we believe that Mr Haggins is an alcoholic. His breath smelled strongly of alcohol and his appearance was not clean, but he seemed clear enough to know what he was talking about."

Morgan suddenly interrupts: "What did you tell these people about Else Henriksen's whereabouts?"

"We told all the tenants that Else Henriksen has gone back to her home country, and that we were interested in finding a male that had visited her apartment on several occasions. The tenants asked a few questions about what the male was wanted for and we told them that we could not disclose that information at this stage."

Morgan nods. "Okay, go on."

Ricketts turns page. "Hum, yes. Next we visited apartment number four, also located on the ground floor but in the far end corner. Tanja Stevic and her four-year old son Nenad answered the door. Mr Stevic, we were told, was at work and wouldn't be home until late. So we proceeded to question Tanja Stevic, who is a thirty-four year old housewife. She told us that the family have lived in the building for about one year. Tanja Stevic looked at the photograph of Else Henriksen for a long time before she told us that she recognized her as, quote: 'someone in the building she had seen around.' Tanja Stevic said that there were, quote: 'a lot of people running in and out of the building all day long especially on weekends and nights, all young, most of them scruffy-looking.' Tanja Stevic remembered Miss Henriksen's face because she looked decent. She had seen Else Henriksen leave in the mornings wearing nice business clothes. And she added, quote: 'she's not like most of the other people in this building who are on the dole or simply weird, she seems responsible.' We asked Mrs Stevic if she had seen anyone with Miss Henriksen, but she had always seen Miss Henriksen alone. Mrs Stevic didn't know which apartment the girl on the photo lived in, only that it was on the second floor. Noises came and went all the time in the building, she said. Mrs Stevic further told us that she doesn't speak to anyone in the building: she keeps her door closed at all times as she doesn't know who she can or can't trust. She hadn't noticed that Miss Henriksen hadn't been home for a couple of weeks."

Ricketts stops reading for a moment and scratches his nose. "Then," he resumes, "we went upstairs to apartment number five, which is located two doors away from Miss Henriksen's apartment. There are three tenants living there: Mr Adams who is twenty-two years old, Mr Zammit who is twenty-one, and Mr Roganoff who is also twenty-one. They are all students but Mr Zammit and Mr Adams also work part-time at a local café. They have lived together in the unit for six months. All three recognized Else Henriksen's face when we showed them the photo, but none of them knew her name. They all agreed that she was", Ricketts looks up momentarily and raises his eyebrows, "and I quote here: 'stuck up and never replied when spoken to'. They didn't know her and they had never had a conversation with her. Mr Adams had seen a man, aged in his late twenties, come out from Else Henriksen's apartment once. He described this male as dark-haired with brown eyes, of medium build, wearing jeans and a dark top. That was about a month ago, Adams said. None of them had noticed noises coming from Else Henriksen's apartment. None of them had seen a car that the male drove." Ricketts looks up from his notes again. "I'd

GAME

like to mention here that there was loud music *and* the TV was on when we knocked on the door to unit number five. We had to knock repeatedly before the door was answered, and both the TV and the stereo were left on until we asked that they were turned off. Neither of the young men seemed disturbed by the noise. And in fact, when we asked, we were assured that if the TV wasn't turned on, there was always music playing or someone was playing computer games with the volume up high. We were further told that the students had agreed not to study in the apartment as there was too much noise." Ricketts scratches his head. "Both myself and Detective Stone made the assumption that these guys wouldn't hear a thing that was going on outside their apartment." He turns page. "We proceeded to apartment number six, which is located next to Else Henriksen's apartment. There we interviewed Miss Turner, who is thirty-one years old. She works as an", Ricketts raises his eyebrows again, "exotic dancer, and has lived in the building for four years. Miss Turner told us that she was on her way out when we knocked on her door, that she didn't know 'the girl next door', and that she had never spoken to her or seen anyone in her company. Miss Turner further told us that she works all kinds of hours, and when she doesn't work she sleeps. She said that she takes sleeping pills that 'knock her out'. Miss Turner hadn't heard any noises from Miss Henriksen's apartment a few weeks ago, or ever. And that was all Miss Turner could or wanted to tell us. Our impression of Miss Turner was that she was taking drugs of some sorts." Ricketts turns page. "There was no one home in apartment number eight, which is located on the other side of Miss Henriksen's apartment. So we, as I mentioned before, left a note under the door." Ricketts closes his notebook and looks at Morgan.

"Okay, good," Morgan says. "Firstly, did you ask any of the tenants if they'd agree to see a police sketch artist?"

Ricketts looks at Stone. "We thought we'd better authorize it with you first. So, no, we didn't ask them."

Morgan narrows his eyes. "You didn't ask them?"

"Well no. We'll get back to them today and organise it." Ricketts red cheeks darken a shade.

"Secondly, since you're going back there, I'll get a warrant for you to go into Else Henriksen's apartment. And you'll bring the forensic team with you. We can't rule out that the apartment was the murder scene, even if no one has seen or heard anything suspicious. And try to be discreet about it, will you?"

Ricketts nods and walks back to his chair.

"You will look for computers, mobile phones, diaries, notes, bills and personal papers and bring it all here, where we can go through it. I can't possibly get a warrant for today so you'll have to go there tomorrow… And yes, I know its Saturday tomorrow, but this can't wait. Is that going to be a problem for you?"

Stone and Ricketts shake their heads. "No worries," they say in unison.

"I take it that you noted the relevant tenants' telephone numbers?"

"Yes we did." Ricketts' face is still suspiciously red.

"That's good, because I want you to call the tenants and give them a time tomorrow to see a police artist at the police station in Newtown. Make it the same time as you're in Else Henriksen's apartment: the less people around when you go in, the better."

Ricketts and Stone agree to organise this.

"Good, then that's sorted." Morgan stands up. "Let's

GAME

take a fifteen minute break and then meet back here."

Everyone in the room scrambles to their feet. Morgan walks over to Amanda's desk and gives her some instructions before he takes the elevator down to the street level where he goes outside and lights a cigarette. He thinks back to the meeting: he got the impression that Ricketts was lying when he said he noted the tenants' telephone numbers. He takes a few quick drags on the cigarette, throws it in an ashtray on the ground and takes the elevator back upstairs. He spends the next ten minutes in front of his computer. Amanda has finished what he's asked her to do and hands him a piece of paper as he walks past her desk. Morgan makes a cup of instant coffee in the kitchen and goes back to the meeting room. As he waits for the detectives to return he reads the notes Amanda have made for him. When everyone is gathered and the door is closed, Morgan announces: "I have organised for a sketch artist to be at Newtown police station tomorrow. Ricketts and Stone will contact the artist and set up times for Else Henriksen's neighbours to meet with him." Morgan hands a piece of paper to Ricketts and then continues: "We have received medical confirmation that the seminal fluid found on Rochelle Stevens and Else Henriksen is from the same perpetrator: which is what we expected. So we are now certain that we're dealing with a serial killer." Morgan pauses for a few seconds to let this information sink in before he changes the subject: "I received a message this morning from the Danish police. Else Henriksen's parents are coming to Sydney next week: they probably want some answers to what happened to their daughter." Morgan looks down at his notes. "Detective Scullion, would you please stand up and tell the rest of us what you have found from reading the investigation reports about Rochelle Stevens and Anne Miller?"

A man, aged in his mid-twenties with freckles and red hair, gets up from his chair and makes his way to the front of the room. He places a folder on the table before him, opens a notebook, turns some pages and clears his throat. "Right," he looks out over the room and blushes. When he starts to read his voice is surprisingly clear and steady: "The first victim was Anne Miller. Anne was murdered six months ago: in November. She was found early in the morning, at six thirty am, by a street cleaner. The body was in a sitting position in an alley in Kings Cross: propped up against a wall next to a wooden cradle. She was naked and bruised, and the throat was cut so deep that the head was barely attached to her neck. She also had marks on her wrists and ankles, which indicates she was tied up for some time before she died. A piece of rope was still attached to her left ankle. No seminal fluid was found on the body but the post mortem examination showed that there was vaginal bruising and also some torn vaginal tissue. We suspect that the perpetrator either used a condom or raped her with an object. There were no fingerprints on the body or the piece of rope. We did however find several sets of fingerprints on the wooden cradle that was found next to the body, but the street cleaner had reportedly seen the cradle in the alley a couple of days before the body was found. The medical examiner estimated that Anne had been dead for about five days, and that the cause of death was the cut throat. He made the conclusion that Anne's body had been transported to the alley only hours before she was found. There were black plastic fragments attached to Anne's skin and hair that showed she'd been in contact with a plastic material: most probably a garbage bag. We believe that she was transported to the alley in this

GAME

garbage bag or plastic material, although no such material was found in the alley." Scullion stops reading and pulls out five enlarged photographs from a folder and attaches them to the whiteboard with blue-tack. The photos are in colour and show a dead woman from different angles. Scullion points to close-ups of the woman's ankles and wrists: "As you will see from photographs taken of victim two and three... these marks are identical on all three women. The piece of rope that was tied around Anne Miller's ankle is a standard kind made of hemp: it is uncoloured and has a thickness of approximately half an inch. It can be purchased from any hardware store in Sydney." Scullion moves to the other side of the whiteboard where he points to a photo showing Anne Miller's naked body leaning against a brick wall covered in graffiti: "These bruise marks on the body are also consistent with the bruising on the other two victims. We think that the killer followed some kind of ritual before and during the murders – where he grabbed the victims' breasts, thighs and upper arms during sexual intercourse. It was possibly done during excitement, but it could also have been to keep the woman down." Scullion points at a photograph that shows a large black wound on the woman's throat: "This cut is similar on all three victims and it was made with a large blade. It is possible that the killer used the same weapon on all three women. We believe that the killer stood behind his victim and then grabbed her hair, pulled her head back and then made the incision. The medical examiner found cotton fibres in all three women's' mouths and has made the conclusion that they were gagged."

Everyone in the room looks at the photos as Scullion continues to read: "Anne Miller was twenty-five years old. She lived on her own in a studio apartment in Petersham.

A.C. Efverman

She worked as a hairdresser in Paddington, where she hired a chair on a monthly basis in a salon. Anne was born in Queensland, where her family still resides, and she was reported missing after no communication to her family had been made for ten days. Anne called her parents or her sister almost daily, according to her mother. She didn't have any close friends here in Sydney, where she had lived for six months. She went out on the weekends with colleagues from work on some rare occasion and there was no boyfriend. Miss Miller's colleagues were questioned, but nothing of interest came up. None of her colleagues were worried when she didn't turn up for work as they assumed she'd gone back to Queensland. Anne's neighbours were also questioned, but none of them had known Anne or seen her with anyone." Scullion stops reading and concentrates on attaching five more photos to the whiteboard. "This," he says, "is the second victim: Rochelle Stevens." He blue-tacks the last picture to the board and then takes a step back so everyone can see. One picture is taken from above and shows a naked woman lying on her side with her arms tied behind her back. The paleness of the woman's skin is offset by the vibrantly green grass that surrounds her body. There is a black mark over the woman's throat that looks like dirt or paint. Her eyes are wide open. The face is coloured blue and black of bruising and dried blood and it is impossible to see what she looked like when she was alive.

"Miss Stevens," Scullion resumes, "was found three months ago, in February. She was found in Hyde Park, at seven forty-five in the morning, by an office worker who was on his way to work. The body was on the grass in full view from the main path. Miss Stevens' injuries were consistent with those found on Miss Miller, and now later Miss Henriksen."

GAME

Scullion points to a close-up of the woman's ankles: "Her legs had also been tied up." The photo shows dark bruises where rope has cut into the skin. "And over here," he points to another photograph, "we can see that the bruise marks on her breasts, upper arms and thighs are similar to those found on Miss Miller's body." Scullion points at a photo that shows Anne Miller's body and then looks down at his notes. "The post mortem examination revealed that there was seminal fluid present on Miss Stevens' body. There was also vaginal bruising. And as Morgan mentioned: the medical examiner has now matched the seminal fluid with the fluid found on Else Henriksen, so now we know that it came from the same offender. The medical examiner also found cotton fibres in Miss Stevens' mouth. We believe that Miss Stevens was killed somewhere else and transported into the park sometime during the night. The medical examiner estimated that she'd been dead for approximately nine days." Scullion pulls his pale fingers through his red hair and turns page. "Rochelle Stevens was twenty-four years old. She was born in Perth in Western Australia and had been in Sydney for two months when she went missing from her work. Her place of employment was a small lawyer's office in Elizabeth Street, where she worked as a legal secretary. The workplace contacted Rochelle's family in Perth and found that none of the family members had heard from Rochelle for weeks. When Rochelle didn't answer her phone, her manager went to her address and knocked on her door but to no avail. Rochelle was reported missing when three days had passed without contact. Rochelle Stevens resided in a unit in Bondi Junction, where she lived alone. Rochelle's family and colleagues reported that she didn't know many people in Sydney and interviews with Rochelle's neighbours

A.C. Efverman

also reported that she had never been seen with anyone. No boyfriend had been mentioned or seen in her company." Scullion closes his notebook. "And that's all," he says and blushes briefly.

Morgan gets up from his chair. "Very good, Scullion." He turns to address the rest of the detectives: "Are there any questions?" The room is silent. "Okay," Morgan says, "you will get a written report of what you've just heard. I want you to keep these images in your head." He points at the photos on the whiteboard. "There is no question in my mind that we're dealing with an organized and intelligent serial killer. And I need to stress that these cases are our highest priority. The decision to keep these murders from the public still stands until further notice." Morgan puts his hands on his hips and leans forward slightly. "Do I make myself clear?"

"Yes sir," the reply comes from a chorus of voices.

Morgan nods. "Okay, good. Now, in the coming investigation Stone and Ricketts will make sure that Else Henriksen's neighbours meet with a sketch artist tomorrow: it will be interesting to see those results. Plus, Osbourne and I will go back to Else Henriksen's workplace and continue interviewing the employees. Stone and Ricketts will also enter Else Henriksen's apartment, together with the forensic team, to see if there is any evidence there, and also to establish whether or not the apartment was the murder scene." Morgan looks at the redhead detective. "Scullion will answer all questions any of us may have in regards to the first two victims. Scullion will be the expert on the Stevens and Miller cases."

"Yes sir," Scullion replies.

Morgan turns his attention to a skinny man in his forties

GAME

with thinning black hair. "Torrone, you will contact Camilla Rogers at the forensic psychological department and let her know that she should forward the profile reports to you. You will be the link between the forensic psychological department and our office, and I expect that you contribute everything Camilla gives you in these meetings."

Detective Miguel Torrone nods slowly as he takes notes. "Understood."

Morgan includes all the detectives in his gaze as he looks out over the room. "The rest of you will read the material that is given to you. And if you have ideas about anything, anything at all, you will come and see me." Morgan turns to Osbourne, who is sitting on a chair in the corner of the room. "Osbourne will hand out copies of the shortened version of Ricketts' and Stone's report now. Everyone gets a copy on the way out."

Osbourne holds a bunch of papers under his arm as he makes his way to the door.

"That'll be all for today," Morgan says as he gathers his notes. "I'll see you back here Monday morning, nine am sharp."

Morgan's hangover hasn't eased and his head pounds as he sits in the café. An empty coffee cup and a half full glass of orange juice stands before him on the table. He knows that he should eat something but the idea of food makes him queasy. Morgan's thoughts are interrupted when Osbourne suddenly appears in the chair next to him. "Hi, mind if I join you?"

Morgan shakes his head. "You already have, haven't you?" He stares at the plate of fish and chips that lands in front of Osbourne. The smell of fried food makes Morgan's stomach turn. "Actually, I was leaving. I've got some things to do." He takes a swig of orange juice and stands. "We're going to Strawberry Hills at one o'clock, don't forget."

Osbourne gives him a strange look but Morgan isn't about to explain that he has a hangover. He pays at the counter and walks out into the windy sunny day, decides to take a walk to get some oxygen into his body and steers his steps towards Darling Harbour.

A Mexican band is playing on the side of the boardwalk. A group of people have gathered on the wide wooden steps: some of them are dressed in business suits and Morgan suspects that they are taking the opportunity to listen to music and get some sun on their faces before they have to go back to their artificially lighted working environments.

He notices that there are more tourists around the harbour area than usual: they stand out from the crowd in their leisure clothes and sun caps. Pickpocket thieves will have a field day during the World Cup, Morgan thinks. The sun comes out from behind a cloud and warms his back and neck, and the wind ruffles his hair as he walks along the harbour. The water is jade green in the sun light and seagulls dot the surface. He stops outside the IMAX theatre and lights a cigarette. For a few seconds he considers turning around and walking back to the office, but then he decides to continue the walk around the harbour and complete the circle by crossing the footbridge. He passes the restaurants and cafés that fringe the water's edge at Cockle Bay and climbs the stairs to the bridge. The wind feels stronger above the shelter from the buildings and the sun has disappeared when he walks across the harbour. Small droplets of cold water drip down on Morgan's face when he reaches Harris

GAME

Street and he runs across the road. The rain is pouring down outside the windows as he enters the office.

Morgan spends an hour in his room where he makes phone calls and sends some emails before he walks into the large room where the detectives sit in cubicles behind grey half wall partitions. He finds Osbourne sitting by his desk: staring blindly at his computer screen.

"Andy, are you ready to go?"

Osbourne doesn't move.

Morgan leans forward and touches Osbourne's shoulder. "Are you alright?"

Osbourne looks up and Morgan sees that his eyes are watery. "Sorry, I was in thoughts. I've had bad news from home: my father has had a heart attack… I just got a call from the hospital."

Morgan frowns. "So what are you sitting here for? Shouldn't you be at the hospital?"

Osbourne closes his eyes: he looks like he's in pain. "But what about… The interviews…"

Morgan walks around Osbourne's table, grabs him under the arm and gently pulls him up. "Don't worry about that. Just give me a call when you know you'll be back… The last thing you should worry about now is work. Okay?" He puts an arm over Osbourne's back and walks with him to the elevator. "Do you want me to drive you?" he asks.

Osbourne shakes his head. "No I should be right… It's just a bit of a shock," he says flatly.

They ride the elevator to the garage in silence. Poor bastard, Morgan thinks when he sits in his own car a minute later and sees Osbourne drive off. He wonders what it would be like to have a heart attack: he has a vague idea that it would feel like being stabbed by a knife.

Morgan sits alone in the small room with the frosted glass door at Thomas & Sons graphic design studio. A cup of coffee that Sarah has provided stands on the table in front of him. Morgan watches the steam rise from the cup and thinks about his decision to let Detective Torrone look after the communication with the psych department. Morgan knows what Camilla's reaction will be: she will tell him all over again that he lacks commitment and that he's hiding from his feelings. But if he can avoid Camilla he can also avoid the sexual arousal he feels when she's around him. He can't afford to be distracted from work. A knock on the door brings Morgan abruptly back to reality. He looks down at his notes and says: "Come in."

The door opens and a man wearing jeans and a short sleeved shirt with prints of yellow ducks enters the room. Morgan is struck by the unusual light blue colour of the man's eyes. "Mr... uh" he searches the list of names. "Mr Welders?"

The man gestures towards a chair. "Yes, can I sit down?"

"Of course, have a seat." Morgan presses the 'play' button on a small tape recorder that he has placed on the table. "Mr Welders, I'm Detective Sergeant Callaghan. I need to ask you questions about Else Henriksen. First of all, how well did you know her?"

The man stretches out his long legs in front of him and sinks lower into the chair. He crosses his arms over his chest. "Please call me Tom. I can't stand formality."

"Okay, Tom. How well did you know Else?"

"Ah well, let me see now... She's been with the company for two years I think. I've been here for more than

GAME

that, so I guess I've known her for about two years." Tom unfolds his arms and lets them dangle down the sides of the chair. "I didn't really know her that well though. Else was a bit of a recluse when it came to socialising, as far as I'm concerned. She wasn't exactly easy to get to know, if you know what I mean?" He crosses his legs and bends forward over the table: minimizing the space between them. Morgan has never seen such light blue eyes on a man: he wonders if they are coloured contact lenses. He breaks the eye contact and looks down at his papers.

"She was an attractive girl so I did my best to get to know her. But she never came out with the rest of us after work." Tom leans back again in his chair.

Morgan raises his eyebrows. "Never?"

"Well, okay, sometimes. But she always left early, before I had time to raise my courage with a drink to talk to her. Anyway, I could probably count on one hand the times she did join us at the pub."

Morgan changes the subject: "What was she like as a person then? Tell me what you know about her."

"She was mystical, that's what she was. She never uttered a word about herself, or what she felt about anything. I guess that's typical of Scandinavian women... I once had a girlfriend from Finland, and she was the same before I got to know her. If it wasn't for her I would have thought that Else was arrogant. But I figured she was reserved towards people she didn't know that well, just like my ex-girlfriend was. Once I got to know my ex she opened right up to me and told me all her feelings and thoughts. And I thought that if I could get to know Else a bit better, she would do the same." Tom exhales loudly. "Of course that never happened. I never got a chance to get to know her, and now it's too late."

A.C. Efverman

Morgan thinks about what he has just heard. "I guess you're right. I never thought that Else would be different because she was from another country. And another culture too, I'm sure."

"Yes. Anja, my ex-girlfriend, she said that she found the Australian people very different to the Finnish. She wasn't used to the way people spoke so openly to strangers here, or that people at work communicated about other things than work. I asked Anja how people got to know each other in her country and she told me that they usually met through mutual friends, or sometimes in bars and clubs when the effect of alcohol had softened their paranoia of strangers." Tom smiles. "But Anja also told me that once you got to know someone in her country, you could talk to them about anything and open up totally." Tom frowns. "Anja left Australia because she couldn't find any close friends. She said that she was too different to Australian women." He suddenly grins. "And I can't say that I disagree with that."

Morgan nods. "Is there anything else you can tell me about Else? Did you notice that she was upset a few weeks ago?"

Tom lets his arms hang down over the sides of the chair again: his fingertips almost touching the floor. "No, I've been busy with a campaign during the last few weeks. I've hardly had a chance to breathe, let alone notice other people's feelings... Sorry I can't help you there." His gaze rests on Morgan's face. "I wish I had noticed though. She probably needed someone to talk to. I can't believe that she is dead... I miss her, even though we weren't close."

Morgan is surprised by Tom's openness. "I know you said before that Else didn't talk about her personal life, but I have to ask: Did she ever mention names of friends or a

GAME

boyfriend to you?"

Tom raises his eyebrows. "I don't think she had a boyfriend. And she never mentioned any friends to me."

"What makes you think she didn't have a boyfriend?"

"Well, I'd like to think that I know women pretty well… They have a different body language when they're in love. I wouldn't have wasted my time thinking about Else if I thought that she was in love with someone else, would I?"

Morgan nods again. "Okay, I don't have any more questions at the moment."

When Tom leaves the room, Morgan writes Tom's name in his notebook and adds: 'In love with Else.'

Since it is Friday many people are dressed in casual clothing instead of the usual business attire, and Morgan gets to see a loud variety of street fashion during the afternoon. One young woman wears a bright blue dress with slits up to her thighs and matching eye make-up when she enters the room. Morgan thinks his face must have revealed his feelings because she instantly offers: "I'm going clubbing after work and I don't have time to go home and change."

Morgan turns the tape recorder on. "Hi, have a seat. Your name's Moira Langer, is that correct?"

She nods as she sits down.

"Could you answer for the tape recorder please?" Morgan points at the machine on the table.

Moira clears her throat. "Yes."

"You are aware that I will need to talk to you about Else Henriksen?"

"Yes."

"How well did you know Else, Miss Langer?"

"Well, I…" She hesitates. "I didn't hang out with her

A.C. Efverman

at work, if that's what you mean. But I did see her out sometimes."

Morgan looks up from his papers. "What do you mean, 'out'?"

"You know, in clubs."

"What clubs were they?" Morgan's interest has woken.

"Uh, just a few different clubs that I go to... Rizzo on Favoe Street, Helium in Redfern, Looks on Oxford Street and Soho in the Cross... just to mention a few."

Morgan writes in his notebook. "Was Else with someone when you saw her?"

"Yes she was, but I didn't get a good look at him. It was probably the same guy though. He was sort of tall with dark hair. But I didn't see his face."

"What do you mean?"

"We didn't talk to each other: I said I *saw* her. She probably saw me too, but I'm not sure. You know what it's like in those crowded, dark clubs."

"Okay. When was the last time you *saw* her in a club then?"

Moira frowns. "It was about three weeks ago... It was at Soho in the Cross, I was with a guy and I remember because he spilled beer all over my new dress. When I walked over to the ladies room I saw Else by the bar. She was kissing a guy."

"Was it the tall guy with dark hair?"

"Yes." Moira Langer pulls her fingers through her hair and Morgan sees that her nails are painted blue.

"Would you be able to describe this guy to a sketch artist?" he asks.

"Good lord no! As I said, I didn't get a good look at him. I mostly saw him from behind."

GAME

Morgan doesn't get more useful information from the remaining employees at Thomas & Sons. When he has interviewed the last person on the list, he spends half an hour going through Else Henriksen's desk. He had hoped to find some personal items but has no luck. He does however feel that he has accomplished something as he now has some new information he can follow up on. All he has to do now is go back to the office and write a report to Travis and send a few emails. Then the weekend is his.

***

Cassandra Saunders sits in her favourite café, 'Craven', in Glebe. She is tired after a whole week's work and is looking forward to catching up on sleep and reading a few books that she has brought with her from work. The book about Feng Shui that she has started to read has lots of promising information: she has tried to furnish her tiny apartment in different ways but she is never happy with the result. With her newfound discovery of Feng Shui she hopes to get some order in both her flat and her life: sometimes she is happy with the way she lives, but most of the time she feels lonely. She is still surprised that it is so hard to meet new people in a large city.

Cassandra sips her coffee while she reads. On a subconscious level she acknowledges the presence of the guy that stands next to her chair, but she thinks he is waiting for someone. When she finally looks up, she realises he had must have been standing there for a while looking at her.

"I'm sorry," he mumbles. "I thought you were someone else."

A.C. Efverman

She raises her eyebrows. "That's alright."

He doesn't move. "I'm sorry, do you mind if I join you? You look so much like a friend of mine that's dead, it's spooky."

Cassandra looks at his arms to see if he's a junkie. But she doesn't see any needle marks and he doesn't smell of alcohol. Besides, she thinks, she was just thinking about how hard it is to make friends in the city, and here is an opportunity to meet someone new: not to mention that this guy is very good looking. She moves her books to the side of the table. "Sure, I wasn't doing anything important."

He puts his cup on the table and places a small rucksack on the floor. "You must think that I'm some sort of weirdo who preys on strange girls." He laughs uneasily as he moves a large pot plant to the side so he can fit himself between the table and the window. When he sits down he rubs his palms over his thighs and smiles.

She smiles back, revealing perfect teeth. "Not at all, I know what it's like to lose someone close. You keep searching for their face in a crowd, like you expect to see them again." She can't help but smile again: he's so attractive and friendly.

"Did someone close to you die?" he asks casually as he spoons sugar into his coffee.

"Yes, my mum and dad: it was a car accident about a year ago." There's grief in her voice.

"Aw, that's tough. I'm sorry, that must be awful."

"Yes, I don't think I'll ever get over it." Cassandra drinks from her cup.

"Shall we toast to the fact that death sucks?" He smiles and his blue eyes are full of humour.

She raises her cup. "I'll drink to that!"

GAME

It's nine pm when they say goodnight. They ordered dinner around seven o'clock and continued to talk over dessert and more coffee.

"Do you want to meet here tomorrow?" he asks casually as they stand outside the café, obviously about to depart in different directions.

Cassandra hesitates for a few seconds. "Sure. Around ten o'clock for breakfast?"

He smiles. "I'll be here waiting for you. Goodnight."

Cassandra laughs in a way she hopes sounds attractive. "Goodnight." She smiles all the way home and doesn't notice the shadow that moves behind her.

***

Morgan is exhausted. He turns the key in his door and throws his briefcase on the hallway table. He takes his clothes off, sets the alarm for eight fifteen pm and falls asleep before any thoughts can enter his mind.

When Lisa rings his doorbell at a quarter to nine he is showered and dressed. She wears high heels and a green dress with deep cleavage.

"Hello party girl." He kisses her red lacquered lips. "You look gorgeous."

"You don't look too bad yourself. But that shade of lipstick doesn't suit you." She rubs her fingers over his lips.

"Sorry about the work bit. But we should be able to get that out of the way quickly," he mumbles into her fingers.

"You *could* tell me what the work bit consist of," she teases as she inserts one finger into his mouth.

He sucks her finger and smiles before he gives it back to her. "Alright, we're looking for a guy who's been seen with a girl in a few clubs. Please don't ask any more questions: you know I can't answer."

"I'm human: I'm curious. But okay, I promise I won't ask more questions."

He grabs his jacket. "Shall we go?"

None of the bar staff at Soho recognises the girls on the photographs that Morgan shows them. Morgan brings back two gin and tonics to the table where Lisa sits.

"What did they say? No luck?" Lisa sips her drink.

"No, we'll try another club later. But since we're out, we might as well have a good time." Morgan raises his glass. "Cheers."

Lisa smiles back at him. "Cheers."

***

Cassandra turns the key in her lock. She doesn't hear the man come up the stairs: he sneaked into the building just before the entrance door slammed shut behind her. He puts his arm over her throat and whispers in her ear: "I couldn't wait til tomorrow sweetheart. Now be a good girl and get inside!" He pushes something sharp into her back and at the same time he presses his arm harder over her throat so she can't scream. They are inside the apartment before she can react, but by then it's too late: he hits her in the back of the head with something hard and she falls moaning to the floor. Blood drips onto her jacket. He exhales and locks the door. Then he opens his rucksack and takes out some rope and two scarfs. When he has tied her hands and gagged her he sits back and waits for her to regain consciousness.

When Cassandra opens her eyes his face is close to

GAME

hers: he is leaning over her. 'No!' she thinks as her mind registers what is happening: he is taking her knickers off. His face is red with excitement and he is breathing heavily. There is a drop of saliva on his bottom lip and she tries to focus her eyes on it. She feels blinded by the strong pain in her head and she can't see straight. Then she feels his hand groping between her legs but there is nothing she can do to stop him. When she realises that she is tied up and gagged she panics: her heart races and her breath gets caught in the gag. She turns her head and sees blood on the floor next to her. She tries to push her mind to think clearly: she is lying on the floor in her bedroom, he must have carried her there when she was unconscious, she thinks. The painful pressure on her body suddenly eases as the man gets off her. He stands on his knees and starts to unbuckle his pants. She wants to say something to stop him but all that comes out through the gag is a hoarse moan. And then he is on top of her again. The weight of his body mangles her to the hard floor. She feels a strange tingling sensation in her fingers and then everything turns black. She is jolted back to reality by a stinging pain on her cheek. "Come on: don't go to sleep on me now. That's not very polite now is it?" He slaps her face until she opens her eyes. "That's my girl. There you are." He grunts loudly and then rolls off her: it's over. She starts to cry: the pain in her head is so immense that she cries out of sheer agony, she has never felt such pain and thinks that she is going to die. He sits up and looks down at her. Then he suddenly grabs her shoulders and turns her so she lies on her side. "What's wrong pussycat? Didn't you like that? You're not very attractive when you cry, you know. Could you stop doing that? It annoys me." He stands and pulls his pants up. "Oh shit, look at that, I can see the inside of your head." He giggles with a hand over his mouth. "I must have hit you harder than I thought." He takes his hand off his mouth. He has a strange look on his face as he buckles his belt. "Well there goes to show you what happens when you hit someone in the head with a hammer."

Her eyes are wide open as she stares at him with disbelief and horror.

"I think I'll give you a little rest now while I have a cigarette. I suggest that you use this time to compose yourself." He walks out of the room and she hears his steps in the hallway that leads to the living room. Her mind feels sluggish as she tries to realise what is happening and how she can get out of the situation. Her mobile phone, she thinks: it's in her bag. But her bag is nowhere to be seen. And even if she could reach the phone she couldn't dial a number. She can't scream: the gag is tied so tightly that it cuts into the corners of her mouth and there is something in her mouth that keeps her from moving her tongue. If she can crawl over the floor and kick the wall she might get attention from the next door neighbour. She tries to move but the pain instantly stops her and she lies paralysed. The hopelessness of the situation almost feels worse than the pain: there is nothing she can do.

***

Morgan doesn't have luck with the photographs at any of the clubs they visit. Lisa doesn't ask questions and follows him around without complaints. At the end of the night they end up in a club on Oxford Street and stay there until closing time. Then they get a cab back to Morgan's place and fall asleep: exhausted and drunk in each other's arms.

GAME

4

It is eleven am when Morgan wakes up. Lisa's head is resting on his chest and shoulder. Morgan looks at her naked body as fragments of the previous night come back to him.

Lisa suddenly opens one eye and looks up at him. "Were you looking at me when I was sleeping, you pervert?" she mumbles.

He smiles. "You look like a painting in the morning light."

Her warm breath on his chest hairs tickles him as she giggles. "You're romantic in the least expected moments, aren't you?"

He doesn't answer: instead he pulls the sheet over their heads and puts his hands over her breasts. They are in an airbrushed world in the filtered light that falls through the sheet. Morgan puts his lips where one of his hands has been. Just then the phone rings. Morgan struggles with the sheet to get his arm free. When he puts the phone to his ear he hears his mother's voice.

"Morgan? Are you still asleep?"

He feels a sting of embarrassment as he sits up, like she can see him through the phone. "No, I'm up. Hi mum, how are you?"

"Today is not too bad."

Morgan touches the stubble on his chin with his thumb. "How's dad?"

"He's in the garden as usual, clearing out some bushes

or something. He'll die from a Redback bite, I'm sure. Listen, I called to ask if you'd like to bring your girlfriend over for dinner tonight. I'd love to see you."

Morgan closes his eyes. "I can't remember telling you that I've got a girlfriend."

"Well you do, don't you? So bring her over so we can meet her."

"You're right. What time do you want us there?"

The sheet suddenly moves as Lisa sits up. She waves her hands back and forwards and Morgan smiles at her.

"How's seven for you, is that too early?"

"No that's fine, we'll see you then."

"Oh listen, bring your swim suits. We're having dinner on the boat. And I expect that you'll stay over; I won't have you driving back in the middle of the night."

"Sounds good, we'll see you at seven. Bye." Morgan turns the phone off and turns to Lisa. "How do you feel about meeting my parents?"

She throws a pillow on his head. "How do you feel about asking me first, you bastard?"

He laughs. "You'll see tonight that I'm not a *bastard*."

She gets out of bed and stands staring out the window. "What should I wear?" she finally asks.

He climbs out of bed and puts his arms around her waist from behind. He rubs his chin over her shoulder: he likes the way his stubble scratches her soft skin. "You're fine the way you are to me," he mumbles in her ear. "But somehow I don't think my parents would appreciate you naked as much as I do."

"Very funny, I'm serious. What should I wear?"

"Mum suggested that we wear swim suits."

"What do you mean, swim suits?" Lisa recalls a scene

GAME

in an Esther Williams' movie where a buffet was served in the middle of a giant swimming pool and dinner guests made pirouettes into the water.

Morgan feels Lisa's pulse under his lips as he smiles against the side of her neck. "We're having dinner on the sailing boat – it's anchored in the bay and sometimes we go for a swim afterwards."

Lisa frowns. "So I wear something that's good for sitting in a boat, having dinner in, and also swimming in? That helps to know."

"What are you on about? My parents don't bite and I'm sure they don't have expectations on you."

She turns to face him. "How do you know? How many girls have you brought back to your parents, huh?" She puts her hands on his chest and takes a step forward as she pushes him. He falls down on top of the bed and puts his hands up in the air. "None, I promise, on my mother's grave."

"That's just it. She's alive. You just spoke to her." Lisa climbs on top of Morgan and tickles his sides. He wriggles under her hands. "Please have mercy on me! I'll do anything…"

***

"Please have mercy on me, I'll do anything." Cassandra's voice sounds shaky and pathetic in her own ears.

The man looks attentively at her. "Yes, I'm sure you will. I want you to eat something. But if you do something stupid like try to scream, I'm going to cut your pretty little neck off. Do you understand?"

She nods with difficulty.

"That's a good girl. Now open your mouth!" He holds a

spoon of cold fried rice in front of her. She opens her mouth and he shoves the spoon inside. She can hardly chew and some of the rice falls out again. She doesn't know if it is day or night now, he has pulled the blinds down in the window and a small lamp on the bedside table gives the only light in the room. She is sitting on the floor leaning against the wall. He is kneeling in front of her: holding a plastic container with rice that he's found in her fridge. The rope cuts into her wrists but she is more worried about the wound in her head: the pain is almost unbearable and she desperately wants to look in a mirror to see how bad it is.

"I need to go to the toilet," she mumbles.

"No, no. Not until you've finished your dinner, young lady. Come on, eat up." As he shoves another spoonful into her mouth she smells rubber. She sees first then that he is wearing thin gloves. This time she manages to swallow most of the food.

He grins. "Good girl. Are you thirsty?"

She nods.

"I bet you would like something to drink, wouldn't you?"

She nods again.

"Well, I wouldn't mind a drink myself. How come you don't have any fucking alcohol at home? Huh?" His voice is aggressive.

She stares at him, too scared to answer.

"I SAID, HOW COME YOU DON'T HAVE ANY FUCKING ALCOHOL AT HOME?"

"I… I've… got a bottle of bourbon... in the cupboard under the… sink," she stammers. Her voice is barely more than a whisper.

He stares at her as he slowly unzips the small backpack

GAME

that is on the floor next to him and pulls out a large knife. He takes the leather casing off the blade and caresses the sharp edge with his fingers.

"Have you seen what I've got here?" He suddenly drops the knife on the floor and takes two scarfs from the bedside table, shoves one scarf into Cassandra's mouth and ties the other one hard around her head: covering her mouth. "That's better. Now you can't object to anything I want to do, can you?"

She closes her eyes when he puts the knife against her throat.

***

"Gently, it's cutting into my skin," Lisa complains.

Morgan fastens the lock on the necklace. "There, all done." He grabs her shoulders and spins her around. "You look great."

She is wearing a strapless dress that falls just below her knees. Her hair is pulled back in a ponytail and she wears a thin gold necklace with a small diamond. On her feet are cotton espadrilles and under the dress she wears a bikini.

"It's a confused look," she says. "It feels like a strange mix of Morrissey and Tigerlily."

He smiles. "You're perfect. Shall we go?"

Traffic is light through the northern suburbs and they reach Palm Beach in forty minutes. Morgan turns off the main road and drives down a small hill on a driveway covered with white gravel. He parks the car in a round courtyard that is framed by large trees. Lisa gets out of the car and stares at the two storey building. "Oh my god, it's huge."

Morgan takes their bag from the boot and holds Lisa's

hand as they walk to the front door. "Just relax," he says.

"You've told me that so many times that I'm getting nervous," she says.

Morgan rings the bell quickly and then opens the door. It takes a few seconds for Lisa's eyes to adjust to the dim light inside. What she had thought was a two storey house, she realises, is actually a three storey house. A wide staircase leads down to a room below where she can see glimpses of the bay through French windows. She can smell food.

Morgan looks down at her. "Hungry?"

"Morgan, is that you?" a female voice asks from somewhere within the house. A silhouette of a woman becomes visible in a door opening: she dries her hands on her apron as she walks towards them and materialises in colours. "Carl!" she calls out. "They're here now!" She holds Morgan's head as she kisses his cheek. "My darling, how are you?"

Morgan turns to Lisa. "Mum, this is Lisa McCall that I told you about."

The woman holds Lisa's hand in both hers. "Morgan hasn't told me a thing about you. He's a terrible liar, don't you think? You can call me Victoria."

Lisa recognises her from the many television shows she has appeared in. But it is first now when Morgan stands next to his mother that she realises his face has many of her features.

"Nice to meet you Victoria," she says.

An older man comes up the stairs. Morgan shakes his hand and pats his shoulder. "Hi dad, how's retired life?"

The man grins. "I'm trying to keep busy." He looks at Lisa. "And who have we here?"

Morgan takes Lisa's hand. "Dad, this is Lisa McCall.

GAME

Lisa, this is my dad, Carl."

Carl grabs Lisa's other hand and presses it firmly. "Hello." He turns to his wife. "Do we have time for a pre dinner drink?"

***

The line between unconsciousness and awareness is a thin edge that Cassandra slips over quickly. She opens her eyes and fear pounds in her every breath as she turns her head to see where the man is: but the room is dark and she can't see him. She realises that she is lying on top of her bed and that she is naked. Her hands are still tied behind her back. She shivers: the room is cold. She wriggles her body sideways until she can reach the corner of the bed cover, holding the fabric firmly between her fingers she rolls around so she ends up under it: lying on her stomach. She breathes quickly through her nose as pain throbs in her head. The lamp in the ceiling is suddenly turned on and she squints with her eyes in the bright light.

"I see that my little pussycat has made herself comfortable. Would you like a drink my dear?" His breath stinks of bourbon as he lowers his face close to hers. "Come on, join the party. It's no fun drinking alone." He grabs her shoulders and pulls her over so she lies on her back again. The bed cover falls off and she shivers as the cold air touches her skin. He reaches around the back of her head and unties the knot on the gag and then he pulls her up into a sitting position and takes a bottle from the bedside table. "This will make you feel much better, I promise." He pulls the scarf out of her mouth and presses the bottle against her lips. She drinks eagerly: thinking that the liquor will take the edge of her pain. But the alcohol burns her dry throat and she involuntarily spits some out. He keeps the bottle to her mouth and keeps pouring. When he finally lets go of her she is soaked in the strong smelling liquid: it is in her hair and on her chest and on the sheets in her bed.

***

"Do you prefer bourbon or brandy Lisa?" Carl stands next to a bar cabinet in the room with the bay view.

Lisa and Morgan sit in a large sofa. Orange flames dance over white pebbles in a fake open fireplace and create a warm light in the room as the last bit of sun disappears outside the window.

"Brandy please," Lisa says.

"And you," Carl turns to Morgan as he hands a small glass to Lisa, "do you still drink bourbon and coke? It's been so long since I saw you I can't remember."

"It hasn't been that long. I've been busy at work; you know what it's like. Actually, you of all people should know what it's like!"

Carl makes a face. "I only know what I missed out on because of work." He turns to Lisa. "Retirement does that to people," he says. "It gives you too much time to think about the things you did wrong in life. And by then it's too late." He looks at Morgan again. "Don't make the same mistake, you'll regret it too." He pours some bourbon into a thick glass, tops it up with coke and picks up ice cubes with a pair of silver tongs from a bucket.

Morgan takes the glass. "Dad, you're getting sentimental. A person has to make a living too, don't forget. And I can't remember that you ever complained when we

GAME

grew up. As far as I remember, you seemed to enjoy your work. Are you going to deny that?"

Carl looks at Lisa and shakes his head. "Either you'll have to shake some sense into him, or hopefully he'll wake up one day when you have children."

Lisa smiles. "He's too stubborn to shake sense into. Believe me, I've tried."

Carl raises his glass. "Here's to stubborn people then."

Morgan was right, Lisa thinks: it's nice to sit under the night sky as they are gently rocked by waves. They've gone out to the boat in a rubber dinghy filled with boxes of food, china and cutlery. Victoria sets the table downstairs and Carl works on opening the roof hatch while Morgan and Lisa sit on deck with their legs dangling over the side, sharing a cigarette. The air is chilly and Lisa is glad she's brought a cardigan. The black sky is covered by stars. House lights on the surrounding bush covered hills look like fairy lights.

Wine helps the conversation flow during dinner. They eat fresh rock oysters followed by fish. When they have finished a platter with fruit and cheeses, Victoria suggests they go for a swim.

The water is cold but Lisa is warmed up by the wine and food and doesn't hesitate to jump in. Lisa and Morgan scream and laugh as they swim around the boat and splash water on each other. She suddenly feels Morgan's body pressed up against her back and is surprised to feel that he is hard against her thigh. "You're a mermaid. This feels so good," he says as he bites her earlobe softly.

She turns her head so he can kiss her wet salty lips.

"Alright you lovebirds, time for coffee and liqueur. We

A.C. Efverman

don't want you to be shark bait." Carl stands on the back of the boat, he holds two towels.

GAME

5

It is six o'clock: Monday morning. Somewhere in the background a vacuum cleaner hums. Stone and Ricketts have left a report on Morgan's desk over the weekend and Morgan reads that Else Henriksen's apartment has been thoroughly cleaned and most surfaces have been wiped carefully. Traces of blood have been found between the tiles on the bathroom floor, on the bedroom floor and on one of the bedroom walls. The blood specks, he reads, have been sent to the lab for analyses. The fingerprints that were found in the apartment have been run through the system and turn out to belong to Else Henriksen and four unknown persons. Morgan impatiently turns a few pages in the report until he sees three drawings of male faces. The men look so different to each other that Morgan shakes his head in frustration. But at least it is a start, he thinks. Now they have something to work with. He looks more carefully at the first picture: it shows a man with a thin long face, large eyes and lips, a long nose, dark short hair and blue eyes. The second picture shows a man with rounder face and stubble, brown eyes, thin lips, wide nose and dark hair: the hair is longer in front and shorter on the sides. The third picture shows a male with a square face and small facial features, brown eyes and short dark hair. Well, Morgan thinks, if you believe the statistics of these pictures, the guy should have short dark hair and brown eyes.

The sound of the vacuum cleaner grows stronger and a

middle-aged woman wearing a grey cleaning dress and ugg boots comes around the corner. Morgan's thoughts shift to the weekend: Victoria had not shown it, but Morgan knows she is in pain. A lot of make-up, false eyelashes, a wig and some carefully drawn in eyebrows might have fooled Lisa, but Morgan knows that his mother is dying of cancer. He feels guilty for not being there for her more and as had Carl pointed out: he is sure to regret it one day. But he has his own life and career, and his mother would never want him to sacrifice any of it for her. He can't stand seeing her in pain when there is nothing he can do for her and he knows that Carl hides his grief by spending most of his time in the garden: hoping that Victoria won't see the fear in his eyes. It's cowardly and wrong and he wishes that both he and his father had the courage to spend more time with Victoria now that she needs them the most. He makes a promise to himself to call his mum more often. She still has some good days when she isn't constantly in pain and they should be grateful for that.

The morning meeting comes and goes: Morgan doesn't want to waste time and decides to hand out copies of all new information to the detectives. They hold a short discussion about the findings in Else Henriksen's apartment. They also look at the three drawings made from Else Henriksen's neighbours' descriptions and Morgan asks the detectives to show the phantom pictures around whenever possible. He doesn't believe that they are looking for three different men as the pictures indicate: to him it is clear that the neighbours have made some grave mistakes in describing the same man, or maybe they aren't sure of what the man looked like. People make mistakes: they see someone in a dark entrance

GAME

or in the stairs, and their minds turn it into something else. In Morgan's experience people are eager to help because they need to feel important, and that can be dangerous.

It is agreed that Stone and Ricketts will show the three images to the neighbours that have seen the suspect: maybe they will remember more if they see how other people have perceived him.

Morgan asks two of the detectives, Barlstowe and O'Neill, to approach Rochelle Stevens' and Anne Miller's neighbours and colleagues with the pictures as well: to see if they can get a reaction somewhere.

Osbourne called Morgan earlier that morning. His voice sounded strained and thin when he told Morgan that his father is not recovering from the heart attack. He asked how the investigation was going and Morgan told him about the findings in Else Henriksen's apartment and the phantom pictures. Morgan also told him to take as long as he needed off work and Osbourne had eagerly accepted. When Morgan hung up after their conversation he thought that Osbourne was a stronger man than he was. His own mother is dying of cancer and here he is: spending most of his time thinking about people who are already dead.

Camilla Rogers calls Morgan around eleven am: she doesn't purr like a cat this time. "Morgan, I've been told that you've been too busy to keep in contact with us and have delegated one of your detectives to do the dirty work for you. Is this true?"

Morgan closes his eyes. "Hi Camilla, good to hear from you, how are you?"

"I would have felt better, to tell you the truth, if you'd

told me to my face that you wanted nothing to do with me. That's for sure." Her voice holds a normal tone but he detects her fury.

"You know it's not like that. You're seeing things that aren't there, believe me."

"Oh, I see what you mean: like the other day when I thought I saw you in my bed. It's amazing how my mind keeps playing tricks on me. I was a normal, intelligent woman who didn't hallucinate on a regular basis before I met you – isn't that funny?"

Morgan opens his eyes and looks through the door opening: the corridor outside is empty but he lowers his voice just in case. "Look, I'm sorry, okay? You know how hard you are to resist. But I've got too much on right now to have a relationship with you. Besides, you know what happened last time."

"I know exactly what happened last time," Camilla snaps. "You couldn't handle the commitment and ran away from your feelings, just like you're doing now."

There it is. He has seen it coming, but he still can't resist the anger that her patronizing comments stirs up. "Yes, you're always bloody right aren't you? I keep forgetting that you're the psycho analyst and I'm just the stupid cop who doesn't know my own feelings as well as you do! I thought we'd agreed that we were too different for each other, or am I hallucinating too?"

There is a loud bang in his ear as she slams her receiver down. Morgan leans back in his chair and stares out through the window. The world is spinning too quickly and he is losing control. He has hurt Camilla's feelings to protect himself and he feels like a coward.

GAME

The rest of the day goes quickly for Morgan. There are telephone calls to make, emails to send, and lots of reports and paperwork to go through. Morgan doesn't mind desk work: he sees it as a chance to brush up on new facts and let information sink to the bottom of his mind.

But in the afternoon he feels like he needs to break up the routine and decides to go with Stone and Ricketts to Newtown. They eat a late lunch together in a Thai restaurant on King Street. Ricketts looks like a chubby Buddha statue sitting on the cushioned floor, Morgan thinks as he his stiff and sore knees remind him he hasn't done any exercise lately. The restaurant is crowded and they decide not to talk about work, instead they discuss rugby and fishing as they pick at their food with thin delicate eating sticks.

The apartment block faces a narrow backstreet that is littered by garbage bins and abandoned shopping trolleys. The red brick building is positioned in the middle of a broken row of terraced houses and raises its ugly head above the Victorian architecture. It's raining: Morgan, Stone and Ricketts huddle together under the small roof over the entrance door. Morgan fights with a wet advertising flyer that is stuck to the bottom of his shoe as Stone presses the buzzer.

"Who is it?" a grumpy voice asks through the intercom.

"Mr Haggins? This is Detectives Stone and Ricketts. We met a few days ago. May we come in please? We have some more questions for you."

The door buzzes and they enter a dark entrance hall that smells like wet socks. The floor is covered with a thick carpet that has a pattern of brown and yellow flowers. What sort of idiot puts wall to wall carpet in the entrance of an apartment building? Morgan thinks as he follows Stone and Ricketts through the dark hallway. The carpet is probably mouldy and filled with fleas. Light suddenly spills out from a door opening and a man with an unshaved face stares at them. "Now what?" He says aggressively. "I already gave up my Saturday to go to the police station so they could make that drawing. How long will this take?"

Stone walks up to the door and places a hand on the handle like he is scared the man might slam the door shut. "We only need a few minutes of your time and then we'll be on our way, I promise. May we come in?"

The man holds his arm up in a mocking welcoming gesture. "My casa is your casa," he mutters and turns his back on them as he walks into the apartment. Stone, Ricketts and Morgan follow him into a kitchen. The sink is covered with dirty dishes; flies buzz in the windows and the air is stale and filled with cigarette smoke. Eric Haggins takes a seat by a small table next to the window. "A drink anyone?"

The three men shake their heads. Haggins raises a glass and drinks a few mouthfuls of brown liquid. There is a moment of awkward silence as the detectives politely wait for an invitation to sit.

"Who's this then?" Haggins finally asks and points a finger at Morgan.

"I'm Detective Sergeant Callaghan," Morgan says. "I'm leading this investigation."

"And what investigation are we talking about here? You see…" Haggins turns his pointing finger to Stone and Ricketts. "They haven't told me what it is you're actually investigating. And I think I should at least know what we're talking about here, wouldn't you agree?"

Morgan nods. "Of course we'll tell you know what's

GAME

going on; you're one of our most important witnesses." He looks at the chairs by the table and wonders if they're clean. "Do you mind if we take a seat?"

Haggins straightens his back. "Am I? Yes of course, sit. Do you want tea or coffee?" The whinging tone in his voice is gone.

Morgan gestures to Stone and Ricketts to have a seat. "Coffee please: strong and black if you've got it."

"Sure. I'll have one myself: it might sober me up."

Haggins turns to the sink and Stone and Ricketts hurry to sweep breadcrumbs and food scraps off the chairs. Ricketts has a disgusted look on his face as he sits down.

Haggins opens and closes cupboard doors and drawers. "I can never remember where I've put things," he mutters.

Morgan looks at the dirty dishes on the bench top. "You know, it's only fair that we provide the coffee. After all, we're imposing on you." He sticks a hand in his pocket and pulls out a twenty dollar note. "Here Ricketts, you go around the corner to the café and get some coffees."

Ricketts looks at the rain outside the window and frowns as he takes the money.

Morgan smiles at him. "Don't forget the sugar." He turns to Haggins. "Do you want something with your coffee, like a cookie?"

Haggins, who has returned to his chair by the table, shakes his head. "Just a long black then, if you're going."

Morgan opens his briefcase as Ricketts leaves the kitchen. "We would like you to look at some pictures," he says and puts three sheets of paper on the table in front of Haggins. "Try to visualise these men as one person, rather than three different men. Do they look like the man you saw with Else Henriksen?"

A.C. Efverman

Haggins holds the pictures one by one. Stone takes a small notebook and a pen from his jacket pocket and sits ready to take notes, but Haggins remains silent. Morgan feels a need to spur him on. "I'm sure that you recognise the picture the police artist made the other day from your description. But the other two pictures are made from other peoples' idea of how the same guy looks."

Haggins looks up. "You know what? I think I need that coffee, can we wait until he comes back with it before we go on?"

Morgan smiles to hide his impatience. "Sure, no worries, there's no hurry, take your time."

"Good." Haggins lights a cigarette and inhales deeply. He holds up the cigarette packet to Stone who shakes his head, and then to Morgan who takes one.

Ricketts is back a few minutes later and places a cardboard tray with paper cups on the table. The men busy themselves for a while pouring sugar into cups and take turns stirring with a spoon that Haggins has found in a drawer. The aroma of coffee fills the kitchen and blend with the tobacco smoke.

Morgan points at the pictures. "How about it Mr Haggins, could you take another look?"

Haggins moves the ashtray and places the pictures next to each other. "Which one was made from my description? I can't remember." He closes his eyes. "Weren't you going to tell me what this investigation was about first?"

Morgan shifts in his seat and crosses his legs. "Sure, what do you want to know?"

"Just why you're looking for this guy I guess." Haggins looks at Morgan with watery eyes. "Did he hurt that pretty girl upstairs?"

GAME

"Yes, he did. He raped her." This isn't untrue so Morgan doesn't feel like he is lying.

Haggins looks out through the window. "Bastard, I knew that he couldn't be trusted when I saw him with her. He looked like a bloody fox. He had this cunning look on his face and I knew that he was up to no good."

Morgan sighs. "Could you take another look at the pictures and tell us which one looks most like him?"

Haggins looks down at the pictures. "No, he didn't look like any of these guys."

Morgan stares at him. "But you told the police artist that he looked like that," he points at one of the pictures.

Haggins closes his eyes. "Did I? My memory fails me."

"But you said that you saw him, can't you remember what he looked like?"

Haggins grabs the bottle and fills his glass. "It was dark and he was turned away from me. Besides, it was a while ago. How can you expect me to remember things like that?"

Morgan tries again. "You just said that he had a cunning look on his face and you told these detectives that you saw a man with dark hair and a handsome face. Remember?"

"Mate… I can't even remember what I did yesterday. There's no way I can remember something that happened that long ago." Haggins drinks from his glass.

Morgan gives up: it would be a waste of time to continue.

They leave Haggins sitting by the kitchen table staring into his empty glass. He looks pathetic.

Morgan knocks on the door to apartment number one. The door opens a few centimetres and a pale face painted with purple lipstick and black eyeliner looks at them over a

A.C. Efverman

safety chain. "Yes? What do you want?"

Morgan holds up his police ID card. "Detective Sergeant Callaghan, you've met Detectives Stone and Ricketts before I believe."

The door closes and they hear the chain rattle before it opens again. "Now what?" She stands with her arms crossed over her chest: a small, defiant figure dressed in a purple velvet dress and black Dr Martins' boots.

"We need you to look at some pictures," Stone says. "It won't take long if we may come in?"

"Uh," she looks back over her shoulder, "now is not a good time, can't we do this some other day?"

Morgan, who has noticed the smell of marijuana, leans closer to her and says with a low voice: "Your name is Trudy, isn't it?"

She nods.

"I give you my word Trudy that we are not here to talk about a few joints that you may or may not have smoked. This is far more important and I would really appreciate if you would let us in."

She hesitates for a few seconds and then shrugs her shoulders. "Alright, but make it quick, I've got things to do." She stands to the side as they walk in. "You can come in here." She walks past them through the hallway and closes a door on the way: the door to the room where she was smoking, Morgan assumes. Trudy turns on the ceiling light as she walks into a living room. A large window is partially covered by dark blue curtains that hold out most of the daylight. Two sofas in different colours are angled in front of a small coffee table and a TV stand on top of two blue plastic milk cradles. There are moisture stains in the ceiling and the paint is peeling on the walls.

GAME

Morgan doesn't wait for an invitation to sit this time: he places himself on one of the sofas and pats the seat next to him. "Could you come and sit here with me Trudy? I would like to show you some pictures."

Stone and Ricketts place themselves on the other sofa. Stone puts his notebook on his lap and Morgan lays the three phantom pictures on the coffee table.

Trudy bites her lower lip. "This is the picture that the police made the other day," she says and points to one of the pictures. "Who are these other guys?"

"Have you seen any of them around here?" Morgan asks.

She shakes her head.

"We think that these images show the same man. Could you take a closer look and see if you recognise him on the other pictures?"

"But they don't look like the same person at all."

"I know, but we believe they are. Other witnesses have described the man looking like this. And we believe that he is a mixture of all three pictures. How close were you when you saw him?"

"It was always at night, but... Maybe he had a smaller mouth, I don't know."

"Are you sure that he had blue eyes?" Morgan asks.

"I thought I was, but maybe he didn't."

"Now that you're looking at these pictures, which one do you think look most like him?"

"My picture for sure, but... I don't know. As I said: it was dark and he was always in a rush. I said 'hello' to him when I saw him but he never replied."

Morgan frowns. "Take a closer look at the other two pictures and tell me if any of them look like the guy you saw."

A.C. Efverman

She bends over the table. "Maybe he's a mixture of all three like you said. I might have exaggerated the size of the mouth and the eyes. They're probably more like this one," she points to a picture. "But I don't think his nose was that big, more medium. The hair is all wrong here: it wasn't so short but longer on the top I think." She stops. "Is that all? I've got a class to go to and I don't want to be late."

Morgan pulls his wallet from his pocket as he stands. "I'll leave the pictures here so you can take another look when you've got more time." He takes a business card from the wallet and hands it to her. "I want you to call me if you think of any more details. We believe that this guy is dangerous and it's important that we catch him."

"What did he do exactly? Angela, my flatmate, saw the police go into that girl's apartment on the weekend. Did he kill her or something?"

"He raped her," Morgan says. "I want you to be very careful if you see him again, he's a very dangerous man. Do you understand?"

Trudy nods.

There is something wrong with the light in the entrance hall and they have to walk up the stairs in darkness. Just as well, Morgan thinks, the stairs are also covered with the horrible carpet and he can just imagine how filthy it is, he doesn't need to see it. Ricketts knocks on a door and they wait for a few seconds. There is music on the other side of the door so there is obviously someone home. Ricketts knocks again: this time with his fist. The door opens almost instantly and a guy with spiky brown hair looks at them. "You again?" he sighs. "I'm the only one home: Josh and Marc are working at the café."

GAME

Stone holds up his notebook. "What time do they finish work?"

The guy scratches the back of his head. "They usually get home around eight. Depends how busy it gets."

"Right, what's the name and address of the café? We'll try them there."

"Jube on King Street, it's close to the cinema. But I don't know if they'll be happy to see you there."

Stone clears his throat. "We won't bother them for long. Thank you."

As they walk down the stairs, Morgan asks: "Have you heard anything from the tenants that weren't home before?"

Stone opens his notebook as they come out in the grey daylight. The rain has stopped. "The couple in number eight, that's the apartment next to Else's, had been trekking in the Himalaya's for a month and got back two days ago. They told us that they hadn't seen or heard anything unusual, nor had they seen anyone come in or out of Else Henriksen's apartment. They both work nine to five." Stone turns a few pages. "The man in apartment number two works as a steward for Quantas and is hardly ever home. He didn't recognise Else Henriksen when we showed him a photo."

Marc Adams has jet black hair with blue streaks and a ring pierced nose. He is dressed in a black tight T-shirt and wears a black apron over black pants. He is clearing tables on the pavement when he spots the detectives. He frowns and glances into the café. The three men take a seat by a table and Adams comes over with a menu. "You've better be here for the food," he says grumpily.

Morgan smiles at him. "We'll have coffee. And we need to ask you some questions when you've got a minute."

Adams nods and disappears inside. He comes back a few minutes later with a tray. "Josh is covering for me so it would be good if you could make it snappy." He places three cups on the table.

Morgan takes the phantom pictures from a folder and places them on the table. He explains that they believe the drawings describe the same man and then asks Adams if he has seen a man that look like any of the pictures go in or out of Else Henriksen's apartment. Adams says that the only guy he has seen was the guy he described for the police artist. "But," he says, "as I told the detectives before," he shoots a glance at Stone and Ricketts, "I didn't get a good look at the guy. So I could have missed some details."

"Do you think that the other two pictures look like him, or have any features that you may have missed?" Morgan asks.

Adams frowns as he looks down at the pictures. "Maybe his hair wasn't that long: it could have been shorter... Look, I really don't know. You don't expect to have to describe some strange guy a month after you've seen him. Do you know what I mean?"

"I'll leave the pictures with you just the same," Morgan says. "If you could have another look at them and call us if you think of anything, that'd be great." He hands Adams a business card.

***

The telephone has been ringing all morning and it drives him mad. He knows that he has to get out of the apartment before someone decides to come looking for the girl. He

GAME

is not comfortable with the situation. He kept the first two girls in his house where no one could disturb them or come looking for them. The third one: Else, she was different... she had been *real* different. But she had been worth the extra trouble. This time he is in an unfamiliar environment. He has to make a quick decision and then there is no turning back. As much as he enjoys savouring the moment he can't afford to stay much longer. He has to kill the girl now, and either leave the body or transport it back to his place. He pulls a chair close to the bed and lights a cigarette. Cassandra's eyes are closed: he isn't sure if she is sleeping or is pretending to. He caresses her figure with his eyes and his gaze lingers on her neck. Soon that slim pretty neck will be no more. A smile curls his lips as he imagines her life drain from her body. It is always an anti-climax for him to watch the moment of death: first there is a rush of energy as the girl struggles for her life and then the energy slowly disappears and leaves the body limp, still and *useless*. But he prefers not to think about that now. Instead he thinks about the eyes. The eyes fascinate him the most. He likes to pull the girl's head back and look into her eyes as he cuts the throat. The eyes will be sparkling with life and then freeze for a second before they go out like a light. It is the moment between the sparkling and the freezing that gives him most pleasure.

He walks into the bathroom, drops his cigarette into the toilet and flushes. After washing his face with cold water he peels the wet gloves off his fingers and takes a new pair from his backpack. He watches Cassandra on the bed as he puts the gloves on. She has opened her eyes and is staring at him.

"Alright pussycat, the moment has come. You're going

to see your mummy and daddy soon. You'll like that, won't you?"

Her eyes widen. He walks up to the bed and puts a hand over her throat. "You can't change anything now. I'm the only person who can change anything, don't forget that. People say that they can form their own destiny, but that's not true. It's always up to someone else to do it for you. Like now…" he looks down at her red face. "Look at you. I'm here to change your fate and you've got no say in it what… so… ever." He lifts his hand from her throat and backs away from her. Cassandra catches her breath and then coughs. She can't see what he is doing but she hears a swishing sound: it sounds like he pulls a plastic bag out of his backpack. He is suddenly by her side again and she sees that he is wearing a black garbage bag with holes cut out for his arms. He holds the large knife in his hand. Cassandra feels how warm urine trickles down her buttocks and forms a puddle under her.

GAME

6

The phone rings. Morgan sits up in his bed. The only feeling he registers is surprise. He looks around the room: it's dark. The phone rings again – he finds it and picks it up.

"Morgan." It's Carl's voice. "I'm at the hospital. You've got to come, she's asking for you."

Morgan closes his eyes. "Which hospital?" His arms and legs suddenly feel icy cold.

"We're at the Royal North Shore in St Leonards, we got an ambulance here. There was no other place to go to they said: all the other hospitals were full."

Morgan hears a distant sob but it is so vague he isn't sure he has heard it at all.

"It took forever to get here and now she's in a private room. I'm downstairs because they wouldn't let me use the mobile phone inside."

"I'll be there in twenty minutes dad. Okay?"

This time the sob is louder. "Okay, okay."

Morgan hangs up and goes to the bathroom to have a quick shower. He is in his car ten minutes later and drives well over the speed limit as he turns a corner and enters the main road.

Carl is waiting outside the hospital. Morgan has never seen his father so upset: Carl's face is yellow and grey under the fluorescent lights over the entrance.

"Dad, I'm here now. Let's go upstairs." Morgan puts his arm around his father's shoulders and turns him towards the sliding doors. The limpness of Carl's body feels heavy and unfamiliar. They take the elevator to level eight and a nurse shows them into a dark room.

"She's asleep now. We gave her quite a bit of morphine so she'll probably sleep for a while." The nurse takes the light from the corridor with her as she closes the door.

Morgan finds two chairs and pulls them close to the large dark shape he knows is a bed. He helps his father sit down and then takes a seat next to him. "What happened dad?"

Carl inhales deeply and when he exhales through his nose it is a loud sigh. "We were going to bed and she was in the bathroom. I heard a noise, like something fell on the floor and that's where I found her: on the floor. She had passed out. When she woke up she screamed with pain. It was horrible. I gave her medicine and called an ambulance. But it took forever until they showed up and when they finally came they told us that all the hospitals in the area were full. So we had to come all the way here."

Morgan's eyes have adjusted to the darkness in the room. A soft glow from the moonlight seeps through the half closed blinds and creates a pattern of lines on the bed spread. The tears on Carl's face look like melted silver.

"She fell in and out of consciousness in the ambulance but she was wide awake when we got here. By then she was screaming with pain so they had to give her a massive dose of morphine. When she was finally falling asleep she asked for you. She wouldn't close her eyes until I promised her that you would come."

Morgan puts his arm around Carl's shoulders. He isn't sure if he wants to give his father warmth or if it is he himself that craves body contact. "Have you told Katherine yet?"

GAME

Carl dries his face on his shirt sleeve. "I didn't want to worry her in the middle of the night, with the kids and all. I'll give her a call her in the morning."

There is nothing more to say so they sit silent in the dark. The sleeping woman's body is a small raised shape in the middle of the large hospital bed. Morgan must have fallen asleep because he jerks back violently when something touches his hand. He feels disorientated for a second before he realises where he is. He looks down and sees that his mother's hand is resting on top of his. The room is still dark but he can make out the contours of his mother's head against the pillow and he sees the whites of her eyes and her teeth.

"Morgan," she whispers. "You came."

Morgan leans forward and touches her cheek with his fingertips. "Hi mum. How are you feeling?"

She draws a shallow breath. "I've been better. I wanted to see you before it's too late. I'm sorry if I worried you."

Tears burn under Morgan's eyelids. "Mum, you'll be alright. Don't talk like that. We're here with you, me and dad, and I'm calling Katherine in the morning."

Her fingernails press into the flesh of his palm. "I'm trying to tell you that I won't be here much longer," she whispers. "And I want you to look after dad and not grieve too much."

Warm tears wet Morgan's cheeks. "Mum, I'm here with you, you're not alone. I love you."

Victoria sighs and the grip of her hand relaxes.

Carl stirs in his chair. "Did she wake up?" He yawns. "I must have fallen asleep. What did she say?"

Morgan dries his face with a corner of the blanket that covers his mum's body. "Not much, but I told her that we're here with her and that I'm calling Katherine in the morning."

Carl strokes Victoria's forehead. "Darling, can you hear me? I'll get the nurse so they can give you your medicine." He stands. "They wanted us to let them know when she woke up. I'll be right back." Carl leaves the room. The open door creates a square of white light on the vinyl carpet.

Morgan holds his mother's hand: it feels warm and dry. He puts his head on her shoulder that feels fragile and small under his weight. He has the weight of the world on his own shoulders. "Mum, can you hear me?" He feels her nod her head slowly.

"Don't go mum, don't go."

It's a cold morning. Morgan stands outside the hospital entrance and talks to his sister on the mobile. Katherine is crying but Morgan can't find any words to comfort her. "I think you should get over here now," he says. "Don't bring the kids, just get over here."

The next call he makes is to the office. He tells Amanda to organize the morning meeting without him, and to ask Ricketts to hold the meeting in his absence.

Amanda says that she will let everyone in the office know what has happened.

Morgan lights a cigarette when he has ended the call. His mind isn't focused on work. The doctors have told him that all they can do now is to give his mother morphine – it is too late for anything else. He is surrounded by death, it's everywhere: he is drowning in it and it feels like he can't breathe. He sits down on a wooden bench and watches the people around him: A man in a wheelchair smokes a cigarette. A woman with bandages covering both her arms sits on another bench next to an old lady who is wearing a

GAME

winter coat and slippers. Doctors and nurses move behind groups of standing people: their white coats are a blur that seem to melt into the yellow brick hospital wall. The sun darts in and out of the clouds and brightens the court yard for a few seconds like a strobe light before it disappears and the world turns cold and grey again. Morgan doesn't want to get up from the bench. He doesn't want to go back to the small room where his mother lies helpless. A childhood memory emerges: He is standing outside the front door of his parents' house. He is crying. He calls out to his mum, asking her to stay. His nine-year old sister laughs and calls him a sissy. His mother, who is stepping into a taxi, turns around and looks at him with tears in her eyes. "I'll be back in three weeks Morgan, don't be sad. Be a brave boy for mummy."

He had cried every time she left. As a toddler he didn't understood why his mummy went away constantly on trips, and why she wouldn't spend all her time with him. Every time she came back she had great presents for him: a set of tin soldiers from Paris, a large teddy bear from New York, or a new technology gismo from Japan or Korea. The gifts didn't ease his pain but he felt an enormous relief that she was back with him. He spent most of his childhood feeling terrified that his mother would never come back. When he was old enough to understand that his mum worked as an actress, he resented her for not wanting to spend more time with him.

And then there was his dad: Carl was barely home enough to know what Morgan was interested in – he worked nightshifts and came home exhausted and quiet. Morgan would ask what he had done at work, but his dad would to shake his head and say: "You don't want to know."

A.C. Efverman

Morgan used to jump up and down in frustration. "Yes I do! Yes I do! Tell me about the bad guys that you've arrested daddy!"

Sometimes when Carl was in a good mood he would tell stories about how the police had caught the 'bad guys' or how they had had a car chase with 'the bad guys' all over town. Morgan loved these stories: he loved to sit on his dad's lap and hear how the 'good guys' had won over the 'bad guys' again.

Katherine, who was four years older than Morgan, played with him and made sure that he brushed his teeth before he went to bed. Katherine happily played the role of a strict mother who never took no for an answer and she could be quite rough with him when no one else was around. There was never a question in Morgan's mind why she bothered to spend time with him: he was her personal doll.

The household kept a maid: an older lady called Mrs Cullen. She cooked for them and took the children to school when their parents weren't home. Morgan doesn't know Mrs Cullen's first name and he can't remember what she looks like: she is a colourless figure in his memory and the features of her face have faded over the years. The only thing he can recall clearly about Mrs Cullen is the day she took him to school for the first time. He had been terrified that Mrs Cullen would leave him in the school building and that he never would see his mum or dad again. He refused to let go of Mrs Cullen's skirt and screamed so loud that the teacher told Mrs Cullen to take him back home. When his mum arrived home a few days later from a trip, she was furious with Morgan. He had never seen her so angry with him before and he hid under his bed and cried for hours: convinced that his mum didn't love him and that she wanted

GAME

to get rid of him. Victoria finally took him in her arms and held him for a long time. Carl entered the room briefly and told her that 'she was weakening the boy and was making a wimp out of him'. Morgan cried in his mother's arms and pressed his body against her warm chest until there were no more tears. She told him that she loved him then and that he would have to be a big boy: he had to grow up to be a brave man like his father. Morgan listened to her soft voice and looked at her beautiful face. He decided then that he would do anything for her.

"Are you sitting out here?"

Morgan looks up and sees his sister: Katherine is forty-two years old and is a younger version of their mother.

"Traffic was mad and I had to take the kids over to a friend's house. How is she?" Katherine sits next to him on the wooden bench.

"She's not good. I've taken the day off to be with her."

Katherine sits silent for a few seconds. "Right," she says finally. "I'm going in, which floor is she on?" She stands.

It starts to rain: small, cold drops of water hit Morgan's face. "I'll go with you."

The smell of hospital is in their noses as they cross the entrance hall. Katherine is silent and doesn't look at Morgan as they take the elevator to the eighth floor. Carl is talking to a nurse in the corridor.

"I'm sorry, but we can't give her more morphine right now. She's had enough for at least another hour," Morgan hears the nurse say.

"What's going on?" Katherine walks up to Carl.

Carl sighs. "Hi honey, the nurse won't give your mother more morphine. She's in pain and is asking for more."

A.C. Efverman

Morgan walks into his mother's room. Victoria's face is almost as white as the pillow that her head rests on. Without the wig and the make-up she looks old. Pain has drawn deep lines around her mouth and eyes. Her hands are clenched into fists.

"Mum, it's me." Morgan sits on the side of bed. "Are you in pain?"

Victoria opens her eyes and starts to cry.

The day goes slowly. Rain drums against the window as the family sits around Victoria's bed. A painfully bright white light snakes its way through the open blinds into the room, and the shadows in the corners are dusty shades of grey. It is afternoon when Morgan's beeper starts to vibrate in his pocket. He goes downstairs and returns the call to the office on his mobile. Ambulance sirens whine loudly behind him as Ricketts answers the phone, and the fear of mobile phone radiation causing cancer cells in his brain enters Morgan's mind briefly as he presses his phone hard against one ear and his hand over the other.

"Callaghan, is that you?"

"Yes, what's news Ricketts?"

"Uh, all of us… we wanted to say how sorry we are for what's happened."

"Thanks Ricketts."

"And I thought I'd bring you up to date on a few things. We've gone through some phone bills that were found in Else Henriksen's apartment. There were quite a few calls recorded there to a mobile phone. But this mobile that Else made regular calls to: it turns out to be stolen. So we still don't know who's been using it. The owner of the stolen mobile says that she lost her phone a few months ago, but

GAME

she didn't report it stolen until last week for some reason. We're looking into it now."

"Okay good. What else?"

"Barlstowe and O'Neill showed the phantom pictures to Miss Stevens' and Miss Miller's neighbours and colleagues. They had no luck though… And the Superintendent called for you. We told him what's happened. He wants you to give him a call as soon as possible."

Morgan sighs loudly into the mobile ether. "Okay, anything else?"

"No that's pretty much it."

"I'll call you when I know I'll be back… And speaking of which: has anyone heard from Osbourne?"

"I'll ask Amanda; hang on." A few silent seconds pass and then Ricketts' voice is back: "No, we haven't heard from him."

"Okay, thanks Ricketts. We'll talk more later." Morgan turns his phone off and lights a cigarette. It is still raining so he stays under the cover of the entrance roof and ignores the no smoking signs. He doesn't see the point in calling Travis just then.

7

A hand is placed on Morgan's shoulder.

"Morgan. Morgan, wake up." Katherine is leaning over the chair where he's been sleeping. He sees tears on her face. "She's asking for you."

Morgan sits up and looks over at the bed where a small lamp shines a white light over his mother's face. The bed head is raised behind her back and she is almost sitting up. Her eyes are closed and he can hear that her breathing is laboured. Morgan goes to his mother's side. His father is sitting on the other side of the bed, holding Victoria's hand. Katherine sits down on the bed, next to Carl.

"Mum," Morgan whispers.

Her sunken cheeks have wet streaks of tears. She slowly opens her eyes and looks up at Morgan. He takes her hand and lies down next to her. He is unable to stop his own tears. "Mum, we're here. We're all here with you," he mumbles. He feels her struggle for air and then she gasps: a long, horrible gasp as she tries in vain to get air down to her lungs. Her body tenses up for a few seconds and then relaxes. Morgan feels her hand letting go of his. He also gasps for air: it feels like he can't breathe. "Mum, mum."

Carl's eyes are black and empty as he looks at Morgan. "I'll get the doctor." He gets up and walks slowly out of the room. Katherine puts her head on Victoria's shoulder and cries. Morgan sits up, he is still holding his mother's hand and he feels the warmth from her body. He looks down

GAME

at her face: it looks like she is sleeping. A small stream of saliva drips from the side of her mouth onto the pillow.

Carl comes back with a woman wearing a white coat. Katherine sits up, she sobs. The doctor leans over Victoria and inspects the instrument above the bed. She carefully opens Victoria's eyelids and shines with a small torch into her eyes and then looks at her watch. "Time of death is 4.08 am," she says softly as she holds two fingers over Victoria's throat.

Morgan's beeper vibrates in his pocket. He takes it out, looks at it and recognizes Ricketts' mobile number. The doctor stands in front of Morgan and looks down at him. "I'm sorry but you'll have to let go of her hand now."

Morgan looks at his left hand that still holds his mother's hand. He looks at the beeper in his other hand and puts it back in his pocket. He gently pulls his hand from his mother's. He feels that there is not enough air in the small room. "I'm going out for a while," he says to Carl and Katherine as he leaves the room. He walks slowly to the elevator and somehow gets to the ground floor: he can't remember pressing any buttons. He inhales the cold night air as the sliding doors close behind him. He lights a cigarette and dials Ricketts' mobile number. Morgan hears his own voice like someone is talking next to him: "Ricketts, what's happened?"

"Another body has been found. She's down at Kirribilli; under the harbour bridge. We're waiting for the forensics and the photographer now."

Morgan drags on his cigarette and exhales loudly. "I'll be there within half an hour. Don't touch anything."

"Okay, see you then." Ricketts ends the call.

Morgan stares blindly into the darkness that surrounds

A.C. Efverman

the lit up entrance. It feels like he is drunk: his mind is foggy and his head is pounding with a dull pain. It must be the shock, he thinks as he walks back inside and through the lobby towards a vending machine. He puts a few coins in the slot and soon holds a plastic cup filled with hot coffee. He burns his lips as he sips the drink, but the caffeine makes his thoughts clearer.

When Morgan walks back into the small room, the doctor is taking the needle out of his mother's arm. She disconnects the monitor over the bed by flicking a switch. On/Off, Morgan thinks. It is as simple as that: his mother is now *off*.

Katherine and Carl stand next to the bed with their arms around each other. Carl looks down at his wife's face over Katherine's shoulder. Katherine speaks softly with a soothing voice: Morgan isn't sure if she is trying to comfort Carl or herself – they are both crying. Morgan puts his hand on his father's shoulder and squeezes it lightly. "Dad, Katherine, I've got to go. The office called; it's an emergency."

Carl turns around slowly. "Your mother just died Morgan. I can't see how anything else could be important." He stares at Morgan without blinking.

"I'm sorry but other people are depending on me. I'll give you a call as soon as I can and I'll come over and see you soon, okay?"

Katherine wipes the tears from her face with a paper tissue. "He's coming home with me. I won't let him sit in that large, empty house on his own."

Morgan nods. "Good, I'll give you a call when I can come over." He looks at his mother's face, abruptly turns and walks out of the room.

GAME

The area under the harbour bridge is lit up by bright lights. Five unmarked cars are parked on the grass by the waters' edge. Morgan has been driving with the radio turned up loud to distract his thoughts and the windows down to allow the cold night air to slap his face, but as he drives into Kirribilli he turns the radio off as he doesn't want to wake the residents.

Ricketts turns around when Morgan approaches the group of people that has gathered under the lights. Morgan catches a glimpse of the dead woman behind Ricketts' large body frame: he can see that she is lying face down and that her hands are tied behind her back.

"She's only been dead for about ten hours," Ricketts sounds excited for some reason.

Morgan lights a cigarette and walks around him. A man dressed in a dark blue overall is taking photos and crouches down to get close-ups. The bright lights are painful in Morgan's eyes.

The dead woman is blond and slim. Dried blood covers her arms, hair and shoulders. The photographer moves away from the body and Morgan sees that the back of the woman's legs are covered in something dark: it looks like excrement. George Demitriades nods in recognition of Morgan and crouches down on the grass next to the body. He carefully turns the woman onto a plastic sheet. A large cut across the woman's throat becomes visible. The front of the body is covered in blood, the face is bruised, and the eyes are open and stare blindly at Morgan. Demitriades holds a small tape recorder in front of his mouth as he records the injuries and the position of the body. Morgan watches him for a while and then turns to Ricketts. "Who found the body?" he says in a low voice as to not disturb the medical examiner.

A.C. Efverman

"It was a fisherman," Ricketts whispers back. He opens his notebook and turns a few pages. "Mr Donald Hooker. He was here at 3.45am: told me that he usually gets here around that time. He said that the fishes bite best between three and five."

"Where is he now?" Morgan looks over his shoulder.

"He's in my car, Amanda is looking after him. He was in a state of shock when we got here."

"Right, make sure that you get a full statement from him and record his ID. You and Stone can talk to him at the office and then give him a lift back home. You might want to contact his doctor as well if he feels he is traumatised. And as usual, make sure that everyone is out of here by day break: no traces for the public to see, okay?" Morgan crushes his cigarette against the sole of his shoe and puts the butt in his cigarette packet. "I've got to go. I'll see you in the office later." He takes a step forward and touches the medical examiner's shoulder. "George, I'll be expecting an autopsy report this afternoon. Did you get my email?'

Demitriades turns around. "Yes, and I'll look after it. Look, here's something interesting for you… See here?" He leans forward and points. "She got a blow to the back of her head. That's different from the others." He sees the look on Morgan's face. "I'll send the report around two o'clock, okay?"

"Okay." Morgan turns his back on the lights and walks towards his car. He feels dizzy and takes some deep breaths of the salt infused night air. He sees that the Opera house is lit up in a strange blue colour on the other side of the harbour and thinks that it must have something to do with the upcoming festivities around the World Cup. The grass under his shoes is wet and moisture seeps into his feet. He

GAME

walks over to the asphalted pavement by the water. He leans on the iron fence and looks over the water towards Kirribilli house and wonders if the Prime Minister is there, sleeping: unaware that they have a serial killer in Sydney – or maybe he knows? From where he stands, behind a wind shelter made of sandstone, Morgan can't see the crime scene. When morning brakes no one will be able to tell that a murdered woman has been lying on the ground under the bridge. All the evidence will have been carried away in plastic bags. The body will be in the morgue. The dead body… Morgan sighs and grief suddenly washes over him like a tidal wave. He holds on to the iron fence and cries silently. His body shakes in convulsions as he recalls his dead mother's face. He slides down against the fence and sits on the cold pavement and stares blindly into the sandstone wall of the shelter. When he can't take the cold any more he gets up and walks over to a wooden bench, sits down, lights a cigarette and watches the sun rise over the harbour. He is inside a picture of beautiful scenery but he is also in hell.

Katherine lives in a pink semi attached house. White tree ornaments decorate the roof and a white wooden gate covered in climbing rosebushes opens into a small front garden that is filled with flowers. Two Frangipani trees stand on each side of the paved path that leads to the front door. Morgan lifts a metal ring on the door and lets it fall towards the wood twice. He sees movement on the other side of the painted glass panel. The door opens and Katherine stands in front of him. "You didn't call."

"I thought I'd get over here as soon as possible. Are the kids at school?" Morgan closes the door behind him and follows Katherine into the kitchen. Carl is sitting by the table, holding a cup.

"Yes they are, I still haven't told them." Katherine turns to face him. "Do you want some tea?"

"That would be great." Morgan takes a seat next to Carl. "Hi dad."

"What was so important that you had to rush off like that?" Carl's voice is flat.

Morgan sighs loudly. "Dad, you of all people should know that I can't discuss that. I had to go, okay?" He buries his face in his hands.

Carl puts an arm around his son's shoulders. "I'm sorry, I'm not myself. I think I'm in shock."

"I think we all are," Katherine says. She puts a cup in front of Morgan and takes a seat by the table.

As they sit together they feel Victoria's absence. She is not with them anymore: never will be. She created their family and she made their family gatherings feel good: she was the one who united them. What is their family without her? What will happen now?

The uncomfortable silence in the kitchen is filled with questions that no one is able to say out loud.

"Have you heard from Thomas?" Morgan finally asks when the silence becomes unbearable. He can't care less about Thomas, but he has to say something: anything – anything except mentioning his mum.

Katherine makes a face. "He's in Milan I think. He calls the kids once a week or so."

Morgan takes a small sip of the hot tea: not because he wants to but because he needs to occupy himself with something. He burns his tongue and puts the cup down again. "And what's he doing now?"

"He's working in some bar there."

GAME

Morgan knows that Katherine only keeps in contact with her ex-husband because of their children. Thomas left her when she was pregnant with their second child. He had expressed a need to 'explore the world', and had never returned. Morgan has never liked Thomas. It was only for his sister's sake that Morgan agreed to be the best man at their wedding. Now he wishes that he hadn't. He wishes that he'd spent more time with people he loved, like his mother, and less time with people he couldn't stand... like Thomas. Victoria who was a caring, loving person has died, and Thomas who is completely rotten is still alive: it's unfair. Morgan thoughts shift to the murder victims: they could have had children and families of their own in a future that is never to be.

Carl starts to cry. His large shoulders shake and tears wet his face. Katherine reaches over the table and puts a hand on Carl's arm. "So, so, dad, do you want a glass of whisky?" When Carl doesn't answer, she goes to a cupboard and pours whisky into a small glass. She holds the glass to Carl's lips. "Here dad, take a sip of this." Carl takes the glass from her and drinks slowly. When he puts the empty glass down Katherine helps him up and leads him out of the kitchen. When she walks back into the kitchen a few seconds later her face is void of any expression. Morgan watches as she silently starts to clean. She washes dishes and frantically scrubs bench tops like there are some hidden bacteria on every visible surface. When she has finished in the kitchen she starts to vacuum in the hallway. Morgan walks into the living room where Carl is lying on a white sofa under a blue blanket; he is staring up at the ornate ceiling.

"Dad, I've got to go to the office for a while but I'll come back tonight and take you out for dinner, okay?" He sees that Carl is still crying.

"She was an organ donor, did you know that?"

Morgan raises his eyebrows. "What do you mean?"

"They will take her corneas and other bits they need. They'll take her eyes out for Christ's sake! They're probably the only bits that weren't eaten by cancer anyway. They made me sign the consent papers at the hospital."

Morgan takes Carl's hand. "Dad, calm down. It'll be alright. It's what she wanted. You can't think like that. Someone will be able to see thanks to mum. That's the way you've got to look at it." He lets go of Carl's hand. "We'll talk more tonight. Try to get some sleep now."

Katherine is on her knees in the hallway dusting the floor skirtings.

"I think dad needs to go home and work in his garden, that's the best therapy for him," Morgan says to her back.

She doesn't look up.

Morgan clears his throat. "I'll come past later tonight and take you all out for dinner. How's that sound?"

She nods and turns around and gives him a quick smile. "What time will you be here?"

"Around seven, is that alright?"

She nods again as she sweeps the feather duster over a neat row of children's shoes.

Morgan sits in a sunny courtyard that belongs to a café on Norton Street. He tries to sort out his feelings so he can concentrate on work. How complicated humans are, he thinks. We have lots of intricate webs of feelings and behaviour patterns but we can never anticipate how we'll react in different situations. Morgan has known his sister his whole life but he has never been able to communicate

GAME

with her: it's like she is from a different country and doesn't understand the language he speaks. Katherine reminds Morgan of his mother in so many ways, but he had been able to communicate easily with his mother; so how come he can't say what he feels to Katherine? Their childhoods have been formed in exactly the same way, but Katherine detached herself early from her fear of being abandoned while Morgan clung to his fear because he was too young to fully understand it. But Morgan later grew to adopt his feelings in a way that Katherine never could.

Morgan realises that he doesn't know Carl that well. Carl wasn't there when Morgan was young and his feelings and behaviour patterns were formed. Morgan had entered the police force because he thought his father wanted him to: he had never even contemplated another career choice. And Morgan likes his work: it has shaped him to be the person he is and he is grateful for the experiences it gives him. But Carl never acknowledges that he is proud that Morgan followed in his footsteps; and that hurts Morgan more than anything.

Morgan's hand shakes when he raises the coffee cup to his mouth. He remembers how his mother looked at him from her hospital bed. She was so beautiful before the disease stole her body. Morgan has always been proud of the photos he has of his mother from the time when she was young and healthy. Victoria was sixty years old when she died, but the cancer made her so much older.

Neither Carl nor Victoria has siblings and their parents are dead. All that remains for Carl now is Morgan, Katherine and Katherine's two children. Morgan feels guilty for not having spent more time with his mum and he suddenly realises that he can't afford to make the same mistake with his dad.

A.C. Efverman

It is close to midday when Morgan enters the office. The surface of his desk is covered with messages and reports, and the in-tray threatens to collapse under the paper weight. He picks up the phone and dials an extension number. "Ricketts, meet me in the boardroom in five minutes. Bring everything that I've missed and prepare to stay there for a while. Have you had lunch yet?"

"No, not yet."

"Alright, I'll order some food. See you in five." Morgan hangs up and quickly connects the line back to voicemail before any calls can come through. He gathers reports and messages and takes the papers to the meeting room. He then goes to see Amanda: he tells her that he doesn't want to be disturbed and asks her to order Chinese take-away for two. "Have you heard anything from Osbourne?" he finally asks her.

"Yes, he called in this morning and said that he doesn't know when he'll be back. He asked for you, but I told him that you weren't here." Amanda gives Morgan a strange look. "How's your mother?"

"She died this morning." Morgan walks off without waiting for a reply.

Ricketts is waiting in the boardroom. He stares at Morgan. Morgan looks down at his shirt and sees that that it is wrinkly and has coffee stains on it. He puts a hand on his chin and feels stubble against his palm. "Sorry Ricketts, I didn't have time to go home and change." He suddenly realises that he must stink. "You don't mind if I go and wash off quickly do you? I won't be long."

Ricketts smiles vaguely. "Not at all, take your time. I'll

GAME

prepare the paperwork."

Morgan notices that people are staring at him as passes through the office. He walks quickly into the men's room and sees a ghost look back at him in the mirror over the sink. Dark shadows surround his bloodshot eyes and his skin is grey under the stubble. His hair sticks out in a funny way on the side of his head and he has large sweat stains under his arms. Morgan takes his shirt off and splashes cold water on his face. He lathers soap and washes his face and under the arms. He then gargles with soapy water. Finally he puts his head under the tap. He pats himself dry with paper towels.

He probably doesn't look much better, but he feels better and he smells better and that's a start, he thinks as he walks back to the boardroom.

"Right," Morgan says as he takes a seat by the table opposite Ricketts, "what happened to the phone bills you mentioned earlier?"

Ricketts turns a few pages in his notebook. "The mobile that was stolen belongs to a young lady called Moira Langer…"

"What? Did you say *Moira Langer*?" Morgan searches his memory: where has he heard that name recently? "Did you meet with her, or did you speak to her on the phone?"

"Stone spoke to her on the phone." Ricketts looks up from his notes.

"Where does she work, where did he call her?" Morgan knows the answer before Ricketts gives it to him.

Ricketts moves his finger down the page. "Place of employment… Thomas & Sons graphic design studio in Strawberry Hills… Hang on… Isn't that where Else Henriksen worked?"

Morgan looks at him with raised eyebrows. "That's

correct. And I interviewed Moira Langer myself – I remember her clearly because she was wearing an unforgettable outfit that day... But more importantly; Moira mentioned that she had seen Else Henriksen in some nightclubs with some guy. She described this guy as 'tall with dark hair' so it's not unlikely that it could be the same guy that was seen outside Else Henriksen's apartment."

"So what are you saying? You reckon this guy... Else Henriksen's boyfriend... you think he stole Moira Langer's mobile phone in a night club?"

Morgan thinks for a while. "Yes, either that, or Moira Langer is not telling the truth. What else did Moira say about her phone?"

Ricketts reads from his notes: "She thinks she lost her mobile a couple of months ago. But she thought she'd left it at her ex-boyfriend's place, so she didn't want to report it stolen. She said that it was a touchy situation with her ex; she called him to ask about the mobile but some girl answered his phone and Moira got 'disappointed'." Ricketts raises his fingers to accentuate. "That's how she put it... Anyway, she decided not to call him again as she was afraid he would think she was 'pestering him'." Ricketts raises his fingers to form inverted commas again. "But then she received a mobile phone bill a week ago and realised that someone was making calls from her phone. And she didn't want to pay for other people's calls, ex-boyfriend or not... And that's when she finally reported the theft of her mobile phone."

"Right," Morgan says. "What's the name of Moira's ex-boyfriend? We should check him out. If not for anything else, we should eliminate him from our list of suspects."

Ricketts hoarse laugh sounds more like a cough. "What list of suspects? I didn't know we had a list?"

GAME

"You know what I mean. What's his name?"

"Uh," Ricketts pulls out his bottom lip and blows his fringe from his eyes. "His name is Ronald Dawson. He lives in unit four, twenty-five Mount Street, Coogee."

"Alright, someone will go and visit Mr Dawson. I'd like to see if he's a tall dark haired guy aged in his twenties. Else Henriksen was making calls to someone who had Moira's lost mobile. This person should have information about what Else Henriksen was doing the weeks before she was murdered, as they seem to have kept in close contact." Morgan looks at the mobile phone bill before him. Moira Langer's mobile phone number is circled with a pink highlighter Ricketts tells him, and is listed eleven times on the bill. The times of the calls are recorded next to the number and Morgan reads them out loud: "Thursday, 2nd of April, 5.45pm. Call duration: 7 minutes. Friday, 3rd of April, 5.03 pm. Call duration: 3 minutes and 35 seconds. Tuesday, 7th of April, 7.15 pm. Call duration: 6 minutes and 10 seconds." Morgan stops. "Do we know what these other numbers are?"

"That one," Ricketts points at a number that is circled with blue highlighter, "is to the reception at Else's work. And this one," he points at a number circled with green highlighter, "is Else's voicemail at work."

There are no other numbers listed on Else Henriksen's phone bill.

"Have you listened to her voicemail?" Morgan asks.

"Yes, but there were no messages, if there were they've been deleted. I spoke to Pete at the technical department, and he said there is no way you can retrieve messages once they've been deleted. Else Henriksen didn't have an answering machine or voice mail at home on her landline.

We tried to check her home phone records, but the phone company she used doesn't keep records for personal calls: they only have that service for business lines. Else used one of those small backyard phone companies that piggy back on Telstra's phone lines – they're cheap as chips and their admin and records are virtually none-existent."

"Was Else's mobile phone found in her apartment?" Morgan asks.

"No, it wasn't."

"Right, and has anyone looked into if Else was on social media such as Facebook yet?"

Ricketts nods. "Yes, I Googled Else Henriksen myself this morning, and all that came up was her school records and some of her work; nothing about her being involved anywhere on social media." Morgan makes some notes in his notebook. "Okay, that's a shame. What about her email account?"

"I am on to that. I have already checked out her email at work, and there seems to be nothing personal in there at all. Pete at the technical department told me that he will contact Yahoo, hotmail and gmail to see who she had her personal email account with, and if we can have access to it."

Morgan writes another note. "What about the other papers that were found in her apartment then, have you got them?"

Ricketts lifts a box from the floor and puts it on the table. "Where do you want to start?"

"Did she have a filing system where she kept bills and personal papers?"

"Yes, those are in here somewhere." Ricketts pulls some papers out of the box.

There is a knock on the door and Amanda enters the

GAME

room. "Your food is here." She puts two plastic bags, two plates and some cutlery on the table. "Let me know if there's anything else you need."

Morgan smiles at her. "Thanks Amanda. That's all."

She nods and leaves the room.

"Right," Morgan says to Ricketts. "Stop that for now. We've got…" He lifts the lid on a plastic container and looks inside. "Looks like beef with vegetables," he lifts the lid on a second container, "and chicken with cashew nuts. Which one do you want?"

Ricketts takes a seat. "I don't care. We can share both if you want."

"Sounds good." Morgan spoons fried rice onto the plates. "We'll share."

They eat in silence for a while. Morgan is starving: the last thing he's eaten was a sandwich at the hospital.

"So," Ricketts clears his throat, "how's your mother now?"

Morgan looks up from his plate. He chews and swallows. "She died this morning. I'd rather not talk about it right now, but thanks for your concern."

"Sure, no worries, god, I'm sorry."

Morgan nods. They finish the meal. Morgan takes the empty containers to the kitchen and makes coffee. "Did you find the filing system?" he asks as he puts two cups on the table in the boardroom.

Ricketts is standing on his knees in front of the box on the floor. He gets to his feet and puts a red folder on the table. "It's mostly bills and correspondence in this one. We'll need a translator for some of the letters; they seem to be in Danish and are probably from her family and friends back home."

A.C. Efverman

Morgan writes in his notebook. "I'll talk to her parents when they get here; they might've heard about the guy she was seeing. But there is a possibility she told her friends and not her parents, so we'll get a translator to have a look at the letters." He looks up. "What else have you got?"

"Let's see... Here are some receipts from credit card transactions. There's an $80 charge from a place called 'La Trattoria' in Crows Nest, on the 3rd of May at 8.58pm. So that would be about a week before she died, is that right?"

Morgan looks in his notebook. "Yes, that's correct. La Trattoria must be a restaurant. What else?"

"Uh, there's a receipt from 'Reeves'; a charge of $65.90, on the 30th of April at 12.37pm. Don't know what 'Reeves' is; probably a shop of some sort."

"Okay," Morgan says. "I'll get some people to go through the receipts and check the places she went to, especially the restaurants during the weeks before she was murdered. There's a good chance she was there with her tall, darkhaired boyfriend, and if we're lucky someone might remember his face."

"Right," Ricketts puts the receipts back in the folder.

"You can leave the folder with me. I'd like to go through the forensic bit now. Can you give me the details on what was found in Else's apartment?"

Ricketts shuffles some papers around to find the forensic report. "Okay, it's here somewhere... The DNA is taking some time: they reckon it will take another two weeks at least. But we do have the results of the blood: it came back yesterday. Ah, there it is." Ricketts turns some pages in a stapled report. "The blood that was found in the apartment was the same blood group as Else Henriksen's, so I guess we can assume that the apartment was the murder scene." He runs his finger down a page. "Most of the blood was found on the floor and on one wall in the bedroom, which seems to suggest that she was murdered in the bedroom. It is likely that the blood splattered up on the wall when her throat was cut. We think that the killer then washed himself in the bathroom and that's when blood ended up on the bathroom floor, in between the tiles. Someone made a pretty good effort to clean the place afterwards; it was spotless. Without the forensics we wouldn't have found anything, I'm sure."

Morgan takes notes.

"A dark brown hair was found that didn't seem to belong to Else Henriksen, but as I said; the DNA-results are not back yet so we don't know. We have, however, analysed the fingerprints, and in total we have clear prints from four individuals other than Else Henriksen. Given the fact that Else Henriksen seemed to be a loner with no friends, and counting in the landlord and possible tradesmen, there should be some fingerprints left by the boyfriend."

"Okay," Morgan nods. "What else was found?"

Ricketts looks up from his papers. "That was it. You should have seen the place. It was like a hotel room: cleaned with perfection. The bathroom and kitchen still smelled vaguely of ammonia."

"Right," Morgan tries to think. "Give me a mental overview of the place then, so I can picture it."

"I can do better than that. The guys from forensic filmed as we went in and I can call them and see if the film is ready for viewing."

Morgan nods. "Great. If you organise that, I'll have some people go through the rest of the papers." He picks up the box from the floor. "And I would like the statement you took from the fisherman this morning, before tomorrow's meeting if you don't mind?"

"Will do, and you'll get the report of the statement this afternoon."

The phone starts ringing as soon as Morgan switches his line from voicemail.

"Sergeant Callaghan, this is Superintendent Travis. I'd like to meet with you if you've got time."

Morgan turns his chair so it faces the window. It has started to rain again, he notices. "Yes, I do. Any time is good for me."

"I can have my driver pick you up at five o'clock. How's that for you?"

Morgan looks at his watch. "That's fine, I'll be downstairs waiting."

Morgan hangs up and looks at the papers on his desk. He takes an empty folder with plastic pockets from a drawer and starts to create a victim's book. When Amanda comes into his room with a report from the medical examiner, Morgan asks her to photocopy the report along with the material in the victim's book. "Make sure you keep everything in the same order," he tells her. She nods, takes the folder under her arm and closes the door. Morgan gets up from his desk and opens the door again. He walks through the corridor to the large room where the detectives are stationed.

Detective Ken Barlstowe has a desk facing the window. He turns from his computer and takes his glasses off his nose as Morgan approaches. "Sergeant Callaghan. How's your mother?"

Morgan sighs and pulls a chair closer to the desk. "I'd rather not talk about it, but thanks for asking." He looks out the window for a second and then faces Barlstowe. "Is

GAME

O'Neill around? I'd like to talk to both of you."

"Yes, he's around here somewhere. I'll find him." Barlstowe walks off and Morgan turns to the window again.

Barlstowe is back a few seconds later with Detective Tom O'Neill. O'Neill remains standing as Barlstowe sits down by his desk.

Morgan hands a folder to Barlstowe. "These are letters and receipts that were found in Else Henriksen's apartment. You will get a Danish translator to have a look at the letters as soon as possible. I want to know if Else mentioned the guy she was seeing in letters to her friends; if that's the case there should be a mention of this guy in her friends' replies. We're lucky that she was still writing letters on paper: not many young people do that these days. You will also go through her credit card statements. There are some receipts in there that show transactions from restaurants she visited only weeks before her death. You will go to these places and show the phantom pictures and a photo of Else to the staff: to see if someone remembers her, or anyone she might have been with."

Barlstowe opens the folder and looks inside. "Okay and when do you want the results?"

"As soon as possible; unless you have something more important to do right now?" Morgan looks at Barlstowe's computer screen where a picture of Miranda Kerr, wearing thigh high boots, a bikini and feathers, is slowly being uploaded.

Barlstowe blushes. "No, of course nothing is more important."

"Good." Morgan gets up from his chair and walks around the grey partitions; for a second he feels lost but then he spots the tall detective with the thinning hairline.

A.C. Efverman

"Torrone," Morgan leans against his desk. "I need you to go to Coogee this afternoon, is that possible?"

The expression in Torrone's brown eyes always remind Morgan of a sad puppy.

"No problem at all."

"There's a…" Morgan opens an envelope and pulls out a piece of paper. "A Mr Ronald Dawson in unit four, number twenty five Mount Street, in Coogee. You will talk to him about his ex-girlfriend, Moira Langer: she thinks she might have left her mobile phone at his place when they broke up a couple of months ago. Someone's been using Moira Langer's lost or stolen mobile, and that someone received calls from Else Henriksen around the time before she was murdered."

Morgan gives the envelope to Torrone. "It's all in there. I want you to tape the conversation and write a report of the interview, and also note Ronald Dawson's appearance. Do not mention anything about Else Henriksen's murder. This conversation will be about a stolen mobile phone. Any questions?"

Torrone shakes his head. "No, that's all clear."

"Good," Morgan says. "I'll expect a report this afternoon. And I've called Dawson to let him know that a detective will be there within the hour, so I suggest you get moving."

Superintendent Travis is dressed in a smoking. For a moment the two men stare at each other. Morgan is surprised to see his boss dressed up: he's used to seeing Travis in a short sleeved polo shirt and chinos or cords. Travis' eyes also reflect surprise when he sees Morgan's unshaved face and crumpled, stained T-shirt. Morgan follows Travis

GAME

through the hallway and into a large bright room. He sits down in a blue and white striped sofa. Flower arrangements in large vases stand on tables made of glass around him. An antique mirror with a gold frame hangs above an open fireplace. Bookcases filled with books and ornaments cover two walls. No framed art is needed in the room: the view from the large bay window overlooking the harbour is a live painting that continuously changes colours and motive.

"In case you're wondering why I'm wearing a smoking; I'm going to the opera tonight." Travis sits down on the sofa opposite Morgan. "How's your mother doing?"

"She passed away this morning." Morgan pulls his fingers through his hair: it feels greasy.

Travis' forehead crinkles and Morgan thinks for a second that Travis might reach over the table and touch him: but he doesn't.

"I'm sorry to hear that. Do you want some time off? I can assign someone else to lead the investigation if you want."

Morgan's body is moulded comfortably into the sofa cushions as he leans back. "No thanks, I'm confident that I'll be able to continue like before."

"Are you sure? We can't slow the investigation down now: we need to find this killer before it's too late."

"It's already too late. We found another body this morning."

Travis taps with his fingers on his knees. "I know, I heard." He stands. "You look like you could use a drink. What do you prefer: bourbon or whisky?"

"Bourbon please; with coke and ice if you've got it." Morgan opens the folder that he has brought with him. "I've made a victim's book about the Danish girl: Else Henriksen.

A.C. Efverman

I thought you wanted a copy. And I brought a copy of the autopsy report of the girl we found this morning. We haven't ID-d her yet. She'd been dead for less than ten hours when she was found, according to George Demitriades." Morgan puts the folder on the coffee table and takes the heavy glass that Travis hands him. "Thanks."

Travis sits back down in the sofa with a glass of whisky in his hand. "What are your feelings on this case?" he asks.

Morgan drinks a mouthful from the glass and places it carefully on the coffee table. "We've received a report from the forensic psychological department: I've made a copy for you." Morgan nods towards the folder. "The profile says that the killer is a man, aged in his mid to late twenties. He's had a bad upbringing, where he most likely was abused or neglected by his mother or another female family member. He's an extremely aggressive person but he hides his emotions, and his surroundings perceive him as normal. He most likely lives on his own, but he could also be in a relationship – he's not socially dysfunctional and he has certainly had relationships in the past. He is well educated and he might work in a white collar job. He chooses his victims based on their looks or behaviour as they remind him of a woman in his life that he hates... most likely his mother or his sister or someone who has rejected him in the past. He is an organized killer and he plans his attacks methodically. Most likely he fantasises about the murders and the rapes before the attacks. And most likely he stalks or befriends his victims in advance. He believes he is superior to women and he sexually abuses his victims to show that he's in control and that he is a masculine creature; this is all part of the sexual gratification he gets. He might have raped girls before but he's not in the register for convicted felons."

GAME

Morgan's throat is dry and he takes another sip from his drink before he resumes: "One theory is that he chose to start his killing spree when he did, because he knew that he would get a lot of attention from the police. He's probably aware of the pressure we're under to find him before the World Cup begins. It's likely that he'll play games with us and he might appear to want to help in the investigation; he would do this to act out his feelings of superiority over the police." Morgan looks down at his hands. He has remembered more than he had thought he would from the report.

Travis clears his throat. "I understand that this is your first experience of a serial killer, but I'm interested to know: do you agree with what the psychological profile says?"

Morgan looks into Travis' brown eyes for a few seconds before he turns his gaze to the harbour view. "Probably, yes, I guess. We don't have a lot to go by at this stage. We've got a vague description of a suspect: a tall man, aged in his twenties, with dark hair. We have the killers' seminal fluid and therefore also his DNA, and possibly his fingerprints: but none of this has been matched to anyone in the register of convicted felons. And no one who matches the psychological profile is out of prison at the moment. But to answer your question: going on the way he murders the girls – and how brutally he appears to act out his fantasies; yes, I do agree with the report in most parts."

Travis swivels the brown liquid around the bottom of his glass. "Okay Morgan. Thanks for coming over. I know that you're going through a tough time now, and I appreciate that you brought the material with you." He stands: a sign that the meeting is over. Morgan quickly downs what's left in his glass.

A.C. Efverman

It is a quarter to seven when Morgan comes home. He calls Katherine and tells her that he is going to be a bit late, has a quick shower and then dresses in a clean T-shirt and jeans.

Morgan is driving towards Leichhardt when he gets a call on his mobile from Lisa. He hears anger in her voice when she tells him that she has left messages both on his voicemail and his answering machine. Morgan is too tired to explain to her what has happened and tells her that he has been busy at work. He also promises her that they'll go out for dinner the following evening.

Morgan stands outside Katherine's door. He hears loud cries inside the house. Katherine opens the door when he has knocked with the metal ring three times. "Come in, don't just stand there," she snaps at him. "Carole's crying and Justine has locked herself in her room. Dad is just sitting in the living room staring at the TV and is no help." She sounds stressed.

Morgan sighs and walks into the living room. "Hi dad, how are you?" He sits down on the sofa next to Carl.

Carl takes his eyes off the TV screen. "Oh, hello, are we going for dinner now?"

Morgan looks up at Katherine but she just frowns and walks out of the room.

"Uh, I'm not sure the girls are up to it dad, they seem pretty upset."

Carl turns to the TV again; two divers are swimming across the TV screen. "Oh, they'll be alright," he mutters.

Morgan gets up from the sofa. "I'll talk to them and find out what they want to eat." He walks into the hallway where

GAME

Katherine is trying to comfort Justine through a closed door. "Come on honey, uncle Morgan is here to take us out to dinner. Please let me in." She turns to Morgan. "You talk to her," she whispers.

Morgan sighs. "Justine, it's uncle Morgan. Do you feel like pizza, sweetheart?" The crying continues and he feels stupid talking to a door. "Justine, come on, open the door so we can talk properly."

The crying suddenly stops, the lock clicks and the door opens a little bit. Morgan looks down at Justine's red, swollen eyes.

"Hi uncle Morgan," she whispers.

He opens the door and picks her up. She has grown since he last saw her: she is heavier and her golden hair is longer. She sniffles against his neck. "Nanna is dead."

He pats her back and looks at Katherine over her shoulder. "I know sweetheart. I know."

Katherine turns her back on them. A second later Morgan hears that she is talking to Carole in the next room.

"Are you hungry?" he asks the little girl on his shoulder.

She sniffles. "Yes, I guess so."

"Well then," he puts her down on the floor. "I'll take you out for pizza if you let me help you wash your face first."

She nods seriously. "Okay."

Morgan takes her by the hand and leads her through the hallway to the bathroom. "You'll feel much better and look much prettier when we've washed your tears away." He helps her up on a footstool next to the sink and turns the taps on.

"Can self," she says with annoyed voice as Morgan lathers soap in his hands.

A.C. Efverman

He rinses his hands under the tap. "I know darling, I was just washing my hands." He sits on the toilet seat and watches her wet her face and pat soap foam on her cheeks in small dollops. "In the eye!" she suddenly yells. "Uncle Morgan, help wash it off!" He gets up and helps her rinse the soap off her face and then pats her dry with a towel. "So, there. Look, that's much better. Do you want a drink before we go, are you thirsty?"

She nods, "Lemonade."

He takes her by the hand and leads her to the kitchen where he finds a bottle of lemonade in the fridge. He watches her drink slowly. It's interesting, he thinks, how easily a child's mind is distracted from sadness and sorrow.

Katherine comes into the kitchen. Carole walks behind her. "Hi uncle Morgan," Carole says shyly. She hides behind Katherine but Morgan sees that her face is swollen from crying. "Hi sweetie, are you hungry?"

Carole peeps at him from behind her mother's skirt. "Mum said we're going out for pizza."

"That's right. I'll get granddad and we'll get going." Morgan walks past them and into the living room. "Dad, we're ready to go. We're having Italian."

Carl turns the TV off.

Dinner is a disaster. Katherine and Carl hardly say a word and Morgan is left in their silence with the children who are crying again. Justine is inconsolable: she is exhausted from crying and the late time of night. The fatty food and the crowded restaurant only aggravate her. Carole craves attention too, but Katherine ignores her children: probably thinking that Morgan will look after them and give her a chance to grieve, and Morgan has to try to calm Justine down

GAME

when she starts to scream with a high pitch. So Carole is left to herself, feeling left out. Her eight year old ego craves attention as she tries to comprehend that someone close to her has died and doesn't exist anymore. Finally the two girls start to push and shove each other in a contest over who can get most attention and Morgan feels that he's had enough. He pays the bill and walks them home. Justine falls asleep on his shoulder and he holds Carole's hand. Katherine ignores them and Carl seems to be in a world of his own. Morgan comes with them inside and tucks Justine into bed. He gives Carole a hug and tells her that everything will be alright and that she will feel better in the morning. He then goes into the living room where Katherine and Carl are sitting, watching TV. They hardly respond to his 'good night' as he walks out of the house.

It's ten o'clock when Morgan is back home in his unit. He pours bourbon and coke into a large beer glass, sinks down in the sofa and kicks off his shoes. He looks around the room as he sips his drink and smokes a cigarette. His plants are dying, he notices without interest. The coffee table and bookshelves are covered by a layer of dust, the ashtrays are full, and empty glasses fill the tabletop. His gaze stops at some framed photos that are standing in the book case. He gets up and brings the photos back to the sofa where he studies them in detail: in one photo Victoria wears a long white dress and holds a martini glass. Her hair is long and blond and her arms are tanned and slender. She smiles at the camera and Morgan feels a sting in his chest as he remembers how she smiled at him from the hospital bed. Warm tears fall from his eyes as he looks at another photo where his mother sits in a deck chair, dressed in a sailor's shirt and shorts. She holds a cigarette in a mouthpiece made of silver and her blue eyes glitter in the sun. Her smile is so vibrant and real that it feels like he is looking at her through a window. Morgan suddenly remembers what Carl said about Victoria being an organ donor: someone else will use his mum's retinas. He dwells on this thought as he stares at the photos but then he shakes his head and pushes all images out of his mind. It is pointless to think like that: he won't allow himself to indulge in self pity like his sister and father have done. He walks into the bathroom and puts his drink on the side of the bathtub.

GAME

8

The office is empty and quiet: there is no sound of a vacuum cleaner this morning. Morgan spoons freeze-dried coffee powder and sugar into a ceramic mug that has a picture of Sylvester the cat sitting on top of the Opera House and the text 'Thydney' underneath. He fills the cup with boiling water and takes it back to his desk.

The autopsy report of the unknown girl in Kirribilli lies in Morgan's In-tray and now that he has time to read it, he opens it to see what George Demitriades has written.

"Female. Dental prints indicate age to be 25 years old. Hair colour: blond. Eye colour: blue. Weight: 51 kilograms. Height: 169 centimetres. Shoe size: 6. Dress size: 10. Blood type: B-.

Tattoo on left shoulder blade, showing a dolphin: 2 inches in length and 1 inch in width (see enclosed photograph), no other visible scars or tattoos on the body."

Morgan turns the page and finds three Polaroid photos inside a plastic pocket that is stapled to the next page. One photo shows a tattoo of a blue dolphin. Another photo shows a wound on the back of a head. A third photograph shows an incision on a throat.

Morgan turns back to page one.

"Cause of death: Carotid throat artery severed causing blood loss.

Wound in the back of the head has sharp edges and is pre mortem; I suspect a sharp and hard object; traces of metal found in wound.

Seminal fluid and vaginal bruising present: sexual abuse is pre mortem. Seminal fluid matched to same found on Rochelle Stevens and Else Henriksen (see previous reports).

Irregular bruises on upper thighs, upper arms, face and torso are recorded.

Wrists tied behind back with rope (identified as same type of rope found on Anne Miller, see previous report), marks on both ankles; tying up was pre mortem.

Fragments of dark blue cotton fibres (identified as similar to those found on Anne Miller, Rochelle Stevens and Else Henriksen, see previous reports) present in mouth; consistent with the material being used as a gag.

Alcohol present in stomach contents and also on skin (exterior front body surface) and in (head) hair.

Excrements (present on exterior body surface of buttocks and back of thighs) and stomach contents contain traces of red meat – not fully digested – rice, corn, egg, peas and prawns – almost fully digested.

No fingerprints found on body or rope.

Time of death: Wednesday 20th of May, between 8 and 9pm.

Place of death: unknown."

There are more plastic pockets in the back of the report that contain more Polaroid photos: most of them show bruises on the dead woman's face and body.

Morgan shuffles the papers in his In-tray to find photos from the forensic photographer. He finds the envelope under a report and opens it. Enlarged photos in full colour paint the horrific scene: A back bound woman lies in the grass. Her blond hair is smeared with blood. Blood covers her back and shoulders. Dark excrements cover the back of her legs.

GAME

Another photo shows the body lying on top of a plastic sheet and Morgan studies this picture closely. He registers the knife wound on the throat and the bruises that cover the torso and upper arms, face and thighs.

Morgan puts the photos back in the envelope and picks up two reports from his In-tray. He quickly reads through the first report and then skims through the second. He goes to the photocopy room where he makes 25 copies of the autopsy report and the two reports from his in-tray. While the machine does the work, Morgan goes to the meeting room and uses sticky tape to attach the photos of the girl in Kirribilli to the wall next to the white board.

Back at his desk he sifts through the papers in the In-tray until he finds a white envelope that has his name scribbled on the front. The envelope contains a DVD disc and a note. The note is from Ricketts and explains that the DVD is a film showing Else Henriksen's apartment. Morgan takes the disc to the boardroom, connects the DVD player to the back of the TV and places the disc in the player.

The film starts by showing a dark narrow hallway with a wooden floor. Paintings with colourful landscapes, people and animals hang on the walls. The cameraman walks through a door opening and enters a dark room.

A voice says: "Turn the light on will you, Rob?"

The ceiling light is turned on and reveals a daybed made from wrought iron with yellow and pink cushions and a green mattress. In front of the bed is a low table made of dark wood. An old wooden desk stands between two windows. The blinds are closed in both windows. The camera zooms in on the items on the desk top and shows vases and bowls filled with brushes, tubes of paint, charcoal pieces and glass bottles with liquid mediums.

A.C. Efverman

A gloved hand opens the drawers in the desk. The first drawer contains a pile of cook books and glossy fashion magazines. The second drawer is filled with electrical cords, envelopes and pens. The third drawer contains a red folder and the fourth drawer is filled with loose papers.

A large cardboard box filled with canvases stands on the floor next to the desk: a gloved hand flicks through them and shows sketches and finished paintings. The camera slowly rotates to show the rest of the room. An older style TV set with an antenna stands on top of a small table against the wall. Four plants with brown dry leaves stand in the window sills. An easel with an unfinished painting is placed in the corner.

The camera films some hallway and then the screen goes black. There is a thumping noise and a muffled voice says: "Damn it." A light is turned on and reveals a small bedroom that is crowded with furniture. A bedside table with a small reading lamp stands next to a simple bed made of wood. There is also a clothes rack filled with clothes and a bookcase stacked with paperbacks. The blinds in the window are closed tight. The cameraman films some more hallway, and then enters a kitchen. The bench tops are empty and the window blinds are closed, but not tightly: some sunlight filters through. A shadow walks past, the blinds are pulled up and bright daylight reveals the colours in the room. A gloved hand opens kitchen cupboards and drawers; showing plates, glasses, cutlery, pots and pans. The camera does a final sweep around the kitchen and then shows a door that leads to a small balcony outside. There is some more hallway, and the next scene shows a combined laundry and bathroom. The gloved hand enters the picture again: this time opening a mirrored cupboard. The camera zooms in on

GAME

bottles and tubes, showing different brands of crèmes and liquids.

The tape shows static for a few seconds and then the screen goes black again. A light suddenly moves through the darkness like a torch and sweeps over the wooden floor, walls and ceiling of the narrow hallway. The camera follows the light to the living room, where the light shows the furniture in quick flashes as it moves over the walls, floor and ceiling.

The next scene is filmed in the bedroom. The light moves over the furniture and is then pointed to the floor where shiny white dots appear in neat rows.

"Stop," a voice says. "There's blood here, note the location."

The light stops moving for a few seconds and then sweeps up over a wall where more white dots appear like shining stars on a dark night sky. This time the dots are in a pattern of a wide arch that starts from about a foot from the floor and thins out a few inches from the ceiling.

"Note that there's blood on the wall in the bedroom, next to the door," a voice says. The rest of the room is filmed in silence. The light moves through the hallway and then shows the kitchen floor, walls and bench tops in quick glimpses before it travels to the bathroom where glowing dots shine in a chequered pattern on the floor.

"Rob, are you getting this?" a voice asks as the light moves again: this time revealing a bathtub, a washing machine and a sink.

"Got it," another voice replies.

The tape shows static for a few seconds. The next scene is shot in the bedroom but this time the window blinds are up and the room is filled with sunlight. Two men dressed in white overalls are crouching down on the floor: they are scraping the thin areas between the floorboards with tweezers and place what they've found between the floorboards in small plastic bags.

There is some more static and then the tape shows the two men in overalls again: this time crouching down on the bathroom floor where they scrape their sharp tools between the floor tiles.

The next scene is filmed in the kitchen. The camera zooms in on a black fingerprint on the edge of the bench top. Then there is a bit of a blur as the camera moves before it zooms in again and shows another black fingerprint: this time on a wall. There is a buzzing sound and the film stops.

Morgan presses the stop button on the player and takes the elevator to the ground floor. He lights a cigarette as he comes out in the cold morning and stands smoking in the shadow of the building. After a while he feels cold and decides to walk over to the café to get some coffee.

A 'closed' sign hangs in the window on the door. Morgan looks at his watch: seven twenty. He sighs – the café won't open for another ten minutes. He starts to pace back and forwards to keep warm.

Morgan starts the morning meeting by going through the forensic report and showing photos of the dead woman under the harbour bridge. He then reads through the statement from the fisherman that has found the body. "You all have a copy of this report on your desks," Morgan points out. "Detective Torrone will share some information with us now from an interview that he held yesterday, and a copy of this report is also on your desks." Morgan nods at Torrone.

Torrone stands up quickly. He scratches his neck as he walks to the front of the room and opens his notebook.

GAME

"Uh, yesterday at three thirty pm I interviewed Mr Ronald Dawson who resides in Mount Street, Coogee. The reason for questioning Dawson was that his ex-girlfriend, Moira Langer, thought she had left her mobile phone at Dawson's apartment when they broke up a couple of months ago. Someone has since used Miss Langer's mobile phone to make calls to Else Henriksen. This person has also received calls from Else Henriksen in the weeks leading up to Miss Henriksen's death. Moira Langer works in the same office where Else Henriksen worked." Torrone pauses and looks up briefly before he turns page. "Ronald Dawson is twenty-eight years old. He is tall and has dark hair and blue eyes. I have a photo here." Torrone hands a small photo to Morgan who looks at the picture but remains silent. Torrone waits a few seconds and then resumes reading: "Dawson stated that Moira Langer had not left her mobile phone in his apartment. When I asked him why she would lie about something like that, his response was that Miss Langer is in love with him and will do anything to get back with him. Dawson further told me that Miss Langer has called him several times since they broke up and that she has used her lost mobile as an excuse to contact him; apparently she wants to come over to his place and look for it. But Dawson has told Miss Langer that he doesn't have her mobile phone and he has suggested that she reports it stolen to the police.

It should be mentioned here that Moira Langer reported her mobile phone stolen only a few days ago. She told the police that she was under the impression that her mobile had been at her ex-boyfriends apartment. But then she received a telephone bill and realised that someone had used her mobile and she didn't want to pay for someone else's calls; ex-boyfriend or not. The mobile phone bill that Moira Langer received consisted only of calls made to Else Henriksen's mobile.

Dawson further stated that Moira Langer is a drama-queen and that she makes things up to get her way. Dawson is now in a new relationship and wants nothing more to do with Miss Langer." Torrone stops reading and looks over at Morgan. "That's all. Since Dawson denied having the mobile I couldn't think of anything else to ask him."

Morgan stands up. "That's fine, thanks Torrone. At this stage I won't consider a search warrant for Dawson's unit. If he did have the mobile phone in his possession, he must have got rid of it by now I should imagine."

Torrone walks back to his seat.

Morgan holds up the photograph of Ronald Dawson. "Detectives Stone and Ricketts will take this photo and make some enlargements." He looks at the two detectives. "You will then go back to Newtown and show the enlarged photo to Else Henriksen's neighbours."

Stone walks up to Morgan and takes the photo. "Understood."

Morgan turns towards O'Neill. "How are you going, O'Neill? Have you organized a translator for the letters from Else Henriksen's apartment yet?"

"We've contacted a Danish translator and she's working on them now," O'Neill says.

"Good." Morgan scratches his chin. "And what about the credit card receipts that were found in Else's apartment?"

"Yes, we're looking into them as well."

"Wouldn't it be better," Morgan says, "if you waited for the enlarged picture of Ronald Dawson, before you go to the restaurants that Else Henriksen visited? That way you could show the photo of Dawson around as well."

GAME

O'Neill looks at Ricketts. "Will you get us some copies?"

Ricketts nods. "Sure. No worries."

"Alright then, it's sorted." Morgan gathers his papers from the table. "That's all for today's meeting, gentlemen. I will see you here again tomorrow morning at nine o'clock."

Morgan is scanning information from the autopsy report when his desk phone rings.

"Sergeant Callaghan? It's Osbourne."

Morgan frowns: it sounds like Osbourne is crying. "What's up Osbourne?"

Osbourne makes some more sniffling sounds – he either has a cold or he's crying.

"I know that you're busy but I was wondering if we could meet for lunch today."

Morgan takes his eyes off the computer screen and looks through the window: outside is a sunny day. "Yes, I am busy. But I guess I can take an hour or so for lunch. Where are you?"

"In the city, we can meet at the Opera house if that's alright with you."

"Okay, I'll meet you there at twelve thirty. See you then." Morgan hangs up and saves the scanned data to a document in his C drive. He then attaches the new document to an email message and sends the information to Interpol, and also to the contact person for a site on the Police Intranet.

At a quarter past twelve Morgan walks to Darling Harbour and from there he takes a taxi to Circular Quay. As he approaches the Opera house he sees that Osbourne is sitting on the steps. Osbourne is dressed in jeans and a short sleeved khaki green shirt. Morgan walks up to him and shakes his hand. "How are you going? I haven't seen you for a while."

Osbourne makes a face. "I've been better, how are you?"

Morgan shakes his head. "Let's not talk about me. Where are we having lunch?"

"I thought the Botanical Gardens would be nice: I've booked a table."

Morgan lights a cigarette and follows Osbourne through the iron gates into the park. Joggers and tourists fill the path by the water. A train on wheels pushes through the crowd and Morgan sees happy faces flash past. Two kids are waving sticks with pink fairy floss and shout something in a foreign language. As the crowd moves to the side to make way for the train, Morgan finds himself pressed up against the stone wall that fences the park from the harbour. He bends over the wall and looks down into the clear green water. The stones on the wall are heated by the sun and the warmth feels good against his chest. Large fans of seaweed are swaying underneath the waves. Morgan can't see any fish but he sees plenty of glass bottles on the sandy bottom. The lower submerged part of the stone wall is covered by oyster shells. Someone bumps into Morgan's back and he straightens up and looks around for Osbourne. He crosses the path and spots Osbourne on the lawn. They walk together through a tropical jungle that is filled with bamboo and palm trees. There is a strong smell of bat excrement and when they look up they see that flying foxes are hanging up-side-down in the tree tops. The path ends in a small clearing where there's a pond covered by water lilies. Ibis storks are begging for food by tables that stand in front of a two story building next to the pond. They walk past the café

GAME

and around to the backside of the building. Morgan follows Osbourne up the stairs to the restaurant. A waiter shows them to a table outside on the large wrap around veranda.

Osbourne orders a gin and tonic as they are seated in large cane chairs with white cushions. "What are you drinking?" he asks Morgan.

"A sparkling mineral water please," Morgan orders and they are left to study over sized menus.

"So what's going on? You didn't sound too good on the phone."

Osbourne looks up from his menu. "I've done a lot of thinking lately: about my dad and all."

Morgan nods. "Right?"

Osbourne puts the menu on the table. "Can I speak frankly with you about some personal problems?"

Morgan raises his eyebrows. Osbourne joined the detective headquarters nine months earlier as a new recruit and Morgan took the young and insecure newbie under his wing a bit as he remembered what it was like to be new on the job. But in all fairness, Morgan thinks, he doesn't know Osbourne that well and he is surprised that Osbourne has chosen him to discuss his personal problems with.

"Sure, if you think that I can help."

The waiter comes with their drinks and they order food.

"Okay," Osbourne says when they are left alone again. "As I mentioned; I've been doing a bit of soul searching lately. And right now I'm not sure if I can continue to work as a detective." He takes a sip of his drink and studies Morgan's face.

Morgan flicks a bread crumb off the white table cloth with his index finger. "I don't know what to say. I thought you were doing great and that you liked the job?"

A.C. Efverman

Osbourne leans back in his chair and crosses his arms over his chest. "I thought so too. Until a few days ago, that is. My dad is not likely to recover from his heart attack, and mum will be on her own when he dies. They live on a farm and mum will have to sell the place because she can't look after it. I don't have any sisters or brothers: it's just me. And that leaves me in an awkward position."

Three white cockatoos are flying over the manicured green lawns and their loud screams provoke a noisy response from Indian Mynahs in the surrounding trees.

Morgan takes a few sips of mineral water as the bird choir abruptly falls silent. "Mate," he says. "I'm not going to tell you that you should quit your job. I think that you've got potential to be a great detective. All I can say is that you've got to do what feels right for you. What are you planning on doing instead: being a farmer? I don't know if I can picture you working on a farm, to tell you the truth."

Osbourne frowns and picks up his drink; the ice clinks against the glass as he swirls the liquid around. "I don't know... I'm just confused. I don't know if I want to work as a detective for the rest of my life."

"So this is more about you not knowing if you want to continue to work as a detective, rather than you feeling forced to quit because of your mother. Is that right?"

Osbourne finishes his drink and waves the glass in the air to catch the waiter's attention. He puts the glass on the table and looks at Morgan. "Maybe, I'm not sure. I think that I'm having a midlife crisis a few years ahead of schedule." He raises a hand and then points at his empty glass. The waiter nods as he hurries past. Osbourne sighs. "I don't know anymore. It feels like the world is upside down and nothing is the way it used to be. I used to get up every day

GAME

and go to work and not think about what I was doing with my life. I was excited that I had become a detective after all the years of training. But now that I've had some time off, I've had time to think about things and I'm not so sure about what I want."

"Is your mother pressuring you to quit your job and run the farm?" Morgan asks.

"Sort of, she assumes that I'll be there I think."

"Well, that's not right. If she can't run the place herself, maybe she should sell the farm and move closer to you. That way you can keep your job and still be there for her."

The waiter approaches their table. Osbourne starts on his second gin and tonic as Morgan cuts into his lamb rack with pesto and red wine sauce. They eat for a while in silence.

Finally Morgan puts his cutlery down. "My mother died yesterday. I didn't spend a lot of time with her when she was sick, and I regret that now."

Osbourne looks surprised. "God, I'm sorry. That's awful. And here I am babbling about myself and my problems. You should have told me!"

"That's alright; I just wanted to tell you that so you don't make the same mistake." Morgan wipes the corners of his mouth with a linen napkin. "I don't think we make our parents happy if we give up our lives for them. I mean, there's no reason why everyone should be miserable. I think we should spend more time with the people we care about. But that doesn't mean we should stop everything we're doing... Like work." Morgan studies a fly that is walking along the veranda railing. He feels emotional and isn't sure if it is wise to show this side of himself to Osbourne.

"I guess you're right. I don't think my mother would be

happy if I wasn't happy." Osbourne drinks from his glass.

"So does that mean you're staying?"

Osbourne gets up from his chair. "I've got to go to the loo."

Morgan pushes his plate to the side. When the waiter comes to clear the table he orders a gin and tonic. He looks at his watch and feels guilty about sitting in the sun ordering drinks when there is work to be done.

Osbourne is back after a minute. "I'm sorry to have troubled you with my personal problems," he says as he sits down. "I didn't know that your mother has passed away and I feel like a selfish pig."

"Don't worry about it: I'm here to help. Have you decided what you're going to do?"

Osbourne finishes his drink as the waiter puts a glass in front of Morgan. "No, I still don't know what to do. But it was nice of you to come; I feel a bit better now."

Morgan sips his drink. "No worries. Let me know soon when or if you'll be back, alright? We need all the people we can get right now." He hesitates for a second and then lowers his voice: "We've found another one."

Osbourne looks at the tables around them to see if anyone is listening. "Another body?" he asks.

Morgan nods. "Yes. She was found yesterday, under the harbour bridge."

"And was she... I mean, was she the same as the others?"

Morgan sighs. "I can't tell you now. I'll fill you in when you get back to the office." He sees the look on Osbourne's face and adds: "Whenever that may be. Don't feel pressured, okay?" Morgan reaches out over the table and touches Osbourne's arm. "You'll be alright; I know you will."

GAME

Osbourne bites his lower lip and Morgan thinks for a second that he is going to cry. He withdraws his hand and quickly downs the rest of his drink. "I've got to get back to work. Give me a call and let me know what you're planning to do, will you?"

Osbourne nods. "I will. And thanks for coming; I appreciate it."

Morgan leaves Osbourne in the restaurant and walks back through the park alone. The tiles on the Opera house are glistening in the afternoon sun and the light is reflecting into his eyes. There is a lot of traffic out on the water: hundreds of sailing boats are milling about and green and yellow ferries are cruising back and forwards. Morgan loves this part of Sydney; even though it's usually crowded with tourists. As he walks away from the Opera house he takes shelter from the sun in the shade from the high-rise waterfront buildings. The buildings represent Australia well Morgan thinks: in the Australian entrepreneurial spirit everything is for sale – even the country's historical landmarks.

Morgan reaches the mid part of the harbour and decides to take a ferry back to Darling Harbour. He buys a ticket and walks along the water to the place where Captain Cook's crew has once set up camp. Morgan looks at his watch: it will be another five minutes before the ferry arrives. He finds an empty bench with a direct view of the Opera house and recalls what he knows of the building's tragic past:

Danish architect Jorn Utzon was excited to win the price in an international competition to design the Opera house in 1957. But the Dane was never paid for his work as the government-funded project run out of money before the building was completed. Jorn Utzon left Australia outraged and wowed to never return. A public lottery was then set up

A.C. Efverman

in 1960 to raise funds, so the half built Opera house could be completed. The family who won the first prize in the lottery had their picture on the front of every newspaper, and little did they know that their newfound wealth would turn to tragedy: only weeks after the big lottery win, the family's eight-year old son disappeared. A call from the kidnapper demanding a ransom of £25,000 came soon after. The ransom was paid: but it was too late. The battered body of the eight-year old boy was found five weeks later: he had been killed the same day that the ransom was demanded.

It's a well known crime: not only because of the controversial Opera house lottery, but also because it was the first kidnapping for a ransom in Australia's recorded history.

Morgan looks at the large grinning face at Luna Park on the other side of the harbour. The dead woman was found meters away from the amusement park. It is hard to believe that it was only yesterday that he sat on a wooden bench there, staring out over the harbour, feeling like his life was over. He shivers and stands up as the ferry pulls in to the boardwalk.

There are only a few people onboard the small boat. The sun disappears as the boat goes under the steel beams of the harbour bridge. Morgan looks up and sees a group of people walking on the arch of the bridge: they are so far up they look like ants. The sun reappears as they leave the harbour bridge behind. Morgan looks up at the large Moreton Bay fig trees as they float past Observatory Hill. The boat makes a left turn and enters the inlet for Darling Harbour. High above the water on a cliff to his left is a row of terrace houses that must have amazing views over the harbour: in the old days these houses were homes to poor people, he knows. Now they

GAME

house millionaires or people who are lucky to have family who had lived there for a long time. Morgan sighs: he is still renting. He might never be able to buy a house or even a unit in inner Sydney. The property prices have skyrocketed and Sydney is now, according to an article he has read recently, the fourth most expensive place in the world to live.

On the other side of the harbour he can see Pyrmont wharf. He remembers Else Henriksen lying naked on the grey wooden planks. He will never forget the awful stench of rotting flesh from her decomposing body. Morgan looks at the other passengers: they are mostly tourists. They are probably experiencing the harbour as something beautiful, he thinks. Ignorance is bliss: not long ago he too was able to appreciate the landscapes, colours and light of the harbour – but all he sees now when he looks around is death. Will he ever see the harbour in the same way again, or will he always associate it with murder and stinking flesh, he wonders. The glittering casino catches Morgan's eye. He has only been inside the casino a few times to see a show or a band – he detests gambling in any form and he knows that Katherine's ex-husband gambled with his wife's money many times. The boat pulls up to the side of Darling Harbour and Morgan climbs ashore after a small group of Japanese tourists.

Morgan's phone is ringing when he unlocks his door. He throws his briefcase on the hallway table and runs to the living room.

"Hi hunny, it's me. What time are we going out?" Lisa sounds tired.

Morgan sits down in the sofa and kicks off his shoes. "Hi gorgeous, I just got home. Did you want to come here and then go out somewhere in the city?"

"Okay, what did you have in mind?"

"I was thinking *'Café thirteen'* maybe?"

"Sounds good, can I stay over at your place? That way I can bring my work clothes and go straight to work in the morning."

"As if I would say no to that," Morgan laughs. "If you're bringing clothes, can I make a request?"

"Like what?" She sounds suspicious.

"Oh, I don't know… maybe that black g-string I bought for your birthday?"

"You're a dirty old man, you know that?"

"I do know. What time are you getting here? I'll book a table."

"Around eight?"

Morgan looks at his watch: it's twenty past six. "Alright, I'll get a table for eight thirty."

They hang up and Morgan goes to the kitchen and makes a large drink of bourbon and coke. He ignores the dirty dishes in the sink, goes back to the living room and puts a CD in the player. The sound of Santana fills the apartment as he takes his glass to the bathroom and turns the bath tub taps on. While the tub is filling up he calls the restaurant and makes a reservation. The water is a perfect temperature when he sinks down in the bath. He holds up a small mirror as he lathers his face with shaving foam and shaves. Then he soaks in the warm water with shampoo in his hair while he finishes his drink and smokes a cigarette. The telephone rings in the living room but he ignores it and lets the machine take the call.

Katherine's voice is loud and clear. "Morgan," he hears her say through the music. "It's me, Katherine. I was just wondering what you're doing tonight, and if you want to

GAME

come over for dinner." She is silent for a few seconds. "But I guess," She resumes, "that you're out already. Give me a call when you get back." There is a loud beep as the call ends. Morgan decides to take a quick shower to rinse the shampoo out of his hair.

'Café thirteen' is located on the thirteenth floor and has a view over the city and the harbour. Morgan and Lisa drink a cocktail at the bar before they are seated at a table by the window. Morgan is already a bit drunk: he's had two drinks in his apartment before Lisa arrived. Still, he orders a bottle of wine to go with the food. Lisa seems tired and is unusually quiet.

"So," Morgan says when the waiter has filled their glasses and left them with menus. "How's everything with you?"

Lisa places an elbow on the table and rests her chin in her hand. "I'm tired. One of the girls at work didn't show up this week and I had to do two double shifts. The owner is too cheap to hire more staff." She takes a sip from her glass. "I guess I can use the extra money, but still... And what about you, you must've been pretty busy yourself, because I haven't heard from you for a while."

Morgan looks at the reflection of his face in the window. "My mother passed away yesterday." He forces himself to turn and look at Lisa.

She stares at him with raised eyebrows.

"I know. I should have told you, but it's been a nightmare. I haven't been able to grasp it myself yet. Plus, work is so full on right now; I had to go back to the office right after it happened."

Lisa reaches out over the table and takes his hand.

"What are you talking about? We saw your mother just a few days ago. What happened?"

Morgan pats her hand. "She had breast cancer: had it for years. It spread and there was nothing the doctors could do. I was with her at the hospital when she… when she went." Tears burn under Morgan's eyelids. He sniffles impatiently and gives a forced laugh that comes out sounding strange. "It's bloody horrible. My dad and my sister are in total shock and are depending on me to be strong. But I…" Morgan's eyes fill up and he wipes the tears from his face with the back of his hand. "I've been busy at work, and to tell you the truth I couldn't talk about it… I'm sorry that I didn't tell you earlier."

He sees that Lisa also has tears in her eyes. "Oh sweetie, it's okay. I'm so sorry, she was lovely."

Morgan pulls his hand back. "I don't think I can talk about it right now." He inhales deeply and takes a large gulp of wine.

Lisa looks into his eyes. "You've got to talk about it sooner or later though. And I'll be there when you're ready, okay?"

He nods. "Thanks."

The waiter appears and puts two plates on the table and refills their wine glasses. "Pepper?" he asks.

Lisa nods and the waiter pulls out a large pepper mill from the pocket of his apron and seasons her rock oysters.

Morgan shakes his head when the waiter turns to him. "No thanks."

After dinner they decide to have coffee across the road. The night is warmer than it has been for a long time and the chairs on the sidewalk are filled with people.

GAME

"Are you working on the weekend?" Lisa asks as she exhales a cloud of smoke and lifts her coffee cup.

"Don't know yet. What did you have in mind?"

"Sleeping in and relaxing. Go for a long walk along the coast maybe. Are you up for it?"

Morgan shrugs his shoulders. "It sounds good: I can use some relaxation." He takes a careful sip of the hot coffee, burns his tongue and puts the cup down. "I've got a better idea. We could hire a boat and go fishing, maybe up in Brooklyn? That would be great if the weather is nice."

"Okay," Lisa smiles. "You look very tired. Do you want to go home?"

Morgan smiles back. "Yes, let's do that." He gets up and goes inside the café to pay.

9

Morgan knows in the back of his mind that there is something he has forgotten: but he can't remember what it is. A phone signal interrupts his thoughts.

"Sergeant Callaghan?" a female voice with a foreign accent asks.

"Yes, speaking."

"I am Kristine Henriksen, mother of Else Henriksen..." The voice halters.

Morgan suddenly realises what it is he has forgotten. "Of course, I've been expecting your call," he lies. "How was your trip?"

"Uh, trip? Oh... fine thank you."

Morgan sighs silently. "Would you like me to come over to your hotel? Are you at the Palisade hotel in George Street?" He tries to imagine what the woman looks like and an image of Else Henriksen passes through his mind.

"Yes. Thank you. Room... wait please." There is a muffled sound in the background and then the voice is back: "We stay in room four five two."

"Do you want me to bring an interpreter, someone who speaks Danish?" Morgan asks.

"No, no. We speak English."

'Sure you do,' Morgan thinks. "Okay, I'll see you soon. Bye now." He hangs up. He has a sinking feeling as he drives out of the garage. He hates this part of his job.

GAME

Morgan can't find parking and has to drive around the block twice. He finally gives up, sticks the police card in his front window and parks in a no standing zone.

He walks through the marbled hotel entrance and announces at the reception that he's there to see Mr and Mrs Henriksen in room 452. A young man dressed in a red uniform takes him up in the elevator to the fourth floor and shows him the way to the room. Morgan hands the bellboy a five-dollar note and knocks on the door. The door opens and a tall man with white hair and a moustache looks down at him over the rim of a pair of reading glasses. "Yes?"

"Detective Sergeant Callaghan. I spoke to your wife on the phone earlier."

The man takes his glasses off and shakes Morgan's hand. "I am Bo Henriksen, come in please."

Morgan walks into the hallway and follows the man to a large, dark room where the curtains are pulled closed and the only light comes from two small reading lamps next to a lounge group.

Bo Henriksen makes a vague gesture with his hand, as to explain the dim light. "We are tired from the trip and my wife has a headache. Sit please."

Morgan sits down in a grey armchair. A woman walks in from an adjoining room. She is dressed in blue cotton pants and a white T-shirt. A blue cashmere scarf is draped over her shoulders.

She takes a seat next to the tall man in the sofa. She looks like Morgan has expected: an older version of Else.

"This is my wife Kristine." Bo's voice is melancholic and he speaks with a strong accent.

"Nice to meet you Mrs Henriksen," Morgan says.

There is an uneasy silence for a few seconds, and

then Kristine Henriksen says: "Would you like some tea or coffee?"

Morgan moves in his seat and crosses his legs. "Thank you. Some coffee would be nice."

The woman gets up and walks out of the room.

"I have some photos that I would like you to look at. You can look at these photos, or you can choose to go to the medical examiner's office and identify your daughter there," Morgan pauses for a reply, but Bo Henriksen remains silent.

"You need to identify your daughter, Mr Henriksen," Morgan repeats.

"I thought that she had been done that already," Bo Henriksen says in broken English; he looks confused.

Morgan sighs. "I'm sorry, but we will need a family member to identify the body. I know that we have established her identity through dental records, but it is our procedure that a family member makes identification as well. After you have identified your daughter you can sign for the body and take her home if you want."

"Yes," Bo says. "We wish to take her home of course." He places his big hands in his lap. "I think it is better if I see the pictures; my wife is not so strong."

Morgan opens his briefcase and places two enlarged photos on the glass table top. The photos show Else as she lies on a table in the medical examiner's office. The blood has been washed off and George Demitriades' assistant has skilfully applied make-up to the face and body. Bo's eyes blink frenetically and his hands shake as he picks up the photos and holds them up one by one under the lamp.

Kristine comes back into the room and sits down in the sofa. Bo quickly pushes the pictures over the table top towards Morgan. "It is Else," he says quietly and wipes his

GAME

eyes on his sleeve. He puts an arm protectively around his wife's shoulders. She looks at him and says something in Danish. Bo replies in Danish and she leans her head against his shoulder and closes her eyes.

Morgan puts the photos back in his briefcase. "I've got some questions that I need to ask you I'm afraid." He places a notebook on the coffee table and looks up. Bo and Kristine Henriksen are watching him intently.

"Right," he starts and opens the notebook. "Did Else ever mention a boy-friend to you: someone she was seeing here in Sydney?"

Kristine shakes her head. "No," she says. Bo takes her hand in his.

Morgan looks at her. "Are you sure? We found letters in Else's apartment from a friend..." He turns a few pages back in the notebook. "A Lotte Sorensen. Does this name sound familiar?"

Kristine looks at him with wet eyes. "Lotte, yes, Lotte is Else's friend."

Morgan doesn't correct her present tense. "The letters from Lotte Sorensen mention a man called 'Patrick', that Else was seeing. Have you ever heard Else mention someone called Patrick?"

"No, I don't know that name," Kristine says. She turns to her husband and says something in Danish. Bo shakes his head. "No," he says. "I never heard her talk about a boyfriend or someone named Patrick."

Morgan writes in his notebook. "Did she mention other friends that she had here in Sydney?"

"She only talked about people that she worked with, but there were no close friends here in Sydney. She was lonely I think. But she liked to stay home and paint." There is a

A.C. Efverman

knock on the door and Kristine quickly gets up and leaves the room. She returns with a waiter that pushes a trolley on wheels. Kristine signs a receipt and the waiter disappears. "Sugar or milk?" she asks Morgan.

"Two sugars please." Morgan takes the cup she hands him. "Thanks."

Kristine places a plate filled with pastries on the table. "Please, take one."

Morgan takes a Danish with red jam in the centre. He takes a bite of the pastry and drinks a few sips of coffee. "Can you tell me a little bit about Else? I'd like to know about her life in Sydney and what she was doing in her spare time." Morgan licks jam off his finger.

Kristine hands him a napkin. "She worked and she painted," she says. "Sometimes she liked to go to the beach. She said she went to Bondi and Manly. Mostly she was home painting. She had, what's it called? …Exhibitions? A few."

"Right," Morgan takes notes. "Where was that? Did she mention the name of a gallery to you, or an area where the gallery was?"

"No, but she said she sold paintings and made some money from it," Bo says as he takes the cup Kristine hands him.

Kristine shakes her head. "She never said the name of a gallery."

"So you think that she spent most of her time alone, is that what she told you?" Morgan asks.

Kristine nods. "Yes, she told me that she was lonely and missed her friends. She liked her work and she liked painting; that was why she was in Sydney."

"How did you communicate with your daughter, was it by phone and letters?" Morgan asks.

GAME

"By telephone, post and email," Kristine answers.

"And how often would that be?"

"Email a few times a week and telephone about every second weekend. The time difference between Denmark and Australia is big. We used the post for photos, birthdays and Christmas and such things."

Morgan looks up at her. "There was no computer, iPhone or laptop found in her apartment. Where did she email from?"

"There was an email café close to where she lived." Kristine sighs and puts a hand over her eyes. She rubs her eyebrows with her fingers.

"Okay, and did Else have her email account with Yahoo or hotmail; do you remember that?"

Kristine nods. "Her email was with Yahoo Denmark; same as me."

Morgan writes it down and then closes his notebook. "Thanks. You've both been very helpful. I'll leave my card here…" He takes a business card from his pocket and hands it to Bo. "In case you think of anything that can help us in our investigation. My mobile number is there and you can call me any time." Morgan stands. "How long are you staying in Sydney?"

"We have tickets back for Wednesday next week," Bo says as he gets up from the sofa.

"I'll talk to the medical examiner. He'll contact you about your daughter's body. There are some forms that you'll have to fill out. Call me if you need help with anything." Morgan takes his briefcase and Bo walks with him to the door. The two men shake hands and Morgan takes a deep breath as the door closes behind him. As he exhales he promises himself to forget the faces in that dark room.

A.C. Efverman

When he comes out on the street he lights a cigarette and decides to walk down to Chinatown and have lunch before he goes back to the office.

***

"Here kitty, kitty."

Linda is taking her usual shortcut through the alley when she sees a man lying on the ground next to the gutter. He looks up at her as she walks past. "Hey, could you help me?" He flashes her a smile. "My kitten is stuck down here and I can't reach it."

She stops and looks down at him. *'He's gorgeous'*, she thinks as she puts her shopping bags down. "How did the kitten get down there?" she asks as she kneels next to him. She lies down on her stomach and peers through the grate that leads to the sewer tunnel below. "Wouldn't these bars be too narrow even for a kitten to get through?" She frowns and starts to get up. But he is quicker than her: she is still on her knees when he hits her in the back of the head with something hard. Linda feels surprised more than anything; although the pain is overwhelming. Her body turns ice cold, then burning hot and then cold again before she passes out and falls to the side. Blood streams from a wound in her head. He quickly looks around and then he grabs her limp body under the arms and drags her to a car that is parked a few meters away. He balances her on his raised knee as he opens the door with one hand and then he pushes her into the back seat. He leans into the car and ties her up and pushes a cotton scarf into her open mouth. He quickly looks around again, throws a blanket over the girl in the backseat, then gets behind the wheel and drives off.

GAME

Left on the pavement are two shopping bags filled with groceries and a small puddle of blood. A cat miaows somewhere in the distance.

***

Morgan is eating barbequed duck with egg fried rice and steamed Chinese broccoli when his mobile rings. He wipes his mouth on a paper napkin and takes the phone from his breast pocket. "Detective Sergeant Callaghan speaking," He looks around the restaurant to see if anyone is listening, but the people around him speak loudly and no one seems interested in what he is saying.

"Hi, it's Ricketts. We just got a call from Surry Hills' police station. Someone's found two grocery bags and some blood in an alley in Surry Hills."

"Right, sounds like some junkie or maniac robbed someone," Morgan doesn't sound interested.

"No I don't think so. A witness saw a guy pull a girl into a car and drive off. He described the guy to be in his twenties, tall, Anglo and with dark hair. The Surry Hills police saw on the Intranet that we were looking for someone with that description and called us. Apparently most of their officers are away on security training in Canberra and they were quick to point out that they don't have the resources to handle this and dumped it on us." Morgan hears that Ricketts draws his breath.

"Right-e-o, I'll meet you at Surry Hills' police station. Bring Stone and the phantom pictures and I'll see you there in half an hour." Morgan ends the call and quickly finishes his meal.

A.C. Efverman

Morgan parks outside the police station in Surry Hills. As he gets out of his car he sees that Ricketts and Stone are walking across the street towards him. They walk together into the small yellow building and when they reach the front desk Ricketts asks for Sergeant Lonigan.

Sergeant Lonigan turns out to be a middle aged man with a large beer belly and thinning hair. His uniform looks to be one size too small.

"So you're from the detective headquarters in Pyrmont, are you?" Lonigan asks as he walks with them around the corner into a corridor.

Morgan nods. "That's right." He wonders where this question is leading: nowhere, it turns out, because Sergeant Lonigan seems content with the answer and the conversation is over. They enter a small room that is furnished with a round table and six plastic chairs. A camera in the ceiling follows their movements as they take seats around the table. A thin man, around thirty years old, Morgan guesses, comes through the door. He wears a bright orange jumper and chews on his thumbnail. Sergeant Lonigan closes the door behind him. Stone places a small tape recorder on the table and turns it on. "Interview starting at 1.38pm," he says after a quick glance at his watch. "Location is Surry Hills' police station in New South Wales. Present are Sergeant Lonigan from Surry Hills' police and Detective Sergeant Callaghan, Detective Ricketts and Detective Stone from the detective headquarters in Pyrmont. Interview with a witness to an incident happening in the district of Surry Hills. Name of witness and details as follows."

Sergeant Lonigan makes his statement for the tape recorder: "This is the witness that saw what happened. Mr Perkins, can you please tell these detectives exactly what

GAME

you saw?"

Perkins takes the thumb out of his mouth. "I was in the bedroom upstairs," he says slowly. "The window there faces the alley behind the house. I was folding some laundry and whilst I was doing that, I looked out the window. I saw a man kneeling on the road next to someone who was lying on the pavement. It looked suss because the guy turned his head quickly like he was checking to see if anyone was watching. Then he picked the girl up under her arms: I could see that it was a girl then, and he started to drag her towards a car. Her feet dragged on the ground and it looked like she was dead or unconscious."

Morgan makes some notes in his notebook. "And what time was this?"

"Uh, it was around twelve. I looked at my watch when I called the police, and it was five past twelve then."

Morgan nods. "Okay, go on. What happened next; after he dragged her?"

"He opened the car door with one hand. He held her with the other hand and raised his knee. He sort of rested her against his knee. Then he lifted her up and put her in the backseat. I could only see the back of his legs for a minute or so as he leaned into the car, and then he stood next to the car and looked around again. And then he went in the front seat and drove off."

Morgan looks up at him. "Did he see you?"

Perkins looks surprised, like the possibility has just struck him. "No I don't think so: he just looked around the street, he didn't look up towards the windows. I've got a thin curtain in my window anyway, so I can look out but no one can see into the room when the light isn't on."

"What did the man look like?" Morgan asks.

Perkins places his elbows on the table. "He was tall and well built, with broad shoulders and thin hips. He wore blue jeans and a black T-shirt with some sort of logo in white on the front. And he had short dark hair. I didn't see his face clearly because he was mostly turned away from me, but I caught a glimpse of it when he was looking around. I'd say that he was aged in his late twenties, and definitely Anglo."

Morgan writes in his notebook. "What sort of car was it?"

"A dark green Volvo station wagon, an old model: you know the square one. Not one of those new sleek things."

"Did you see the license plate?" Morgan holds his breath as he waits for the answer, but when Perkins sighs he knows that there will be none.

"I only saw the car from above when it was parked. And he drove so quickly around the corner that I didn't get a chance to see it."

Morgan exhales. "Right, can you tell me what the girl looked like?"

Perkins leans back and crosses his arms over his chest. "Her hair was covering her face. It looked like a young girl though. She was dressed in a short skirt and by the look of her legs I would guess that she was quite young."

Morgan takes notes. "A child or a woman?"

"A woman; probably in her twenties or late teens. But I can't be sure, because I didn't see her face. And she was quite tall, which is why I got the impression she was an adult." He hesitates for a second before he adds: "And her bust was quite large."

"What else was she wearing?"

"A red sleeveless top and black shoes, the skirt was black too."

GAME

"Did she carry a handbag?"

"No, I didn't see a handbag. But there were two shopping bags on the pavement filled with groceries."

"What colour was her hair?"

"Dark brown and wavy, quite long: it reached over her shoulders."

"And you couldn't see her face at all?"

Perkins shakes his head slowly. "No."

"Okay Mr Perkins," Morgan says as he looks up from his notes. "We'd like you to take a look at some pictures now." He nods at Ricketts who takes the phantom pictures from a folder and places them on the table in front of Perkins.

"Do you recognise the man in any of these pictures?" Morgan asks.

Perkins leans forward and studies the pictures. "No," he says. "He didn't look like any of these guys."

Morgan sighs. "Would you consider seeing a police sketch artist and try to make a picture of the man you saw?"

"Yes, okay."

Morgan turns to Sergeant Lonigan. "Do you have a police artist here today?"

Sergeant Lonigan stands. "I'll find out if we can set one up for you." Morgan watches him leave the room and then turns to Perkins. "For the record Mr Perkins, where do you live?" he asks.

"At number 5 Cornello Street, here in Surry Hills."

"And that's a house is it?" Morgan writes in his notebook.

"It's a two storey terrace house."

"And what's the name of the street behind your house?"

"Uh, I think that's Greens Lane. It's really just a small alley."

A.C. Efverman

"But it's big enough to drive one way?"

"It is on a day when there are no garbage bins. On garbage day it's impossible to drive there at all."

"Right, and what day is garbage day in your neighbourhood?" Morgan asks.

"Uh, Tuesdays. But most of the garbage bins are still there on Wednesdays. I've tried to drive through the alley on a Wednesday but I couldn't get through and had to back out. The garbage men throw the bins all over the place when they've emptied them and I remember thinking that people were lazy to leave their bins like that."

Morgan takes some more notes. "Okay, good," he says finally. He closes his notebook and puts the pen in his shirt pocket.

Sergeant Lonigan sticks his head through the door opening. "I've called the police artist and he can be here in half an hour. Does that suit you?"

Morgan looks at Perkins. "Can you wait for half an hour Mr Perkins?"

Perkins nods. "Yes, I guess so. I might go and have a coffee and come back, if that's alright?"

Morgan nods too. "That's fine." He looks at his watch. "Interview finished at 1.53 pm." He leans forward and turns the tape recorder off and then looks at Lonigan. "Thanks Sergeant. We'll go and have a coffee as well and come back here at half past two."

Lonigan nods. "I might not be here when you come back. But ask for Constable Stewart if you need help with anything. He's one of the men that responded to Mr Perkins' call."

Stone and Ricketts walk across the street to a café as

GAME

Morgan walks a block down the road to a pharmacy to buy a bottle of contact lens solution. Stone and Ricketts are sitting by a table next to an open window as Morgan walks into the café. All the other tables are vacant. Morgan orders a coffee at the counter and takes a seat on the cushioned window sill. He looks at Stone. "What's your opinion on all this?" he asks.

Stone's pale blue eyes are void of any expression. "Well, I guess it could be the guy we're looking for. But it could also be a nutcase who bashed his girlfriend, or a pro that overdosed... Or, anything, really."

Morgan nods. "I can see where you're coming from. Perkins didn't recognise the guy on the phantom pictures. But those pictures are so bloody vague: none of Else Henriksen's neighbours were sure about what her boyfriend looked like. Personally I think there's a good chance that this guy could be the killer. And when I say that, I'm thinking of the description mostly. The overdose theory doesn't fit with the blood that was found on the scene, and why would someone bash his girlfriend when she was carrying the groceries home? No, this points more to a stranger who attacked a woman he knew would be alone and unable to defend herself." Morgan stops abruptly when he sees that the waitress is approaching their table. She places a cup in front of Morgan. When she's disappeared into the kitchen, Ricketts speaks: "So we're definitely dropping that guy in Coogee; Ron Dawson, with the mobile phone then? Or do you want us to keep an eye on him?"

"There's no use." Morgan looks out on the side street. "O'Neill and Barlstowe didn't have any luck with Dawson's photo. And since no one recognised him, I reckon he's out of the picture. It was all too easy anyway: the killer wouldn't be that careless. You read the profile report: it said that the killer is above intelligence. He's not insane. He's a psychopath." Morgan takes a sip of his coffee. "Not that it helps to know that he's smart bastard," he mutters.

Stone clears his throat loudly. "But why did he attack another woman so soon after he killed that bird in Kirribilli?"

Morgan raises his eyebrows. "Why not? The girl in Kirribilli was killed about a week after Else Henriksen was murdered. And as I said: he's a psychopath. These guys don't follow any rules. They make up their own agendas. Serial killers have been known to escalate their murdering sprees when they have work experience." Morgan falls silent as the waitress comes out to pick up Stone and Ricketts' empty cups.

"Did you want anything else?" she asks.

They order another round of coffees and the waitress disappears back into the kitchen.

"Basically," Morgan resumes, "you never know with serial killers, and you can't predict what's going to happen next. It seemed like he was following a set pattern when he killed a girl every three months. But he broke that pattern when he killed the girl under the bridge."

"That's true," Ricketts says.

Morgan's mobile rings. He swings his legs over the window sill and walks a few steps down the road before he answers.

"Sergeant Callaghan, it's Superintendent Travis. I've called for a meeting with some of our colleagues on Monday… Let's call it a crisis meeting. I want you there too: can you be at the Blue Prince Hotel at eight thirty, Monday morning?"

Morgan watches as an Ibis stork sticks its long beak

into a garbage bin and pulls out a plastic bag. "Right, sure."

The plastic bag opens and miscellaneous garbage items fall out onto the pavement. The bird makes a clumsy jump to the ground and starts to pick at a piece of bread.

"Good," Travis says. "It's suite 10078 on the tenth floor. Bring all material regarding the investigation."

"Okay. I'll see you there." Morgan ends the call and walks back into the café through the door.

"Ricketts," he says as he pulls his notebook from his jacket pocket. "Can you hold the morning meeting on Monday?"

Ricketts raises his eyebrows. "Sure. What's up?"

"I've got a meeting with the big boys: it's about the investigation."

Stone scratches his nose. "Maybe they'll give us some more people."

Ricketts laughs. "Yeah right, dream on. All police units have been delegated for the World Cup safety; you know that. We're on our own with this one."

Morgan frowns. "We'll see what they've got to say." He writes the details of the meeting in his notebook. "I've got to get back to the office and put together some information for the meeting. You will go back to Surry Hills' police station and supervise the making of the phantom picture with Perkins. Record him when he describes the guy. And when you're done, come back to the office and give me a copy of your report."

Stone nods as he takes notes.

Morgan puts the notebook back in his pocket. "And ask Constable Stewart if you can get a photo of the crime scene where they found the blood and the grocery bags. I want samples of the blood: we'll forward them to the lab ourselves. And I want a typed report of all interviews with Perkins."

Morgan calls George Demitriades on his hands free as he drives back to Pyrmont. As always, the medical examiner's voice mail is activated and Morgan has to leave a message: he asks Demitriades to call the Henriksen's at their hotel and organise the pickup and release of Else's body.

When he walks into the office, Amanda is reading a magazine. She blushes when she looks up and sees Morgan.

"Hello you," he says. "Keeping yourself busy, I see."

She quickly opens a drawer and throws the magazine in it. "Hi, I was just…"

He smiles. "Don't worry about it. Look, if you're not *too* busy…" to his amusement Amanda's cheeks turn a darker shade of red. "I'm joking. But seriously, I need you to gather all new material and make two copies of everything."

Amanda nods. "I'll do it right away."

He leans over her desk. "Is it true that the Beckham's are divorcing?"

"Yes, David has…" Amanda interrupts herself and frowns. "You're pulling my leg, aren't you?"

Morgan straightens up. "Not at all Amanda, not at all." He walks off with a smirk on his face.

Morgan's desk top is covered by papers again. He turns the computer on and makes an effort to clean his desk by shuffling the papers into a pile. The mobile starts ringing just as he gets up to go to the bathroom. He presses the green button on the phone and sits back down in his chair.

"Morgan, I haven't heard from you. We need to discuss the funeral arrangements you know," Katherine sounds annoyed.

GAME

"Sis, hi, I'm at work at the moment, can I call you back?" He doesn't have time to discuss funeral arrangements while he's at work. Katherine can be so bloody ignorant, he thinks.

"Right, are you going to call me later then? What time, so I know."

Morgan sighs. "I'll give you a call as soon as I leave. Around four thirty, okay? How's dad?"

"He's alright. He just sits in front of the telly all day. I'll talk to you later then." She ends the call before he has a chance to reply.

Ricketts walks into Morgan's room at a quarter to four. He places a phantom picture on Morgan's desk. "This is the result," he says. "It turned out that Perkins didn't get a good look at the guy's face after all. He was very vague in his descriptions."

Morgan studies the picture. "Right, can you type up the interviews and give me everything else that you've got on this, tonight before you leave?"

"No worries, Stone is on it already. Are we working on the weekend?"

"No, I'm keeping the roster as it is. We need some time off to relax and regain our strength, so we can think clearly. But I do need you to gather some material for my meeting on Monday. I'm making a presentation on the investigation, so I'll need all the facts. Can you do that for me now?"

Ricketts nods. "I'll get on to it as soon as I've finished this."

"We should focus on the abduction now. Did the police in Surry Hills say that they were looking into who the girl is, with missing persons et cetera? Or did they leave that to us as well?"

Ricketts scratches his chin. "They didn't mention it. I guess they figured we'd look after all of that. I'll find out: I'll give them a call."

"Good. Before you go; I've got a printout here from missing persons. Looks like we've got an ID on the dead girl in Kirribilli." Morgan hands a paper to Ricketts. "Take it and make copies for the morning meeting on Monday. I'll need the original back when you're done."

Morgan spends half an hour going through reports and other paperwork at his desk. When he leaves for the day he carries a thick folder with papers under his arm.

He calls Katherine from his car on his way home and they decide that he will come over to her place for dinner. Morgan never sees the car that swings out from the curb and follows him home.

The red button on the answering machine is blinking. Morgan fills a wine glass, the only clean glass he has left, with bourbon and coke and goes to the living room. He kicks his shoes off under the coffee table and presses the play button on the answering machine. A loud beep followed by another beep tells him that someone has called without leaving a message. Morgan looks around the room: it looks like a disaster zone. He will need to have a clean up this weekend, he thinks. The answering machine beeps again and plays the first recorded message. Katherine has called two times earlier, she says, she has yet to hear back from him and she demands that he calls her back. Morgan sighs. The next message starts: "Morgan honey, it's Lisa. I'm a bit upset; can you call me back please? It's two o'clock in the afternoon now, but I'll be home tonight." A loud beep ends the message. Morgan drags on his cigarette and looks

GAME

out through the window. A long beep from the answering machine tells him that there are no more messages. He picks up the cordless phone and dials Lisa's home number.

She answers after one signal. "Morgan is that you?"

"Hi, yes it's me. How are you?" Morgan stubs his cigarette out in the ashtray and lies down on the sofa.

"Not too good. Thanks for calling back."

"No worries, what's up?"

She draws her breath. "One of the girls at work has been murdered. I didn't know if you knew."

Morgan sits up. "What was her name?"

"Cassandra: Cassandra Saunders."

Morgan thinks back to the missing persons' report he's read in the office. He gets up and walks over to the dining table where he's left his folder.

"Are you there?" Lisa asks.

"Yes, sorry, I just want to have a look at something. Hang on a second." Morgan turns some papers over and finds the report. He holds it up and reads the name 'Cassandra Saunders' on the front page. He searches the text for the dead woman's occupation and finds it on the second page: 'Shop Assistant, Bermuda Book Shop, 457 George Street, Sydney'. Morgan is amazed that he hasn't noticed this information earlier: it's the same bookshop that Lisa works in.

"Are you going to be home tonight?" he asks her.

"Yes, of course. I don't feel like going out. Did you know what had happened?"

"Well yes, but I didn't know that she worked with you until now. Can I come over to your place later on? I've promised to have dinner at my sister's place. We're organising the funeral for my mother."

A.C. Efverman

Lisa is silent for a few seconds before she answers. "Yes, I'd like you to come. You might as well sleep over at my place. You're not working tomorrow are you?"

"No, I'm not working tomorrow. I'll give you a ring before I come over. It'll probably be pretty late though, is that alright?"

"I'll be here waiting for you. I'm going to order Indian food and have a bath."

"Okay, I'll talk to you later then. Love you." Morgan hangs up and goes to the bathroom: he has planned to have a quick shower before he drives over to Katherine's. After the shower he wipes the steam off the bathroom mirror and has a shave. Then he brushes his teeth and walks naked into the bedroom where clothes are spread out all over the floor. Morgan finds a clean T-shirt in the bottom of the cupboard and pulls his jeans on without bothering with underwear. After a bit of looking around he finds his sandals under the sofa in the living room and leaves the apartment.

Morgan thinks that he has avoided rush hour until he reaches Anzac bridge. All three lanes on the left side of the bridge are filled with cars that move nowhere and Morgan swears to himself: he is already late. He calls Katherine on the mobile.

"It's me. I'm stuck in traffic on Anzac bridge so I'm going to be a bit late. Just thought I'd let you know."

"Alright." To Morgan's relief she doesn't sound upset. "I'll see you when you get here."

"Okay. See you then." Morgan pulls the window down and lights a cigarette. The water in Glebe bay is coloured by patches of golden orange and purple in the twilight. A dragon boat is a dramatic black slash through the colours.

GAME

The fish market is a landscape of shadows, and masts on anchored boats are creating a pattern of lines against the pink sky. Sea gulls are screaming over the muffled noise of humming engines. The traffic starts to move slowly and Morgan passes a car that has broken down in the left lane. The pace picks up and a minute later he reaches the exit for Leichhardt.

Morgan can smell food and realises that he is starving. Carl is sitting by the table reading the paper when Morgan walks into the kitchen.

"Hi dad, how are you?"

Carl looks up. "Oh hello, look who's here. How's work?"

Morgan sits down next to him. "Busy." He looks up at Katherine. "That smells great. What are you cooking?"

She bends down and opens the oven door. "Just a roast with garlic and vegies: I hope you're hungry."

"I am. I haven't had a home cooked meal for a while." He smiles at her but she turns to the stove and stirs something in a pot. "Could you let the kids know that dinner is ready? They're in their rooms."

Morgan walks out into the hallway. Vague music comes from Carole's room and he knocks on the half closed door. "Carole? Dinner is ready sweetheart." He pushes the door open. Carole is lying on her stomach on the bed; she is reading a fashion magazine. Morgan recognizes the music that comes from a stereo in the corner: it's Lady Gaga.

"Hi uncle Morgan," she sits up and pushes the magazine down on the floor. Morgan picks it up and places it on the bedside table. "How are you sweetie?" he strokes her hair.

"I'm okay," she mutters and looks up at him under

her fringe. "Do you know if granddad is going to live here forever?" she whispers.

Morgan laughs and ruffles her hair. "No sweetheart, it's only temporary. Are you coming? Dinner is ready."

"Okay, I'm coming." She climbs off the bed and pats her hands over her hair to smooth it down.

Morgan sees the gesture of vanity and suddenly feels angry for a reason he can't define: perhaps Carole has reminded him briefly of Katherine when she was younger, or maybe he's just responding in self defence to Carole's need to remove his touch from her hair. Morgan mentally pushes his feelings away and smiles. "Good, I'll tell your sister that dinner is ready. Wash your hands and then go in the kitchen and help your mother set the table." Morgan walks out in the hallway and knocks on Justine's closed door. "Justine? It's uncle Morgan, can I come in?" There is no answer so he opens the door. Justine is sleeping in her bed. Blond plaits frame her face on the pillow. Morgan walks up to her and shakes her shoulder lightly. "Justine, dinner is ready. Wake up."

She opens her eyes and looks sleepily at him. "Uncle Morgan, hi."

"Hi sweetie, are you hungry?" Morgan sits down next to her on the bed.

She rubs her eyes and yawns.

"Do you want some dinner?" Morgan asks.

She sits up. "What are we having?"

"Your mummy has made a yummy roast. You like that, don't you?"

She nods and Morgan lifts her warm body up, he carries her to the kitchen and places her on a chair next to Carl.

"Hang on, I'll get her pillow." Katherine takes a large

GAME

pillow from a cupboard under the sink. She lifts Justine up and places the pillow on the chair under her. "There, now she can see the rest of us and not be so lonely under the table."

Justine giggles. "Yes, because I'm only little."

Morgan smiles at her. "That's right. You're the smallest person in the whole world." He turns to Carl. "Isn't that right dad?"

Carl looks surprised. "What? I'm sorry, I wasn't listening."

Justine stops giggling and looks down at her plate.

"That's alright dad. How are you? You look a bit tired," Morgan says.

"There's nothing wrong with me, would you stop babying me!" Carl snaps.

Katherine puts the roast on the table. "Let's eat. There's gravy on the stove if anyone wants some."

Morgan looks at Carl: he looks tired and angry. "I'm sorry dad. I didn't mean it that way. I was just worried, that's all."

"Well, you can stop worrying about me. I am capable of looking after myself. Always have been and always will be." Carl avoids Morgan's eyes and starts to fill his plate.

Morgan sighs and decides to ignore Carl's outburst. He has to remember that his father is mourning, he thinks as he clenches his teeth around angry words that want to come out.

After dinner they sit in the living room while the children watch TV in Carole's room. Carl hasn't said a word to Morgan during dinner and sits quiet, looking down at his hands as Katherine makes tea in the kitchen. Katherine finally comes in and breaks the silence. She puts some brochures on the coffee table.

"I got these brochures from a funeral parlour yesterday," she says. "I thought we'd have a look at them to get ideas about the ceremony."

Carl suddenly looks up. "I've got a place in the grave yard; we bought it years ago."

Katherine sighs. "We know dad. We're just trying to organise the ceremony now. You know: what sort of casket, flowers and music we should have."

Carl looks angry. "You don't know what sort of music or flowers she liked. I'm the only one who knows what she liked," he blurts out.

"Alright dad, tell us what she liked and we'll organise it," Morgan says gently.

Carl turns around and looks at him. "You, you were always mummy's boy, weren't you? You always ran to mummy when you hurt yourself, you never came to me," Carl blows air through his nose.

Morgan puts a hand on his shoulder. "Calm down, dad. All we're trying to do is organise the ceremony for the funeral. We want to make sure that you're happy with the results. Unfortunately this can't wait and I know it's hard for you, but it's hard for us too."

Carl takes a few sips from his cup and sits silent. Katherine stares into the wall and says nothing. Finally Morgan picks up a brochure. There are three pictures on the front cover that show three different styles of caskets and flower arrangements. He studies the photos. He pictures his mother lying in a casket with purple velvet lining; her head resting on a small silk pillow. He wants his mother to be comfortable. If they make the coffins look like beds why

GAME

don't they have blankets, he wonders.

"You haven't even read her will!" Carl says suddenly and Morgan looks up at him. "What? I didn't know that mum had a will." Morgan is surprised.

"Of course you didn't know. You didn't know anything about your mother, did you?" Carl spits the words out. His voice is loud and angry.

Morgan puts the brochure on the table and stands up. "I need some fresh air. I'll be back in a minute." He takes long strides over the living room floor and through the hallway and resists the urge to slam the front door behind him. He sits on the cold stone step under the door and lights a cigarette. He can hear traffic swish past outside the gate but he can't see the cars behind the trees and bushes. He watches the glow on the cigarette move in the dark and tries to hold back his anger. If he hadn't left the room he would have said something rude to his father and they probably would have started an argument. He drags on his cigarette and shivers: it's cold. After a minute he stubs the cigarette out and walks back inside.

The TV is on in the living room and both Katherine and Carl are silently watching it.

"Right," Morgan turns to Katherine after a minute of watching the news. "Tomorrow I'll go to some different places and have a look at prices. Then I'll give you a call." He gets up from the armchair. "Thanks for dinner and say goodnight to the girls for me."

Katherine's eyes are on the TV as she nods.

Morgan turns to Carl. "Goodnight dad."

Carl looks up at him and then turns to the TV again. "Goodnight."

A.C. Efverman

Morgan dials Lisa's number on his mobile and leaves it on hands free as he turns left onto Parramatta Road. He turns the heater on; even though he knows it will make him sleepy.

"Morgan, is that you? I was in the bath." Lisa sounds out of breath.

"Yes, I'm leaving Leichhardt now. Do you want me to bring anything?"

"Only clothes for tomorrow if you're spending the night."

"Okay, I'll swing past my place and pick some up on the way. I should be at your place in less than an hour." Morgan stops for a red light and hits the auto lock key as three guys with beer bottles in their hands cross the road.

"Good, see you then," Lisa says. "Drive carefully."

"I will. See you." Morgan ends the call and realises that he doesn't have any clean clothes. He'll just pick up a pair of shorts and his contact lenses, he thinks.

When he reaches Coogee he stops at a bottle shop and buys two bottles of chilled Chardonnay and a packet of cigarettes. The pavement outside Coogee Bay Hotel is packed with young people singing loudly. Even during the winter months there is never a shortage of backpackers in Coogee, Morgan thinks as he drives away from the noisy crowd and passes the beach. He pulls the window down and breathes in the salty air. The old traffic slogan 'stop, revive, survive' comes to his mind when he parks by the side of the road: he can do with some reviving.

Lisa opens her door almost immediately and Morgan gets the impression that she's been standing in the hallway waiting for him.

"Come on in," she says and kisses his mouth.

GAME

"You smell nice," he comments as he walks into the kitchen. He puts one of the wine bottles in the fridge and takes a corkscrew from a drawer.

Lisa watches as he opens a bottle and takes two wine glasses from a cupboard. "My god, you certainly know where everything is, don't you."

"I've been watching you for months, I should know by now," Morgan says over his shoulder as he walks into the living room.

The sofa table is filled with lit candles and the walls are covered by shadows that are jumping up and down as the flames move in the draft from the open balcony door. Morgan gets a dizzying feeling that the whole room is moving.

Lisa sits on the sofa and pats the seat next to her. "Come and sit."

Morgan hands her a wine glass as he sits down. "So how well did you know Cassandra?"

She takes a sip of wine before she answers. "Quite well: we used to have lunch together and sometimes we went shopping."

Morgan frowns. "I will probably come to your work next week and talk to the employees. How do you feel about that?"

She shrugs her shoulders. "That's not a problem."

"Can you pretend that you don't know me?"

"Why would I do that?" Lisa raises her eyebrows. The flickering shadows are making her face look distorted and grotesque.

Morgan looks away and picks up his glass. "Because I'm not supposed to have personal involvement in an investigation that I'm working on: I'll be taken off the case if anyone finds out."

She shrugs her shoulders again. "Sure, I can do that. No problem."

He puts his arm around her. "Let's not talk about it now, I've had enough for this week and I can see that you're upset. We'll discuss it later, okay?"

Lisa makes a face. "I don't want to think about it either but I have to know: why Cassandra? Was it someone she knew?" She takes a cigarette from a packet and leans forward to light it on the flame from one of the candles. She hands the cigarette to Morgan and lights another one.

"This is complicated. You know I'm not allowed to discuss work with anyone, but I think that this is personally affecting you and therefore you're entitled to know certain things."

Lisa watches Morgan's lips move. Why does he sound so formal? She isn't sure she wants to hear what he is going to say.

"We believe that Cassandra was murdered by a serial killer," Morgan touches Lisa's chin and looks into her eyes. "This is strictly confidential information, you do understand that don't you?"

Lisa nods. Her eyes moves to Morgan's mouth again.

"Good," Morgan sighs. "We don't know how or where he finds his victims, so I want you to be careful."

Lisa pulls her knees up to her chest and puts her arms around her legs. "Stop it. You're scaring me!"

Morgan stubs out his half smoked cigarette in the ashtray. "I need to tell you. Cassandra worked with you and you knew her. That worries me." He turns and looks at her. "Do you want to move in with me for a while – just until this whole thing blows over? I don't think it's a good idea that

GAME

you live here on your own right now."

Lisa takes a sip of wine. "I don't know... I must admit that I'm scared, I really am. And you're right: this place is not exactly high security." Her hand shakes as she puts her glass on the table. "I don't know."

Morgan puts his hand on her knee. "Come on, it'll be fun to live together. We can see each other all the time. Please? It's for your own safety."

She smiles. "Alright, but I'm not going to do all the cooking and cleaning for you, if that's what you're thinking."

"Actually, my place is a mess. But if you give me a few hours I can clean it up before you move in."

"I know that your place is a mess, I saw it the other day. But I'm not going to move in tonight, we can do it on Sunday. That leaves us time to rest this weekend, and I can pack before we go to your place. How's that sound?"

"That sounds good to me." Morgan gently pushes her down on the sofa and kisses her. "But now we should rest: you said so."

***

A phone signal breaks the silence in the empty office on the fifth floor. The phone rings once more before the call is diverted to an answering machine. A taped message is played and there is a beep as the answering machine starts to record. "Help me; he's going to kill me! Somebody? Please! I'm..." Another beep confirms that the call has ended.

10

Morgan wakes early, he feels like a lazy cat: rested and *content*. He looks at Lisa who is sleeping next to him and thinks about waking up next to her every morning. Carefully, so he won't wake her up, he gets out of bed and walks to the bathroom. When he turns the taps on in the shower he starts to plan their day. He will call the marina in Brooklyn and book a boat and some fishing gear. He is looking forward to sitting in the sun surrounded by calm green water with a fishing rod in his hand. He knows a restaurant in Brooklyn where they can bring their catch and have it cooked for them.

Morgan can smell coffee as he walks out of the bathroom and follows the aroma to the kitchen. Lisa stands on her tip-toes under a cupboard and reaches for cups. Morgan puts his arms around her waist and kisses her neck. "Good morning," he whispers.

She starts to turn around when a ring tone from a mobile phone startles them both.

Morgan sighs. "No way, not today," he goes to the bedroom and takes the phone from his jeans pocket. "Yes?" he answers impatiently.

"Sergeant Callaghan? This is Detective O'Neill. Sorry to bother you so early, but I wanted to inform you of what's happened."

"Right?" Morgan sits down on the bed. He keeps the phone pressed between his ear and shoulder as he pulls his

GAME

shorts over his feet.

"We got a strange phone call over night: it's recorded on the answering machine."

"What, the answering machine on Amanda's desk?" Morgan stands as he pulls his shorts up.

"Yes, and on the message a girl is screaming that someone's going to kill her. It sounds like an emergency call: she's screaming for help."

Morgan sits down on the bed again. "Did you say that the call was recorded last night?"

"Yes it must have been. Barlstowe was the first person in this morning: he checked the answering machine and heard the message. He told me that he was here at ten to eight, so the call was recorded before that."

"Get Pete from the technical department to analyse the tape from the answering machine – his mobile number is in the back of the black diary on my desk. He might be able to tell us when the call was made. Ask him if there are any background noises and if we can trace the call."

"Okay, I will. Barlstowe and I discussed the message before I called you: why would someone call here and scream for help? Anyone in an emergency situation would surely call triple 0 – it's a number everyone knows and help is instant. We have never received calls like this before."

"No we haven't. It's very strange."

"Strange indeed: the main number where the answering machine is connected is not known to the public as far as we know – it's only used internally between the departments, isn't it?"

A cold realisation starts to grow on Morgan. "You're right: it is."

"That's why we have voice mail on our personal lines

– on numbers that we give out to the public. And everyone knows that it is a strict policy not to give the main number to the public as it's only used internally. It doesn't make sense. Surely the girl didn't call the wrong number?"

Morgan shakes his head. "No, I wouldn't believe that."

"Neither do we, so how did an outsider get a hold of this number then?"

"That's a good question. Ask Pete if the line at Amanda's desk is listed as silent and give me another call if you need help with anything. I'll keep my mobile on," Morgan presses the red button on his phone to end the call.

Lisa is sitting in the sofa reading the morning paper. "What was all that about?" she asks.

"You would not believe it; that was work. It never stops." Morgan picks up a coffee cup from the table and takes a few sips.

"Hey, that's mine! Get your own cup in the kitchen. I didn't know if you were staying or going."

"Sorry, I'll get my own then." Morgan puts the cup on the table and walks into the kitchen. "I told work that I'll be available on my mobile, but this is my day off," he says as he comes back to the living room. "I was thinking that we could rent a boat up in Brooklyn and go fishing if you still want to?"

"Yes, that sounds good. The weather will be fine today according to the paper."

"Alright, I'll give the marina a call to book a boat." Morgan looks around the room. Lisa doesn't own a computer or smart-phone, and his own mobile is a standard police phone so he can't Google the marina's phone number there either. "Where do you keep your Yellow Pages?"

Lisa puts the paper down. "It's in the hallway I think,

GAME

under the telephone table."

Morgan walks out in the hallway and finds the telephone directory on a shelf underneath the telephone. He sits down on the floor and flicks through the pages. Suddenly he freezes. A number is circled under the heading 'Pregnancy Counselling' in the health services section. Next to the circled number is a scribbled note in Lisa's handwriting: 'Mon 25/5, 1pm. 4th floor, St Vincent's. No food or drink 12 hours before surgery.' Morgan stares at the note.

"Did you find it?" Lisa calls out.

Morgan slowly gets up and walks into the living room. He sits down on the sofa and stares at Lisa. "Is there something you would like to tell me?" his voice reveals anger and confusion.

Lisa looks at him with raised eyebrows. "What do you mean?"

Morgan throws the opened Yellow Pages on the sofa table.

Lisa looks at it and then closes her eyes. "You weren't supposed to find out. I have already made the decision," she whispers.

Morgan stares at her in disbelief. "What did you just say? YOU made the decision? What about me? Don't I get to have a say? And was that your plan? To go and have my child aborted and not tell me?"

Lisa turns her head and looks out through the window. "I thought that you would leave me if I told you I was pregnant: that you would think it was a trap to marry me. Some girls do that you know."

Morgan tries to calm down but it feels like an electrical storm is raging inside his head. "But why didn't you talk to me? I can't believe that you were going to do this without even telling me."

He sees that Lisa's cheeks are wet with tears. "You didn't seem to want to have children. You always said that you would rather have a dog."

"Oh my god," Morgan leans forward and places his head in his hands. "How could you base your decision on that?"

Lisa stands up and crosses her arms over her chest. "But face it Morgan: you never took our relationship seriously. For you it was just a bit of fun, not something that you based the rest of your life on. Was it?"

He looks up at her. "I don't know. We've known each other for less than a year and I guess I was just trying to get to know you."

"Well, I know you. And I don't want to have a child with you." She turns away from him and stares out through the window again. "And if you don't mind, I would like to be alone now."

Morgan sits paralysed for a few seconds and then he gets to his feet slowly. "Okay, I'm going. If that's what you want." He walks into the bedroom and pulls his shirt over his head, picks up his jeans from the floor and grabs his things from the bathroom. He slams the front door hard behind him as he leaves.

Morgan sits in his car and tries to figure out what he should do next. His hands shake violently on the steering wheel when he pulls out from the curb and he decides to find another parking spot and pull over. What he needs to do now is to get drunk and forget about everything, he thinks. He parks in a 'no standing' zone and dials a number on his mobile.

GAME

A few signals go through before the call is picked up. "David speaking," a voice says.

"David, it's Morgan. How are you going?"

"Well, hello, hello. I haven't heard from you for a while. Where have you been hiding?"

"Nowhere, I'm calling you now aren't I? What are you doing tonight, fancy grabbing a beer somewhere?" Morgan closes his eyes and leans back in the car seat.

"Maybe; hang on."

Morgan can hear a female voice in the background and then David's voice is back in his ear: "Yes, alright; where at?"

Morgan opens his eyes. "How about Nags Head in Glebe, around seven if you'd like to grab a bite to eat as well?"

"Sounds good, I've got to go; the missus wants me to get my gear on. We're off to the beach."

"No worries, catch you later then?"

"Yes, I'll see you there at seven."

Morgan hangs up and realises that he is sweating. He wonders if his anger has started a chemical reaction in his body and then he suddenly decides to go for a swim at Clovelly beach. He puts his phone and wallet in the glove box, pulls out from the side of the road and drives slowly up the hill. A few minutes later he parks his car and walks down some wooden steps that lead to a small sandy beach. He hides his car keys in the sand, places his sandals on top and takes his shirt off. There are not many people on the beach. Morgan walks slowly into the cold water and then lounges forward and swims with long strokes towards the open sea. There is a rumour that a giant blue Groper is swimming around just off Clovelly beach and as he swims further out he wonders if it is true. He feels the tug of a rip as he comes to the opening of the channel and decides to swim back. The waves out on the ocean are big and splash against the rocks on both sides of the channel. As Morgan turns he sees something in the corner of his eye: it's dark and shiny and goes under the surface so quickly that he first thinks it is a reflection from the sun on a rock. Then he sees it again as it surfaces: it's a dark grey triangularly shaped dorsal fin. Morgan's heart races. His body freezes in sheer fear and refuses to move. Then the adrenalin kicks in and he starts to swim as quickly as he can. He only looks up every third stroke to catch his breath and his feet paddle madly as he tries to propeller his body as quickly as possible through the water. Suddenly his hand scrapes against the sandy bottom and he stands up and runs the last few meters to land. He turns around and holds a hand over his eyes as he looks out over the water and catches his breath.

"What was all that about?"

Morgan turns and looks at the young guy in shorts who is standing next to him.

"I saw a large dorsal fin out there," Morgan points to the water.

"No, are you serious?" The guy looks at Morgan doubtfully and then he turns and looks at the water.

"Yes, it scared the crap out of me!" Morgan sits down in the sand and wipes the salt water from his eyebrows with his fingers.

"What do you think it was: a shark?"

"We don't get dolphins in these waters as far as I know, so yes; it must have been. And it didn't look like a dolphin: the fin was straighter and more rugged looking. Anyway, I didn't hang around to see how big the shark was... Or if it

GAME

was hungry," Morgan smiles wryly.

"Can't blame you for that... Hey, you're a good swimmer! I've never seen anyone swim that fast around here." The guy turns to two other guys that are walking down the wooden steps and calls out: "Martin, Robbo, come here! This guy just saw a shark!"

Morgan stands up and notices that his knees are shaking. He walks slowly over the warm sand and picks up his shirt and keys. He slips his wet feet into his sandals and walks towards the steps. When he passes the guy in shorts he nods. "Take care out there if you're planning to go for a swim, alright?"

The guy nods back. "Okay, will do."

Morgan pulls the window down in his car and smokes a cigarette while he listens to the radio. He feels exhausted and realises that he is hungry when his stomach makes a growling sound. He shivers and puts his shirt on. As he turns the key in the ignition he thinks about his messy, dirty apartment. He doesn't feel like going home to a mess and he knows that his fridge is empty, but he can't think of anywhere else to go. He desperately wants a hot shower, eggs on toast and a cup of coffee, so he decides to stop at a seven eleven shop and pick up some groceries on the way home.

He parks outside the convenience store around the corner from where he lives and buys food, cigarettes and cleaning products. Then he carries the grocery bags up the hill. His shorts are still wet from the swim and he feels cold in the shade from the buildings. Part of the reason he is shivering is probably that he is still in shock, he thinks as he climbs the stairs up to his apartment.

The first thing Morgan does when he comes home is to open all the windows to let the warm sun light in. Then he turns the stereo on and listens to the radio while he fries eggs in the kitchen. He wipes old breadcrumbs off the top of the toaster and puts two fresh slices of bread in it, boils some water and makes a cup of instant coffee. With a plate in one hand and the coffee mug in the other he walks into the living room and sits down in the sofa. He looks at the blinking red light on the answering machine but chooses to ignore it and starts to eat instead. Just then the phone starts to ring: three signals ring and then a beep comes, followed by Lisa's voice: "Morgan, it's me. We need to talk. Can you give me a call back please?" There is a pause and then Lisa's voice resumes: "Okay, I'll talk to you later." Another beep follows.

Morgan finishes his breakfast and takes the plate back to the kitchen. He walks into the bathroom, takes his clothes off and throws them on the floor. He stands under the hot water in the shower for nearly half an hour before he finally turns the taps off and dries himself on a towel that has a damp smell to it. Naked, he walks into the bedroom and tears the sheets off the bed. He takes the bedclothes to the bathroom and throws them in the washing machine together with towels, clothes, underwear and socks that he collects off the floor around the apartment. While the machine is filling up with water he washes the dirty dishes that are piled on the kitchen bench tops.

Two hours later Morgan sits in the sofa and looks around his living room. His hands smell like cleaning spray and he feels dirty again. But the apartment is spotless: he has polished every surface except the windows. He looks at his watch: it's nearly one o' clock. Six hours to go before he is meeting David at the pub. While he was cleaning he was thinking about Lisa. He is still angry at her for what she had

GAME

planned to do; and as far as he knows she is still going ahead with the abortion. The thought strikes him: she is going to murder his baby. Morgan suddenly feels helpless and lonely. His life is falling to pieces and he has no one to talk to. His mother is dead and his family has shut him out emotionally. Lisa's words echo in his mind: 'I know you, and I don't want to have a child with you.' He moans. Her words hurt him badly. What sort of a person is he if his girlfriend says something like that? She must think that he will make a lousy dad.

Morgan gets up from the lounge and walks into the kitchen to make coffee. He feels like drinking something stronger but controls the urge: becoming an alcoholic won't help – he knows that he has drunk more lately than what is good for him.

While the coffee brews he smokes a cigarette in front of an open window in the living room. He looks out over the water. A sailing boat is floating past below and he can see the people aboard clearly: a woman is sitting in the front with her face turned towards the sun and a man is standing behind the steering wheel. Suddenly the woman opens her eyes and Morgan blushes when he realises that she is looking directly at his naked body. He quickly closes the window and sits down in the sofa. His heart pounds hard as he finishes the cigarette. Finally he shakes his head and gets up to get the coffee when a phone signal cuts through the music. Morgan stops and looks at the phone; who can it be: Lisa? His sister? Or is it David calling to cancel dinner? He walks slowly up to the phone and picks it up. "Hello?"

"Hi, it's O'Neill again. Sorry to bother you at home. Your mobile's switched off."

"Is it?" Morgan sits back down on the sofa and looks

around the room. He spots the mobile on a chair and goes to pick it up: the battery is dead and he realises that he's forgotten to charge it the night before.

"I got in touch with Pete from the technical department this morning," O'Neill says. "And he just got back to me. He's been in contact with the telephone company and apparently they swore to him that no one can get our main telephone number from them. The number is listed as silent and the phone company's got a security code on our number in their computer system and only the account manager's has access to this code and he says he hasn't given it to anyone."

"Right," Morgan tries to think. "What about the switchboard? Aren't all numbers in our office connected to the switch?

"Apparently not: the phone company told Pete that our main number is excluded from the switchboard. That's why it's the only line that's connected to the answering machine. You know how the phones at the desks are on the switch? If someone calls a personal extension number during office hours and it's not connected to voice mail, the call goes automatically to another desk after a certain number of signals. Well, that's where our switchboard ends, according to Pete. So I can't think how an outsider could have called our main number. Everyone here knows that we shouldn't give the number to the public."

"Well, obviously someone at our office has given our main number to someone: it's the only explanation I can think of. I believe that this person knew where he or she was calling."

"He or she? I'm sure it's a girl on the tape."

"Yes, but I'm thinking if this is the girl who was kidnapped in Surry Hills, the killer probably dialled the

GAME

number for her and let her scream on the phone: to give us some sort of message. Did Pete listen to the tape from the answering machine? I need to know if there are any background noises. If we're lucky the killer's voice might be in the background somewhere; maybe he told her when to scream or something like that."

"Right, no, Pete's at his country house this weekend and it's a two hour drive from Sydney apparently. He didn't mind calling the phone company, but he said he couldn't make it to the office this weekend. He'll listen to the tape first thing on Monday. And he's also promised to make a list of everyone who has access to our main number."

Morgan sighs. "Okay. Thanks for letting me know. I'm in a meeting away from the office on Monday morning, so if anything else comes up you can give it to Ricketts: he's holding the morning meeting in my absence."

"Okay, will do. Have a nice weekend."

"You too O'Neill, I'll see you on Monday." As Morgan puts the phone on the coffee table he realises that O'Neill probably isn't going to be in the office on Monday as he is rostered to work on the weekend.

Ignoring the coffee as he comes into the kitchen, he takes a clean glass from the drying rack and makes a large drink of bourbon and coke that he takes with him to the living room. He picks up the remote control and switches the TV on.

By five pm Morgan has drunk four glasses of bourbon and he has watched one fishing show, a rugby game and bits of an old black and white movie. He feels slightly drunk and decides to have a shower to try to sober up a bit. He is glad that the phone hasn't rung during the afternoon to disturb him in his blissful drunken state. As he stands under the warm water he is in a good mood. He sings loudly as he scrubs his body with a wet towel that he's found on the floor under the sink. He thinks about how good it will be to meet David and get drunk, like they have done so many times before: before all this crap happened.

Still naked and wet from the shower, Morgan pulls the laundry from the drier and throws the pile on top of the bed. After a few minutes of rummaging through the laundry he manages to find a towel, underwear, socks and a shirt. He spends five minutes looking for his jeans around the apartment before he finds them in the bottom of the pile on the bed. Fully dressed at last, he walks into the kitchen and pours himself a cup of coffee from the brewer. The coffee tastes burnt from having been in the brewer all afternoon. He looks at his watch: it's half past six and he knows that he is too drunk to drive to Glebe. 'But what the hell,' he thinks. He has planned to drink anyway so he might as well get a cab. He can probably find a taxi on the street rather than wasting time calling for one, he thinks as he finishes the coffee. He grabs his wallet and keys from the hall table on the way out. When he closes the door he realises that he has forgotten to shave and brush his teeth. He puts a hand on his chin and feels stubble. Another hand against his mouth while exhaling proves that his breath can be improved. He sighs and unlocks the door. When he comes inside he sees that he has forgotten to turn the lights off and when he walks into the kitchen he sees that the coffee brewer is still turned on. He turns it off. If he isn't careful he will come home to a burnt down unit, he thinks.

The phone rings while he is shaving in the bathroom. "Fuck you," he says out loud. He continues to shave and

GAME

spills shaving foam on his shirt.

The beep comes after three signals and then Lisa's voice says: "It's me, Lisa, why don't you return my calls?"

"Why don't you return my calls?" Morgan repeats with a mocking tone in front of the mirror. He makes a face and pokes his tongue out.

Lisa continues: "I wanted to talk to you, but I guess you're not home. Or maybe you don't want to talk to me; because you're not answering your mobile either. Anyway, I didn't want to say this on your answering machine, but I guess I'll have to... I'm sorry for what happened this morning."

"I bet you're fucking sorry… that I found out, you bitch!" Morgan says to the mirror.

"Anyway, I'll give you a call in the morning and hopefully we can talk then," Lisa's voice says and a beep from the answering machine follows as she hangs up.

Morgan stares at his reflection in the mirror. His eyes are bloodshot and he has a shaving cut on his chin. A drop of blood falls on his shirt. "FUCK YOU!" he screams. He walks into the bedroom and starts to go through the laundry pile in search of a clean shirt. He pulls his stained shirt off and wipes his face with it before he puts a clean shirt on. He walks back into the bathroom, splashes his face with after shave and puts a piece of toilet paper over the shaving cut. He finds a bottle of eye drops and squirts some into his eyes. He watches in the mirror as the whites of his eyes turned whiter. As he waits for the shaving cut to stop bleeding, he smokes a cigarette in front of the window and drinks bourbon straight on ice as he's out of coke.

It takes Morgan less than a minute to hail a cab on the

main road. The driver makes eye contact with him through the open window. "Where are you going?"

Morgan quickly opens the back passenger door and gets in the back seat before the driver can see that he is drunk and refuse to drive him. "Glebe, 'Nags Head'."

The driver looks at him in the rear view mirror as he pulls out from the curb. "Nags Head, where's that?"

Morgan briefly meets his gaze in the mirror. "It's a pub. Go to Glebe Point Road and I'll direct you from there." Morgan looks out through the window as they pass Kings Cross. The traffic moves slowly. Pink and yellow neon signs light up the side walk outside the strip clubs. The crowd is a blend of prostitutes in short skirts, drug addicts looking to score, alcoholics begging for money, tourists and party goers. Morgan shakes his head with disgust as they drive past an old woman dressed in a hot pink miniskirt. She holds a bottle of beer and sings Waltzing Matilda.

The cab driver laughs. "How would you like to have her as your grandma?"

"It would make family gatherings more interesting, that's for sure," Morgan replies.

The driver shoots him a glance in the rear view mirror and nothing else is said until they reach Glebe Point Road and Morgan gives directions to the pub.

David is sitting at the bar when Morgan walks into Nags Head. He nods at Morgan. "You look like shit. What are you drinking?"

Morgan takes a seat on a barstool. "Bourbon and coke."

David catches the barmaid's attention, orders two drinks and then turns to Morgan. "What's up?"

GAME

Morgan sighs. "Everything."

The barmaid puts two glasses on the bar and Morgan grabs his drink and drinks eagerly.

David gives him a strange look. "Are you alright?"

Morgan looks up. "I'll be alright, don't worry about me. We're out to have a good time, aren't we?" He lifts his glass. "Here's to a good time!"

David lifts his beer glass and nods. "Cheers."

Morgan places his elbows on the bar. "How are the wife and kids?"

David smirks. "They're good. They're still with me, aren't they? Marie did a good job on the house; you should come by and have a look at it."

Morgan nods. "Yes, I might do that. I'd like to see the kids again."

"You should see how much they've grown." David drinks some beer and looks around the room. "Do you see any babes?"

Morgan raises his eyebrows. "Married with children and still on the prowl?"

David wipes his beer moustache off with a finger. "I feel sorry for women who are left out when all good men are married or gay." His eyes search the room.

There is a screeching sound from a microphone behind them and someone strums a guitar. Morgan turns around and sees that a band is setting up their instruments on a small stage. He lifts a hand as the barmaid walks past behind the bar. "Hey, could we get some drinks over here please?" His last words are drowned out by loud music as the band starts to play.

David taps him on the shoulder. "I thought we were going to eat?" he shouts through the music. "We can order more drinks in the restaurant." He stands up.

"Alright," Morgan follows David down a hallway and through a door: the noisy crowded pub is on the other side of the door as it closes behind them. They are in a court yard that is surrounded by ivy covered brick walls. Morgan has been here before with Lisa: it is a romantic place for dinner.

There are no romantic thoughts in his head this evening.

"So what's up? Are you going to tell me, or do I have to guess all night?" David asks as they are seated by a table under a wall mounted heater.

Morgan puts his empty glass on the table. "I'll tell you what's up: my mother died, work is a bloody nightmare and I found out this morning that my girlfriend is pregnant but has decided to abort the baby. And to cap it all off I was chased by a bloody shark this morning when I went for a swim."

David stares at him. "Bloody hell."

Morgan shrugs his shoulders. "Yes you can say that: bloody hell." He burps and doesn't bother to cover his mouth. "Are we going to get served here or what?" He looks around for a waiter.

"What about the shark; where was that?" David pulls his attention back.

"At Clovelly: I saw a large dorsal fin at the end of the channel."

"No shit? I went there for a swim the other day." David looks dubious.

"Yes shit," Morgan says impatiently.

"Did you contact the coast guards?"

Morgan raises his eyebrows. "Should I have?"

"I think that would be common courtesy, yes; to let other swimmers know there's a shark in the water."

GAME

"Shit. I never thought of that. But I told a guy on the beach. He might have told others."

David smirks. "That's very thoughtful of you."

"How the hell should I know what to do? I've never seen a shark before."

"True. Anyway, I'm sorry to hear about your mother. What happened to her?"

"Cancer: she died a few days ago." Morgan waives at a waiter that walks past. The man nods and comes back with two menus that he places on the table before he hurries off.

"I wouldn't worry about the girlfriend if I were you." David keeps his eyes on the menu. "Women get weird when they're pregnant. I know all about it."

Morgan frowns. "What, like mixed up in the head because of hormones? Is that what you mean?"

"Yes, they go mad. I don't have a medical explanation for it but it's probably the hormones rushing around in their bodies or something like that. Marie went bloody bonkers when she was pregnant. I had to move in with my parents for a while as I couldn't stand to be around her."

Morgan raises his hand as the waiter hurries past. "Can we order some drinks here?" He turns to David. "What are you having?"

David looks up from the menu. "Uh, I'll have a schooner of VB thanks."

"Right," Morgan turns to the waiter again. "We'll have a schooner of VB and a bourbon and coke." He yawns and adds: "Please."

The waiter nods and walks away.

"So I wouldn't be too heavy on the girlfriend if I were you," David says.

Morgan turns to him and accidentally knocks his glass

over with his elbow. He manages to grab it just as it falls off the table. "At the moment I don't give a shit about her." He slams the glass down on the table with a bang that is louder than he has meant it to be. "I can't believe that she has booked herself in for a bloody abortion without even telling me that she is pregnant!"

David looks around and puts a hand on Morgan's shoulder. "Calm down, mate. People are staring."

Morgan turns around. Two middle aged women at a table behind them frown as they avoid his gaze.

"Right, sorry." Morgan picks up his menu. "What are we eating?"

***

Lisa is on her way out when her phone starts ringing. She closes the front door and walks back into the hallway. She sees that the number display window is empty as she picks up the phone. Fiona, she thinks: Fiona has a silent number.

"Yes, hello?"

"Is this Lisa?" a male voice asks.

"Yes, Lisa speaking."

"This is Detective Thompson calling from the detective headquarters in Pyrmont. Sergeant Callaghan has been in an accident."

"What?" Lisa sits down on a chair. All the blood in her body seems to rush to her feet.

"Morgan Callaghan is in hospital and he's asking for

GAME

you. Can we pick you up and drive you there?"

"My god, what happened? Is he alright?"

"It was a car accident and I'm afraid he's hurt quite badly. What's your address? We can have a car pick you up and drive you to the hospital."

Lisa stares at her shaking fingers as she wipes her nose with the back of her hand. "I live in unit five, number twelve Alexandra Street, in Coogee."

"Right, I'll send someone over straight away."

"Okay, thanks." Lisa hangs up and remains motionless in the chair. Finally she picks up the phone again and calls Fiona: the friend she has promised to meet for dinner. There is no answer so Lisa leaves a message on Fiona's answering machine. She curses the fact that Fiona doesn't have a mobile.

A.C. Efverman

11

It is midday when Morgan wakes up. He has a crushing headache. He turns around, realises that he's under a pile of clothes and throws the laundry on the floor. He can't remember how he's ended up in bed and thinks that he must have substituted the clean laundry for a lack of sheets.

He walks slowly through the hallway. The wind outside is shaking the glass in the windows and he hears that something falls to the floor.

For a second he stands in the doorway to the living room and looks at the open window that is banging against the wall. Was he that drunk he forgot to close the window when he left the night before? He tries to remember: is it possible that he opened the window when he got home in the morning? He walks up to the window and closes it. He looks around the room and picks up a stapled bunch of papers from the floor. Everything else seems to be as he's left it. When he walks into the kitchen he feels dizzy. He leans against the wall as he opens a cupboard and takes two pain killers from a packet. A quick look in the refrigerator confirms that there is nothing to drink. He grabs a glass from the drying rack, fills it with tap water and swallows the tablets. The water makes him burp and he feels a sour taste mixed with garlic.

After a warm shower Morgan feels a bit better. He decides to make coffee and watch TV while he recovers.

GAME

***

Lisa feels a sharp pain in her head when she opens her eyes. Her hand hurts too: she tries to move it and realises she can't. Something holds her wrists and ankles together and there is something in her mouth. She looks around. She is lying on a floor that is covered with vinyl carpet. In front of her is a large bundle of see-through plastic. Something is rolled up inside the plastic. Lisa gasps when she realises what it is she's looking at: there is a naked person in there. And there's blood: lots of blood. Lisa's instinct is to scream but the only sound that comes through the gag is a moan. She closes her eyes but fear makes her open them again. Now she looks over the bundle and sees a white painted wall and a small dirty window covered with spider webs close to the ceiling. The window glass is rattling in the wind outside. Her eyes move and she sees a staircase made of stone or concrete in the corner of the room. She realises that she must be in a basement. She can't see through the window but she imagines that it is close to the ground outside. An uncovered light bulb hangs from a cord in the ceiling and spreads a harsh light.

The room is cold and damp. Lisa shivers. Her eyes move to the bundle next to her and she knows that the person who is rolled up inside the plastic sheet is dead. She tries to remember what has happened; she was on her way out to see Fiona when she got a call from a detective who said that Morgan was hurt – she clearly remembers that. Oh my god, Morgan – he's been hurt; there was something about a car accident. She blinks through her tears. But wait... was that really true, because there had been a knock on her door and she had opened it and outside was a good-looking guy who said that he was Morgan's colleague and that he would drive her to the hospital to see Morgan. She remembers walking down the stairs behind the man and walking with him to a car that was parked by the side of the road, and then she had gotten inside the car... She tries her hardest to concentrate her thoughts, but she can't remember anything more. She shivers again. Morgan – she suddenly thinks, he had been so furious with her; she has never seen him so angry before. But surely Morgan wouldn't want to hurt her?

Suddenly there is a squeaking noise: a door opens somewhere above and Lisa hears that someone walks down the stairs towards her.

***

Morgan is lying under a blanket in his sofa. Cold winds from the ocean are blowing through the gaps around the windows and make the apartment icy cold. Morgan's electrical heater is broken and he has promised himself to get a new heater every time the weather turns cold; but he has been busy and has forgotten all about it.

Morgan reluctantly moves one arm from the warmth under the blanket and grabs his phone from the coffee table. He remembers the number to the pizza shop by humming the commercial jingle. He dials the number and puts his arm back under the blanket: leaving only his head and one hand out in the cold.

As he is placed in a phone queue he thinks back to the night before: After dinner they had some more drinks in the pub and then David got the bright idea that they should go to a nightclub so they hailed a cab on Glebe Point Road.

GAME

They ended up in a dark bar with a tiny dance floor and loud music. Morgan can't remember the location of the club but he remembers that David tried to chat up some girls and that he had felt left out and bored. He'd drunk more than he could handle and he had thrown up in a toilet. He also remembers that some girl had helped him into a taxi.

"Pizza Club, delivery," a voice says in Morgan's ear.

"I'd like to make a home delivery order please," Morgan's voice is hoarse and he clears his throat.

"Could I have your telephone number please?" the brisk voice asks.

Morgan gives the girl his phone number and confirms that they have his correct address in their database. He orders a large pizza, a bottle of coke and garlic bread.

"That comes to a total of twenty-one dollars and fifty cents. If you could have the correct change ready, that'd be great. Our driver will be with you in approximately forty-five minutes." The girl sounds like a parrot that has repeated the same words a hundred times.

"Okay. Thanks." Morgan feels sleepy and is making himself comfortable under the blanket when a thought strikes him. He picks up his phone again and dials Lisa's home number. Four signals go through and then he hears Lisa's voice say: "You have reached Lisa's phone, leave your details and I'll return your call."

"Uh, hi, it's me... Morgan. You called earlier. I'll be at home for the rest of the day, so maybe you can call me when you get this message." He hangs up and reaches for the cigarette packet on the table, lights a cigarette, picks up the phone again and dials Lisa's mobile number. The call is diverted to voicemail and he doesn't bother to leave another message.

A minute later the phone rings and he grabs it again.

"It's me, Katherine. What are you doing?"

"Nothing, what's up?"

"Well that's a surprise," Katherine's voice is patronising. "I called to see if you've got those prices that you promised to check?"

Morgan closes his eyes. "Bloody hell, I forgot about that. I'm sorry. I've been busy and today I'm sick. I'm in bed."

"Right, well I'm glad I called then. I guess I'll have to check those prices myself."

"Yes that would be good." Morgan waits for Katherine to say something but she remains silent. "So…" he says. "How's everything? How's dad?"

"Oh right, like you care? Give me a call when you've got time so we can to start to organise things. We're planning to have a funeral next week, just so you know… Get your act together by then, will you?"

The call is disconnected as she hangs up.

Morgan stares at the phone in his hand. "Bitch," he says and throws the phone on the table. He looks at his watch: it will probably be another half hour before the pizza arrives. He decides to take a hot bath while he waits.

***

A pair of black shoes stops in front of Lisa's face. She doesn't dare to look up at the man who stands in front of her.

"Hello, hello. So we're awake now, are we? You've been sleeping all day you lazy little bitch," the owner of the black shoes says. "Do you like your company? She's a bit

GAME

quiet now but she was lively last night, let me tell you." He gets down on his knees and puts his face close to Lisa's.

Lisa looks into his eyes to see if there is a glimpse of compassion in there somewhere, but all that stares back at her is cold hate. She squirms as he touches her face.

"My beautiful girl, you're my pretty girl, aren't you?" He sits down in front of her and crosses his legs. "Are you hungry?"

She nods and stares down at the floor: she doesn't dare to look at him anymore. Her body is tensed up with fear and her neck is so stiff that her neck muscles make small jerky movements: causing her head to shake against the floor. Her hands are icy cold, she has lost all movement in her fingers and her hip hurts from lying on the hard floor.

"Well, good; I'm hungry too. Come on." He gets up on his knees and pulls her into a sitting position by grabbing her upper arms. Then he pulls her up with a hard grip. He holds her under the arms as he drags her backwards over the floor. Her shins hit every step painfully on the way up the stairs but she is too stiff and scared to move her legs. They enter a small dark room at the top of the stairs and from there she is dragged into another, warmer room.

"Here you are gorgeous." He dumps her on a chair in front of a table.

Lisa stares at the table that is set for three people. There is dried up food on the plates. A cooking pot stands in the middle of the table: it is filled with something that smells like baked beans in tomato sauce. There is also a bottle of bourbon, a bottle of coke and three glasses. Lisa can see mould in the glass that stands in front of her.

"Have I forgotten something?" He looks down at the table. "Oh yes, cutlery. I'll be right back."

A.C. Efverman

Lisa looks around the room when he has left. A small fire on logs in an open fireplace creates warmth and is the only light source in the room. A mattress is propped up against the window and effectively blocks out any day light.

"I don't think we'll need forks or knives." He is back. Lisa watches as he places three spoons on the table. "I'll get my second guest." He turns in the doorway and looks at Lisa. "Don't you start now, be patient."

Lisa stares at his back as he leaves the room. A few seconds later she hears a door open and then a thumping noise from somewhere below. Lisa knows that he is dragging someone up the stairs, the same way he has dragged her from the basement. The warmth in the room has softened her muscles but her body is still sore from lying on the cold floor. She has a terrible headache and the smell of baked beans makes her nauseous even though she is hungry.

"Here we are."

Lisa turns her head and sees that he is dragging someone behind him as he walks backwards into the room. When he comes closer she sees that he is holding a naked woman. Lisa stares at the blood on the body. The woman's face is hidden behind a curtain of dark hair.

He tries to seat the body in a chair next to Lisa's but the body is stiff and refuses to bend.

"Damn it," his face is red and he breathes heavily. He drops the woman on the floor and a dark stain immediately spreads out on the carpet.

"No not on the carpet!" He hurries out of the room. Lisa hears a door open. A few seconds later he is back with the large plastic sheet from the basement. He puts the plastic on the floor and puts the body on top. When he stands up Lisa sees that his T-shirt is stained with blood. He looks

GAME

around and then suddenly moves towards Lisa. She turns her face away as he comes closer but he is reaching for something behind her. Then she sees that he is pushing an armchair towards the table. He crouches down next to the dead woman, lifts her up in the plastic sheet and places the body over the armrests of the armchair. Blood drips from the plastic sheet onto the carpet but he doesn't seem to notice.

"So, now that we're all here we can start to eat." He looks at Lisa. "Sorry, I forgot."

Lisa closes her eyes as he walks behind her and unties the knot of her gag. She pictures the blood from his hands smearing onto her hair.

"But remember: if you scream or make any noise I'll take your pretty little head off. Are we clear on that?" He bends his head down in front of Lisa's face. She opens her eyes and nods slowly. His hand moves towards her face. He pulls the cotton scarf out of her mouth and she feels wet blood on her cheek. She coughs: her throat is dry.

"Good girl." He takes a seat by the table. "See this?" He takes something from his pocket and points it at her. "This is what I'll use on you if you're not a good girl." He puts the gun on the table next to his plate. "Now, let's say our prayers… Thank you god for bringing me these well behaved girls," he blinks at Lisa, "and for giving us the meal we are about to receive." He uncaps his hands and spoons beans onto the plates, pours bourbon into two of the glasses and tops the drinks with coke.

"Cheers." He raises his glass, looks into Lisa's eyes and drinks.

***

A.C. Efverman

Darkness grows rapidly out of the corners in the apartment. This painful day will soon be over, Morgan thinks as he puts his bathrobe on. The intercom buzzes. A few seconds later Morgan pays a young delivery guy and receives a warm cardboard box and a plastic bag. He opens the pizza box in the living room and eats quickly. When he has killed most of his hunger he walks into the kitchen and pours bourbon into a glass. Back in the sofa he fills the glass with coke and drinks thirstily. He ignores the annoying voice in his head that tells him to not drink alcohol.

He has just started eating again when the phone rings. He quickly chews and swallows.

"Yes hello?" Morgan's hand leaves grease prints on the telephone.

"It's me, David. Are you recovering?"

"Uh, yes, I'm as well as can be expected. When did you get home last night?" Morgan looks at the pizza and wishes that David hadn't called.

"Wouldn't have a clue… Listen, I've been talking to some of the guys and we've decided to play cricket in the park on Tuesday night. Are you in?" David's voice is loud and Morgan holds the phone a few centimetres from his ear.

"Maybe, which park?"

"Jubilee Park, in Glebe: they've got night lights there. We're meeting there at seven. We need you or we'll be one man short."

Morgan thinks for a few seconds before he answers. "Okay, I'll play. Who else is coming?"

"Tommy, Pete, Steve and some others. See you on Tuesday then?"

Morgan is eager to hang up. "Okay, see you then." He

GAME

puts the phone down and starts eating again.

It is late evening when Morgan realises that he has to prepare some material for his meeting the following morning. He searches the wardrobe in his bedroom, finds a knitted jumper that he puts on and then sits down in the sofa with a cup of coffee and a pile of papers.

He suspects that Travis wants him to present the investigation and that means he has to put his material in some sort of order or make a list of facts. He decides to write a summary. He isn't sure what sort of people will attend the meeting, and he can't include medical terms and police acronyms that outsiders won't understand. He feels that it will be best to mention as little as possible about the investigation but he needs to present the main facts and prepare himself for a lot of questions.

It is two am when he finishes writing and puts his alarm on for seven. He thinks about Lisa as he drifts off to sleep.

A.C. Efverman

12

It is raining hard and traffic is chaotic when Morgan drives through the CBD. He is wearing a suit and a newly ironed shirt and he has fuelled himself with two cups of coffee before he left the apartment.

He drives up behind a large tour bus that is parked outside the hotel entrance. A man in blue uniform takes his car keys. Morgan zigzags around groups of German tourists that have gathered in the entrance on his way to the elevators.

He finds a brass sign in the corridor that shows him the way to the right suite.

About twenty people are seated around a large oval table in the room. Morgan recognises the police Commissioner at the end of the table, as well as some members from the World Cup committee that he has met some months earlier during a briefing on FIFA's security practices. Travis is sitting close to a podium next to the window.

A girl stands by the door and asks his name. She gives him a name tag and points out a breakfast buffet that is set up on a table. Morgan fastens the name tag on his breast pocket and helps himself to a cup of coffee.

"Detective Sergeant Callaghan," Travis says as Morgan takes a seat by the table. "Thank you for coming."

Morgan nods. "Good morning."

Travis gets up from his chair and stands behind the podium. "And now ladies and gentlemen, I think that

GAME

everyone is present, and we can start." He looks at the girl by the door. She walks out and closes the door behind her. Travis turns to face the people around the table. "I'd like to thank everyone for turning up with such short notice; I know how busy you are in times like these… But I'm sure you will appreciate the importance of this meeting once we have explained why we've brought you here." Travis turns to Morgan. "Detective Sergeant Morgan Callaghan will give you all the details." He steps down and takes his seat by the table.

Morgan grabs his notes and takes Travis' place behind the podium. He clears his throat as he considers what to say. "Thank you Superintendent Travis. I am Detective Sergeant Callaghan, and I'm in charge of an investigation of four murders that have occurred in Sydney during the last six months. We have established by medical evidence that one killer is responsible for all four deaths." Morgan pauses and then feels the need to clarify: "We're dealing with a serial killer." He pauses again and looks at the faces around the table. He has everyone's attention as he continues to read from his notes: "I am not here to give you details of the murders, but I can tell you that all four murder victims were young, respectable women. They were brutally raped and murdered and their bodies were then dumped in public places around the city. One of the dead women has been identified as a Danish citizen who was here in Sydney on a working holiday."

"Oh my god," someone at the table says.

"So far we have managed to keep these murders from the media and we are continuing to treat this investigation as top secret. We'll have the world's eyes on us in one week's time when the World Cup begins and if the public finds out that we have a serial killer in Sydney there will be mass hysteria. Following that, there will be cancellations of match tickets and hotel rooms, cancellations of plane tickets, et cetera." Morgan pauses for effect. "We are," he continues, "concentrating on finding this killer and even though the investigation is moving forward, I cannot assure you that we will catch the killer before the World Cup begins… We do not want to alarm you, but it is necessary that you are aware of the situation." Morgan looks at Travis: he isn't sure if he has chosen the right words but Travis nods. "Are there any questions?"

A young woman from the World Cup committee clears her throat. "I've got a question: What are we doing to prevent the press and the public finding out about this, and how can we be sure that they won't find out?"

Morgan looks at her. "We are, as I mentioned earlier, treating this as a top secret investigation. Our legal department has created a document that all the witnesses and people we have interviewed have signed: these documents are legally binding and have heavy penalties attached. Basically the documents prevent anyone involved in this investigation to mention the murders. We have also updated the security of the police departments' computer and telephone systems, to ensure that the media cannot listen in on police activities…" Morgan holds out his hands. "Of course we can't guarantee that this won't leak out somehow, but we are doing our best to prevent it from happening."

The woman nods. "Okay, but say if this *would* leak out, what do we do then? Is there a plan? I'm mostly thinking of the World Cup now: something like this would obviously scare people from coming to Sydney to watch the matches."

"We are aware of that, but all we can do if this leaks

GAME

out is to assure people that we are investigating the murders and that we hope to catch the killer soon." Morgan looks at Travis for support but Travis sits quiet with a frown on his forehead. Morgan wonders if Travis would have answered the question differently.

The police Commissioner suddenly speaks and everyone turns towards him. "How many men are working on this investigation, Sergeant Callaghan?"

Morgan meets his gaze. "We currently have twenty-three men working on the investigation."

The Commissioner holds the eye contact. "If you are confident that you can carry on with the investigation with your current resources, I don't see the point in bringing in detectives from other parts of the country. We don't want to compromise the security around the World Cup: we have placed a large part of the police force on security and I don't think we can allocate more men to your command."

Morgan nods. "I agree with your view. I am confident that we have enough resources at present. And as the investigation hasn't been covered by media, there is no need to set up of a call centre to respond to the public."

The Commissioner seems content with this answer as he remains silent. Morgan and Travis answer more questions from the people around the table. Everyone has an agenda and needs to be assured that everything is continuing to plan and a few people have questions about the possibility that the murders can be part of a terrorist attack. Travis hands over more and more questions to Morgan and in the end Morgan is the only one answering questions. When there is nothing more to say, Travis hands out a piece of paper to everyone around the table. "This," he says, "is the legal document we mentioned earlier. If you could all sign at the bottom of the page and then hand the form back to me before you leave, that would be appreciated." He hands a form to Morgan and Morgan looks at him with raised eyebrows.

"Yes you too, Sergeant Callaghan." Travis looks at him with his small brown eyes. "I have signed one myself."

Morgan signs the paper and hands it back to Travis without a comment.

It has stopped raining. Morgan leaves his car in the hotel car park as he knows it will be impossible to find other parking in the area. He crosses the road and finds a vacant table at Hyde Park café. The air feels free from pollution. Everything is wet. A waitress sweeps water off the tables and chairs with a towel. Morgan feels something that resembles a small earthquake stirring in his stomach but he ignores it and orders a coffee; he needs the caffeine to stay awake. He is reading his notes when someone touches his shoulder.

"Hello, what are you doing in my neighbourhood?" Camilla stands next to Morgan's table. She is dressed in grey pants and a white blouse and her hair is pinned into a French twist. She smiles at him. "Can I sit down, or are you going be a bore and just stare at me?"

He automatically returns the smile. "Have a seat. How are you?"

She unfolds a chair that is leaning against the table and he suddenly recalls what the skin on her breasts and stomach smells like.

"I'm fine," she says. "But how are *you*? You look like crap."

A waitress turns up at their table with a notepad in her hand. Camilla turns to her. "I'm just having coffee: a long black. And could you wipe the water off this chair please?"

GAME

The girl wipes the chair and walks off. Camilla sits down by the table. "I'm sorry that I got upset with you the other day on the phone." She smiles apologetically. "Are we still friends?"

"Of course we are. And I'm sorry too. I've been busy lately."

"How's work?"

Morgan places his elbows on the table. "I was going to call you actually. There have been some recent developments in the investigation. A girl called our office the other day: she screamed that someone was going to kill her. The call was recorded on the answering machine in our office but I haven't heard the tape yet."

Camilla raises her eyebrows. "That's odd. Was it an emergency call?"

Morgan nods. "Yes, apparently it was. But that's not all: a girl was abducted a few days ago in Surry Hills. We have a witness who saw the kidnapper and his description matches other descriptions we have of the killer. I believe it's all connected with the phone call somehow. Maybe it was the killer who called our office and let the girl scream on the phone... The girl he kidnapped, I mean."

Camilla leans in closer. "It seems far-fetched. Why are you dismissing the possibility that the girl made the phone call herself?"

"Why would she? Anyone in an emergency would call triple 0, wouldn't they? And if it was her who called, how did she get our number?"

Camilla frowns. "What do you mean?"

"The call was made to our main number that is connected to the answering machine: this is a silent number that is not given to the public."

"This is not making sense at all."

Morgan nods. "I know. Maybe the killer is playing games with us."

Camilla looks down at the table top. "Well, I guess that could be true. Serial killers have been known to show off: to show that they are clever and that they can get away with things. That's part of the reason they kill: to show that they're in control. These murders haven't been covered by media so maybe he wants attention." Camilla pauses and then asks: "Do you have any suspects?"

"No. None of the known offenders who match the description or profile is on parole or out of jail right now."

"But hang on, if the call was made to a silent number that is not known to the public, I guess you need to ask yourself who has access to this number."

Morgan frowns. "I thought of that too. The main line is only used internally by the police departments."

Camilla looks up as the waitress puts a cup on the table. "Thanks." She pours one teaspoon of sugar into the cup and stirs the coffee. "So you're saying that someone within our organization gave this telephone number to someone outside, is that it?"

"Either that, or the call was made by someone who works within our organization."

Camilla frowns at him over the rim of her cup. "What? You're thinking it's a cop? Are you seriously suspecting that the killer is a cop?"

"Well how else would this person know our number? And don't forget that the person who made the call must also have known that we investigate the murders."

"If the call wasn't made by the girl herself... I mean: that is as much a possibility as anything else, isn't it?"

GAME

"I guess so." Morgan sighs and looks into the wet park. "Anything is possible. But I still think it was the killer who called and let the girl scream: to give us some sort of message."

"Okay, let's assume that you're right. But we still have to ask ourselves who has access to your main number."

Morgan thinks for a second. "To start with, there are all the police stations around Sydney. And then all the different departments that we deal with: like your department. There's also the technical department, the legal department, the lab and so on…. But I don't see why any of these people would have given our main telephone number to an outsider, and it has never happened before."

"I guess that if you're looking for someone who has access to your main telephone number and who also knows that your department is investigating these murders, it seems possible that this person is someone who works in one of our departments or at the police," Camilla says calmly.

"It seems more than possible." Morgan puts his notes in his briefcase. "But I haven't even heard the tape from the answering machine yet." He looks into Camilla's green eyes for the first time since she joined him at the table. "I should head back to the office, but it was good to see you again." He gets up from his chair.

She smiles. "You too, take care."

Morgan feels weak and dizzy as he walks into his office. He has to eat something, he thinks as he sits down at his desk. He shouldn't have spent the weekend drinking and indulging in self pity. He feels bad thinking about it now: he still has a hangover and needs to think clearly.

He picks up the phone and dials Ricketts' extension.

Two signals go through before Ricketts answers.

"It's me, Morgan. I just got back from the meeting. How did you go?"

"It was alright. Do you want to go through it?"

Morgan looks at the grey coloured day through the window. "Yes, that would be a good idea. Have you eaten yet?"

"No, I was on my way out to get something. Do you want me to get you a sandwich or something?"

"Yes, you can get me a chicken schnitzel on white bread with mayo, avocado and tomatoes. I'll occupy the boardroom meanwhile."

"No worries, I'll see you soon then."

Morgan hangs up and sorts through the papers in his In-tray. He then listens to messages on his voicemail and makes notes of people he needs to call back. Finally he walks over to the boardroom.

Ricketts enters the room a few minutes later. "I don't know about you, but I'm starving."

"Yes me too, have a seat." Morgan takes the paper bag that Ricketts hands him.

"So, what's new?" Morgan asks after he's taken a few bites of his sandwich.

"The morning meeting went well. I updated everyone on the abduction in Surry Hills. I think we've found out who the girl was from missing persons." Ricketts takes a sip of Sprite from a can.

"That's good news. Who is she?"

Ricketts wipes his fingers on a paper napkin and flicks through some papers. "The name we have is Linda Kasinski. Miss Kasinski's flatmates reported Linda missing on Saturday morning after she had failed to return home

GAME

from work on Friday afternoon. The flatmates got worried as they had organised a party at their house on Friday night and Linda was supposed to buy the food for the party on her way home from work. The clothes that Linda wore on the day she disappeared also fit the description that Mr Perkins gave. Linda Kasinski is twenty-two years old and she works part time in a second hand clothes store in Surry Hills. She usually takes a shortcut through Greens Lane on her way home from work according to her flatmates."

"Did O'Neill tell you about the phone call that we got on the weekend?" Morgan asks.

If Ricketts is surprised that Morgan changes the subject so quickly he doesn't show it. "Yes he left a message for me. The tape is still with the technical department so I haven't listened to it yet. We're waiting for Pete to get back to us with the results."

Morgan scrunches up the brown paper bag that has contained his sandwich and throws it into a waste paper basket that stands in the corner. "I think we should play the tape for Linda Kasinski's flatmates and see if they recognise her voice. You and Stone will go to Linda's house this afternoon and interview her flatmates. I want all details of Linda's personality and habits. And while you're in Surry Hills, you might as well go to the clothing store where she works and talk to the employees there as well."

Ricketts writes in his notebook. "Okay, will do."

"Did you announce the phone call to our answering machine at the meeting?"

"Yes I did, but just briefly because I didn't have all details."

Morgan considers letting Ricketts in on what he has

discussed with Camilla about the internal phone number but decides not to.

"Ask Torrone to contact the psychological department for an update on the killer's profile in regards to the kidnapping and the phone call," he says instead.

Ricketts makes more notes. "Okay, was there anything else?"

"Yes, someone needs to go to Cassandra Saunders' workplace and interview her colleagues. See who's available and send two men. We also need to go into Cassandra Saunders' apartment with the forensic team: I can go with them if no one else is available. Let me know before you go to Surry Hills." Morgan has decided not to go to the bookshop. "Do you know if Cassandra Saunders' relatives have been notified yet?"

Ricketts looks up. "I'm not sure actually."

Morgan frowns. "Find out if this has happened. If not, organise it now. We can't have delays: it doesn't look good."

"Okay, I'll find out." Ricketts turns page and makes another note.

Morgan stays in the boardroom after Ricketts has left. He reads reports and makes notes. Then he goes to his desk and collects two empty folders. Back in the boardroom he creates a victim's book about Cassandra Saunders, by filling the plastic pockets with papers containing all the information they have on her. The second folder is considerably thinner as it only holds a report from missing persons.

There is a knock and Ricketts puts his head through the door opening. "I've told Scullion and Whitfield to go to Bermuda Bookshop and talk to the employees. They're

GAME

on their way now. The only man who's available to go to Cassandra's apartment is Braun. Do you want to go with him?"

Morgan looks at his watch. "Yes I do, can you call the forensic department and ask them to send two men with relevant equipment to Cassandra's address? Me and Braun will meet them there this afternoon. Let me know what time they're available, will you?"

Ricketts nods. "Will do, I'll get back to you." His head disappears and Morgan continues to read.

A few minutes later Ricketts' head is back in the door opening. "The forensics said to meet you there at four o'clock. And according to Cassandra's employee form; her parents are dead and the closest relative is an aunt who lives in Newcastle. The aunt has been notified by local police in Newcastle of her niece's death but there has been no contact made to her about an identification of the body." Ricketts hands a piece of paper to Morgan. "Here's the aunt's phone number. Me and Stone are leaving for Surry Hills now."

Morgan looks at the note. "Okay. Leave a printed copy of the interviews on my desk tonight before you leave."

"Alright."

Morgan walks back to his room and puts one of the folders in the bookcase behind his desk. He then picks up the phone and calls information service and asks to be connected to the real estate agent that is listed as Cassandra Saunders' landlord in the report.

"Grey's Real Estate Glebe, Diana speaking. Can I help you?"

"This is Detective Sergeant Callaghan from the detective headquarters in Sydney. May I speak to the manager there please?"

A.C. Efverman

"Yes, may I ask what it's in regards to?" The woman sounds curious.

Morgan adds an arrogant tone to his voice. "Just tell him that Detective Sergeant Callaghan is calling please."

"Hold please."

Music fills Morgan's ear for a few seconds before a male voice says: "This is Boris Delaney, how may I help you?"

"Mr Delaney, this is Detective Sergeant Callaghan. I'm calling in regards to one of your tenants." Morgan reads from the report in the murder bible that lies open on his desk: "Unit eight, thirty-two Fraser Street in Glebe."

There is silence. "What's the problem?" Mr Delaney asks finally.

"No problem. Can I come and see you? Will you be in your office at three thirty this afternoon?"

"Yes, but may I know what this is about?"

"I'd rather not discuss it over the phone, but I can tell you that I will need the keys to that apartment. What's your address there?"

"It's 352 Glebe Point Road: we're next to an art dealer on the corner."

Morgan writes the address in his notebook. "Thanks. I'll see you in your office at three thirty then."

"Okay, I'll see you then."

Morgan hangs up and makes another note in his notebook. Then he dials the number that Ricketts has written on a piece of paper. A breathless voice answers: "Hello?"

"Ms Estelle Saunders?"

"Yes, who's calling please?"

"This is Detective Sergeant Callaghan calling from Sydney. I believe that you have been contacted recently by

GAME

Newcastle police in relation to your niece Cassandra, is that correct?"

"Yes, the police were here yesterday."

"I need to inform you now Ms Saunders that our standard procedure is that the person listed as next of kin makes a formal identification of the body. Do you have any questions in regards to this?"

The woman starts to cry. "The police that were here just told me that Cassandra was dead, they wouldn't tell me what had happened. How did it happen?" she whispers.

"I'm afraid that I can't go into details over the phone, Ms Saunders. Would it be possible for you to come to Sydney within the next few days?"

"Yes… of course… I'll have to take the train down, and organise time off work… But I should be able to come down tomorrow."

"Good, I'll give you my telephone number, have you got a pen?"

"Hang on." There is silence for a few seconds and then her voice is back: "Okay, I've got pen and paper."

Morgan gives her his telephone number and makes sure that she writes down the address to the headquarters as well. They agree that she will call him as soon as she comes to Sydney and they will meet. Morgan doesn't want her to go to the morgue alone. He sighs as he hangs up. He is not looking forward to meeting Cassandra's aunt and bringing her to the morgue.

He suddenly realises that he should call George Demitriades to make sure he makes Cassandra look presentable for the identification. For once he gets the medical examiner on the phone, rather than a recorded message.

"Hi it's Morgan Callaghan, nice to hear your voice live for a change."

"Morgan, hello, what can I do for you?"

"A few things actually; firstly, have you contacted Mr and Mrs Henriksen at their hotel yet?"

"Yes, yes. We spoke the other day. They're coming here tomorrow to sign the release forms for their daughter."

"Good. I'm glad that it's been taken care of. Secondly, I've spoken to Cassandra Saunders' aunt. She'll identify Cassandra tomorrow. I don't know what time she'll be here because she's getting a train from Newcastle, but I'd appreciate if you could put some make-up on Cassandra before she sees her."

"Sure, I'll make her up and put her in the presentation room. Don't worry, she'll look fine. She isn't decomposed like the others."

"Thanks George. I'll be joining Ms Saunders tomorrow, so I'll see you then."

"Alright, see you then."

As soon as Morgan hangs up the phone rings.

"Morgan?"

"Yes, who's this?"

"It's Pete. How are you going?"

"I'm alright, what have you got for me?"

"About the tape from your answering machine: there's traffic noise in the background, but it's very vague. We had to erase the girl's voice and magnify the background sound seventy-five points before we could pick it up. I'd say the call was made from a phone booth, or inside a house or unit where there's heavy traffic on a road nearby. That was all we could find. The time of the call can't be established: the phone company only records times of outgoing calls, not incoming calls. It's not like voicemail where the time of a call is recorded. I don't know why you have an answering machine there at all actually; you should have voicemail on all your lines."

"Yes, but this line is used internally and not by the public. That's why we keep it separate from the switchboard."

"Right... But I don't get it: how come this girl called your internal number then? How did she get a hold of this number, and why did she call it?"

Morgan sighs. "We don't know. Did you give the tape to Ricketts?"

"Yes I did, he came down and collected it about half an hour ago. I've made a copy that I'm keeping here for our records."

"Okay, good. So that's it then? Isn't there anything else you can do to get more information from the tape?"

"We've done everything we can, believe me. From one thing to another: are you playing cricket with us tomorrow night?"

"Yes I am, David talked me into it. Is he there today?"

"No he's down in Wollongong on a training course."

Morgan turns his computer on. "Okay. And another thing; have you checked out Else Henriksen's email yet?"

"Else Henriksen's email? No, I haven't."

"Ricketts said that you were looking into her personal email account and that you would contact Yahoo and some other email providers – and by the way; I found out that Else had her personal email account with Yahoo Denmark."

"Right, yeah I just haven't had a chance to follow up on that as yet. We've been flat out here, and like I said; David isn't here today either."

"Okay, I know that you're busy but can we prioritise

the email for now – I think it's important."

Morgan hears that Pete sighs. "Okay, I'll do my best, but I can't promise anything soon, alright?"

"Alright, and thanks for the report. Can you send me a written copy of your findings of the answering machine tape as soon as possible? And I want a list of everyone who has access to the private number connected to our answering machine."

"That is on its way."

"Okay, thanks. I'll see you tomorrow night." Morgan hangs up and looks at his watch: almost two thirty. He yawns and feels that he needs a cup of coffee and some fresh air.

It's raining again. Morgan runs down the road to the coffee shop. He smokes a cigarette under the roof of the cafe entrance as he waits for his coffee. There are hardly any people on the street and the few he sees hurry along under umbrellas. Morgan shivers: he has left his jacket in the office. The waitress comes out and hands Morgan a paper cup and two sachets of sugar just as his mobile phone starts to ring. He takes the cup and mouths the word 'thanks' as he flicks his phone open. "Yes, Sergeant Callaghan speaking." Morgan looks at the waitress who remains standing on the pavement.

"You haven't paid. It's three dollars twenty," she says when Morgan looks at her with raised eyebrows.

"Hello? Morgan, are you there?" Katherine's voice asks in the phone.

"Hang on; I'll be right with you." Morgan puts the coffee cup on the ground and digs in his pocket for coins. "Keep the change," he says as he hands the girl two two-dollar coins.

"Katherine, sorry about that; I was in the coffee shop."

GAME

Morgan picks up his cup and starts to walk back towards the office.

"We've set a date for the funeral. I'm just going to call people and not worry about written invites. We're buying the casket tomorrow. I chose a basic coffin for a reasonable price. And I've contacted the priest in Palm Beach. It's all taken care of. All I have to do now is to organise the flowers. Should we have coffee afterwards at dad's place? What do you think?"

Her words have tumbled out like a waterfall: a hundred miles an hour.

"Are you alright?" Morgan asks.

"No I'm NOT BLOODY ALRIGHT!" she blurts out.

Morgan frowns. "What's wrong?"

"My mother is dead and I'm organising the whole bloody funeral on my own, while you're fart-assing around, doing god knows what. And dad's missing; he's not here and he's not at his house. I've tried to call him all day but there's no answer…" Morgan hears that she draws her breath.

"My god, calm down please. You know that I'm at work... I've got some appointments this afternoon, but I can come over to your place when I'm done. We'll find dad, don't worry. He's probably in his garden, that's all. You know what he's like."

Katherine draws another deep breath. "But he just left: he didn't leave a note or anything. Doesn't he realise that I get worried?"

Two detectives walk past in the entrance and Morgan nods at them. "Alright Kath, I've got to go. I'll give you a call as soon as I can. Don't worry, okay?"

"Alright, I'll talk to you later."

Morgan sighs and turns his mobile off in the elevator on

the way up to the office: he can't afford distractions.

The traffic is a nightmare because of the rain and it takes Morgan almost twenty minutes to get to Glebe. As they near Glebe Point Road Morgan gets stuck behind a moving truck that is parked in the middle of the street. The truck driver, dressed in a pair of shorts and a singlet, finally comes out of a house and makes a gesture with his middle finger when Morgan beeps his horn. Morgan shakes his head and chokes an urge to shout something abusive. Braun, who is sitting next to Morgan, laughs. "Professional drivers are the worst."

"Yes they are," Morgan says with a deadpan tone and drags on his cigarette – the car is filling up with smoke despite the air con but he doesn't care. He finds a parking spot around the corner from Grey's real estate and they run to avoid getting soaked by the rain.

A woman is sitting behind the front desk in the real estate agent's office. She looks up as they walk in through the door. "Yes, can I help you?" Her eyes stop at Braun's wet shirt that has become see-through.

Morgan is glad that he is wearing a jacket. "Detectives Callaghan and Braun, we're here to see Mr Delaney for a three-thirty appointment."

The woman takes her eyes off Braun with difficulty and picks up a phone receiver. "Mr Delaney, I've got two detectives here to see you… Right," she hangs up and looks at Morgan. "You can go through. It's the first door on your left."

A man is seated behind a desk in the corner of the room. A badly designed hairpiece rests on his head: it looks like a dead guinea pig. The man stands up as they get closer and Morgan sees that he is dressed in an out-dated double

GAME

breasted suit. No wonder that the receptionist is hungry for eye candy if this is all she has to look at every day, Morgan thinks.

"I'm Boris Delaney," the man says. "How can I help you?"

Morgan shakes his hand over the desk. "I'm Detective Sergeant Callaghan: we spoke on the phone earlier. And this," he nods at Braun, "is Detective Braun."

Delaney makes a gesture with his hand towards two plastic chairs. "Please, have a seat. What can I do for you?"

Morgan crosses his legs in the uncomfortable chair. "It's a rather sensitive matter, and you need to treat this conversation as confidential. The tenant in the unit that I mentioned over the phone is dead, and we need to enter the premises as part of our investigation."

"Good lord!" Mr Delaney exclaims. "She didn't die in the apartment, did she?"

Morgan looks at him. "So you know who I'm talking about?"

Mr Delaney looks confused. "Of course I do. I checked immediately after I spoke to you."

"But you didn't go to the apartment did you?"

"No... Why?"

Morgan looks into Delaney's eyes. "Well, it *is* possible that she *did* die in the apartment. That's why we need to go there: to establish if it's a crime scene. And if it turns out to be a crime scene, we wouldn't want anyone to contaminate it. You can see how important that is, can't you?"

Mr Delaney looks shocked. "What do you mean, 'crime scene'?"

"I can't disclose any details surrounding Miss Saunders' death. All we need from you is the keys to her apartment."

A.C. Efverman

Morgan wonders how Ricketts handled Else Henriksen's real estate agent and if he had been as difficult.

Delaney stands. "Alright then but I'm going with you."

Morgan is happy to get up from the uncomfortable chair. "That won't be possible, I'm afraid. We're bringing in equipment to make a thorough investigation of the apartment. This is a matter for the police."

Delaney stares at him. "But I'm in charge of that apartment: I need to be there to supervise you."

Morgan feels his patience drip away. "I can get a court order to enter the apartment. But that would waste everyone's time, and we could possibly loose vital pieces of evidence during that time. Is that something you would like to be responsible for Mr Delaney?"

Delaney sits back down in his chair. "I don't know," he mutters. "I don't like it. I don't like it at all."

Morgan looks at his watch. "How about giving us those keys, Mr Delaney? We're meeting some officers at the apartment in ten minutes, and I'd hate to let them wait. Let us do our job."

Delaney opens a drawer in his desk and takes out a large key ring. He flicks through some keys and finally unhooks two of them. "Here you are." He hands the keys to Morgan. "But you are responsible for any damages, is that understood?"

Morgan takes the keys and puts them in his pocket. "Sure, as long as the damages weren't there before we went in." He turns to Braun. "Come on, let's go."

Braun gets up from his chair and hands a business card to the real estate agent. "Have a good day, Mr Delaney."

They walk out of the room.

"I want those keys back when you're done!" Delaney

GAME

yells after them.

Unit eight at thirty-two Fraser Street turns out to be a tiny one bedroom apartment that is located on the second floor in a high rise building. The hallway is dark when Morgan and Braun enter the apartment with Freedman and Campbell from the forensic department. Freedman, who is recording their entry with a small video camera, opens a door and an overwhelming stench bellows out into the hallway. Freedman's gloved hand touches the wall and finds a light switch. The light reveals a small bedroom furnished with a single bed and a bedside table. There are built in wardrobes along one wall. The bed clothes on top of the bed are tangled and covered with dark stains. The blinds are shut tightly in a window next to the bed. As they walk around the bed they see more stained sheets on the floor.

"Looks like bed sheets. The stains smell and look like excrements and alcohol, and it looks like there's blood as well," Freedman's voice is recorded by the video camera as he films the floor.

There is a sudden flash of white light as Campbell takes a photo.

Morgan and Braun step out of the room into the hallway. They draw a few deep breaths. Morgan feels nauseous. "Guys," he calls into the bedroom. "We'll go outside for a while. There's not enough room in there for all of us."

"No worries, we'll give you a call on the mobile when we're done," the reply comes.

"Come on, let's go outside and have a smoke." Morgan walks towards the front door and Braun holds a hand over his mouth and nose as he follows Morgan.

They take the plastic covers off their shoes and close

the door behind them.

It has stopped raining and the sky seems to contain all grey tones imaginable. Morgan lights a cigarette and offers his packet to Braun.

"That was a full on nose-full; I don't think I've experienced that smell before." Morgan exhales a cloud of smoke.

Braun lights a cigarette. "Neither have I, that's for sure. I don't know how those guys from forensics do it. They're in there now scraping that *shit* or whatever it was, from the sheets. What a job!"

Morgan shrugs his shoulders. "Yes I guess. But it must be interesting to see the investigation from their angle. They only see the evidence: not the people involved in the cases, like we do."

Braun looks out over the wet tree lined road. "You're right; they're only a part of the big picture. And we're another part I guess."

Morgan looks at him. "No we *see* the big picture, that's what we do. We're the ones who put the whole puzzle together. Didn't they teach you that in training?"

"Yes but that's not what I meant though. I mean, sometimes you get so caught up in all the details that it's hard to see the woods for the trees." Braun looks flustered.

Morgan frowns. "Look, I know that you're new, but you should focus on seeing the investigation as a whole. The other departments like the forensics, the technical department, the psychological department and so on… They're our tools: they give us information that we need to find answers."

Braun looks down at his shoes. "Sure, I know that."

Morgan smiles. "Relax; I'm not giving you a hard time.

GAME

You're already a detective: you don't have to prove yourself to me."

"Sometimes I forget that I've completed the training… I do. I like working as a detective though; it's everything that I imagined it'd be." Braun keeps his gaze on the ground.

Morgan remembers how he had felt the first year on the job. He was proud that he had succeeded in his exams, but he was also scared: scared that he would fail doing a job that was so important and affected people's lives. These days he is in charge of a lot of young detectives and he feels old amongst most of them.

"Don't worry," he says. "You'll be old in the game before you know it. But I'm here to help if you have questions meanwhile; that's why I'm here."

"Actually, there's a question that I've been meaning to ask you, if I may."

"Okay, what's that?"

"Do you ever get personally affected by a case, like this one?" Braun looks curiously at Morgan and Morgan gets the feeling that it is more than a casual question.

"Well, we like to think that we don't get affected by what we see. But of course we do. We're only human after all."

Braun squints with his eyes. "No, I meant *you* personally. Are *you* touched by this investigation?"

Morgan hesitates. "I guess I am…Work is a big part of my life and solving these murder cases are by far the most important thing I've had to do in my career. So, yes, there you go, are you happy now?" Morgan isn't going to tell Braun how he feels.

Braun blushes. "I'm sorry; it's just that sometimes it's hard to know how much you're allowed to freak out at work.

And I guess it's comforting to know that I'm not the only one feeling like that."

"As I said, we're only human…" Morgan stops when he sees that two young men are approaching them. "Can we help you?" he asks.

One of the men – a tall guy wearing a blue shirt and a black scarf, sticks his hands in his jeans pockets. "We saw that the police were here and we wondered what's going on."

"Do you live in this building?" Morgan asks.

"Yes we do, we're on the third floor."

Morgan takes his notebook from the pocket of his jacket. "Well, we'll be talking to all the neighbours soon, so we'll be contacting you then, Mr…?"

"My name is Wayne Taylor. This here is my flatmate Jim Wheatley. We're in unit twelve."

Morgan writes the names in his notebook. "And is your unit located through this entrance?"

"Uh, yes, we're in a one-bedder: they're all one bedrooms on this side of the building. The two-bedders are through that entrance there." He points towards the corner of the building. "And those units come with a garage as well."

Morgan looks up. "Where's the garage located?"

"Underneath the building, the entry's on the other side."

"So tenants with one bedroom apartments don't get a parking spot, is that right?"

"That's right. But you can hire a car space if you like. We get notes in the letter box with offers of parking all the time."

"Okay," Morgan closes his notebook. "As I said: we'll be in contact with you shortly. Before then we can't disclose what has happened here."

GAME

The two men nod and walk off.

Braun turns towards Morgan when the men have walked a short distance down the road. "Two guys in a one bedroom unit… It doesn't take a genius to work that one out, does it?"

Morgan gives him a cold look. "Keep your personal ideas to yourself, Braun. I don't want anyone to hear them, is that clear?"

"Yes sir," Braun blushes.

"Good, come on. We'll go back inside and wait. I don't want the whole street to know we're here."

The forensic investigation of Cassandra Saunders' apartment is completed. All surfaces have been dusted with black powder and fingerprints have been collected. Campbell and Freedman have found blood specks on the bedroom wall: in a pattern that is almost identical to what they found in Else Henriksen's apartment.

Freedman turns the lights out in the bedroom. Under the portable Luma light Morgan and Braun sees a large glittering arch that reaches from the floor to the ceiling. The arch is broken where circular wipe marks show that someone has wiped the wall with a cloth. A large amount of blood has been trapped between the pieces of parquetry on the floor below the wall. The sheets in the bed and on the floor also have blood on them. And Freedman tells them that there is blood in the bathroom as well. The rest of the apartment is extremely clean.

Freedman and Campbell carry their equipment, their samples and Cassandra's bed sheets placed in large plastic bags as they leave Morgan and Braun in the apartment.

Morgan tells Braun to stay in the hallway and turns the lights on as he walks slowly from room to room. He spends a few seconds in the bedroom and then walks through the hallway to the living room. The living room is also very small, but it contains a surprising amount of furniture: there are two armchairs covered in a dark blue velvety fabric and a two seater sofa in a corduroy brown fabric. On the sofa are three white pillows and a grey blanket. A coffee table with a glass top stands in the middle of the room. A bookcase filled with books stands against a wall next to the window. A long narrow table stands against another wall: the table top seems to act as storage for clutter and is covered with jewellery, loose bits of paper, sunglasses and make-up items. Eight white boxes are stacked on top of each other under the table. Morgan walks between the furniture and looks carefully at everything. He pulls out a few books and picks up pieces of papers to study them closer.

Finally he walks into the kitchen and opens all the cupboards and drawers and looks inside. From the kitchen he walks into a tiny bathroom where a shower head is attached to the wall above the toilet seat. A shower curtain hangs on the side of the door frame and reveals that the room also acts as a shower cabin. A large Huntsman spider runs down the side of a wall mounted cabinet and startles Morgan as he opens the mirrored door to look inside.

When Morgan walks out of the bathroom he sees that Braun is standing in the kitchen.

"What's wrong with you? I thought I told you to stay in the hallway?"

"Sorry, I wanted to watch you. You know, for learning purposes." Braun's neck is red.

"I meant what I said when I told you to stay put. An order is an order, do you understand?" Morgan shakes his head in frustration.

GAME

Braun nods. "Yes and I'm sorry."

Morgan turns his back on him and walks into the living room. "Come on; help me gather all the papers you can find in here. I'll start in the bedroom meanwhile." He takes a clear plastic bag from his pocket and puts it on the sofa table. "Put all the papers in the bag," he says as he walks into the hallway.

Braun stands frozen for a few seconds before he walks into the living room. He starts to pull the white boxes out from underneath the table.

Morgan takes a deep breath before he enters the bedroom: the stench is overwhelming even though the bedclothes have been removed. He breathes through his mouth as he pulls out a drawer in the bedside table. The drawer only contains a birthday card. Morgan opens the card and reads the hand written note inside: *'To our dear Cassandra on her eighteenth birthday, all our love forever, xx Mum and Dad.'* Morgan turns the card over: it's thumbed and doggy-eared.

He turns his attention to the built-in wardrobes that are filled with clothes, shoes, towels and sheets. He leans in and moves some long coats and dresses to the side and reveals a large cardboard box that stands on the floor of the wardrobe. He pulls the box that seems to contain letters, photo albums and magazines out on the floor. Sitting on the edge of the uncovered mattress, Morgan carefully opens an envelope and reads the letter that is inside. He puts the letter back in the envelope and searches the rest of the contents in the box. He places loose papers, letters and photos inside the plastic bag he has brought with him and then walks around the bed. The floor under the bed is empty. Morgan stands up and brushes the black fingerprinting dust off his pants with his hands. He carries the bag with papers to the living room.

Braun sits on the floor. He is rummaging through a box. On the coffee table next to him, the plastic bag is filled with a neat pile of papers.

Morgan stands in the doorway and watches Braun's back. "How are you going there, are you almost done?" he asks.

Braun turns his head. "Yes, this is the last one." He puts a lid on the box. He gets up from the floor and brushes the fingerprinting dust off the back of his pants with his hands. "I'm done." He looks at his hands: they are black.

Morgan is locking Cassandra's front door when his beeper starts to vibrate in his pocket. He looks at the display window and turns his mobile on as he walks down the stairs. Braun silently watches the road as Morgan dials Scullion's number.

"Hi, it's me, Morgan. You called."

"Yes I did, we're at Bermuda Bookshop and one of the employees here hasn't turned up for work today. There's no reply on her home phone or mobile. Do you want us to go to her address and check if she's alright?"

Morgan feels his heart beating hard in his chest. "What's her name?"

"Uh, Lisa something, hang on... I've got it written here somewhere... Lisa McCall."

Morgan's mind races and then it hits him: he should call the hospital where Lisa has an appointment for an abortion of his child according to the note in her Yellow Pages. He tries to think: what time had the note said?

"Scullion, I'll call you back. Don't go anywhere, stay put." Morgan presses the red button on his phone and then

GAME

calls the 'number information service'.

Braun frowns as Morgan asks for the number at St Vincent's hospital. Morgan gets connected to the main switch at the hospital and asks for the abortion clinic. He is transferred to a secretary who refuses to give him any information. "We cannot give out such information over the phone," she says.

Morgan thinks for second. "But I know that Lisa McCall had an appointment to see you today, I'm her fiancée and this is an emergency. Lisa is missing and I need to find out if she came to the hospital today. She's not answering her mobile or her home phone. Try to call her to see for yourself," he says.

"Right, please hold; I'll see what I can do." There is silence for half a minute before the woman's voice is back. "We usually don't give this information out, but I have tried calling her and you're right: she's not answering. Lisa McCall had an appointment at the clinic at one pm today – what her appointment was for I cannot tell you – but I can tell you that she never showed up."

"Thank you." Morgan stares blankly into space as he ends the call. He starts to walk towards the car and Braun follows. Morgan unlocks the car absentmindedly and then sits in the driver's seat and stares out through the window.

Braun touches Morgan's shoulder. "Are you alright?" He holds his hands out and Morgan stares at them before he realises that he still has the bag with papers and albums in his lap.

"What's going on?"

Morgan shakes his head. "Hang on a minute." He dials Scullions number again on his mobile. "It's me, Morgan. I'm going over to Lisa's apartment now. I want you stay at the bookshop and continue to talk to the employees."

"Okay, will do. I'll give you the address, hang on a sec…"

"That's alright, I know where she lives." Morgan hangs up and puts the key in the ignition. "Put the sirens on Braun, we're going to Coogee." He starts the car and drives out on the main road. Cars stop and pull over to the side as Morgan drives past; the sirens give them clearway. Braun has one hand on the car door and the other firmly on the corner of his seat. Nothing is said during the trip to Coogee.

Morgan slams the brakes outside Lisa's apartment building and rushes inside without looking over his shoulder to see if Braun is with him or not. Upstairs he bangs loudly on Lisa's door with his fists, but there is no reply. Another door opens and a woman pokes her head through the opening. "*What* is going on out here?"

Morgan turns towards her. "Have you seen the girl who lives here today? Do you know where she is?"

The woman looks startled. "Who are you?"

Morgan walks up to her. "I'm from the police. We suspect that something has happened to Lisa. Do you know where she is?"

The woman gives him a strange look. "I recognise you, haven't I seen you here before? How do I know that you're from the police?"

Morgan pulls the wallet from his pocket and shows the woman his police ID card. "Who's got a key to her apartment, who's your landlord?"

The woman looks closely at Morgan's ID card. "Uh, it's Pino's Real Estate up on Coogee Bay Road, next to the post office."

GAME

"Thanks." Morgan runs down the stairs. Braun sits quiet as Morgan floors the gas pedal and speeds up the hill. Morgan double parks outside the real estate agent's office and flings the door open. A middle aged woman sitting behind the front desk turns a surprised face towards him as he walks inside.

"Who's the manager here?" Morgan asks her.

"Hang on, we're actually closed." The woman stands up behind her desk.

Morgan pulls his ID card from his wallet again. He should have brought Braun with him: he's wearing a police uniform, he thinks. "I'm from the police, this is an emergency. I need to see the manager NOW!"

The woman backs away from Morgan when he raises his voice.

Morgan frowns. "Come on now, I need…"

A man opens a door at the back of the office and stares at Morgan. "What the hell is going on here? Didn't you see the sign in the window? We're closed."

"I'm from the police. I need the key to one of your apartments, it's an emergency." Morgan holds up his ID card.

The man puts on a pair of glasses that hangs in a chain around his neck as he walks up to Morgan.

"I have to go with you, which apartment is it?" he says after he has satisfied himself that the ID is legit.

"Fine, it's apartment number five, number twelve Alexandra Street. Hurry up." Morgan waits impatiently as the man walks to the back of the office to get the keys.

The man finally comes back and puts a jacket on. "Okay, I've got the keys."

Morgan takes him by the arm and leads him to the car.

"Get in the back seat," he says sternly and slams the car door shut when the man has got in. He speeds up the hill, makes a U-turn, drives back down the hill, around the corner and double parks in front of Lisa's building. "You stay here," he tells Braun as he gets out of the car and opens the back seat door for the real estate agent.

Morgan runs into the building and has to wait as the older man slowly makes his way upstairs. Finally the man puts the key in Lisa's door and Morgan goes inside. Nothing looks different to when he was there a few days earlier. He walks through the kitchen, bedroom and bathroom and is on his way to the living room when he suddenly stops in the hallway. The red light on the answering machine is blinking. Morgan presses the 'play' button and hears his own voice; he quickly glances over at the real estate agent, but the man doesn't seem to react to the voice on the tape. The short message ends and a long beep tells Morgan that there are no more messages. He picks up the receiver and presses the 'redial' button on the phone. After a few ring tones a female voice says: "You have reached Fiona, I'm not here at the moment, please leave a message."

Morgan leaves his name and number, says that it is an emergency in regards to Lisa and hangs up. He walks around the apartment once more and restlessly touches the clothes that lie on top of the bed: they are Lisa's evening wear – he recognises a black sleeveless top with glitter and a pair of skinny black pants.

As he walks back through the hallway he suddenly realises that he should call the 'last number dialled service', to get Fiona's telephone number. He gets the notebook and a pen from his pocket and picks up the phone again. The real estate agent watches him from the doorway as he scribbles a

GAME

number in his notebook and hangs up the phone.

"What's this all about?" he asks.

Morgan looks up at him as he puts the notebook back in his pocket. "What?"

"What's all this about? You only said that it was an emergency but you never told me what it was."

Morgan takes a seat on the chair next to the telephone. He looks down at his hands and sees that they are shaking. "Lisa McCall is missing, but I can't tell you any details. This is police business and you need to treat this confidentially." He looks into the man's eyes. "Are we clear on that?"

The older man nods. "I was in the army, I understand."

"Okay, I think we're finished here. Let's go, I'll give you a lift back to your office."

As the real estate agent locks the front door, Morgan says: "I will need the keys from you again, but when I do I'll come and see you."

He drops the man off outside the real estate office and drives back towards the city. Braun looks out through the window and doesn't say a word.

Back at the detective headquarters they take the elevator to the fifth floor in silence. Braun walks around the corner to his desk with the papers from Cassandra's apartment. Morgan sits down by his desk and stars into the wall without seeing. Suddenly he picks up his phone and dials a number.

"Where are you?" he asks as Scullion answers.

"We're on our way back to the office."

"Good, I'll see you soon then." Morgan hangs up and continues to stare into nothingness. His mind is stuck and he can't think clearly. Pictures of dead women are flashing through his mind.

"Morgan?" Someone pats Morgan's shoulder. He looks

up and sees Ricketts. "Are you alright?"

Morgan rubs his eyes. "Yes, what's up?"

"We just got back from Surry Hills. Linda Kasinski's flatmates couldn't tell if it was her voice on the tape or not: one girl said that she thought it was Linda and the other girl said that it didn't sound like her at all. But they gave us a tape from their own answering machine. Linda's voice is on the tape so I've sent it to Pete to compare it to the voice on our tape."

"Right," Morgan says absentmindedly. "Write it all in a report and give me a copy before you go home will you?"

Ricketts doesn't move.

"I said, write it in a report and give it to me." Morgan turns away from Ricketts and stares out through the window.

"Yes sir," Ricketts mumbles and walks off.

Morgan takes his notebook from his pocket and flicks through the pages until he finds the page where he has written the number to Lisa's friend, Fiona. He picks up the phone and dials the number.

"Fiona speaking."

"Fiona hi, this is Detective Sergeant Morgan Callaghan. I left a message on your answering machine earlier today."

"Hi, I haven't listened to my messages yet, I just got home from work."

"Well, anyway, I'm calling in regards to a friend of yours... Lisa McCall."

"Sorry, what was your name again?"

"Morgan Callaghan."

"You're Lisa's boyfriend, aren't you?"

"Uh, yes I am. But I'm actually calling more in the role of my job: I work at the detective headquarters in Sydney."

"Yes I remember that Lisa mentioned you're a cop.

GAME

What's this about? I haven't spoken to Lisa since Saturday, we were supposed to meet for dinner but she never showed up. She left a message on my answering machine saying something about an emergency and I figured it had something to do with her parents, because I tried to call her that night and the following day and she didn't answer. So I thought she'd gone home to see her parents. You know: to Melbourne."

"I'm trying to find her. Are you sure you don't know where she is?"

"As I said: I thought she'd gone to Melbourne to visit her parents. Do you think that something's happened to her? I thought it was a bit strange that she didn't answer her mobile."

"Let's just say that I have reason to be worried about her. When was the last time you spoke to her, and what did she say then?"

"She called me at home on Saturday afternoon: it was around half past one. She said that she needed to go out and have a good time and talk. She was upset and stressed." Fiona pauses. "She told me that she'd had an argument with you that same morning."

Morgan frowns. "Yes, we did have an argument that morning. But that's not why I'm worried... What else did she say?"

"We agreed to meet at a restaurant in Coogee that night at 7pm. I was there on time and waited for an hour before I realised that she wasn't going to show up so I went home and saw that she had left a message on my answering machine. On the message she said that she was sorry that she couldn't make it and that she had an emergency to attend to. Those were her words."

"And you thought then that she was referring to her parents, why is that if I may ask?"

"She has mentioned before that her father's been sick a lot, he has high blood pressure and Lisa was worried about him. Didn't she tell you?"

"Yes she did," Morgan tries to think of something else to say. "And you can't think of any other reasons why she didn't come to the restaurant?"

"No, not at all, it's not like Lisa not to show up. But why do you think there's reason to be worried?"

Morgan sighs. "I wish I could tell you, but I can't until I find out where she is. I'll try to contact her parents: you wouldn't by any chance have their phone number would you?"

"No, I would have called them myself if I did. Will you let me know if you find out where she is? I'm getting worried now."

"Sure, I'll let you know. Thanks Fiona." Morgan hangs up and stares at his reflexion in the dark window. Lisa hasn't been home since Saturday night according to Fiona, he thinks. He has to contact her parents: what was her dad's name? Bryan: that's it. Bryan McCall. He recalls that they live in the Melbourne suburb of Narre Warren. Morgan calls the 'number information service' and is given a phone number that he dials.

"McCall," a female voice answers.

"Mrs McCall, my name is Morgan Callaghan. Are you a relative to Lisa McCall?"

"Yes, I'm Lisa's mother. I'm sorry, what was your name again?"

"My name is Morgan Callaghan, I'm calling from Sydney."

GAME

"Oh, you're Lisa's boyfriend aren't you?"

"Yes I am, is Lisa there with you?"

"No, no. She's in Sydney. Why would she be here?"

"Right, I'm sorry. I haven't been able to reach her and I thought she might have gone to Melbourne to see you. She's probably at work then." Morgan thinks it's unnecessary to worry the woman.

"Unless she is planning a surprise visit that we don't know about. Anyway, it's nice talking to you finally. Lisa has told us so much about you. I'm looking forward to meeting you someday soon."

"Yes, me too, okay, I won't bother you any longer then. I'll try to call Lisa later."

"No bother, bye now."

Morgan holds the receiver in his hand until it starts to make beeping noises that prompts him to hang up.

"We're back." Robert Scullion and Nick Whitfield are standing in front of Morgan's desk.

Morgan crosses his arms over his chest. "What did you find out?"

"Uh, not much, no one at the bookshop has noticed anything different about her lately. Do you want us to write a report?" Scullion seems embarrassed. He must have talked to Ricketts, Morgan thinks.

"Who are you talking about now; Cassandra or Lisa?" Morgan stares at Scullion with bloodshot eyes.

"Uh, I meant Cassandra."

"And what did you find out about Lisa?"

"Nothing, only that she didn't turn up for work today… Didn't you go to her apartment?"

Morgan turns to look at the dark window again. "Yes I

did… Alright, leave a copy of the report on my desk before you leave."

"You got it." Scullion and Whitfield leave the room quickly.

Morgan walks to the elevator and takes it to the street level. When he gets outside, he lights a cigarette. Cars are moving past in the dark: the quick flashes of colour and light turn into a blur. Morgan takes the mobile from his pocket and dials Lisa's mobile number. Three signals go through and then comes a recorded message: 'The mobile you are trying to call is switched off or is out of range. Please try again later.' Morgan dials Lisa's home number and the answering machine comes on after four signals – he doesn't bother to leave a message but hangs up. He has just put the phone back in his pocket when it rings.

"Morgan? It's Katherine. Are you still at work?"

Morgan sighs deeply. "Kath, hi, yes, something came up and I don't know if I'll be able to come over, did you manage to get in contact with dad?"

"Yes and you were right: he was in the garden. He finally picked up the phone about an hour ago. So you're not coming over then?"

"No, it doesn't look like I'll have time to, sorry about that." Morgan drags on his cigarette.

"My god, they're really getting their money's worth with you, aren't they? Do you work twelve hour days or what?"

"It's just one of those days…" Morgan suddenly feels angry that he has to justify himself to his sister. "I *am* in charge of this investigation you know – I do have responsibilities."

GAME

"Right, yes I guess so." Katherine is quiet for a few seconds. "Okay, I'll talk to you later then. Can you give me a call tomorrow? I want to go through the details of the funeral."

"Sure," Morgan snaps at her and ends the call. He steps angrily on the cigarette, swipes his security card in the slot next to the door and goes inside. In the elevator on the way up he takes some deep breaths.

Most of the detectives have left for the day and only five of them remain by their desks. Ricketts, Stone, Scullion and Whitfield are busy tapping on their computer keyboards while Braun is sorting through the papers they found in Cassandra Saunders' apartment.

"Right, all of you; can you please listen to me for a second?"

Everyone looks up at Morgan.

"I feel that I should explain my behaviour this afternoon. I want you to understand why I have acted a bit strange." Morgan looks at the floor for a second before he continues: "Lisa McCall, the girl at Bermuda Bookshop who didn't turn up for work today and is still missing... She's my, well, she's my girlfriend. We all know that we're not supposed to have personal involvement in the cases that we work on, so I didn't want to mention our relationship to anyone. And I would appreciate if you could keep it so... for now, anyway. Can you do that?" Morgan looks around at the detectives.

They all mumble a 'yes'.

Morgan nods. "I really appreciate it, thanks." He turns around and walks off before anyone can say anything.

Back in his room Morgan takes the victim's books from his bookshelf. Once the computer has started up he clicks on the writing program and starts to make notes.

Ricketts comes in to Morgan's room and gives him the reports from the interviews with Linda Kasinski's flatmates and colleagues. A few minutes later Scullion comes in with the report of the interviews from Bermuda Bookshop.

By eight o'clock Morgan is alone in the office. He sorts through the papers in his In-tray and creates a new document where he notes all significant details from the reports that have come in during the day.

It is ten o'clock when he finally gets up from his chair and stretches his back. He calls Lisa's number again; for the fifth time in one hour. But there is no reply on either her home phone or mobile. Morgan takes his empty coffee mug to the kitchen and puts it in the dishwasher. He walks back to his desk and takes his jacket from the back of the chair.

The red light on the answering machine is blinking in the darkness of Morgan's living room. He doesn't bother to turn the lights on and hits his knee on the corner of the coffee table as he presses the play button.

"It's me, Katherine. Obviously you're not at home so I'll try your mobile."

Morgan clenches his teeth and rubs his knee with one hand. There is a beep as the message ends and another one follows.

"Hello Morgan, my name is Bryce Banks. I'm a solicitor and the executor of your mother's will. I got your number from your sister, Katherine Irving. Your mother's wish was that I read her will to you one week after she had passed away. So it would be good if you could give me a call at my office and organise a time on Wednesday when you, your

GAME

sister and your father can come and see me. My office is in on Elizabeth Street in the CBD and my number is nine, nine, nine, five, five, four. Hope to speak to you soon."

Two more beeps confirm that there are no more messages.

Morgan hobbles over the living room floor and turns the light on. He has a massive headache. And he is starving. He opens the paper bag that he has dropped on the coffee table and tears the wrapping off a hamburger. When he has finished eating he walks into the kitchen with a half empty coke can and tops it up with bourbon. Back in the sofa he lights a cigarette, leans back and sips his drink. A loud burp comes from his mouth and he looks with disgust at the paper wrappings on the table that have contained two large hamburgers. He is turning into a pig, he thinks. But he doesn't have time or energy to cook healthy meals. He hasn't exercised for weeks and he can feel that his waist is growing rapidly: which reminds him of his promise to play cricket the following evening. There is no way he can play cricket with everything that is going on. He hates to let his mates down, but he has to cancel. He sighs. His life is a mess. Lisa is gone and nothing he does will bring his mother back: she is gone forever. Tears suddenly wet Morgan's face and something deep inside him bursts. He can't stop the tears and his body shakes with convulsions. He pulls his knees towards his chest and wraps his arms around his legs. With his chin resting on his knees he starts to rock slowly back and forwards.

13

When Morgan wakes up it is still dark outside and the rain is pounding against the windows. He moans when he realises that he has fallen asleep on the sofa with his clothes on. His eyes are stinging when he slowly gets up and makes his way to the bathroom. He removes his contact lenses and stares into the mirror. He hardly recognises the face that is staring back at him. Dark grey circles surround his red eyes and his skin has a grey tone and sags along the jaw line. He splashes cold water in his face and quickly brushes his teeth as he avoids looking at his reflection in the mirror. He almost falls over as he slips on a shirt that lies on the wooden floor in the bedroom: the laundry pile is still there. But at least there are clean sheets in the bed that he has made up the night before.

He sits on the edge of the mattress and bends down to set the alarm when he sees what time it is: ten past five.

"Fuck," he says out loud. He might as well stay up and make coffee and use the extra time to have a thorough shave and a shower. He stands up. An intense pain hits his chest so strongly that he falls back on the bed. He tries to breathe calmly but the pain hits harder with each breath and he thinks that he is going to suffocate. He coughs and rolls over on the bed as the pain responds sharply. It feels like a knife is cutting into him.

The phone: he has to get to the phone, he thinks through the fog of pain. He tries to sit up but when he moves his arms the pain strikes with a paralysing power that leaves

GAME

him gasping for air.

After a long time that seems like hours the pain finally subdues enough to allow Morgan to pull himself up into a sitting position. The telephone on the bedside table is finally close enough. He dials the three zeros with shaking fingers.

"Emergency, do you want police, ambulance or the fire department?"

Morgan tries to clear his throat. "Ambulance, heart attack... I think I've had a heart attack." His voice sounds strange in his own ears and he hopes that the person on the other end can understand him.

"I'm connecting you now."

A few seconds later another voice says: "This is St Vincent's Hospital, ambulance dispatch. What's your address there?"

"Unit seven, number forty-three Bulgarah Road... Potts Point." Morgan feels his strength return bit by bit as he speaks.

"And what's your name?"

He can hear clicking noises as the woman writes on a keyboard.

"Morgan Callaghan."

"How old are you?"

"Thirty-eight."

"And you think that you've had a heart attack, is that correct?"

"Yes."

"Are you alone there?"

"Yes, yes I am."

"How will the ambulance men gain entry to the building; is there anyone we can call?"

Morgan tries to think. "No, I can open the doors. They

need to buzz the intercom downstairs."

"Are you sure you're in a condition to walk?"

"Hang on; I'll try to stand up." Morgan pushes his body up into standing position with one hand on the bed.

"Hello? Are you there?"

"Yes, I'm here. Please hurry, I'll be alright to open the doors I think."

"The ambulance is almost there, I need you to sit down and keep talking to me. How do you feel now?"

Morgan tries to laugh but the sound that comes out is more of a moan. "It feels like I've been hit by a truck." He slowly sits back down on the bed.

"Which room are you in, how far away from the front door are you?"

"Um, I'm in the bedroom. It's not far to the door, I should make it." Morgan hears sirens and has a strange feeling of déjà vu that he cannot connect an image to.

"Okay, the ambulance should be there now. The medical staff will be with you shortly."

"Yes, I can hear the sirens." Fire trucks – that's it, he remembers now; he had a dream about a bush fire and the sound of fire truck sirens was really the ringing phone. But that was in a different time: a different life – or someone else's.

"Okay, I need you to hang up and slowly make your way to the door. Can you do that?"

"Yes, okay. Bye." Morgan slowly gets up from the bed. He feels weak and dizzy as he walks across the floor in slow motion. He stops and leans against the door frame for a few seconds before he can continue. The intercom buzzes in the hallway and it feels like forever before he gets there. Finally he presses the button to let the paramedics in. He

GAME

leans against the wall. There is a knock on the door. Two men holding a stretcher are standing outside. The men put the stretcher on the floor in the hallway and help Morgan to lie down.

"Where's your wallet and keys?" one of the men asks.

"Uh, they're on the coffee table in the living room I think." Morgan closes his eyes as the second man places a blanket over him.

"Is there anything else that you want to bring?" the man asks as he places the wallet and keys on Morgan's chest under the blanket. He tucks the blanket tightly around Morgan.

"No... no that's fine. Just turn the lights off please. And slam the door on your way out, otherwise it won't lock." Morgan feels like he is floating even before he is lifted up and carried down the stairs. Cold raindrops hit Morgan's face outside but he hardly feels it. He is so sleepy. There is a sound of metal on metal as the stretcher clicks into place on rails and slides into the back of the ambulance. Morgan closes his eyes and starts to drift off.

"Morgan, you can't go to sleep. We need you to stay awake, okay?" One of the paramedics sits next to the stretcher. As the ambulance starts to move the sirens come on and the loud sound jolts Morgan back to reality.

"I'm not sleeping." Morgan voice is slurry.

"Okay, good. When did you start to feel the pain?"

Morgan squints with his eyes under the bright light. "It was ten past five this morning."

The paramedic writes something on a piece of paper that is attached to a clipboard. "Do you remember what happened; were you standing up or sitting down?"

"Can we turn the light off please? It's hurting my eyes."

A.C. Efverman

The man stretches his arm out and flicks a switch in the ceiling and the lights are turned off. "Is that better?"

"Yes, thanks...Uh, I was sitting down, and when I stood up I felt the pain."

"So you didn't wake up by the pain, you weren't asleep?" The man leans over Morgan and holds a small torch over his eyes. "Just look up for me... thanks."

"No, I was already awake." Morgan blinks as the sharp light is taken away.

The man takes a pill out of a bottle. "Open your mouth and hold this under your tongue," he says. Morgan does as he's told.

"It's an Aspro; it will dissolve under your tongue and it will help to thin your blood out."

Morgan nods.

"What do you do for a living?"

Morgan looks at the man and wonders how he will be able to reply with the tablet in his mouth. "I'm a Detective Sergeant." The words come out with a slight lisp.

"Do you work shifts, different hours every day?"

"Uh, no, it's pretty much the same hours every day." Morgan feels cold fingers against the skin on his arm. His arm is lifted up and a plastic material is wrapped around it. The paramedic squeezes a pump and the material tightens.

"Okay, have you had any major shocks lately, something that sticks out of the ordinary?" The man puts a stethoscope in his ears. "Try to breathe normally for me... Okay, good."

"Shocks, yes: a few actually."

"Okay, like what?"

The Velcro makes a swishing sound as the plastic material is pulled off Morgan's arm.

"First my mother died. Then I found out that my

GAME

girlfriend is pregnant and has been kidnapped."

"Those are certainly things that would shock you… How old are you?"

"Thirty-eight."

"And how's your general health?"

Morgan looks up at the face that hovers above him. "Do you mean if I'm looking after myself with healthy food and exercise?"

"Yes that, and have you had any major health problems lately?"

"I haven't had time to look after myself properly lately. I've had a few more drinks than what's good for me. And I can't say that I've been eating healthy food either… But no, I haven't had any health problems before." Morgan feels how the ambulance tilts slightly to the side as the driver makes a sharp turn. The sirens stop abruptly.

"Okay. Well, we're here now." The backdoors open and the paramedic jumps out.

Morgan is wheeled out of the ambulance. The cold fluorescent light in the hospital entrance gives him a headache and he closes his eyes again.

"Hello, you're not asleep are you?"

Morgan opens his eyes and sees that a white dressed nurse is looking down at him. "No," he mumbles. "The light is hurting my eyes."

"Okay, you'll get a room of your own soon. Just wait here for a few minutes." The nurse walks off.

Morgan lies with his eyes closed. The blanket is tucked so tightly around him that he can hardly move. People rush back and forwards. Someone moans loudly behind a curtain.

"We've got a heart attack here," someone says next to Morgan and he opens his eyes. A woman wearing a purple polo neck jumper and a white robe stands next to the stretcher: she has a stethoscope around her neck and a pair of black rimmed glasses on her nose. She looks at a sheet of paper. "Let's get him to a proper bed. Get nurse Bronwyn."

Morgan feels cold hands touch him. "Can you roll over on your side Morgan? That's it…" He is lifted over to a bed that has a real pillow and it feels good to have soft support under his neck. Someone puts another blanket over him. He closes his eyes and starts to drift off. He is so sleepy. All he wants is to be warm and go to sleep.

A hand shakes his shoulder gently. "Mr Callaghan. Mr Callaghan, wake up. You can't go to sleep: didn't you hear what the nurse said?" The woman with the purple polo neck jumper is looking down at him.

"I'm awake," Morgan mumbles.

"Good, we need to ask you some questions, and then we'll do some tests and scans. After that you can sleep. Okay?"

Morgan feels disorientated when he wakes up and at first he doesn't know where he is. He looks around the room and sees that he is lying in a bed next to a large window. The rain is pouring down outside. A green curtain hangs on the other side of the bed. Across the room he can make out the contours of another bed. There is someone in the bed, but Morgan can't see what the person looks like. When he tries to turn over he feels a stinging pain on the back of his hand. He pulls the hand out from underneath the blanket and looks at the white patch on the back of his hand. Under the clear bandaid that holds the patch is the end of a needle. A plastic tube leads from the needle to a plastic bag that hangs on a steel frame next to the bed. He looks at his watch and

GAME

sees that it shows a quarter past ten. It must be morning; according to the grey light outside. He looks around for a button he can press to get attention. Finally he finds a red button next to his pillow and presses it long and hard.

A nurse is standing next to the bed a few seconds later. "Oh good, you're awake."

"Can I use the phone please? I'm expected at work."

The woman looks at him with a serious look on her face. "I can get you a phone, but you can't get yourself worked up. You're supposed to take it easy. You've just had a heart attack."

Morgan nods. "I promise, but I really need to use the phone now. Please?"

"Of course." The nurse walks off and comes back a few seconds later with an old fashioned pay phone on wheels. "Your wallet is in the drawer in the bedside table, do you need help to get it?"

Morgan shakes his head. "No thanks, I should be alright." When he pushes himself up with one hand on the bed and reaches down towards the bedside table, he notices that there are more plastic wires attached to his body and that he is connected to a machine that stands behind the bed. He opens the drawer in the bedside table and finds some coins in his wallet, puts them in the slot on the phone, picks up the receiver and dials the main number at the office. Amanda answers after two signals.

"Amanda, it's me, Morgan. I'm sorry I haven't called you earlier, I'm in hospital."

"Morgan? Are you alright? We've been so worried!"

"It's okay, I'm alive, but I've had a heart attack."

"Oh my god!"

"I know, is Ricketts there? I need to talk to him."

"Yes he is, I saw him a minute ago. Hang on; I'll get him for you."

"Sergeant Callaghan, are you alright?"

"Ricketts, hi, no, I've had a minor heart attack. The doctors want to keep me for observation for a while so I need you to look after things at work for me, can you do that?"

"Sure, of course I will. Don't worry. Which hospital are you in?"

"St Vincent's, in Darlinghurst."

"Are you allowed visitors? We can pop in, me and Stone, if you'd like."

"Not today, but I'll give you a call and let you know how I am tomorrow. Could you do me a favour and let everyone in the office know? And I need you to look after the morning meeting. We need to keep everyone updated on what's going on, that's important."

"No problem."

"Good, you'll find all material that I've collected in separate victim's books. They're in the bookcase behind my desk. There's one for each girl. It would be good if you could recap all new information in the meeting to update everyone of what's going on."

"I'll do that. I didn't want to start the meeting before we knew what had happened to you, but I'll call everyone in now."

"Good." Morgan leans back and rests his head on the pillow. "What else is new?"

"Some real estate agent in Glebe called this morning, he was furious that you didn't return the keys yesterday…"

Morgan smiles.

"… So Braun went over there with the keys. Don't

GAME

worry; we're looking after things here. You just rest and get better."

Morgan sighs. "Easier said than done, but okay, I'll give you a call later on… Oh shit, I just remembered: Cassandra Saunders' aunt is coming down from Newcastle today and I am supposed to meet her and go with her to the morgue so she can identify Cassandra. She is going to call me when she gets to Sydney. Can you ask one of the detectives to switch my line to their desk and have him answer my calls? I promised Cassandra's aunt that she wouldn't have to go alone, so you need to have someone go with her."

"Sure thing, we'll look after it."

"Oh, and one more thing: I've promised to play cricket tonight with Pete and David at the technical department, can you give them a call and let them know what's happened? I would really appreciate that."

"Alright, I'll call them straight away. Is there anything else that you want me to do?"

"No, that should be it. I'll talk to you later."

"Okay, you rest now. Don't worry about things here. As I said; we'll look after everything."

"Right, I'll talk to you later then." Morgan hangs up and stares up at the ceiling.

The curtain next to the bed suddenly moves as a hand pulls it to the side. "I'm sorry but I couldn't help to overhear." A man sits on the edge of a bed and holds out his hand. "Hi I'm Dennis, Dennis Lane, pleased to meet you."

"Morgan Callaghan." Morgan shakes the hand and studies the man that is dressed in red pyjamas: he looks to be around forty years old.

"So, what are you in for mate?" Dennis lies down on his side. He places an elbow on the bed and rests his head in his hand.

"You make it sound like we're in jail."

Dennis makes a face. "To me it is, mate. And you'll feel the same once you've been here long enough, believe me."

"Alright, I'm here because I've had a minor heart attack. What about you?"

"The same actually – this must be the department for small heart attacks. I wonder if the department for big heart attacks has a better view... But I guess they don't; if you know what I mean," Dennis smiles, "I'm starving, aren't you? They're skimpy on the food in this joint."

Morgan tries to turn on his side; his neck muscles are feeling stiff.

Dennis gets up and comes over to his bed. "You've never been in hospital before, have you?"

Morgan shakes his head. "No, I can't say that I have." Up close he sees that Dennis' pyjamas have a pattern of flowers and rainbows.

"Because if you had, you'd know that there's a switch down here," Dennis bends down, "that pulls up this part of the bed."

The bed head is raised behind Morgan's back.

"Just tell me when you're comfortable mate and I'll let go."

Morgan leans back. "That's good. Thanks."

Dennis walks back to his bed and sits down. "I'm sorry if I was rude to listen in on your conversation earlier on... So you're a cop?"

Morgan frowns. "I didn't realise that you were there, but yes I'm a detective sergeant."

"That's a coincidence. I used to be a detective myself not so long ago."

GAME

"Really? Where at?"

"In Melbourne; that's where I'm from. But I live in Sydney now."

"Right," Morgan pulls the blanket up over his chest. "So what do you do these days?"

"Now I work as a private investigator. So maybe life hasn't changed so much after all, the biggest change is probably that I work on my own these days… Yes, it's just me and my partner Bob now," Dennis smiles, "Bob's my Labrador."

Morgan returns the smile. "Sounds good, and how's business?"

"I can't complain. There are enough people out there who don't trust their wives and husbands, let me tell you. And then there are always the trusty insurance companies when everything else fails to keep me afloat. What about yourself?"

Morgan sighs. "Well we're busy enough… That's partly why I'm here, I guess."

There is a sound of rubber soles moving over the floor.

"Mr Callaghan, you should be resting, and you too Lane." The nurse turns to Morgan. "Are you finished with the telephone so I can take it back?"

Morgan sits up. "No, actually I need to make another call."

The nurse sighs. "Alright, do you want something to eat? I believe you missed breakfast."

"I'm hungry, could I have a sandwich or something?"

The nurse turns to Dennis. "You had breakfast just a few hours ago, didn't you?"

Dennis grins. "But I'm hungry. Please?"

"Alright," The nurse turns to Morgan again. "How

about it; do you want some food?"

Morgan nods. "Yes please."

"Alright, I'll get you both something; you'll need to take your medicine anyway. But you both need to rest, so enough with the chit-chat, okay?" The nurse walks off.

Dennis smiles at Morgan. "Isn't she charming?"

Morgan nods. "Lovely." He bends down towards the bedside table and picks up his wallet and takes a dollar coin that he sticks in the slot on the phone. "Excuse me for a minute: I need to make a call."

Dennis lies back on his bed and sticks his hands under his head. "No worries. Don't mind me."

Morgan dials Katherine's number and hears one signal go through before she answers.

"Kath, it's me, Morgan. I'm in hospital."

"What? What for?"

"I've had a heart attack."

"Are you serious? Where are you?"

"Yes I'm serious, but it's only a minor heart attack. I'm at St Vincent's." Morgan looks down at the telephone and reads from the label: "Level five, the cardiac department. Could you do me a favour? I need you to go to my apartment and pick up my contact lenses – I'm blind as a bat without them. I've got the keys here."

"Yes of course I can do that. Lucky you caught me at home: I was just on my way out. Level five, did you say?"

"Yes, thanks Kath. See you soon then?"

"I'll just make a phone call and I'll come straight over after that. Bye."

Morgan hasn't realised how hungry he is until he starts eating the pumpkin soup and toast with scrambled eggs, and

GAME

he finds that the food is surprisingly tasty. He has always imagined that hospital food would be bland for some reason. After the food he is given some tablets. He swallows the medication, lays back and falls asleep.

When he wakes up the curtain next to his bed is closed again, and he can vaguely make out the contours of a person who is standing by the foot of his bed. It has to be Katherine, he thinks. The nurse is a dark shape behind her.

"…So remember what I told you, no longer than a few minutes. This is not visiting hours."

"Right, I heard you the first time," Katherine snaps.

Morgan raises himself up on his elbow. "Hey, thanks for coming."

"My god, you look like a wreck. What happened?" Katherine walks around to the side of the bed and sits down on the edge of the mattress.

"I don't know. I had this terrible pain in my chest when I woke up this morning. I guess it's been a bit too much lately." Morgan smiles weakly.

"What, with mum?"

"Yes that too, but it's more than that... Who would have thought that a healthy thirty-eight year old would have a heart attack?" Morgan moves his arm and flicks the switch on the side of the bed. The bed head moves up and he leans back against it.

"What other things?" Katherine looks concerned.

"Oh you know, it's mostly work…" Morgan stops and looks down at his hands. "No, I'm not going to lie to you. I haven't told you; but I have a girlfriend called Lisa." Morgan lowers his voice to a whisper. "I just found out that she's pregnant. She was planning to have an abortion without telling me, so we had a fight… And then I found out that she's probably been kidnapped. Well, that's part of work. We're looking for this guy – a serial killer – and I think he was the one who took her. I don't have a clue where she is, and I'm in charge of this investigation."

Katherine stares at him. "My god, that's terrible. Why haven't you told me this before?"

Morgan keeps his voice low. "Well, you know, the investigation is not official and I haven't been able to tell anyone. Besides, you've been busy with work and the funeral and everything…"

Katherine puts a hand on Morgan's arm. "Come on, I'm not that busy. I just freaked out a bit with dad and that. And of course mum's death shocked us all."

"Well, anyway, that's what caused the heart attack I think. I mean, I haven't exactly been looking after myself properly lately, but ultimately I think that everything that's happened finally took a toll on me."

Katherine strokes his arm. "You poor thing, you should have told me. I've been terrible to you; thinking that you didn't care about us: and all this time you've been weighed down with all this."

Morgan looks up at her and sees that she has tears in her eyes. "Come on, you've got your own life to worry about. I couldn't expect you to worry about me."

Katherine sniffles. "No I've been terrible to you, and look what happened: you could have died." She digs around in her handbag and pulls out a handkerchief that she dries her eyes with. "What does the doctor say and how long do you have to stay in hospital?"

"The nurse said that I'll find out today; when the doctors make their round in the afternoon."

Katherine stands up. "Okay, I better go before that

GAME

dragon of a nurse comes back. Where are your keys?"

"In the bedside table," Morgan points. "Can you grab them? I'm not so mobile right now."

Katherine opens the drawer and picks up the keys. "I'd better come back tonight during visiting hour, the dragon probably won't let me come back before then. Is there anything else you need?"

"Yes I'd like my shaver, my shaving cream, my toothbrush and my aftershave. They're in the bathroom, and there's a toiletry bag in the cupboard under the sink. My contacts and the eye solution are next to the sink and everything else is in the cupboard I think."

Katherine puts the keys in her bag. "Okay, no problem. I'll see you tonight then."

"Thanks Kath." Morgan smiles sleepily.

She pulls the sunglasses from the top of her head and puts them on. "You rest now. See you later." The weight on the mattress shifts and she is gone.

The green curtain next to the bed is pulled to the side and Dennis' face grins at Morgan. "Mate, was that who I thought it was?"

Morgan raises his eyebrows. "That was my sister Katherine."

"Yes, the chick on TV; channel nine, isn't it?"

"Yes, she works for channel nine."

"My god, I don't believe it! I've had a crush on her ever since I moved to Sydney."

Morgan smirks. "Don't tell her that; she'll hit you over the head. She hates attention."

Dennis looks up into the ceiling with dreamy eyes and a goofy smile on his face. "*And* she's passionate. Is she coming back here?"

"Yes, she'll be back at visiting hour. She's bringing me some stuff from home."

Dennis sits up in his bed. "I'm going to have a shower." He presses the red button to call the nurse.

Morgan flicks the switch to lower his bed head. When the nurse looks in on him a few minutes later he is asleep.

Morgan hears voices and someone says his name. He opens his eyes and sees three blurry figures by the foot of his bed.

"Mr Callaghan, are you awake?" a male voice asks.

Morgan rubs the sleep from his eyes with the hand that is not connected to the drip. "Yes."

"I'm Doctor Collins, how are you feeling?"

"Uh, I feel better now. The pressure over the chest is gone." Morgan tries to sit up. A nurse is instantly by his side and flicks the switch on the bed and pulls the pillow up behind his head.

The doctor looks at the chart by the foot of the bed. "Uh um, you've had a minor heart attack, but nothing too serious." He turns to the nurse and asks her about some medication. Morgan tries to focus his eyes but he still can't see the doctor's face clearly: he is too far away. He clears his throat. "When can I go home?"

The doctor turns to face him. "Heart attacks are serious in all shapes and sizes…" he pauses. "But you were lucky to have a mild one. You should be on your feet within a few days given that you take the right medication, but you'll have to stay overnight for further observation. You should be able to go home tomorrow. I'll prescribe some medication for you and then you should rest for a few days at home."

Morgan nods. "Okay. Thanks."

GAME

The doctor walks around the bed and stands next to Morgan. He pulls a small torch from his breast pocket and shines it into Morgan's left eye. "Look up for me... Okay good, and now the other one..." He puts the torch back in his pocket and holds the end of a stethoscope. "Could you pull your gown down please?"

Morgan unties the bow on his back with one hand and lets the white cotton gown slide down over his shoulders. First now he sees the plastic stickers on his chest and stomach that are holding the plastic wires that connect him to the heart monitor behind his bed.

The doctor presses the stethoscope to Morgan's chest while he listens. "Breathe deeply for me."

Morgan takes a few deep breaths.

"Good, now bend forward for me."

Morgan bends forward and the doctor presses the stethoscope to his back.

"Breathe deeply again please."

Morgan takes a few more deep breaths.

"Okay, it sounds good." The doctor straightens up. "I've had a look at your scans and you've been very lucky. There doesn't seem to be any damage. We'll do another check-up in a few weeks' time though, just to make sure. You can get dressed again."

Morgan pulls the gown up over his shoulders. The doctor turns his back on him and walks off and the two blurry figures by the foot of the bed move away with him. Morgan lies back down and closes his eyes; he is so very tired.

The day goes slowly. Morgan drifts in and out of sleep and is woken up a few times to take his medicine and to eat lunch. Dennis is sitting up in his bed when Morgan is served dinner on a tray. The curtain between their beds is pulled to the side. Morgan can smell aftershave and sees that Dennis' hair is wet.

"Mate you're lucky to get out of here so soon, I heard what the doctor said to you earlier on." Dennis takes the lid off his plate. "Oh goodie, baked beans and pork chops. I'm starving."

Morgan pushes the switch for the bed head. "How long have you been here for?"

Dennis frowns. "Too bloody long, if you ask me. Four days."

Morgan smiles wryly. "Come on mate, four days. What's that?"

"And counting, don't forget. They're not letting me out of here. I'm telling you: it's like a bloody prison." Dennis makes the words sound dramatic.

"Why?" Morgan swallows some beans. "I thought you said you only had a mild heart attack, like me."

Dennis chews and stares past Morgan out into the darkness through the window. "I guess it becomes more complicated after you've had a few of them," he says finally. "The first time was a breeze, they let me out after only one day and everything was dandy. The second time they kept me a bit longer, and so on."

Morgan stops shovelling food into his mouth and swallows. "How many heart attacks have you had?"

"It's been five, but I'm still here aren't I? And they've just been mild ones. I'm a lucky bastard, really."

Morgan feels like he is looking down a corridor of years that lies ahead of him. Is his life going to be like that? Maybe he can't handle the stress of work and life. Maybe he will spend the rest of his time floating in and out of hospital

GAME

like this poor bastard. He clears his throat. "Mate, do you mind if I ask how old you are?"

Dennis chews and swallows. "I don't look it; but I'm forty-three."

They eat during silence for a few minutes and then Dennis pushes his tray table to the side. "Don't worry; lots of blokes have mild heart attacks, and they never get bothered by the old ticker again. I didn't mean to scare you."

Morgan pushes some beans around the plate with his fork. "I know, but it's a scary experience. And it gives you a new perspective on life, doesn't it?"

Dennis raises his eyebrows. "You're not wrong there. But it's a good thing mostly, because you start to appreciate life's little wonders. You wake up and smell the roses, like my old man would say."

Morgan keeps his eyes on the plate. "Why do you think it's happened to you though?"

"Oh, I know why it happened to me. It's the stress mate. That's what happens in most cases. That's why I quit as a detective." He sees the look on Morgan's face and quickly adds: "That doesn't mean that it's not the right thing for you though; we're all different. The stuff that I had to see and deal with at work was too much for me, but hey, a lot of guys work as detectives their whole life without having heart attacks every five minutes, don't they?"

Morgan nods slowly. "Yes, my dad did."

"There you go. Don't go scaring yourself like that. Remember what I said about stress? It's a vicious circle mate." Dennis abruptly stops and quickly lies down in his bed as a nurse approach them.

"Did you finish your food?" the nurse asks briskly.

"Morgan, meet Miss Dagger," Dennis says in a dead

pan tone.

"Mr Lane! How many times do I have to tell you that my name is Ms Dabber?" The middle aged woman takes their trays and staples them on a trolley. She walks off with a stiff back.

Dennis chuckles. "She's the night nurse; very strict. And you never hear her coming; she sneaks up on you."

"Thanks for the warning." Morgan straightens his back and for the first time he has a view over the whole room as all curtains between the beds are pulled to the side. He can make out blurry contours of eight beds and he can see that he is in a large room with a high ceiling.

Suddenly there are voices in the room and people are moving around: it must be visiting hour, Morgan thinks.

Dennis leans over towards him. "Psst! Hey, you wouldn't mind introducing me to your sister, would you?"

Morgan smiles at him. "No worries, as long as you behave yourself."

Dennis nods and quickly grabs a book from his bedside table that he pretends to read when Katherine walks up to Morgan's bed. Morgan sees that she is holding a large plastic bag as she gets closer. Katherine puts her hand in the bag and pulls out a dark grey morning gown made of thick corduroy fabric. "Here you go. You can't walk around in that daggy dressing gown you had at home; you'll look like an old cleaning lady." She puts her sunglasses on top of her head. "Try it on."

Morgan puts the gown over his shoulders: it is soft and warms him. "Thanks, it's nice."

Katherine hands over a black toiletry bag as she sits down on the side of the mattress. "I took the liberty of buying you some new razors and shaving cream as well,

GAME

yours looked a bit grubby to tell you the truth."

Morgan takes the bag and looks inside. "Thanks, you didn't have to do that."

Katherine sighs. "It's the least I can do for behaving like such a bitch to you." She pats his arm. The gesture feels unnatural but Morgan knows that she means well.

"So have they told you how long you have to stay here yet?"

Morgan places the toiletry bag on the bedside table. "Yes, I'll be released tomorrow."

"Aren't some people lucky?" Dennis' voice says behind them. Katherine turns around and looks at him.

Morgan places a hand on her arm, as to prevent her from saying something rude. "Kath, this is Dennis Lane. He's been keeping me company since I got here. Dennis, this is my sister Katherine."

"Hello, nice to meet you," Dennis says.

Katherine doesn't reply.

"He's nice," Morgan whispers theatrically, "really."

"Nice to meet you too," Katherine says finally. She turns to Morgan. "So you're getting out tomorrow? That's great. Do you want me to pick you up?"

Morgan blinks at Dennis who has put on a sad face when Katherine turned her back on him. "That would be great, I'm counting on being out of here first thing in the morning, but you've better clarify that with the nurse before you leave."

"Okay, I will. I'll shout you breakfast and we can celebrate that you're out of here."

Morgan smiles, "Thanks. I'll need to swing past a pharmacy on my way home as well: I've got a prescription."

Katherine stands up. "I'll go and talk to the nurse. I'll

be here tomorrow to pick you up; whatever time she tells me you can go." She bends down and gives Morgan a quick hug: this time the gesture feels more natural. "Take care of yourself and I'll see you in the morning."

Morgan looks over at Dennis as Katherine leaves the room: he is still pretending to read his book, and now he sees that Dennis is the only patient in the room that doesn't have a visitor.

"What are you reading?" he asks.

Dennis looks up. "God knows; some half-wit's idea of life through the eyes of a dog. Can you believe it?"

Morgan struggles to free his legs from the sheet that is tucked tightly around the mattress. "Sounds interesting, hey listen; what do you have to do around here to go to the bathroom?" He looks at the needle in his hand that is connected to the drip.

Dennis stands up and comes over to Morgan's bed. He points at the drip. "See this frame? It's got wheels on it, so you can move it around." He pulls the frame from the corner. "All you have to do is pull it along with you. And you can disconnect the heart monitor yourself by pulling the wires out."

Morgan wins the battle with the sheet and swings his legs over the side of the bed. He pulls his gown down and pulls out the wires that are connected to the stickers and then puts his bare feet on the cold floor. His legs feel shaky and he has to stand still for a while to find his balance before he grabs his toiletry bag and puts it under his arm. He takes a steady grip around the metal pole that holds the drip. "Right," he says to Dennis, "which way to the bathroom?"

GAME

14

It feels good to be outside. Morgan inhales the clean morning air as he walks next to Katherine towards her car. Raindrops cover the grass and the sunlight warms his face – he feels like he has been given a second chance; the positive ions must be making him delirious.

Katherine holds Morgan's arm and helps him into the passenger seat and closes the door for him.

"Where are the kids?" Morgan asks Katherine as she pulls out on Oxford Street.

"They're at a friend's place: she looks after them and takes them to and from school when I'm busy. And the kids love it there, because she's got kids their own age." Katherine pushes her sunglasses up on her forehead. "I know this great little café up the road, if you're up to it?" she glances over at him.

Morgan nods. "Yes sure, I could do with some food and a good coffee." He looks out through the window as they drive up the street. There aren't much people in this part of the city on a weekday morning and Katherine easily finds a parking spot at the top end of Oxford Street. As they step out of the car Katherine pushes her sunglasses down to cover her eyes.

They walk through the café and come out into a small courtyard. Heaters are mounted on stands next to the tables. Sun light filters down through leafy tree branches and Morgan takes a seat in a corner where the sun can reach his face. They have the courtyard to themselves but Katherine places herself with her back towards the café and keeps her sunglasses on until they have ordered and received their food; first then she places her glasses on the table. "God I hate these things, it's like seeing the world in shadows. Sometimes I forget what colour things outside have."

"I can't imagine what it's like." Morgan doesn't envy his sisters' celebrity status.

Katherine chews on a piece of bacon and swallows. "It's bloody horrible."

They finish their food in silence. Morgan feels comfortable in his sisters company: and he can't recall to have ever felt this way before. He looks at her as he puts his fork down. "How are the funeral arrangements going?"

Katherine puts her cup on the saucer. "Good, it's all done. The service is on Friday afternoon. Do you think you're up for it?"

Morgan nods. "Yes, I should be right. It has to be done. Do you need help with anything? Just let me know."

"No seriously, it's all been taken care of. Just concentrate on resting and getting better so you can be there." Katherine takes a cigarette packet from her bag and holds it up in front of him. "I thought you wanted one of these; I'm not sure if you should smoke though. What did the doctor say?"

Morgan takes a cigarette from the pack and Katherine lights it for him.

"Ah." He exhales a grey cloud of smoke. "That's better. What the doctor doesn't know doesn't hurt him." Morgan grins when he sees the expression on Katherine's face. "I'm kidding. He said to cut down, but no one expects you to quit just like that... Thanks," he adds.

"So," Katherine lights a cigarette and inhales, "did the

GAME

lawyer call you about mum's will?"

"Shit, I totally forgot about that. Yes, he called me the other day. He wanted us to come and see him on Wednesday… That's today isn't it?"

Katherine frowns. "It is," she says slowly. "But I can call him and delay the meeting. I don't think it's a good idea for you to go there today."

Morgan nods. "I agree. It will have to wait a few days."

"Okay, I'll give him a call and organise it."

Morgan empties his coffee cup. "That was good. Thanks for breakfast."

"No worries," Katherine smiles. "Do you want to go past a pharmacy on your way home?"

"Yes, that would be good. There's one around the corner from where I live."

"Alright I'll fix the bill and then we'll go." Katherine puts her sunglasses on and gets up from the table.

Morgan sits in an armchair that he has pulled up in front of his window. He is drinking a cup of tea and smokes a cigarette. Katherine has cleaned his whole apartment; done the dishes, folded his laundry and dusted every surface so that all rooms smell fresh and clean. Large white tiger lilies stand in a vase on the coffee table with a card that reads 'Welcome Home'. She has even filled his freezer with gourmet health food in microwaveable containers. And she has placed a new electric heater next to the sofa.

The sun warms Morgan through the open window. The solitude of his apartments is welcome after being prodded and poked at the hospital. He doesn't sleep well in a room full of strangers and the hospital was noisy: ambulance sirens howled outside the window and people snored; god he hates snoring. Good thing he is a man, he thinks, and a straight one at that: he doesn't have to sleep in the same bed as another man. The apartment is his piece of the world: his piece of silence. For the first time in days Morgan feels calm and relaxed. He intends to feel this way; with his mind cleared of any thoughts, for exactly fifteen minutes more before he calls work.

The doctor has told Morgan to stay away from stressful situations within the near future but that is difficult when it comes to the line of work he is in; Morgan pushes the thought out of his head – he knows what he needs to do.

He sips his tea and looks out over the harbour: the water is covered by a light grey mist. Every minute of the day the harbour looks different. He likes the view most in the early morning before every man and his dog decides to go sailing or fishing. The rent he pays for his unit is for this view: the moments he can be alone with the harbour. Except for the standard necessities, his unit holds little else for him: it is cold and drafty in winters, and cockroach infested and hot in summers. But it is his private space. Morgan thinks of Travis' large house on the other side of the harbour: Travis has a very different view, and a different lifestyle to go with it. Morgan knew this lifestyle when he grew up in Palm Beach but that belongs to his past now: a different life.

When the fifteen minutes are up, Morgan walks over to the sofa and sits down with the phone. He dials Ricketts' number.

Ricketts is chewing on something when he answers the phone. "Yes, Ricketts speaking." Morgan hears that he swallows.

"Hi, Morgan here, how's it going?"

"Hi, good, how are you feeling?"

GAME

"Better, I'm out of hospital, which is an improvement. I'm planning on popping in to the office this afternoon."

"Oh really, don't you think you should take it easy for a while?"

"Ricketts, I'm not dying, okay? I've just had a mild heart attack. And yes, I should be resting according to the doctor, but how can I rest when I know there's a serial killer maniac out there somewhere?" Morgan stretches his legs out under the coffee table and leans back in the sofa. "So what's new?"

"Uh, I don't know if I should tell you, knowing that you should stay away from shocks."

"Don't mind that; tell me what's going on!" Morgan sits up straight.

"Okay, we got a call last night at the office and it was recorded on the answering machine again."

"Yes, and? What was it?"

"Well, it was for you. It was a girl who said her name was Lisa, and she mentioned your name."

Morgan stares into his teacup. His voice doesn't reveal any feelings when he speaks: "And what did she say?"

"Uh, she was screaming, screaming that someone was going to kill her. Then she screamed that her name was Lisa and she said your name."

Morgan leans his forehead in his hand and stares down at the floor. "Okay, have you sent the tape to Pete yet?"

"Yes, it was the first thing I did this morning when I came in and heard the message."

"Okay good, I want you to do something for me. I want you to fingerprint everyone who has access to our internal number, and that includes all the cops in all the police stations around Sydney, as well as all the departments that we deal with. There's a list of the departments and police stations on my desk in the In-tray. And Ricketts…"

"Yes?"

"This includes our department as well."

There is silence for a few seconds and then Ricketts says: "I understand."

"Now, I know that this won't be easy. A lot of people are going to be upset and feel that their rights are being violated but you can tell them that we're not keeping their prints on file: they will only be used this once. And Ricketts: do not exclude anyone. Have you got that?"

"I've got it."

"Good, contact the forensic department and get them to do the fingerprinting. This is a forensic part of the investigation, and it should be carried out by the forensic department. Are we clear?"

"Yes. What time are you coming in?"

"I'll be in sometime this afternoon. I'll expect this to take some time because I know that a lot of police officers work shifts, so let's start with the departments. And don't worry about the personnel that are away in Canberra; I'm not interested in them."

"Okay. I gather that you want prints of the personnel in the forensic department as well?"

"Yes I do, but let's do them last since we need them to do the fingerprinting."

"I'll get on to the forensic department straight away."

"Alright, give me a call if you get any problems. And if not, I'll see you this afternoon."

Morgan hangs up and runs his fingers through his hair. He wishes that he knows how to meditate or do yoga; to relax his mind and force himself to think clearly – but he

GAME

knows no breathing techniques and all he can do is to try to breathe calmly and think positive thoughts. He gets up and walks over to the armchair in front of the window; he sits down in it and stares out over the water below.

In the early afternoon he eats one of Katherine's health meals; it's some sort of meat stew with vegetables and he finds it surprisingly tasty. After the food he sits down on the sofa and flicks through the channels on the TV with the remote control. But after a few minutes of trying to watch a midday movie without being able to concentrate on the storyline he abandons the sofa and goes to have a shower instead.

The phone rings as he comes out from the bathroom wrapped in his new morning gown. He takes the call in the bedroom, sitting on the bed.

"Sergeant Callaghan? It's me, Ricketts. We've found another one, another body I mean."

Morgan feels his heart beat hard and fast. "What does she look like Ricketts? Does she have blond hair?"

"I don't know what she looks like – we just got the call from Bondi police station. She was found early this morning on the beach."

"Where's the body now?"

"She was taken to the city morgue in Annandale, but I've already contacted George Demitriades and he's organised a transfer of the body to his office this afternoon."

"Why didn't the Bondi police contact us directly?" Morgan voice is filled with frustration. "My god, I hope they took photos at least."

"Their computer system was down so they didn't check the Intranet and they thought it'd be best to take the body to the city morgue. I was told they took photos of the body where it was found and I've sent Stone to Bondi to get the pictures."

Morgan rubs his hand over his forehead and feels that he is sweating. "What time is the body expected at George's office, do you know?"

"George said that he's expecting the body around three o'clock; that's when the deliveries usually arrive from Annandale."

Morgan looks at the alarm clock on his bedside table: it shows two thirty. "Ricketts, could you pick me up? I don't think that I'm in a condition to drive, and I'd like to get to the morgue as soon as possible."

"Sure, no problem, I'll leave now. What's your address?"

Morgan gives him the address and Ricketts promises that he will be there within twenty minutes. Morgan feels dizzy as he stands up. He suddenly realises that he's forgotten to take his medication with his lunch as he is supposed to.

He is sitting on the sofa smoking nervously when Ricketts presses the intercom buzzer fifteen minutes later. He stubs his cigarette out in the ashtray and grabs his keys from the hallway table on the way out.

Morgan sees the surprised look on Ricketts' face as he gets into the car.

"I know that I don't look too hot, but I've just had a heart attack and to tell you the truth I don't like sleeping with strangers around me." He gives a short nervous laugh as he fastens the seat belt. "I don't expect you to understand how I'm feeling, but could you stop staring at me and start driving now please?"

Ricketts' red cheeks darken a shade. "Sorry, it's just a bit of a shock to see you like this." He turns the key in the

GAME

ignition and drives slowly up the hill. "George is expecting us; I gave him a call after we spoke on the phone."

Morgan turns his head and looks out through the window. "So how did you go with the fingerprinting?"

"It's done. I mean; I spoke to Pete and he said that he was going to take some time this afternoon to start organise it."

Morgan turns his head and looks at Ricketts' profile. "Organise it this afternoon? What do you mean? Didn't you explain to him that it's urgent?"

Ricketts stops at the top of the hill and waits for a gap in the traffic on the main road so he can turn the corner. He turns and looks at Morgan. "No, I mean, you didn't say… I wasn't under the impression that it was urgent."

Morgan leans his elbow against the car door and looks straight ahead. "You do understand that I'm not supposed to get upset, don't you?"

"Yes I do."

Morgan turns his head and looks at Ricketts again. "Well, you *are* bloody upsetting me now. Pull over and give Pete another call." Morgan's voice is ice cold: "*Now*."

Ricketts looks up in the rear view mirror and reverses down the hill a few metres. He swings the car over to the side of the road and parks behind another car in a no parking zone. Morgan opens the door as soon as the car stops and gets out. He bends down and looks at Ricketts. "I'll wait out here; let me know when you're finished."

Ricketts nods. "Alright."

Morgan slams the door shut and pulls the cigarette packet from his pocket.

Morgan and Ricketts are seated in comfortable

armchairs when the medical examiner enters the room. George Demitriades pulls a pair of thin rubber gloves off his hands and throws them into a waste paper basket that stands next to the desk. "Sorry to keep you waiting, I had some work that couldn't wait." He sits down behind the desk and rubs his hands together. "It is cold down there," he explains when he sees Morgan's expression.

Morgan leans forward and places his elbows on his knees. "Has the body arrived from Annandale yet?"

"Yes, it came in a few minutes ago. She's been treated the same as the others by the look of her." Demitriades picks up a stapled bunch of papers from his desk and flicks through the pages. "This is the report from the city morgue: it was couriered over to me earlier." He clears his throat. "They've already performed the autopsy and it says here that the body is female, age is twenty-two years, hair colour is dark brown, eye colour is brown, weight is fifty-eight kilograms, dress size is ten and shoe size is seven. The serology report says that her blood type…"

Morgan suddenly interrupts: "Okay, we don't need to know her blood type right now. Can we see her?"

Demitriades looks up at Morgan with raised eyebrows. "Alright, I'll ask my secretary to make a copy of the autopsy report so you can take it with you; it'll save me money if I don't have to courier it to your office." He stands up. "The body's downstairs."

Morgan and Ricketts follow Demitriades through the door and wait in the corridor as Demitriades exchanges a few words with his secretary.

"This way," Demitriades says as he comes back. They turn a corner and enter a corridor that is built wide for transports of gurneys and curls downwards. At the bottom

GAME

of the corridor, Demitriades disappears behind a pair of plastic doors and Ricketts holds one square of plastic open for Morgan. A sharp smell of disinfectants is in their noses as they enter a cold room where unforgiving florescent light reveal every detail: stainless steel gurneys are parked along the walls and small tables that hold sharp instruments, scales, bottles filled with clear liquid and small electrical saws stand next to each gurney. The saw cords are plugged into wall sockets and create a graphic pattern of repeated thin black lines against the shiny white walls. The green hoses that hang in chains from the ceiling remind Morgan of a carwash.

"She's through here." Demitriades opens a door and Ricketts and Morgan follow him into a small and even colder room. Morgan sees the contours of a body under a white sheet on a table. He suddenly puts a hand on the wall for support. Demitriades walks up to the table and unceremoniously pulls the sheet off the body. Morgan exhales loudly.

The girl on the table has been cleaned and the blood has been dried or washed off, but the gaping hole in her throat still looks grotesque: pieces of blackened skin and meat hang loosely around the neck and cover parts of the collarbones. Black autopsy stitches forms a large Y from the pubic hairline up to the chest. The stitches on the scalp are hardly visible under the dark brown curly hair but Morgan knows that the cranium has been sawed open so the brain can be removed and examined.

"So," Demitriades says, "she's been dead for five or six days. That's why she doesn't smell so good. I've got Vicks if you want some under your nose?"

Morgan shakes his head: he is breathing through his

mouth out of habit. "No, that won't be necessary. We've seen what we came to see. Thanks George."

"Okay, I'll take you back up then." Demitriades places the sheet back over the body and leads the way out of the room. Morgan feels dizzy as they reach the top of the winding corridor: he leans against the front desk in the reception and inhales deeply.

Ricketts looks concerned as he touches Morgan's shoulder. "Are you alright?"

Morgan looks into the mirror behind the reception desk and sees that his face has a strange pale shade. "I think I need to sit down," he mutters.

Ricketts holds Morgan's arm as he helps him over to a chair. The girl behind the desk gets up and fills a plastic cup with water that she hands to Morgan. He drains the water and stands up a bit too quickly: the whole room spins as he turns to Demitriades. "We need to go over some details with you: can we go into your office?" He places the empty cup on the reception desk and nods a 'thank you' to the girl.

"Sure." Demitriades walks ahead and closes the door to his office when Morgan and Ricketts are seated in the armchairs.

"So, what can I do for you?" Demitriades takes a seat behind his desk.

"Ricketts," Morgan turns to look at Ricketts, "can you take notes please?"

Ricketts nods and takes a notebook from his pocket.

Morgan turns to the medical examiner again. "We've got a possible ID for the body: a girl was reported missing who fits the description. We'll contact the relatives and let you know when they can come and view her."

Demitriades forms his fingers into a pyramid under

GAME

his chin. "Okay."

Morgan's mouth feels like sandpaper and he rolls his tongue around his mouth to encourage the saliva to return. "I need to ask you George: in your opinion, would you say that the killer is left handed or right handed?"

Demitriades leans back in his chair. "I couldn't say for sure, but I believe that he's right handed. I have examined the knife wounds and have come to the conclusion that the killer must have stood behind his victims when he cut their throats. The force of the cut is emphasised on the right side from the middle, which means that's where he ended the incision. If you were a right handed person, like me, it would be natural to start the incision on the left side." Demitriades makes a cutting movement with his hand in the air to demonstrate.

"I have also read the forensic reports, and the blood splat marks on the walls in Else Henriksen's and Cassandra Saunders' apartments confirm my theory. If the killer was standing in front of the victim as he cut her, the blood drops on the wall would not have been in a pattern of a perfect arch, the killer's body would have interrupted the blood flow and it would have partly hit him before it hit the wall. When the carotid throat artery is severed with the force that has been recorded in these cases, the blood spurts out with extreme speed and in a huge amount. I believe that the killer stood behind his victims and that the victims were on their knees, facing the wall."

Morgan glances over at Ricketts who is taking notes, before he addresses Demitriades again: "Okay, thank you. Now to something different: did you organise the release of Else Henriksen's body to her parents?"

"Yes, all the papers have been signed and the body

will travel to Denmark by air this Friday."

Morgan closes his eyes and mentally ticks the question off in his head before he goes on to the next one: "And did Cassandra Saunders' aunt come here yesterday to ID the body?"

Demitriades nods. "Yes she was here in the afternoon with one of your detectives: Braun, I think his name was. She positively identified the body as Cassandra."

Morgan gets up from his seat. "Thanks George, I know you're busy so we'll get going."

Demitriades stands up behind his desk. "No worries. My secretary will give you a copy of the autopsy report on your way out."

Morgan lights a cigarette as they come outside. He walks up to a railing by the edge of the cliff and looks out over the harbour. The setting sun casts an orange-pink light over the water and the bridge. "It's a nice view from here, isn't it?" he asks Ricketts.

"Yes, there's nothing like the harbour," Ricketts replies as he walks up to the edge.

"Where do you live Ricketts?" Morgan asks casually as he supports himself against the railing: the nicotine is giving him a rush and he feels dizzy again.

"Uh, I'm in Petersham." Ricketts turns his head to look at Morgan. "No water views there, I'm afraid. But you must have a pretty good view where you are."

Morgan nods. "Yes, it's not bad."

"Isn't it human to want to be close to the water? Don't we all yearn for the fresh breeze from the ocean and the therapeutic sound of whispering waves?"

Morgan pats Ricketts' shoulder. "I didn't know you

GAME

were a poet." He crushes the cigarette under his shoe. "Let's go."

Ricketts frowns as they walk towards the car. "To the office you mean? Shouldn't you go home and rest? You don't look too good. You certainly didn't look good in there." He gestures with his thumb towards the medical examiners' office.

Morgan holds his hand on the car door. "I'm fine Ricketts, open up."

"Okay, if you say so." Ricketts presses the remote key and unlocks the car doors.

Morgan gets inside and breaths in through his nose: he knows that he would have fainted if he hadn't been allowed to sit down. He opens the side window and breathes in the cool air as Ricketts drives up the hill to the freeway. Despite the afternoon traffic that is building up on the bridge it takes them less than ten minutes to get from Milsons Point to Pyrmont.

Morgan insists on walking by himself when they reach the office. He lets Ricketts help him out of the car, but he doesn't want the whole office to see him as a cripple. He doesn't get far: after a few steps he feels that the room is spinning. He pretends that he wants to stop and talk to Amanda and he casually leans against her desk until he feels strong enough to continue. As soon as he reaches his room he turns to Ricketts who is walking behind him: "Get me a glass of water will you?" He sits down in his chair and breathes heavily. "And close the door."

Ricketts nods and closes the door behind him as he walks out.

Morgan looks out through the window until Ricketts

returns with the water. "Thanks." He takes the glass from Ricketts. "I'm going to make some phone calls but I'll let you know when I've got time to go through…" Morgan waives his hand in the air vaguely. "You know: everything. As I said; I'll let you know."

"Okay, I'll leave you to it." Ricketts leaves the room and closes the door behind him.

Morgan takes a small bottle of pills from his pocket. He takes two pills and swallows them with some water.

There are two telephone messages from Travis on Morgan's desk, but Morgan chooses to ignore them: he suspects that Travis has heard about the heart attack and wants to take him off the investigation. Travis is also going to find out about his relationship with Lisa sooner or later – he'll better stay away from Travis for now. He picks up the phone and dials the number to the technical department. Pete's voice answers before Morgan hears any signals go through.

"Pete? Morgan here."

"Morgan, how are you mate? We heard about the heart attack."

"Yes, no I'm alright. It's not life threatening. How are you going with the tape from the answering machine?"

"We've identified Linda Kasinski's voice on the tape: it's the same voice that's on the tape from her answering machine."

"Right," Morgan doesn't hide his impatience, "and what about the second tape from our answering machine? Have you had a look at it yet?"

"Yes we had a look at it this morning. Same thing: there's traffic in the background, but we can't determine anything else."

GAME

Morgan stares at the piece of gauze that covers the needle prick on his hand. "Is it the same distance away from the traffic as the first call?"

"I can't answer that to be a hundred percent accurate, but this call seems to be a similar distance away from the traffic as the first call."

"And what about the fingerprinting, have you started the process yet?"

"I've got four guys on it; they're doing the departments in alphabetical order and we're starting on the police stations after that... Are you really suspecting someone internally for the murders?"

Morgan deliberately avoids the question. "We'll need to speed up the fingerprinting process. Do you think you could put some more people on it? And I'd like to hear the message from our answering machine – the second tape that is. Send a copy to me this afternoon, will you?"

"Okay, sure. Me and David can do fingerprinting as well if you like. That's if you can put a priority on this; we've still got other jobs here that will fall behind."

"This is definitely a priority, so if you get any problems in regards to the other work you can quote me on that. I want you to compare the prints you get with the prints we found in Else Henriksen's apartment. And I'll be expecting the tape from the answering machine within the hour."

"Right, of course, I'll send the tape over straight away."

Morgan hangs up and rubs his jaw thoughtfully as he stares through the window. It is dark outside and as his eyes refocuses he sees his face in the reflection. He suddenly wonders if Katherine has told their father about the heart attack: he hopes not. He sits lost in thoughts for a few more minutes before he suddenly gets up and walks out of the room.

Stone is sitting next to Ricketts: they are both looking at something on Ricketts' computer screen. Morgan takes a seat on the edge of Ricketts' desk. "Stone, can I have a look at the photos that you picked up from Bondi please?"

Stone walks over to his desk and pulls out a large white envelope that lies under some papers. He hands the envelope to Morgan. "Here you go, how are you feeling now?"

Morgan opens the envelope and grunts. "I'd feel a whole lot better if everyone could concentrate on work instead of my well-being." He looks up and sees the expression on Stone's face. "Shit, I'm joking with you Stone. Thanks for asking, but I'm fine; really."

Stone nods. "Good to hear."

Morgan holds up a photograph. "What's this wall that she's leaning against?"

Stone slumps down in a chair. "The body was found leaning against the stone wall on the northern end of the beach. She was well out of reach for the tide."

"Who found her?" Morgan has taken all the enlarged photos from the envelope and flicks through them.

"A surfer, I can't remember his name but all his details are in the police report. I gave the legal document to Bondi police so the surfer can sign it; the officer I spoke to said that he would get right on it."

Morgan looks up at Stone. "Were there any other witnesses?"

"No, lucky for us it was still early morning when the body was removed by police – they put her in a body bag and got her out of there as quickly as possible."

GAME

"Okay, good." Morgan stands. "Just make sure the surfer signs the document before tomorrow, I don't want to read about this in the morning papers."

"Okay, I'll see to it."

Morgan turns to Ricketts. "Oh yes, before I forget; did you get the profile report from Torrone that I asked for?"

Ricketts closes the computer program he is in and holds the cursor over the Intranet icon. "I've got it on e-mail. But I can't print it right now; the printer's down."

"No rush, we can go through it tomorrow. And could you," Morgan includes Stone in his gaze, "contact Linda Kasinski's flatmates and locate her relatives? We need to identify the body at the morgue as soon as possible."

"Sure," Ricketts says, "we'll do that first thing."

"Okay." Morgan tries to think if there is anything else that needs to be done. "That's all for today. I'll be heading home soon." He walks off with the white envelope under his arm.

The tape from the answering machine is inside a padded envelope on Morgan's desk. Morgan reads the short note that Pete has written and takes the tape to Amanda's desk. Amanda is on her way home and has her coat on and her bag over her shoulder. "Do you need me for anything else today?" she asks as Morgan bends over the answering machine and places the tape inside it.

He shakes his head. "No, you can go. Have a nice evening."

"Thanks, you too." She walks off, and Morgan presses the play button on the answering machine.

"Help! He's going to kill me! It's me, Lisa! Help! Morgan! Morgan! I'm…" the tape stops abruptly and Morgan stares at the answering machine and then presses rewind' and play. Scullion and Whitfield walk past on their way to the elevator and nod at Morgan. He nods back. Lisa's voice starts screaming again and Morgan presses the stop button quickly. He takes the tape out of the answering machine: he has heard enough.

It isn't until Ricketts' and Stone have put their heads through the door opening to his room and said good night, that Morgan realises he is without transport. For a moment he contemplates running after them to ask for a lift, but then he relaxes. He can always call a cab, he thinks. He has been sitting behind his desk, he doesn't know for how long, thinking about Lisa. When he stands up he feels that his back is sore. He pushes his shoulders back to take the pressure off the muscles around his spine. What he needs is rest and food: to his own surprise he is hungry. Someone walks past in the corridor outside his room and Morgan thinks it is Wendy; the woman who works the midweek evening shifts. He opens the door fully and looks out. "Wendy? Is that you?" But there is no reply. Morgan sighs and takes his empty coffee cup to the kitchen and puts it in the dishwasher. He turns the kitchen light off and has one foot in the corridor when he catches a glimpse of someone walking around the corner. Morgan slowly walks around the corner to the room where the detectives' desks stand, but there is no one there. He turns around and starts to walk back towards his room when he hears a vague noise behind him: the sound of a chair moving over the floor. As he stops he suddenly detects danger and his adrenaline pushes him in the direction of his office. As he comes around the corner he starts to run and he reaches his room in seconds. He slams the door shut behind him and reaches for the mobile phone on his desk. For a

GAME

second he stares at the phone and doesn't know who to call. Then he suddenly makes up his mind and dials Katherine's number with shaking fingers. He silently curses the architect who hasn't put locks on the office doors as he sees the door handle move. The door slowly opens.

Morgan quickly reaches out and grabs his jacket from the back of his chair, sticks the mobile in the inner pocket and puts the jacket on.

***

Lisa is in pain when she wakes up. She feels that she is laying in something warm and wet. At first she thinks that she has urinated in her sleep, but when she manages to move her head to look down at the floor she sees that the puddle under her is red.

***

Morgan's strongest feeling as he sits in the visiting chair in his office; is anger. "What the hell are you talking about? Have you lost your fricking marbles, or what?"

Travis sits in Morgan's chair behind the desk. His voice is calm. "We've got reason to believe…"

"What reason? While we're wasting time here, the real killer is murdering my girlfriend for Christ's sake!"

Travis sighs. "Lisa is one of the reasons; on the tape she clearly says your name."

Morgan shakes his head in frustration. "She's pleading for my help; isn't that obvious?"

"It really doesn't sound that way to me." Travis squints with his eyes. "It sounds to me like she is trying to tell us that you're the killer."

Morgan stares at him. "You can't be serious! You know me, you know my father…"

Travis leans forward and shakes a finger in front of Morgan's face. "That's right, and if it wasn't for your father you wouldn't be here. You know that, as well as I do."

Morgan's mind goes blank. "What do you mean? I worked my way up like everyone else."

"No you didn't. Your father came to me and asked for a favour… And I gave him that favour. *That's* the only reason you're here."

Morgan breathes angrily through his nose. "Right, so give me your reasons why you think I'm the killer; I can't wait to hear it!"

"Well," Travis says. "First there's the forensic profile. The report clearly states that you're a top suspect. Camilla Rogers, our forensic psychiatrist, seems to know you pretty well. And it's my understanding that you know her too… intimately."

Morgan blushes. "What's that got to do with anything?"

Travis bangs his fist on the table. "It's got everything to do with this! Camilla Rogers states that you forced yourself upon her in her apartment and that you… let me see what her exact words are…" Travis flicks through some papers. "She says that you practically raped her; and I quote her exact words now: 'Morgan came into the bathroom when I was having a shower, brutally forced himself upon me and secured my hands behind my back so I couldn't resist', end quote." Travis looks up at Morgan with a triumphant smile.

Morgan closes his eyes for second. "That's not what happened."

Travis stares at him with his small brown eyes. "That's

GAME

how it happened for Camilla and you're goddamn lucky she didn't file charges against you for rape! She says in her report…" He looks down at his papers. "Where is it? …She says here that you are; in her professional opinion, quote: 'unstable, suffer from hair-trigger anger outbursts and fits the profile of someone capable of considerable violent acts'; end quote."

Morgan feels hot and uncomfortable. "You asked her to profile me? We had a relationship; or did she forget to mention that too?"

"No, she mentioned that. But your relationship was over, wasn't it? Or were you having two girlfriends at the same time? And I can inform you that she was happy to comply with my request for a profile of you."

Morgan closes his eyes briefly again. He will deal with Camilla later. So now everyone knows. "What other evidence have you got?" His voice is filled with irony as he emphasizes the word 'evidence'. "Let's clear this up once and for all."

"I have testimonies from some of the detectives that you have been acting strange lately; Ricketts?" Travis turns to Ricketts and Stone who stand leaning against the wall.

Ricketts blushes. "Well," he says slowly. "You haven't been yourself lately. And we called the Royal North Shore hospital to check that your mother was there; when you claimed to have been there with her just before Cassandra Saunders' body was found. But the hospital denied that Victoria Callaghan had been a patient there."

Morgan blows air angrily through his nose. "You fucking imbecile! She was there incognito! We told the hospital staff not to give her name to anyone. The bloody reporters would have hunted her to the grave if they knew she was there. Or didn't you know that Victoria Callaghan was one of the most famous actresses in Australia; or that she was the mother of Katherine Irving; the news presenter on channel nine?" Morgan catches his breath. "And how do you explain Else Henriksen's neighbours? I was there, remember: I spoke to them. Wouldn't they have recognized me if I was the killer?"

"Not necessarily. You know as well as I do that those neighbours couldn't tell shit from clay: they only saw the guy when it was dark. We took those phantom pictures to all the restaurants and shops where Else Henriksen had been and no one recognised any of the faces. Besides, we don't know if her boyfriend was the one who killed her."

Morgan tries to think. "Okay. But what about Mr Perkins; the guy who saw Linda Kasinski get dragged into a car? I was there, I spoke to him too: remember?"

There are no emotions on Ricketts' face as he looks at Morgan. "Yes, but Perkins never saw the guy's face. The police artist couldn't even make a decent sketch from his descriptions."

"But listen to what you're saying; it doesn't make any sense." Morgan looks at the three men. "All witnesses said that the suspect was around twenty-five to twenty-eight years old. ... Look, it doesn't really matter what you think, because I've got alibis. You can check with the Royal North Shore hospital again to start with. And then call St Vincent's hospital: I was there, having suffered a bloody *heart attack* when Lisa made the call to our office." Morgan crosses his arms over his chest. "Go on; do it."

"Come on Morgan." Travis leans forward over the desk. "We knew it had to be someone in our office when the calls came to the answering machine on our internal line.

GAME

It added up with the murder scenes that were cleaned so thoroughly: it pointed to someone with forensic awareness. And then your girlfriend called and said your name on the tape. Lisa obviously managed to get to a phone while you were in hospital; to make the call. So just tell us where she is now."

Morgan stares at him. "You are out of your mind, do you know that? Why do you think I had a heart attack? Because I was worried sick about Lisa; that's why!"

"Yes that's what you say. But I think you couldn't handle the stress of being both a killer and a detective. And I believe that you are craving attention; so much so that you want to be caught, don't you Morgan?" Travis leans back in the chair and stares at Morgan without blinking.

"What about the fingerprints that we found in Else Henriksen's apartment? I can tell you now that they don't belong to me. Take my fingerprints right now and I'll prove it to you." Morgan holds Travis' gaze.

"Those prints could have been left by anyone who was in the apartment: they don't have to belong to the killer. Surely you realise that I would say that, don't you Morgan?"

"Alright, but I can prove to you that they *were* left by the killer, after we get fingerprints from all our staff. I can prove that someone who works for the police department was inside Else's apartment and left his finger prints!"

Travis fiddles with a pen and looks down at the desk. "We will not go around fingerprinting our personnel at the departments and police stations. This charade stops now." Travis taps the pen against the table. "I think we should take a sample of your body fluids and see if they match the seminal fluid found on the victims." He suddenly looks directly at Morgan and smiles. "Don't underestimate me

Morgan; I might have suffered a nervous breakdown but I'm still in charge here and for a good reason." He exhales loudly and looks at Ricketts. "Have you got the number for the medical examiner Ricketts?"

Ricketts pulls his fingers through his hair and frowns. "Uh, I don't have the number on me… Morgan?"

"It's in my black diary. There, next to the computer." Morgan points.

"Right," Travis opens the diary and finds the number in the back pages, after Morgan has pointed it out to him. He calls Demitriades' mobile and his eyes are on Morgan as he speaks: "George? This is Superintendent Travis, have you got a moment? …Good. Look, I need to ask you a favour. Can you come to your office and meet us there? …Yes, right now if you could. I'll bring some detectives with me. We'll need you to do some tests; to match the seminal fluid from the victims to a suspect …That's right; the victims of the serial killer… I'd prefer if you did the tests on the suspect yourself; it would take longer if we had to order them through pathology and then send the lab results back to you for comparison… I'm sure you understand my point. Okay thanks, I'll see you soon then." Travis hangs up and looks at Morgan. "Come on let's go; we'll take my car."

Travis turns the engine off in front of the medical examiner's office. The street is dark and empty but the lights are on over the entrance when Stone knocks on the glass door. A light comes on inside and they can see Demitriades walk over the carpet towards the door, he turns the lock and lets them in. "You'd better come into my office." He stops and looks around. "Where's the suspect?"

Travis pats Morgan's shoulder. "Here he is. Is it okay if

we wait out here while you do the tests?"

Demitriades stares at Travis. "Are you joking? Morgan is the suspect?"

Travis takes a seat in a chair in the reception area and crosses his legs. "I'm not joking. And if you don't mind; we'll wait here. I'd like to cover the exit."

Morgan looks at Demitriades. "It's okay. It's just to eliminate me from the list of suspects, that's all." He shoots an angry glance at Travis and ignores Ricketts and Stone as he follows Demitriades to his office.

"Leave the door open!" Travis yells after them.

Demitriades sticks his head through the door opening. "I can't, this door is heavy and it closes automatically."

Ricketts walks over to the door. "I'll keep it open for you," he says.

Morgan looks up at him from where he is sitting. "You're enjoying this, aren't you Ricketts? I'm tempted to believe that you wouldn't mind if something happened to me. Have you always been after my job or did you become ambitious over night when I was in hospital?" He smirks. "Is that it? Is that why you accused me; so you could get my job?"

Ricketts doesn't answer; he stands rigid by the door and looks in the opposite direction.

"Hey Ricketts, you remind me of one of those door men you see at nightclubs. Maybe that could be a good career choice for you when this is over?" Morgan turns and looks at Demitriades. "I'm sorry about this, but you can understand how it's pissing me off."

Demitriades frowns. "I sorry too Morgan, I will do this test but I want you to know that I am doing it because I've been ordered to."

A.C. Efverman

Morgan gives him a tired smile. "That's alright. You're just doing your job."

Demitriades puts a pair of rubber gloves on and pulls a small table on wheels towards the armchair where Morgan sits. "Okay, give me your arm."

Morgan takes his jacket off and rolls up the shirt sleeve. Demitriades picks up a rubber cord from the table and ties it around Morgan's upper arm, asks him to make a fist and sticks a needle in a vein. Morgan watches as his dark red blood fills a plastic tube.

Demitriades comes back into the office twenty minutes later. "I've got the results."

Morgan nods. "Good, but give it to the idiots out there." He nods his head at Ricketts by the door. "It's no use telling me; I already know the answer."

Demitriades ignores Ricketts as he puts his head through the door opening. "We're ready."

"Alright, let's see what you've got," Travis says as he takes a seat in the armchair next to Morgan.

Demitriades leans against his desk. "First of all, I want you to know that this blood test is a hundred percent accurate."

Travis frowns. "Blood? I thought we were testing seminal fluids?"

Demitriades nods. "Let me take this opportunity to educate you in the science of serology: the analysis of blood that is. The serial killer is a secretor: as is eighty percent of the human population." He sees Travis' expression and explains: "A secretor is a person whose body fluids contain the same genetic substance as their blood. Basically it means that you can get a secretor's blood type from all their body

GAME

fluids. As it happens; Morgan is also a secretor." He looks at Travis over the rim of his glasses. "Through the seminal fluid that we collected off the murder victims, we have established that the killer has blood type AB. Type AB is the rarest of all blood groups as it has both antigens present." Demitriades pauses for effect. "Through Morgan's blood test I have established not only that he is a secretor, but also that he has blood type O. Morgan is not the killer."

Morgan looks at Travis. Travis stares down at the floor.

Morgan gets up and shakes Demitriades' hand. "Thanks George. And again, I'm sorry about all this."

Demitriades looks tired as he takes his glasses off. "No problem."

There is a loud bang as the door to the office slams shut: Ricketts is no longer standing in the doorway. When Morgan comes out in the reception area he sees through the glass door that Ricketts and Stone are standing out on the street. Travis says something to Demitriades in the office: their voices are a soft murmur through the closed door.

Morgan walks out through the glass door and lights a cigarette. Stone looks embarrassed as Ricketts turns his back on Morgan.

Morgan exhales a cloud of smoke into the cool night air. "So, now that we've cleared that little mistake up, I'd like to suggest that we concentrate on finding the *real* killer before more time is wasted and another girl gets killed." His voice is filled with controlled anger. "You wouldn't like to have that on your conscience, would you?" He looks at Stone who is staring at the ground. Ricketts' back doesn't move. The glass door opens behind them and Travis comes out. "Alright, let's go," he says. He holds his hands in his pockets and his head bent down as he crosses the street.

Morgan follows him and steps on his cigarette before he climbs into the front seat. Stone and Ricketts get in the back seat and Travis drives up the hill towards the bridge. There is an uneasy silence in the car; each man is submerged in his own thoughts as they cross the harbour bridge.

Finally Travis clears his throat loudly. "Hrm, Morgan, I owe you an apology. But you know that we are under a lot of pressure at the moment and the evidence pointed firmly in your direction; you understand that don't you?" Travis keeps his eyes on the road.

Morgan looks out through the window and sees that the Opera house is lit up by a pink light.

He turns to Travis. "So now that this has been cleared up; can we continue with the fingerprinting process of our personnel?"

"Where do you live?"

Morgan points him in the right direction.

"Well, I guess we don't have a choice right now, do we?"

Morgan shakes his head as Travis looks at him.

"Alright, I'll put some more men onto it first thing in the morning." Travis' voice is flat.

The silence that follows is only broken when Morgan gives directions. The car finally stops and Morgan opens the door. Without a word he slams the door shut behind him. The car drives away quickly.

Morgan feels exhausted, cold and hungry as he unlocks the entrance door. He slowly makes his way up the stairs.

***

Someone is singing somewhere above: Lisa can't make

GAME

out the words, but the melody sounds like a lullaby. She has been lying on the cold hard floor for so long that the side of her body has turned numb. And her stomach still aches: the sharp pain comes in short waves now and she knows that she has lost a lot of blood. She also knows that the foetus is gone. A few days earlier she was determined to have an abortion, but now that the pregnancy is over she feels a huge loss: it feels like a part of her soul has been ripped out. The pain and fear paralyse her. Tears that have dried on her cheeks dissolve as she cries again from pain and exhaustion. She knows that she can't take this much longer. Floorboards creak as someone walks around, around in the room above.

***

Morgan sits in his sofa with his head leaning in his hands. One of Katherine's health meals is spinning around in the microwave and spreads an aroma of lamb and herbs in the apartment. He shakes two pills from the small bottle that he keeps in his jacket pocket and swallows them with some organic orange juice that he's found in the fridge. The light on the answering machine is blinking and beckons his attention. Morgan rubs his eyes and then presses the play button.

He leans back in the sofa and smokes a cigarette while he listens to the recorded message that Katherine has left. When the beep comes he picks up the phone and dials her number.

"Katherine, I got your message. I'm sorry about that call earlier."

"That's alright. What happened? You just disappeared."

"I was at work. I was going to call you straight back,

but something came up and I got busy."

"You're supposed to take it easy for a while, remember? Anyway, I called the solicitor and changed the appointment for Sunday. He made an exception for us since you're not well and he wanted to get it done as soon as possible. I told him that Sunday was the earliest we could make it."

Morgan stubs his cigarette out in the ashtray on the table. "Good, thanks for that. How's everything going? Have you heard from dad?"

"Yes, I spoke to him tonight on the phone. He's alright I think. He spends his days fossicking around in the garden."

The microwave oven beeps in the kitchen and Morgan stands up. "Okay, good. Look, I've got to go; I've got one of your health meals in the microwave. But I'll talk to you tomorrow. And thanks again for everything."

"Don't mention it. You just look after yourself and I'll talk to you soon. Goodnight."

"Goodnight." Morgan switches to auto pilot: he walks into the kitchen and takes the container from the microwave, grabs some cutlery from a drawer and returns to the living room. He picks up the remote control and turns the TV on to distract himself from any thoughts.

GAME

15

The sun is low on the sky when Morgan drives into the garage under the office and takes the elevator to the street level.

A young girl wearing an apron is hanging the Open sign on the door as Morgan walks into the café. He makes his order by the counter and sits down to read the paper as he waits for his coffee. He flicks through the pages quickly and is relieved to see that there is nothing about a body on Bondi beach. Several pages in the paper cover the upcoming FIFA World Cup and the cost of the World Cup is a well covered topic: a lot of money has been spent on upgrading Sydney stadiums to FIFA's standards and some people argue that this money has been robbed from future years of other sports budgets. Supporters of AFL and NRL seem particularly upset as the rugby season is not allowed to continue during the soccer cup.

Did the sports clubs have the same dilemma during the Olympics when Sydney hosted the Games? Morgan can't remember. But he is looking forward to the World Cup. He has never shared the pathological hatred that some of the Australian people seem to have for soccer. Morgan associates the soccer pet name 'poofter game' with hate campaigns against homosexuals in the old days: maybe there is a connection.

The articles in the paper show that plenty of people

are unhappy that Sydney is hosting the World Cup. No one mentions that most local businesses in Sydney can use the boost in tourism.

Morgan turns page and reads that all tickets for the cup have been sold out. Apparently some tickets have cost eight hundred dollars on the black market. You'd think the ticket sales will recover some of the costs, Morgan thinks as he walks up to the counter and pays for his coffee.

There is hardly any traffic on the street as Morgan walks back to the office with a paper cup in one hand and a cigarette in the other. He ducks under a branch of a flowering bottlebrush tree that is planted on the pavement and his head is for a moment surrounded by noisy parrots that fight over nectar. The sun feels unusually hot. Morgan throws his cigarette in an ashtray on the ground and swipes his security card in the slot at the entrance door.

The office is still empty as he reaches the fifth floor and walks through the corridor to his room. Morgan's In-tray is overflowing with papers and reports and he has about an hour and a half before the morning meeting starts. He sips his coffee as he turns the computer on, listens to telephone messages and makes notes in his diary. He keeps his door closed and no one calls him or comes to see him. At ten to nine he dials Amanda's extension and asks her to call everyone to a meeting.

Morgan leans against a table in front of the detectives that have gathered in the meeting room. Pictures that show the body on Bondi Beach are blue-tacked to the wall behind him. Stone and Ricketts sit in the middle of the room next to each other and they both avoid looking directly at Morgan.

GAME

Some of the men hold conversations as they wait for the meeting to start and their voices are a low mumble in the room.

Morgan suddenly presses the play button on the answering machine that stands next to him on the table and the screaming voice catches everyone's attention. The short message ends and Morgan turns the answering machine off and looks around the room.

"I understand that you have all been informed that this message was left on our answering machine, here at the office. That was the first message, and I know that the voice on the tape belongs to a woman named Linda Kasinski." Morgan points at the enlarged photographs on the wall behind him. "I believe that this is Linda Kasinski. An autopsy found that she was killed by the same man who killed the four previous victims." Morgan presses the play button on the answering machine again. His face doesn't reveal any feelings as he listens to Lisa's screaming voice. He presses the stop button. "That," he says, "was the second message recorded by the answering machine in our office. This voice belongs to a woman called Lisa McCall. She disappeared from her unit in Coogee on Saturday the fourth of June, and the technical department has informed me that this call was made from the same phone that Linda Kasinski called from." Morgan pauses. "You all know that the answering machine in our office is connected to a telephone line that has an internal and silent number, and that this number is never given to the public. Therefore we have reason to believe that the killer is someone who works at one of our departments or at the police."

A loud murmur is heard in the room.

Morgan stands up. "Be quiet!" he yells.

A.C. Efverman

Stunned faces turn and look at Morgan's red face.

Morgan draws a deep breath and sits down on the edge of the table top behind him. "We are running out of time to catch the killer and I'm telling you this so you can be on your guard. We can't rule out the possibility that the killer is right amongst us; in this room."

The detectives glance around at each other.

"Right," Morgan continues briskly, "back to what I was saying before; the last body was found on Bondi beach and we have reason to believe that she is the missing girl: Linda Kasinski. Ricketts and Stone were going to talk to Linda's flatmates in Surry Hills and find out where we can contact her relatives, so they can identify the body; Detective Ricketts?"

Ricketts still avoids looking at Morgan. "We have contacted Linda Kasinski's parents, and they have agreed to view the body this afternoon."

"Good, you can update everyone on email as soon as you find out if it was a positive ID." Morgan holds his gaze steadily on Ricketts who is stubbornly looking at the wall next to Morgan. "Now," Morgan continues and looks away from Ricketts' red face, "I must inform you that everyone in our departments will be fingerprinted. We will match these fingerprints with the prints that were found in Else Henriksen's and Cassandra Saunders' apartments. Are there any questions about this?" Morgan looks out over the room, but no one moves or says anything. Morgan stands. "Okay, just one more thing before I let you go: as you've probably heard, I suffered a minor heart attack a few days ago but I'm better now, so everything is back to normal." Morgan glances over at Ricketts' face: it is redder than ever. "So, if no one wants to add anything, I'll see you all here tomorrow morning at nine am." Morgan gathers his notes. He sees that

GAME

Ricketts and Stone hurry out of the room. Morgan walks slowly back to his office and the detectives look down at their desks as he passes them. Morgan sighs as he takes a seat behind his desk and picks up his phone: who else has thought that he is a killer? He wonders if Stone and Ricketts have talked to the other detectives about their ridiculous suspicions.

"David speaking," a voice says in Morgan's ear.

"David, it's Morgan. How are you going?"

"Morgan, are you back so soon? I heard about the heart attack."

"Yes, it was just a minor version. Look, I'm sorry about the other night. Did you end up playing anyway?"

"What, the night cricket? Don't worry mate, I called my brother instead. We didn't win, but we had a good night at the pub afterwards." David gives a short laugh and then gets serious again. "So what can we do for you?"

"Did Superintendent Travis call you? He was going to delegate some more men to assist with the fingerprinting process."

"Hang on, I'll ask Pete; I just got here."

A few seconds passes and then David's voice is back: "Yes, apparently Travis called this morning and said that he was going to put some more people on it."

Morgan leans back in his chair. "Okay good; that's what I wanted to hear. Where are you up to now?"

"Uh, today..." There is a rustling sound of papers in the background. "Today we're doing *your* department first actually, so I guess I'll see you later if you're there."

"I'm not going anywhere except for lunch, but you'll be here before noon won't you?"

"Yes we should be leaving here soon, we're just

printing a stack of fingerprinting forms now – we're not used to taking fingerprints of so many people at the same time. We're not used to fingerprinting people who are alive either actually. And we can't use our standard computerized fingerprinting process when we're out of the office: we're still to receive iPads for that."

Morgan isn't interested in discussing budget issues. "Okay. Well I'll see you later then." He puts the receiver down but changes his mind and picks it up again. He dials Amanda's extension.

"Amanda? It's me, Morgan. Could you make sure that no one leaves the office before noon please? I need everyone here for the fingerprinting process ...You can tell them it's an order from me ...thanks."

Morgan spends the following hour making notes on his computer and reading reports from the beginning of the investigation. He finally stretches his back and contemplates going downstairs for a smoke when there is a knock on his door. David sticks his head through the door opening. "Good day, we're here now."

Morgan stands up behind his desk. "Come in."

The door opens fully and David and Pete walk in. They carry black bags and for once they aren't dressed in blue overalls: David wears a colourful Mambo shirt and jeans and Pete has on a dark blue polo-shirt and jeans. Morgan has jokingly threatened Pete a few times that he will put him on the roll call for Australia's Next Top Model: he has an unusually handsome face, striking blue eyes and a tall sculptured body. Pete is aware of his good looks but he seems to get annoyed by the attention he gets from girls when they are out – he isn't like David who sleazes on to any girl. It surprises Morgan that Pete is still single: but for

GAME

all he knows he might be gay and hiding in the closet. He shakes David and Pete's hands. "How's it going?"

David smirks. "You don't look better than you did the other night; you still look like shit!"

Morgan smiles, "Thanks mate, you know just what to say to make me feel better."

David pats him on the shoulder. "No but seriously; I'm sorry for what happened. You're lucky that it wasn't worse than it was."

Morgan nods. "I feel very lucky."

"We must catch up some night and go out for drinks when you've recovered." Pete puts his bag on the floor. "We haven't been out for ages."

Morgan nods again. "I'll let you know when I'm up to it. So, are you ready to start the fingerprinting process? All the detectives are here so you can get to it right away. I'll show you where you can set up your equipment." Morgan leads the way through the corridor.

"Alright everyone," Morgan says loudly as they stop in front of the detectives' desks. "We're taking fingerprints today as I mentioned earlier. And if you could assist our friends here from the technical department I would be grateful." He turns to David. "You know where I am: just give me a yell if you need anything."

Morgan smokes a cigarette in a sunny spot on the pavement. He thinks about the funeral that will be held in Palm Beach for his mother and tries to remember if he has a dark suit that is clean enough to wear for the occasion. Then he wonders who will come. Victoria's friends from the area will be there, and probably her friends from her acting days as well: most of them are older ladies now but they still look like they have stepped out of the pages of a fashion magazine. Morgan remembers the dinners and cocktail parties his mother held in their garden during the summers: he used to sit in his room and watch the guests through his window. He loved to watch the beautiful women in their amazing clothes. Morgan takes a last drag on his cigarette before he throws it in the ashtray and walks back inside.

David and Pete have started the fingerprinting process and their equipment is laid out on one of the desks. A queue leads to the door to the men's room where the detectives are waiting to wash the black colour off their fingers.

Morgan nods to Pete as he walks past. "Hey, let me know when it's my turn."

Pete nods back. "Sure, will do."

Morgan goes to his office and closes the door behind him. He picks up a report that he has been reading and flicks through the pages. Something nudges his memory when he sees Osbourne's name in the report. He picks up the phone and turns the pages in his diary to find Osbourne's home number. He dials the number and waits. Six signals go through before a breathless Osbourne answers.

"Hi it's me; Morgan. Sorry to bother you at home, but I just thought of something."

"No bother at all. It's good to hear from you, what's up?"

"I was just going through some of the old reports from the beginning of the investigation and it hit me that you have some reports that I haven't seen. Do you know if they're still in your computer?"

"Uh, yes, they should be."

"Right, I know it's not ethical to ask: but can I have your passwords so I can go into your computer and have a look?"

GAME

"Oh gosh, I don't think I can remember them now. You know; we change the passwords every month."

Morgan rubs his jaw. "Alright, I guess I can get someone with authorization from the IT helpdesk to access your computer. Would you mind?"

"No, do what you have to. How are you going with the investigation?"

There is a knock on Morgan's door and Pete's head appears in the opening. "You're next," he whispers.

"Good, good," Morgan says into the telephone. "Look, I've got to go. So you don't mind if we hack into your computer then?"

"No, not at all, it was good to hear from you."

"Take care Osbourne, and let me know soon when you'll be back will you?"

"I will, say hello to everyone from me."

"Okay, I will. Bye now." Morgan hangs up.

"We're all done here," David says as Morgan comes up to him. "It's only you left."

Morgan holds out his hand. "Print away."

Pete looks at a list on the table. "Yes, everyone except for Osbourne, that is."

"Osbourne's on leave." Morgan looks up. "I just spoke to him on the phone. I should have asked him to come in. If you can wait a minute, I'll give him another call."

David presses Morgan's finger down on a sheet of paper. "We can't, we've made an appointment with another department. But maybe Osbourne can come and see us this afternoon when we get back?"

Morgan looks down at the desk. "Or maybe you could lend me one of your printing kits and I can get his prints myself."

A.C. Efverman

David looks at Pete. "What do you say? We've got enough haven't we?"

Pete shrugs his shoulders. "Okay, sure. Here, take one of mine." He hands a small box and a folder to Morgan. "You know how it's done, don't you?"

"Yes, thanks."

The sun is glary through the car windows. O'Neill drives. Morgan tries to call Osbourne's home number on his mobile for the third time; but it is still engaged. He looks at O'Neill's sharp profile against the bright light. "No, he's still on the phone. Do you know where we're going?"

O'Neill keeps his eyes on the road. "No worries, it's on Parramatta Road just after Leichhardt."

Morgan leans back in the car seat, he feels dizzy. He should eat and drink something to keep his strength up, he thinks. The traffic is not bad: the cars keep a steady pace and it takes them less than fifteen minutes to get to Haberfield. Morgan keeps an eye out for the house number but they miss it and have to turn into a service station and have a look in the street directory as the computerized map system can't localise the address. O'Neill makes a right turn by a set of lights and drives in the opposite direction before he swings back out on Parramatta Road. This time they find the house and O'Neill turns into the driveway directly from the busy highway.

"How can you live so close to this traffic?" Morgan asks as he opens the car door and gets out. He looks at the dark brown bungalow that is located only metres from the road. The short driveway leads to a garage next to the house. The windows that face the road are covered by dark curtains.

"I can tell you all about it: my house is right on Princess

GAME

Highway," O'Neill says as he locks the car. They walk up a short flight of stairs to the front door.

Morgan presses the doorbell: it gives a sharp sound and they hear steps approach on the inside. The door opens and Osbourne is looking at them. "Hello! What are you doing here?"

Morgan makes a gesture to the plastic bag in his hand. "We're fingerprinting everyone in the office. I should have mentioned it on the phone, but I forgot."

Osbourne open the door wide. "Come in and have some coffee. I was just about to make some."

Morgan and O'Neill walk into the hallway and follow Osbourne into a small, dark kitchen. Osbourne points at some chairs that stand around a kitchen table. "Grab a seat."

Morgan still feels dizzy and doesn't need to be asked twice. O'Neill takes a seat in the chair next to him.

"So how have you been?" Morgan asks as he looks around. The walls are covered with dark brown wallpaper that is patterned with red flowers. The cupboards are also painted brown. The kitchen must have been renovated in the fifties or sixties, Morgan guesses.

"Yes, I'm not too bad. I've been helping my mother to sell the farm. The paperwork is complicated and it takes a lot of time," Osbourne says over his shoulder as he washes cups in the sink.

"Do you live here on your own?" O'Neill asks as he looks at the dark coloured walls.

"Yes, I do now. The house belongs to my parents but when they moved to the farm I got it to myself." Osbourne puts three clean cups on the table, turns to the sink and spoons coffee powder into a coffee pot and turns the gas on. Suddenly there is a thumping noise somewhere below.

A.C. Efverman

"What's that noise?" O'Neill asks.

Osbourne turns from the stove and frowns. He holds a cigarette in his hand. "What noise?"

"That thumping noise downstairs."

"Oh that. That's my dog, Bluey. I lock him in the basement when I have guests: he gets excited and jump on people. He's a cross between a Border collie and a Blue Cattle dog and he'd be better off on the farm where he can run around, but he's my mate and I can't part with him." Osbourne sticks the cigarette in his mouth and lights it on the gas flame on the stove.

"I don't believe it: you're smoking," Morgan says. "Are you the same person who always tells me that you hate tobacco smoke?"

Osbourne leans against the kitchen bench and drags on his cigarette. "Have I said that? No I've smoked for years; but never at work."

Morgan takes a packet of cigarettes from his pocket.

"Since we're all smoking, do you mind if I have one too?" O'Neill asks as he holds his hand out.

Morgan raises his eyebrows. "You too, O'Neill; I've never seen you smoke."

O'Neill takes a cigarette from the packet that Morgan offers. "I don't like to smoke at work either. It's not politically correct these days, is it?"

Morgan shrugs his shoulders as he lights a cigarette. "Maybe I should quit smoking at work too."

Osbourne takes the pot from the stove and pours coffee into the cups. He sits down next to O'Neill and pushes an ashtray to the middle of the table. "I can't offer you something to go with the coffee; I didn't expect guests."

Morgan takes a sip of hot coffee and puts the cup down

GAME

again. "No worries." He takes the plastic bag from the floor and puts a metal box on the table.

"So you're fingerprinting everyone at the department," Osbourne says. "What for?"

Morgan sticks his hand back into the plastic bag and takes out the folder. "We're doing it to eliminate prints from the murder scenes mostly."

Osbourne shrugs. "That's fine by me, but I wasn't at any of the murder scenes."

Morgan looks at him. "Yes you were: you were at the wharf when we found Else Henriksen."

Osbourne flicks ash from his cigarette into the ashtray. "Yes, but that wasn't the murder scene, was it? I thought you meant the place where the girls were killed."

"I meant both."

"Okay, fine. You can take my prints; I don't mind. Let me just go and wash my hands, I've been out in the garden." Osbourne gets up. "I won't be long." He walks out of the kitchen.

Morgan looks at O'Neill. "Did he just wash these cups, or am I imagining things?"

O'Neill nods. "He did."

"So how can he still have dirt on his hands from the garden?"

"Doesn't make sense," O'Neill says and drags on his cigarette.

Morgan suddenly stiffens in his chair. "O'Neill, have you got your…"

O'Neill raises his eyebrows. "My what?"

But Morgan doesn't answer; he is staring at something behind O'Neill's back.

O'Neill slowly turns around to see what it is.

A.C. Efverman

Osbourne stands in the doorway. He holds a gun. "You're fucking smart-asses, aren't you? You come here and pretend you don't know what's going on. But we'll soon see who the smart one is; won't we?"

Morgan glances down at O'Neill's waist to see if he is carrying his weapon. He is: Morgan can see the bulge under his jacket. Morgan moves his hand in slow motion towards the gun. He is partly covered by O'Neill's body and hopes that Osbourne can't see the movement from where he is standing.

"I want you to stand up, both of you." Osbourne waives his gun in the air.

O'Neill starts to get up and Morgan quickly pulls up O'Neill's jacket, uncaps the gun and pulls it out.

"What the fuck are you doing back there?" Osbourne yells.

A shot is fired. The bang is so loud Morgan thinks he's lost his hearing: until he hears the thud of O'Neill's body hitting the floor. Blood seeps through the fabric of O'Neill's pants and the front of his left leg quickly turns dark. He moans and holds his leg. "You fucking bastard," he mutters between gritted teeth.

Osbourne laughs. "Ha ha, who's the smart ass now, hey? You're not so smart now, are you?" He seems to have forgotten Morgan who ducked when the shot went off. Morgan is crouched down in the corner and O'Neill's gun is hidden in his lap.

Osbourne laughs again. "You don't look so tough now, do you smart ass? Ha, ha." He suddenly takes a step forward and points the gun at Morgan's face. "Get up!"

Morgan hides the gun behind his thigh as he stands up. "Think before you act Osbourne," he says slowly, "don't do

GAME

anything that you'll regret."

But Osbourne isn't listening: he waves the gun in the air. "Get out of the fucking corner… NOW!"

Morgan slowly takes a few steps forward. O'Neill remains on the floor: he is moaning. Osbourne bends down and keeps the gun pointed at Morgan as he pulls O'Neill to his feet. O'Neill holds onto the back of a chair for support. Morgan doesn't dare to take a shot at Osbourne from where he is standing as he will risk hitting O'Neill. He slowly pushes the gun up under the sleeve of his jacket.

"Right;" Osbourne waives with his gun again. "Go out in front of me. Morgan, help O'Neill."

Morgan walks up to O'Neill and puts his arm around his waist. O'Neill jumps out of the kitchen on one leg.

"Go through that door." Osbourne waives with the gun towards a door.

Morgan opens the door and sees a staircase that leads down into darkness.

"Get down there. Do it!"

They take a few steps down and Morgan turns his head to see if Osbourne is following them when the door slams shut with a loud bang. They hear a key turn in the lock.

They slowly make their way down the rest of the steps. When they reach the bottom Morgan helps O'Neill to lie down on the floor and then he starts searching for a light switch. There is a small window close to the ceiling but it is so dirty it hardly gives any light. Morgan walks around the room and touches the walls. Suddenly his feet touch something he thinks is a rolled up carpet. Someone moans and he crouches down on his knees. His hands fumble in the dark as he strains his eyes to see. "Oh my god," he mumbles. "Lisa?"

A.C. Efverman

There is another moan. Morgan sits down on the cold hard floor and moves his hands over Lisa's body to find the gag. Finally his fingers find the fabric and pull it off.

Lisa's mouth is so dry she isn't sure she can speak. "Morgan?" she whispers.

Morgan bends down and lifts her up into his arms and buries his face in her hair. "I thought that I would never see you again," he whispers. Tears wet his face. He gently puts Lisa back on the floor. "I'll turn the light on", he whispers. Touching the walls with his fingers he slowly walks around the room. He finally finds the light switch close to the stairs. "We must get these ropes off," he mutters as he crouches down next to Lisa and carefully turns her over. First then he sees that her lower body is soaked in blood. "Oh my god, what has he done to you?"

Lisa shakes her head slowly. "It wasn't him ...I think I've had a miscarriage."

There is a creaking noise from the floorboards as someone walks around in the room upstairs.

Morgan looks up. "What's he doing now?"

Lisa opens her eyes wide. "Is he still there?"

Morgan bends over her and struggles with the knots around her wrists. "Don't worry; I'll get you out of here." Suddenly he remembers that he has his mobile phone in his pocket and pulls it out. He gets up and walks over to O'Neill who is lying on the floor by the bottom of the stairs. "O'Neill," he pats his shoulder, "O'Neill, I've dialled triple 0; can you tell them where we are when you get through?" He places the mobile in O'Neill's hand. O'Neill looks up at him with watery eyes. "Sure."

Morgan walks back to Lisa and tries to untie the rope

GAME

around her wrists: the knots are tied hard and his fingers are shaking.

They hear a clattering noise as something falls on the floor. Morgan walks over to O'Neill and sees that the mobile is lying next to him: O'Neill has passed out. Morgan picks up the phone and holds it to his ear. "Hello?"

"Yes hello. This is emergency services. Do you want police, ambulance or the fire department?"

"Police."

"I'm connecting you now."

"This is the police. What's your emergency?"

"Uh, we're locked in a basement. There's an armed man in the house…"

"What's the address there?"

"We're at 568 Parramatta Road, in Haberfield, hurry." Morgan walks back to Lisa and sits down next to her on the floor.

"What's your name?"

"Detective Sergeant Morgan Callaghan. There's another detective here; he's been shot. And there's an injured woman here as well."

The door upstairs opens: Morgan hears the hinges on the door screech.

"Are you in a freestanding house or in a unit? …Hello, are you there?"

Morgan takes the phone from his ear. He sits quiet listening and then he slowly puts the phone on the floor and pulls the gun from his sleeve.

"What are you doing down there?" It is Osbourne's voice: it sounds like he is crying. "You can't just come into my house like that. Now you've ruined everything." Morgan hears that Osbourne slowly walks down the steps. Morgan creeps backwards until he feels the cold wall behind his back. He points the gun towards the stairs.

Osbourne's legs become visible and Morgan sees that he bends down to look around the basement. He holds the gun steady and fires. Osbourne falls down the stairs and lands on the floor with a loud thump. Morgan sits still and waits. There is silence for a few moments and then Osbourne starts to cry. "Oh my god that hurts! Help me!"

Morgan pushes himself up with a hand against the cold wall and stands still for a few seconds. Osbourne stops crying and the room is suddenly very silent. Morgan's heart beats fast and hard as he slowly makes his way over the floor to where Osbourne and O'Neill lay next to each other. Both men are motionless.

Osbourne suddenly opens his eyes and looks up at Morgan. "Help me Morgan. You've got to help me."

Morgan stares down at him. He has never felt so tempted to shoot someone. He holds the gun over Osbourne's head. His hand is shaking.

"Kill him Morgan!" Lisa suddenly yells. "What are you waiting for? Kill the bastard!"

Morgan nods with his eyes on Osbourne. "I'm tempted; and don't you think I won't. If you move, it will be the last fucking thing you ever do!" Morgan spits the words out.

Osbourne squirms back on the floor and then suddenly reaches out and grabs Morgan's leg. Morgan screams as he loses his balance and falls. He lands hard on his tailbone. Pain shoots up through his spine. In that split second he makes his mind up: he knows that he doesn't have to kill Osbourne – he can just point the gun at him until help arrives. He looks at the blood on the floor next to Lisa and knows that the blood is their unborn baby. Pictures of dead women and cut throats

GAME

and wounded bodies flash through his mind. Somewhere to his right Osbourne laughs. Morgan turns and points the gun that he still holds hard in his hand. With an odd feeling of warm satisfaction he fires straight into Osbourne's laughing face. Blood spurts out and Morgan instinctively turns his face away. The loud bang from the shot echoes for a long time between the walls. After that there is absolute silence. Morgan stares at the body on the floor: Osbourne's face is gone and a large pool of blood grows rapidly under his head. Morgan gets up on his knees and crawls over the floor to Lisa. She is curled up in a foetal position with her knees against her chest: she is shaking. When Morgan touches her shoulder she screams hysterically. Morgan takes her in his arms and rocks her back and forwards. "Shush! Shush! Everything's alright now; he's dead."

But Lisa continues to scream until her voice dries up – then she lies motionless in Morgan's arms and stares into the wall.

A.C. Efverman

16

The sunlight bleaches all colours: a small lizard that runs across the path appears to be white under the harsh sun. The winds that blow in from the ocean are strong and Morgan struggles to push Lisa's wheelchair up the hill. The grass is wet. A group of people have gathered in the shade from a large gum tree and it looks staged: like they have taken positions there for a scene to be played out. And in a way it is a staged scene: the final scene of Victoria Callaghan's life. Morgan takes his place next to his father. They have a view over green hills and the endless blue ocean below. Morgan holds Carl's arm. Katherine stands on Morgan's other side and Lisa sits in front of them in her wheelchair.

"We have gathered here today…" A female priest reads from a book and Morgan's thoughts starts to drift. He remembers his mother's face and the warmth in her eyes. Someone sings a song: a beautiful sad song; and people step forward to put flowers on top of the casket that is lowered into the ground. The priest continues to read and the words cut into Morgan's thoughts:

"Victoria will live on in our memories as the beautiful person we knew. We all have different memories of Victoria as we all knew her differently. But we all loved her. And we still do. This love is eternal and will stay with us forever…"

Katherine is shaking. Tears stream down her face but she makes no attempt wipe them off.

GAME

Carl stands motionless. He has a look of disbelief on his face.

Morgan looks down at Lisa. They have spent the night together at the hospital. Lisa has suffered a miscarriage and has infected wounds on her wrists and ankles where the rope has cut into her skin. She is also suffering from dehydration and blood loss. When she arrived at the hospital she was in a state of shock and was unable to communicate with anyone. Morgan knows that her experiences in the house on Parramatta Road will stay with her for the rest of her life.

The police officers told him at the hospital that the basement looked like a scene from a horror movie when they got there; and at first they thought that everyone in the room were dead.

The police haven't found a diary or any notes that explain what Osbourne has done. But they found papers that show that both Osbourne's parents have been dead for a long time: Osbourne lived a lie in many aspects. He must have possessed supreme self confidence to join the police force just months before he started his killing spree. He probably got a kick out of being both the offender and a part of the team that was trying to catch him. When Morgan thinks back to the time he has known Osbourne he can't detect anything that would have made him suspect what Osbourne really was – and that is a hell of a scary thought.

A psychiatrist at the hospital told Morgan that people's behaviour can always be explained, but hidden parts of personalities can't always be detected. Morgan spoke to the psychiatrist for a long time while Lisa slept, and the psychiatrist's conclusion stuck in his mind. He said that: 'Everyone puts up a different face to the outside world. We even hide parts of ourselves to our friends, children and spouses. Who can say that they really know someone? We only know as much about another person as that person allows us to. Most people have dark secrets. And everyone has secrets.'

Morgan will never know what drove Osbourne to do the things he did: dead people don't speak.

Lisa squeezes Morgan's hand as the priest throws a handful of dirt on the top of the casket that contains his mother's body.

"Ashes to ashes, dust to dust."

That night the sky explodes outside Morgan's window as fireworks are set off over the harbour to mark the beginning of the World Cup. Morgan looks at Lisa's sleeping face: she finally looks peaceful. "Let the games begin," he mumbles.

Books by A.C. Efverman

Borta
Skuggspel
Game

Available from Amazon.com and other online stores.
Available on Kindle and online stores.

Printed in Great Britain
by Amazon.co.uk, Ltd.,
Marston Gate.